Once an
Innocent

Elizabeth Boyce

Author of *Once a Duchess* and *Once an Heiress*

CRIMSON
ROMANCE

F+W Media, Inc.

Crimson Romance
an imprint of F+W Media, Inc.
10151 Carver Road, Suite 200
Blue Ash, Ohio 45242
www.crimsonromance.com

ISBN 10: 1-4405-7349-2
ISBN 13: 978-1-4405-7349-1
eISBN 10: 1-4405-6196-6
eISBN 13: 978-1-4405-6196-2

Printed in the United States of America.

10 9 8 7 6 5 4 3 2 1

This book is available at quantity discounts for bulk purchases.
For information, please call 1-800-289-0963.

Dedication

Mama, this one's for you.

Acknowledgments

Many thanks to my wonderful editors on this project, Jerri Corgiat Gallagher and J.C. Kosloff.

My deepest gratitude to Jennifer Lawler, for . . . everything. Lady, you rock.

Tara Gelsomino, thank you for championing my novels. You're an absolute gem.

To my Crimsonistas: Thank you for the nonstop laughs, commiseration, and inspiration—CR Sisters style.

Carrie Allen, thanks for allowing me use of your eyeball.

Tavish Brinton, midwife extraordinaire, thank you for the wealth of knowledge you imparted.

Oasis, I appreciate the many years y'all have put up with me. Thanks for humoring my history rants, laughing at my bad jokes, letting me brainstorm about grouse hunts and poisoned horses, and telling me those are Great Ideas, even when they're half-baked and probably not very good yet. When I hit the big time, I'll pony up the down payment for the island in Fiji.

SareBear and "Hell Shell," you ladies always help me get it started, even when I don't want to. In then end, I'm always glad you did. Thank you, sweet dears.

As ever, Jason, your support and encouragement mean the world. I love you!

Finally, thanks so much to my readers who have read and enjoyed my novels. Hearing from you via reviews, blog comments, and e-mails makes all the pain worthwhile. You're all the very best!

Chapter One

London, 1814

When the liveried footman in front of Jordan stumbled over a lump in the rug, a bottle of claret and two wine glasses toppled from his laden tray. Jordan sprang forward, caught the bottle 'round the neck in one hand and a glass by the stem in the other. The second wine glass he intercepted with his leg; it rolled down his shin to settle, unharmed, on the treacherous floor covering.

As he stooped to retrieve it, an audience of one applauded off to his side. "Lord Freese, my hero! You saved my rug, wine, and stemware all from unfortunate demise."

He turned to the speaker and bowed with a flourish. "Your servant, madam."

Isabelle, Duchess of Monthwaite, smiled warmly as she stepped off the bottom stair and crossed the entrance hall to where he stood. "We didn't know if you'd come tonight, Jordan. Charity events are not nearly so tempting to single gentlemen as other amusements."

Jordan affected an affronted demeanor. "And where should I rather be, if not at 'An Auction for the Benefit of King's Cross Vocational School for Young Ladies,' as the invitation so enticingly described?" He poured wine into the two rescued glasses then returned the bottle to the red-faced footman before turning to offer Isabelle a drink.

She took both it and his proffered arm as they strolled toward the salon, following the faint sounds of pianoforte music and laughter. "Still, it was good of you to come," Isabelle continued. "I know Lily will be grateful for whatever material support you offer, and I'm just glad to have another body in the room. This far into summer, it was difficult to fill out the guest list." Her sigh was thick with fatigue, and she leaned heavily upon his arm.

Jordan looked down at his friend's wife. Though the arm hooked through his own was still willowy and her face as slender and lovely as ever, Isabelle's lithe figure had given way to the heavy fullness of late pregnancy. Her breasts were larger than they'd ever been—scarcely contained by the bodice of her light green dress. Even so, they were overshadowed by the great roundness of her belly.

Though politeness prevented him from directly alluding to her delicate condition, he was concerned she might overexert herself. "Are you sure this is not too much?" he asked. "Would you like to take a rest?"

A frown line creased her brows. "I've just come down from taking a rest," she answered testily. "Pray do not stare at me like that, Jordan. I'm perfectly aware of my limitations."

"Forgive me, Isabelle," he said with a quick smile. "If I seemed to stare it is only because I am dazzled by the becoming new cut of your hair." He nodded toward the blond curls framing her face. "That short style suits you—very modish."

"You're forgiven, since you not only noticed my new hairstyle but complimented it. Poor Marshall is mourning the length I cut off."

They rounded a corner; the salon was directly in front of them, its doors thrown open wide, spilling light and music into the corridor. Inside, a respectable crowd of several dozen mingled over drinks. Jordan smiled mischievously and bent to speak in a low voice near her ear. "Since you'll not go rest, at least say you'll leave Marshall and elope with me, Isabelle. I'll take you to Paris and buy a hundred hats to adorn your new hair."

Isabelle threw back her head and laughed as they entered the room, drawing admiring gazes from the assembled guests. "You grow more outrageous by the day," she scolded, her blue eyes swimming with mirth. "If you don't hurry up and marry, you'll soon be so scandalous, no decent woman will have you."

"You've uncovered my scheme," he replied in jest, raising his voice slightly to be heard over the hired musician seated at the pianoforte in the far corner. "If no decent woman will have me, then my dear stepmama must stop badgering me to shackle myself to one."

Their private conversation ended as Marshall broke away from a group of gentlemen to meet them. His arm slipped protectively around Isabelle's expanded waist, concern etching his features. "Are you feeling better?" he asked. "You don't have to do this, darling. I'm sure among Lady Thorburn and Naomi and myself, we have everything well in hand."

Isabelle laid a reassuring hand against her husband's cheek. Their sweet, open affection moved Jordan. He was happy for the joy his friends found in one another but very much doubted he was meant for any such relationship. The permanence of marriage scared the daylights out of him. Jordan couldn't bear to stay in one geographic location longer than a month or two at a time—how could he be expected to remain at one woman's side for the rest of his life?

The duchess moved on to speak with her guests. Marshall turned nonchalantly to face Jordan, lifted his wine, and swirled it beneath his nose. "There's someone in my study to see you," he murmured, his lips concealed by the glass.

Jordan frowned. "Who?"

Go, Marshall mouthed silently. His dark eyes cut to the door.

Feeling foolish for leaving almost as soon as he'd arrived, Jordan retreated from the social gathering. Curiosity put a spring in his step as he found his way upstairs to the study. He knocked once on the door and entered. The smell of leather and ink greeted him as his eyes sought out his summoner.

A head of close-clipped, graying hair looked up from where it had been bent over papers. Jordan shook his head ruefully as he shut and locked the door behind him. Was there nowhere the man could not engross himself in work?

"Freese." Lord Castlereagh nodded once and gestured to a chair across the desk.

"Fine," Jordan said as he took a seat. "Thank you so much for asking. And how does the night find you, Robert?"

The Foreign Secretary's lips turned up in a small smile. He tossed his quill onto a sheet of paper, his hard eyes glinting in the light cast by the candelabra on the end of the desk. "I don't waste time on idle chitchat, Jordan Atherton—and if you knew what was good for you, neither would you."

"I find it singular," Jordan rejoined, "that I've been turned away from your office every time I've attempted to see you this year. But here you are," he said, spreading his hands wide, "running me to ground at a charity auction, pulling my strings as deftly as a puppet master. I should like to have a word with you."

"And I with you," Castlereagh said, leaning back in the borrowed chair. "That's why I've come."

"I'd hoped to accompany you to Paris." Jordan hadn't meant to blurt it out. He only hoped he hadn't sounded like a petulant child.

Castlereagh pursed his lips. "You'd have been no good to me there, Freese. You're no diplomat."

Jordan's teeth ground together. "There was intelligence to gather before the treaty was signed. I could have done that."

"You have your assignment."

"I'm *sick* of my assignment," Jordan seethed. "Four years is long enough. Send me somewhere, Robert—anywhere. Let me be useful again!"

Lord Castlereagh's brows shot up. "I *am* sending you somewhere." Amusement tinged his words. "Home, in fact. What in the name of God Almighty are you still doing in Town this late in the summer? You're lucky I haven't strung you up for dereliction of duty, Freese."

Jordan swiped a hand down his right cheek; his fingers automatically traced the scar he had obtained carrying out Castlereagh's orders. It ran from his ear almost to the corner of his mouth.

How could he make the impassive Foreign Secretary see that this assignment was killing him? He was hobbled, tied to England like a dog staked on a short rope, when all he wanted to do was stretch his legs on foreign soil and engross himself in meaningful work once more.

"I've always done my duty, Robert," he protested. "You cannot question my loyalty."

Castlereagh spread his hands flat on the desk, long, ink-stained fingers splayed wide, and leaned forward, pinning Jordan in his fierce gaze. "Then why are you still here?"

Because Lintern Abbey is the dullest place on Earth, he wanted to say. Because estate ledgers, crop rotations, and rent tallies bored him to tears. Instead of anything approaching the truth, which Robert would only interpret as sniveling, he opted for sarcasm. "I've taken a keen interest in charity schools, you see. I had to stay to lend my support to Her Grace's benefit."

His superior leveled an incredulous look at him, his jaw working side to side. Finally, Lord Castlereagh rummaged through the papers before withdrawing one and handing it across the desk to Jordan. "Home may have just become more exciting for you."

Jordan read the intelligence report with mounting alarm. When he reached the end, he turned disbelieving eyes on Castlereagh. "French agents? Are you sure?"

The Foreign Secretary shrugged. "*I'm* not sure, but our man in York is, and that's good enough for me. Frenchmen have been sighted in villages and towns in the North, asking questions."

"But it doesn't make sense," Jordan said in a rush. He swiped his fingers through the mop of black curls atop his head. "The monarchy is restored." His eyes lit as an idea took shape. "Perhaps King Louis has sent them?"

"No." Castlereagh shook his head. "Louis would approach the government directly. They're Bonapartists."

"But Napoleon is on Elba," Jordan pointed out.

"Where he is already expanding his army and navy," Castlereagh snapped. "His exile is not secure, damn it all. And now we have nine, ten, perhaps more of his men nosing around Yorkshire, getting closer to Lintern Abbey."

With fingers and thumb pressing into his eyes, Jordan growled in frustration. "To what purpose? Do we suspect assassins?"

When he opened his eyes again, he saw the Secretary's lips drawn into a grim line. "Of course they're assassins. When have you last laid eyes on Enrique?" The pang of guilt aroused by the mention of his ward's name must have shown on his face. Castlereagh scoffed. "Go home, Freese. Do your goddamn job." He shoved another paper at Jordan. "I want you to take these men with you. Set a patrol; do whatever it takes."

Jordan glanced down at the list. He recognized the ten names as well-placed gentlemen: some sons of *tonnish* families, some men attached to high-ranking government officials—and all agents of the Foreign Office, as well, it would seem.

He scowled at the paper as a problem presented itself. "If I run home with ten men, that will draw attention. If those same ten men start patrolling, asking after these Frenchmen, that will certainly draw attention. As it is, Bonaparte's agents can't know anything for certain. They're looking, yes? Otherwise, they'd be on my doorstep in an instant. Setting out a guard like this is as good as lighting a beacon for them. It would be better to allay their suspicions. 'Nothing to see here; move along,' as it were."

Castlereagh pressed his hands together in prayer fashion and rested his chin on his fingertips. "How do you propose to do that?"

"I don't know," Jordan admitted. "But I'll think of something."

"Do whatever you'd like, Freese, but you have to take those men. You're good, but I'll not pit you alone against ten Bonapartists."

Jordan squeezed his eyes shut and pinched the bridge of his nose. Despite an overwhelming desire to be released from his assignment, he found himself even more tightly bound to it. He'd wanted Robert to relieve him of his burden and give him something more exciting, more compelling to do. Instead, he not only had to hurry home to Lintern Abbey, but he had to concoct a front, something perfectly ordinary and domestic to cover the sudden influx of almost a dozen armed men. Something boring. But, blast it all, this was his job—his duty. And no matter how it rankled, Jordan Atherton, Viscount Freese did his duty.

"At the end of September, I'm leaving for Vienna," Castlereagh announced. "There's to be a meeting in November, a congress of the Allies. I want this settled before my departure. Anything untoward that suggests Bonaparte is still wielding power could upset negotiations."

"It's already the eighth of August," Jordan protested. "You want me to carry out a covert manhunt and eliminate all these French agents by the end of next month?"

"Yes, I do," Castlereagh stated.

"If I do this, if I succeed, will you take me with you to Vienna?" Jordan asked. "I would be useful to you there, Robert, I swear. If you only needed me to act as your page, I would do it."

"No." Lord Castlereagh's mouth held the tight O shape of his refusal for a moment as though making sure his edict was understood. "I know it's not as thrilling as your old days on the Continent or in Spain, Jordan. But it's vitally important. You must understand that your work is crucial to the very survival of Europe. If Bonaparte's agents succeed . . . If he escapes and returns and we can't fight him off again . . . Castlereagh's mouth pressed in a grim line. "I don't have to tell you it would be devastating. Political stability *must* be maintained while Europe rebuilds. That's what you're guarding at Lintern Abbey. Stability. Peace."

Well.

When he put it that way, Jordan couldn't formulate any further argument against his assignment. While stability and peace weren't his cup of tea personally, he certainly valued them for the world at large.

"You're in this for the long haul," Castlereagh concluded. "You might as well resign yourself to it and find some pleasure in living a more domestic lifestyle. Get married, my boy. My Amelia has been a good and constant companion these last twenty years."

Jordan rose and bowed. "Thank you for your advice, sir. I shall consider it." He tucked the intelligence report and list of Foreign Office agents into his coat pocket before taking his leave.

As he made his way back downstairs to the auction, Jordan scoffed to himself at Lord Castlereagh's final words. The last thing he needed—or wanted—was a good and constant companion. A good companion was marvelous for a night or two, but the constant part was right out.

*

When he rejoined the party in the salon, Jordan attempted to regain his typical, jovial manner, but the tight pull of his scar told him he still frowned. In Town, he found it very easy to forget about his responsibilities at Lintern Abbey and throw himself into entertainments and the company of his friends. This collision of his worlds was most unwelcome.

What the devil was he going to do? He could not carry out Castlereagh's orders without amending them. If his home were being watched, an action such as the Secretary desired would bring the Bonapartists down upon his head and ruin four years of careful intrigue. Lintern Abbey itself held little draw for him, but he didn't want harm befalling those who lived there. Uncle Randell and Enrique would be as helpless as lambs before wolves without Jordan's protection. Leaving them to face the threat alone was out of the question. But how to go about it?

"I didn't think anyone could scowl as fiercely as my husband, but you may have bested him."

Lily Helling, Viscountess Thorburn, regarded Jordan with a bemused expression on her face, full lips twisted in a wry smile. The statuesque female was sheathed in chocolate satin, touched here and there with gold lace and beading—a smashing complement to her own dark hair and eyes.

"If I am scowling fiercely," he said, his charming smile once more in place, "it is only because you look—"

"You used that one on me already." Isabelle joined them and playfully swatted Jordan's forearm with her fan. "Pen some new material."

"Save your flirtation for the other ladies, in any event," Lily said. "Handsome you may be, but I am utterly immune to your charms, my lord."

The two ladies' husbands joined the group. Ethan Helling handed a cup of punch to his wife. "Freese, I warn you. If you attempt to flirt with Lily, she will almost certainly skewer you for it. I still must couch remarks in innuendo and entendre."

Jordan grinned. "I'm well aware of the lady's formidable parlance. Indeed, I admire Lady Thorburn's forthright manner." He nodded to Lily, who blushed and shared a smile with Ethan. Despite his claims of walking softly around her, Jordan knew a woman as strong as Lily could only be matched by an equal force—and any fool could see the Thorburns were as deeply in love as Marshall and Isabelle.

Good God, I'm surrounded by willing prisoners, he realized with a start. Jordan was the odd man out in the group, the fifth wheel in the midst of couples wallowing in marital felicity. He scanned the other guests for someone else to talk to. How had it happened that everything tonight kept pointing to the subject of marriage, even as he was dunked into a crisis of international security? When he should be thinking of nothing but how he would outsmart Napoleon's dogs, he found himself forced to reflect upon the distasteful institution of matrimony and all the choking restrictions it entailed.

His restless gaze landed upon Lord and Lady Hollier—married since the beginning of time—who socialized with Lady Thorburn's parents, Mr. and Mrs. Bachman—likewise possessed of a long, seemingly happy union.

A gorgeous vision stepped into the group of older guests and made Jordan suck in his breath. Naomi Lockwood made a polite curtsy to Lord Hollier. She bent her neck, and the light from the chandeliers skimmed across her strawberry-gold hair, which was knotted on top of her head and adorned with a charmingly frivolous blossom. The rose color of her dress brought out the healthy glow of her creamy skin.

Lord Hollier took her hand and patted it fondly. Mr. Bachman bowed when she greeted him. Jordan noted how the faces of all four guests lit with pleasure as Naomi moved gracefully amongst them, sharing a few words with each. She leaned over to put an arm around the seated Mrs. Bachman's shoulders, giving Jordan a view of the gentle swell of her breasts, filling out the low, square neckline of her gown.

An unexpected tightening in his groin startled him. This was Naomi—Marshall's little sister, for God's sake! He'd known her since she was a schoolroom miss in braids. And while he'd always been aware—academically speaking—that she was a lovely female, it had been the awareness of an older sibling-esque personage toward a younger quasi-sisterly individual, a reason to help look over her since she'd made her debut last year.

And yet, he couldn't take his eyes off of her.

She flagged down a footman to bring punch for Mrs. Bachman. Then Naomi took her leave of the older group and made her way to other guests, a welcoming smile at the ready for each.

That warm, open way of hers contradicted the rumors Jordan had heard of late. She'd been branded an ice queen, an untouchable. Two Seasons out, and the beautiful, generously dowered, younger sister of an obnoxiously wealthy duke was still unattached. Naomi was *the* catch last year, a diamond of the first water. She should have been snatched up within minutes of making her bow. But for two years she had deftly, delicately rebuffed the advances of every gentleman who had attempted to court her.

The grumbling in the clubs among her thwarted suitors was that she was cold, heartless—made in the same mold as her imperious mother, Caro Lockwood.

Jordan knew that wasn't a true or fair characterization. Naomi had one of the kindest natures he'd ever encountered. His eyes followed her as she continued to move through the assembly with the ease of a natural-born hostess, helping everyone feel noticed and included, seeing to the comfort of her brother and sister-in-law's guests.

No, Naomi Lockwood was anything but heartless, Jordan reflected. The conclusion he drew was that she was content with her single status. Marshall would never force his sister to marry against her will, and she would always be amply provided for. Perhaps, he thought with rising admiration, Naomi shared his unfavorable view of matrimony. It would be an unconventional opinion for a female—especially for one as well-bred and raised to convention as Naomi—but that only made it all the more fascinating.

"Do you mind," rumbled a dangerously low voice against his ear, "extricating your eyes from my sister, Freese?"

Marshall stood beside him, matching every one Jordan's six feet and four inches, glowering and tight-lipped. A quick glance around the group confirmed the others all had fallen silent and had been engaged, for some indeterminate length of time, watching Jordan watch Naomi.

Bollocks.

Jordan flashed his annoyed friend a smile. "If you don't want her admired, Marsh, you'd best put a sack over her head. Otherwise, I fear it's hopeless. Besides," he said, glancing back to where Naomi stood, quickly appraising the people around her, and snagging on the first likely suspect his eyes found, "Augustus Gladstone has been dogging her heels all night. I'm surprised you didn't notice," he added with a hint of rebuke. Marshall's head snapped to where Naomi was, in fact, exchanging words with the pup Gladstone, who was known to be trying to prove his manhood by making his way through all the bawdy houses in London.

Marshall frowned. "I'm sorry, Jordan. I didn't realize—"

Jordan clapped his friend on the arm. "It's all right; I know your mind is elsewhere." He nodded toward Isabelle. "I just thought someone should keep an eye on things."

The duke's jaw tightened, and Jordan still wasn't certain his friend wouldn't call him to account for so publicly ogling his sister. Isabelle intervened with a hand on her husband's arm.

"We're blessed to have a good friend who shares our concern for Naomi's welfare, aren't we, my love?" She steered Marshall away to go converse with the Bachmans.

Jordan impulsively glanced back to where he'd last seen Naomi, but she was no longer there. Frowning, he scanned the salon but couldn't locate her anywhere among the guests.

A few minutes later, the musician on the pianoforte stopped playing, and Marshall's voice rang out over the crowd. "Ladies and gentlemen, if you'll please take your seats, the auction will begin."

As Jordan filed along with the others to the several rows of padded chairs standing at one end of the room, he saw Naomi slip in. She stopped just inside the salon with her back to the wall, and even from this distance, Jordan noticed the high color staining her cheeks.

Another group wandered in— several young bucks and a lady. They passed Naomi, and she reached a hand out to stay one of the gentlemen, Wayland Hayward. The flaxen-haired young man turned and leaned while Naomi spoke to him, her fingers twisted together at her waist.

Hayward straightened, a light smile touching his lips. Then he glanced around, and—apparently supposing them unnoticed—grasped Naomi's hand and pulled her out into the corridor.

Jordan frowned. "What's that about?" he muttered to himself. A sharp prod in his back pulled his attention away from Naomi's peculiar behavior.

"Lord Freese, sit down!"

He glanced at the seat behind his. The Lockwood siblings' spinster aunt, Lady Janine, cast a look of sharp disapproval at him. Jordan saw that everyone else had settled into their chairs. He pressed a hand to his chest, bowed briefly by way of apology, and took his seat at the end of the row.

Lady Thorburn stood at the front of the room. "Ladies and gentlemen, thank you for coming," she began. "And a special thanks to Their Graces, the Duke and Duchess of Monthwaite for hosting this benefit. I would like to take just a moment before we start the auction to tell you all about the purpose and vision behind King's Cross Vocational School for Young Ladies—"

Jordan maintained a look of polite interest while his mind wandered back to his conversation with Lord Castlereagh. How was he ever to solve this problem? What could he do, quickly, to cover an armed patrol of his property?

Lily nodded and everyone clapped. Jordan joined in, having not heard another word of her speech. Then Marshall stood and presented the first item up for auction, a sitting with the portraitist, Lawrence. The bidding opened at a hundred pounds and quickly rose. Lord Cunnington won with a bid of seven hundred fifty pounds.

While the guests applauded Cunnington's generosity, Jordan glanced at the door. Naomi was still gone. And he still had a mess of international security to sort through, by Jove! Why the devil was he even thinking about Naomi's whereabouts, much less obsessing over them?

Two more items came and went. Jordan's feet tapped restlessly against the immaculately polished floor. Another poke to his back had him turning in his seat.

"You haven't bid on anything," Lady Janine said in a stage whisper.

"Nothing's caught my eye, my lady," he replied.

"You'd better dig into those deep pockets of yours," Lady Janine insisted. "This is for my niece's school."

Jordan raised a quizzical brow. "Lady Thorburn is not your niece, ma'am."

"Don't contradict me, boy!" Her blue eyes sparked behind the lenses of her gold-rimmed spectacles. "Mind your own damned business and do as I say."

He chuckled. Jordan had always appreciated Lady Janine's spunk, even if she was a hopeless bluestocking. He turned around to see Marshall standing at the front of the room again, balancing a pie on each hand.

"The winner of this lot is in for a special treat," he announced. "These fruit pies were baked by the Duchess of Monthwaite herself, especially for tonight's auction."

Another round of applause. Isabelle nodded from her seat, acknowledging the attention.

"What are the fillings, Duchess?" someone called.

"One cherry, one blueberry," Isabelle answered.

Jordan glanced once more at the door. Still no Naomi. He huffed. *Get out of my head,* he thought in frustration. He had far more important matters to think about.

"Very well," Marshall announced, "for one cherry and one blueberry pie baked by the Duchess of Monthwaite, who will open the bidding at fifty pounds?"

French agents at his home. They would be former military, he reasoned—as well trained themselves as anyone he could bring to counteract them.

David Hornsby raised his hand.

"We have fifty pounds!" Marshall called. "Who will offer seventy-five?"

These would not be brutes, no, Jordan thought, tapping a finger against his upper lip. Their actions so far had demonstrated an organized elegance, working in small groups to cover more ground. That meant they had established a communication network. They wouldn't rely upon the English post to carry their reports to one another. Couriers of their own, then. A French intelligence network—in Yorkshire! His mind reeled.

"One hundred pounds," Mr. Bachman called.

The door still stood vacant. No Naomi. Jordan's toes tapped out a rapid tattoo.

"Thank you for your generous bid, Mr. Bachman," Marshall said. "Can one of you best it?"

Lady Janine's finger dug into the back of his shoulder. Jordan ignored it. "Where the devil is she?" he muttered. He looked at the door again and sighed.

"One hundred fifty!" Hornsby called.

Jordan shook his head. One hundred fifty pounds for two pies? Ludicrous! Lintern Abbey had twenty thousand acres. Jordan had to patrol it with ten men—eleven, including himself. And make it look innocuous. It was preposterous.

Poke.

Scowling, he turned fully to face the door. "Get back in this room," he whispered. Why was he growing agitated at Naomi? She hadn't done anything to earn his ire. Except look utterly delectable this evening and arouse an awareness in him that had never been there before.

"Two hundred," said Lord Hollier.

"Two hundred pounds from Lord Hollier," Marshall called. "Are there any more bids?" No one spoke. "Two hundred once."

Poke.

Where is she? Jordan scanned the room to make sure he hadn't missed seeing her come back in. No, she was not in the salon, he was certain. What if something had happened to her? An uneasiness tightened his chest.

"Two hundred twice!"

Poke.

"Fifteen hundred pounds!"

A collective, startled gasp filled the room, and every face turned to see who had bid such an outrageous sum for two fruit pies. It took Jordan a moment to realize they were all looking at him.

"Sold," Marshall called, grinning broadly at Jordan, "for fifteen hundred pounds to the gentleman with the sweet tooth."

The audience laughed and clapped appreciatively. Jordan stood, feeling like the biggest fool imaginable. Lady Janine wore a satisfied expression.

He realized what he'd really purchased was the right to leave. With a sharp nod to no one in particular, Jordan turned on a heel and stalked out of the salon to find Naomi.

Chapter Two

Two hours earlier

Naomi looked over her shoulder into the full-length mirror in the corner of her dressing room while her maid adjusted the bow at the back of her ensemble. Her dress was rose gauze and split at the back to reveal the darker mauve, silk slip beneath. Lace the color of buttercream adorned the short sleeves and low, square neckline.

"Thank you, Brenna," she said when the bow was just right. She pressed a hand to her fluttering stomach and drew a deep breath as she scrutinized her appearance once more. Her blond hair, marked with strawberry highlights, had been twisted high at the crown of her head, with a single braid wrapped around the knot. A silk peony—its petals touched here and there with glittering crystals—was tucked under the braid. Around her neck, she wore the necklace Marshall had given her for her twentieth birthday, a strand of pearls with a diamond-accented, filigreed pendant.

"Do I look all right?" she asked Brenna.

Her lady's maid smiled warmly, crinkling the corners of her kind eyes. "As beautiful as ever, my lady—more than usual, if it's possible."

Naomi smiled wryly. "I doubt very much that my looks are improving. I'm steadily closing in on one-and-twenty."

"But still in the first bloom of youth," Brenna said firmly.

Naomi nodded. "You're right, of course."

But she wasn't so sure.

After two Seasons, Naomi was as unattached as she'd been the day she made her bow. In just a couple days, Monthwaite House would close up, and they'd all retire to the country to Helmsdale until next spring.

She slipped out of her room and padded downstairs to join Isabelle and Lily in the salon. Along the way, she noticed familiar family portraits and heirloom furnishings—all the features of home. But increasingly, Naomi had begun to feel as though Monthwaite House was not truly *her* home. This was Marshall's house, and Isabelle was mistress here. And then there was Marshall's collection of estates: Helmsdale, the ducal seat, Bensbury, just outside of London, and several more scattered across the country. All Marshall's. All Isabelle's.

Marshall was the very best of brothers and Isabelle was both sister and friend to Naomi. They had never once uttered a syllable to make her feel unwelcome, and Naomi knew she could live with them forever, if she so chose.

But she did not so choose.

The time had come for Naomi to have a home of her own, a place where she was mistress, a life to share with a husband and children. She was ready.

At the moment, however, her marriage prospects were dim. And they would be dimmer yet during the long months when eligible gentlemen guests at Helmsdale would be few and far between. Tonight might be her last chance this year to catch a gentleman's eye.

In the salon, a footman wearing the maroon Monthwaite livery was lighting the candles on one lowered chandelier, filling the air with a clean, waxy aroma. The other chandelier was already fully illuminated and in place near the ceiling.

Isabelle and Lily stood at the far end of the large room, directing two other footmen in setting up chairs for the evening's auction. Isabelle turned to say something to Lily, giving Naomi a view of her full profile. The pale green silk of her dress hugged her pregnant curves. As Naomi approached, Isabelle's hand drifted to the side of her belly and rubbed a small circle there, caressing her unborn child.

A twinge of guilt darted through Naomi. How could she worry about her lack of suitors at a time like this? With less than two months before the arrival of her nephew or niece, Naomi should focus instead on helping Isabelle. What a selfish beast she was to think about setting up her own house when Isabelle needed her.

Her sister-in-law glanced her way and smiled at her approach. "What a fetching dress!" Isabelle exclaimed. "Turn around, please."

Naomi did so; the gauze overdress swirled around her hips.

Lily wore a look of frank admiration. "I don't suppose you'd allow me to put *you* on the auction block? We would raise a million in one go, and I'd never have to fret about soliciting support again."

Naomi rolled her eyes at her friend's suggestion. "And why not you, Lily? That brown is positively luxurious with your complexion."

"I'm afraid poor Ethan couldn't bear to part with Lily at any price," Isabelle said, "not even for a cause as worthy as ours."

With the chairs arranged in neat rows, the footmen brought in the lots to be auctioned off. The ladies walked to the table where the refreshments would stand and discussed where everything should be placed. When Naomi looked back, she saw the servants were making a muck of arranging the auction items.

She briskly crossed the room. "No, no," she said to one of the footmen. "That won't do at all. You see how this is a lopsided configuration? Bring that easel with the landscape down to this side," she said, gesturing. "That will give some balance to the grouping."

The footman hesitated. "My lady, Her Grace—"

"Her Grace told him exactly where to place everything," Isabelle said, hurrying from the refreshment table. She raised a brow at Naomi before directing the servant to keep the easel right where it was.

Heat flushed Naomi's cheeks. "I'm sorry, Isa. I didn't mean anything by it. I just thought . . ."

Isabelle sighed. "Not at all, dearest. And now that I look, you have the right of it." She called to the footman, "Put the painting where Lady Naomi says."

Isabelle squeezed her hand before rejoining Lily. Naomi smiled but inside she chilled with humiliation. "It's not your house," she whispered softly to herself. Her duty here was to assist, not direct.

Marshall, Lord Thorburn, and Aunt Janine came in just ahead of housemaids bearing trays of food. Ethan greeted Lily with an arm around her waist and a brief kiss full on the lips. Naomi averted her eyes only to see Marshall take Isabelle's hands in his own and kiss the backs of her fingers.

Naomi sighed. Would she ever have such a love of her own?

Aunt Janine pulled Naomi aside. "A little much for public consumption, isn't it?" she said in a low voice.

"Oh, I don't mind, Auntie," Naomi said. "I think they're sweet."

Aunt Janine shrugged; her overlarge, lavender frock, with no pretension to style, scarcely moved. "Sweet, yes. But for maidens such as ourselves with delicate sensibilities . . ." She interrupted herself with a decidedly indelicate snort, unable to get through the misrepresentation of her own character with a straight face.

"I don't think they can help themselves," Naomi mused. She smiled lightly at her bemused aunt. "Propriety seems not to cross one's mind when one is possessed of a strong passion." She quoted a couplet of poetry.

Aunt Janine's eyes narrowed shrewdly. "I didn't know you read Marlowe, my girl."

"John Donne," Naomi corrected. Aunt Janine cocked a brow, and Naomi realized she'd stepped into a trap. "That is," she started, "I might be mistaken. Indeed, I almost certainly am. There was a dusty, old book of poetry I picked up off the floor once, and I just happened—by chance—to see a few lines."

Aunt Janine smiled smugly. "I didn't discover Donne until I was thirty. And even then, I wouldn't own to having read some of his more shocking verses." Leaning in, she added in a whisper, "I always knew you had it in you, my dear. Educating yourself is nothing to be ashamed of."

Naomi's lips pressed together. She glanced at the others, who were talking amongst themselves and paying no attention to Naomi and Aunt Janine's conversation. "I received a proper lady's education from my governess and tutors," she hissed. "Beyond that, I have no idea what you—"

Isabelle suddenly gasped. Her eyes squeezed shut and her hands covered her abdomen.

For a moment, everyone froze with shock.

Marshall moved first; he reflexively wrapped a supporting arm around her waist and took one of her elbows with the other hand. "Isa, what's wrong?" His dark eyes were wide and his lips white. "It's too soon, isn't it?"

"I'll go for the midwife," Ethan offered.

"That isn't necessary," Isabelle said weakly. She opened her eyes and drew a breath. "It was just a pain, but it's gone now."

Marshall's hand moved to her belly. "Hard as a rock," he murmured.

"For God's sake, get her off her feet!" Naomi snapped. Everyone turned to look at her as though she'd sprouted horns. "Listen to me."

She moved to Isabelle's other side and rubbed her back. Her sister-in-law's eyes were filled with fear. Naomi tried to convey a sense of calm and reassurance. "It's probably nothing but the effects of too much activity. You should have a drink, lie on your left side for a while, and see if that brings an end to the pains. If it does not, then I'm afraid the midwife will have to be sent for."

Lily's brows furrowed. "Why the left side?"

Briefly, Naomi considered going to her room to retrieve the French book about pregnancy and birth she'd been secretly studying ever since learning of Isabelle's condition. "It's an old wives' tale," she said instead, shrugging. "But it's worth a try."

"I'd rather consult the midwife," Marshall said. "We should cancel the auction."

"No." Isabelle shook her head; the short waves framing her face bobbed. "We promised Lily we'd do this for her school. Please, darling. Let's try Naomi's way first. If the contractions continue, we'll summon the midwife."

Marshall cast a disapproving glance at his sister then scooped Isabelle into his arms and strode from the salon.

Naomi exhaled a breath she hadn't known she'd been holding. She blinked and looked around at the others. Lily tilted her head and studied Naomi as though seeing her in a new light.

Ethan regarded her with admiration. "Left side, you say? File that tidbit away, princess," he said to his wife. "Might be useful sooner or later."

Naomi felt Aunt Janine's eyes boring into her back. She did not wish to turn around and face her knowing smirk again. She cleared her throat. "The guests will arrive shortly," she announced. "Let's finish preparations." With a lift of her chin, she turned back to the refreshment table and made minute adjustments to the platters of food.

Fifteen minutes later, Marshall returned, his posture and demeanor considerably eased. "Isabelle feels much more the thing," he told the group. "She's resting comfortably and will join us later if she's up to it."

Lily put a hand to her chest and breathed a sigh of relief. "Oh, thank heavens. I couldn't have gone on with the benefit, knowing Isa was in peril."

Marshall surprised Naomi by pulling her into a hug. "Thank you," he rasped. "If anything happened to her—"

"She'll be fine, Marshall," she assured him. "Isabelle is a strong woman. She'll give you a perfect, healthy child when the time is right."

He held her back but kept a grasp on her upper arms. A thoughtful look passed across his face. "I don't know how anyone can stand to have more than one baby. Isabelle might have the fortitude for it, but I don't know that I do. The nearer her time comes, the more . . ." He stopped himself and patted her shoulder. "Well, that's not for you to worry about."

Naomi shook her head. "*Now* you remember my maidenly innocence?" she teased.

A footman announced the first guests, Mr. and Mrs. Bachman. Marshall squeezed her hands before going to greet them.

Soon, a fair crowd mingled and chatted. Lily and Ethan made an elegant-looking pair as they spoke to everyone about King's Cross Vocational. Naomi was awed by her friend's massive undertaking—a school to train disadvantaged young women in good-paying trades. The institution was scheduled to open its doors for Michaelmas term on the first of October, a date fast approaching. Ethan matched his wife's enthusiasm for the institution; between her force and his charm, Naomi did not think anyone could help but be persuaded to contribute to the cause.

Naomi had spent a great deal of time at the school, helping in whatever small ways she could. Another benefit to her eventual marriage, she thought as she nodded to some new arrivals, was that she could sit on the board for King's Cross as Isabelle already did.

She exchanged a warm greeting with her friend Emily—now Lady Gerard. "How lovely you're looking, Em." Naomi admired her friend's canary dress. Emily raised a hand to touch her auburn hair—and to display the large, yellow-sapphire ring gracing her finger. "Oh, my!" Naomi exclaimed.

"Do you like it? Charles gave it to me just tonight," Emily gushed. She glanced to where her husband, Lord Gerard, conversed with Mr. Hayward.

Naomi watched her friend's features closely. There was a pride about her that she'd acquired since the June wedding. She was proud of her husband, Naomi saw, proud of the good match she'd made. But she did not love him. Not yet. Naomi hoped her friend's marriage would become a true love match before long. Lily and Ethan's marriage had not begun on the warmest terms, after all, but now Naomi could not imagine one without the other coming to mind.

The sound of laughter drew their attention. It was Isabelle, looking much recovered from her earlier discomfort. She entered the salon on the arm of Lord Freese. Naomi felt a little sigh in her chest at the sight of the inordinately handsome viscount. His tall, broad frame and dark hair and brows should have made him intimidating. The prominent scar on his cheek should have spoiled his looks. But he was saved from ferocity by an easy, jovial nature. Unruly curls lightened the effect of their black hue, and even the scar was turned to an asset, because it lent him an air of experience. Here was a man who had been out and seen the world, fought bravely, and lost blood for his country. The only feature about him Naomi found the slightest unsettling were his eyes, a striking blue, sharply contrasting with his coloration.

His personable demeanor made him popular with other gentlemen while his looks made him a great favorite of the ladies. Indeed, Naomi considered Lord Freese to be perhaps the most attractive gentleman of her acquaintance—truly *attractive*, in that he drew females to him like shards of iron to a lodestone. Women could not help but lose their heads over Jordan—and they did so in droves.

And he'd never looked at her twice.

Well, she amended mentally, that wasn't quite true. He had looked at her numerous times—countless, even. But only as the younger sister of his friend. Never as a young woman of marriageable age might wish to be looked upon.

Which was why Naomi had resisted the urge to lose her own head over the man. When a god descended from on high to mingle amongst mortals, one was wise to keep one's distance. She contented herself in enjoying the view from afar and relishing the brief exchanges they shared when he visited Marshall. Their one dance at her debut ball was a highlight of her first Season. But she knew Jordan was not interested in making a match with someone as ordinary as Naomi. No, her own husband would be a man more of this sphere than the Adonis-like Lord Freese.

"Now, there's a gentleman who could pay me court anytime," Emily said in a low, lusty tone.

Naomi's eyes widened at her friend's statement. Her eyes cut to Lord Gerard. "Em, you've not been married two months!" she whispered.

Emily crossed her arms and clucked her tongue. "Oh, Naomi, you're still such a girl. You'll understand one day." Her lips turned up in a smile that held a hint of meanness. "Or not. I'm sure your marriage will be perfection, just like everything else you touch." Emily sauntered off to join her husband and the other gentlemen.

Naomi blinked, stung by her friend's lowering words. She glanced back to where Jordan had been, just in time to see him depart. The well-lit room seemed dimmer somehow. Why was he leaving so soon? Her mood sank, but when Sir Simeon greeted her, she gave him her most dazzling smile. Tonight, she had to help Isabelle and Lily. There was no time for sulking.

After a while, Naomi was able to discount Emily's hurtful words and enjoy herself. *She probably didn't mean anything by it at all,* she reasoned. Naomi was in an odd mood and had probably misinterpreted Em's comment.

As she chatted with the Holliers and the Bachmans, Naomi's neck prickled as though someone was watching her. She shrugged it off as another symptom of her own aberrant frame of mind and concentrated all the harder on her brother's guests. The sensation persisted, however.

Even as Mr. Gladstone paid her copious compliments on her appearance, she could no longer ignore the feeling of being watched. Naomi glanced over her shoulder. Lord Freese had returned, she saw, but he was not looking at her, of course. He stood talking to Marshall, with Isabelle, Lily, and Ethan all looking on.

With a start, she realized the sensation had gone away. *It was just a fancy,* she told herself. "Mr. Gladstone," she said at a pause in the man's profuse praises of the faux blossom adorning her hair, "do you have the time?"

The gentleman fished a gold watch from a pocket. "It's ten minutes before eight o'clock, my lady."

"The auction will begin at the hour," Naomi said. "If you'll please excuse me, I must see to rounding up the guests who have stepped out for air."

Just outside the salon, she bumped into the Holliers. "My lord, my lady, the auction will commence momentarily, if you'd like to go ahead and take seats."

"Thank you, m'dear." Lord Hollier patted his wife's hand, tucked into the crook of his arm. "We shall do so. I saw a group of young people go toward the library." He pointed an unsteady finger down the hallway.

Naomi thanked him before searching for the others. The library door stood open and she heard Emily's laughter. Smiling, Naomi started forward, but the sound of her own name halted her before she appeared in the doorway.

"Be kind, Charles!" Emily admonished her husband. "Naomi may not know how to encourage a gentleman's attentions. Why, just tonight she was shocked to her toes by some mild comment I made."

"To the contrary, my dear," Lord Gerard said, "she toys with men quite ruthlessly. Gets their notice with that pretty face, lets 'em put a foot in, then slams the door on their toes. I tell you, they aren't calling her the 'Snow Angel' at the clubs for nothing."

Naomi's jaw dropped and she covered her mouth to keep from making a sound. *The Snow Angel?*

"She could have been married a year and more by now if she'd wanted to be," Emily said.

"She has it all, by gad," said a man whose voice Naomi did not know. "I suppose she can afford to be choosy."

"Yes, but will anyone still come calling?" Emily mused. "If she's as cold-hearted as you say, who would have her?"

Tears pricked the backs of Naomi's eyes. "Oh, Emily," she whispered. How could her friend believe her to be a heartless tease? It wasn't Naomi's fault she'd had to discourage gentlemen from courting her. Her brothers had each forbidden her from making a match the last two Seasons. The year of her debut, Marshall had insisted she was too young to make such a decision. This year, Marshall had been in South America during the Season, and Grant had refused to take responsibility for allowing a betrothal. Naomi thought she was doing gentlemen a kindness by gently turning them away, rather than stringing them along.

"I would have her," said a voice she recognized as Mr. Hayward's. A man's steps paced the floor. "Indeed, were it not for the fact that Lady Naomi has rebuffed the attentions of all comers," Hayward continued, "I would have paid my addresses long since. She is, by far, the loveliest lady in Town, and in possession of both wealth and connections. Lucky will be the gentleman who wins her hand."

Naomi's heart lurched, grateful for Mr. Hayward's unexpected friendship. He alone spoke up for her, while the others dragged her name through the gutter.

"Maybe it will be you," Emily teased.

There was a long pause, and Naomi wished she could see Mr. Hayward's face. Did the idea of winning her hand please him? Was he indifferent?

"I think not," the gentleman said at last. "Greater men than I have been cast aside by the lady. What chance has the younger son of a baron, where loftier peers have failed?"

Her mind reeling, Naomi's eyes squeezed shut. Her fingertips curled around the chair rail running the length of the corridor.

She heard the sound of crystal clinking together. "Make mine tall," said one of the men. While someone poured drinks, the conversation inside the library turned to less personal topics.

Of all the gentlemen she knew, did Mr. Hayward alone still hold her in good esteem? Naomi had followed all the conventions since stepping foot in London. Well, she thought, there was that one instance when she and Lily had followed Lord Thorburn down Bond Street and spied on him in the lending library. Other than that indiscretion, however, she had walked straight and done her duty to her brothers. Despite following all the rules society and family placed on her, her reputation had suffered.

"I believe the auction begins at eight, yes?" Lord Gerard's bored drawl snapped her out of her reverie. "We'd best get back before we are missed."

Startled by the sound of footsteps, Naomi ran back to the salon on the balls of her slippered feet, praying she made no sound. Her cheeks burned as she skittered into the room and pressed herself against the wall, chest heaving. The guests were taking their seats. Lord and Lady Gerard's group entered and passed by an unnoticed Naomi.

Impulsively, Naomi shot a hand out and caught Mr. Hayward's sleeve. He turned, surprise evident in his gray eyes. *He really is a good-looking man,* she thought. His hair was dark gold and hung in loose waves to his jawbone.

"Mr. Hayward," she said. She glanced nervously at the assembled guests, not wanting to draw attention to herself. Everyone was seated—everyone but Lord Freese, that was. He looked straight at Naomi and Mr. Hayward. The lines of his posture suggested a hound *en pointe,* altogether rattling her nerves.

Mr. Hayward bent his neck. "Yes, Lady Naomi? Is there something I can do for you?"

It was an effort to escape the snare of Jordan's eyes and return her attention to Mr. Hayward. His own demeanor was much softer than Jordan's. Curiosity and amusement tugged at the corners of his mouth. *You can marry me,* she almost blurted. What if he really was her last chance? She couldn't afford to let him slip away.

Color flooded her face. Naomi's eyes dropped and she wrung her hands at her waist. "I'm feeling rather flushed," she said, "and I wondered if I might beg your escort for some . . ." She raised her gaze to Mr. Hayward's astonished face. "For some air," she finished quietly.

Mr. Hayward's brows rose a fraction; his smile vanished. "Of course, my lady." Rather than offer his arm, he took her hand and spirited her out of the salon and back down the corridor to the library he and the others had just vacated. He swung the door to, but did not close it completely.

Naomi started to pull her hand free of his, but Mr. Hayward instead tucked it into his arm. He looked seriously at her, but she caught a hint of something . . . heated . . . in his gaze. Swallowing around a bundle of nerves in her throat, she smiled. "Thank you, Mr. Hayward. The salon has grown intolerably warm."

He led her on a turn around the room. A moment passed in silence before he spoke. "It is a pleasure to serve you, my lady, but I do wonder that you should require an escort in your own home." Abruptly, he stopped and faced her. Naomi's back was almost against Marshall's prized collection of botanical research volumes. He held her in a sharp gaze.

"I . . ." she began. Her heart pounded in her ears while her mind went blank. How on earth did women go about catching themselves a husband? This all felt so awkward and unnatural. "I must admit I desired your company," she said at last.

Mr. Hayward's eyes dropped to her lips. Lifting her hands, he pressed a kiss against the back of the right and then the left. He lowered their arms and slipped his hands around her waist. "I have long desired your company," he murmured.

As he drew her close, Naomi caught a strong whiff of alcohol on him. She held her breath as she tilted her chin up, certain he would only press his lips chastely against hers for a second.

But he did not.

His mouth crashed down on top of hers with a force that made her eyes fly open in alarm. Mr. Hayward's arms clamped around her middle and drew her body full against him. Naomi's head swam. She brought her hands to his shoulders, uncertain whether she ought to force him away or draw him nearer. It wasn't an altogether unpleasant kiss, but so, so . . . sudden. And forceful.

Mr. Hayward decided the issue by breaking away. He sucked spittle and air between his teeth, a sound that made Naomi cringe inwardly. "My dear Lady Naomi, I have long admired you but thought myself beneath your notice." His mouth turned up in a half smile. Naomi thought his lips rather too full, now that she had the opportunity to examine them at close proximity. "How can it be that you have singled me out?" he marveled.

She frowned. She couldn't very well tell him he'd come to her notice because she'd eavesdropped and now believed him to be the only man left in the *ton* who truly wanted her. "Well, sir . . ." she started.

His finger covered her lips. "No, don't." He chuckled low in his throat, allowing more of his liquor-tinged breath to roll into her nostrils. "One doesn't look a gift horse in the mouth—one *kisses* the gift horse's mouth."

Oh my, he's drunk. The realization struck her even as he took her mouth again, more urgently this time. He groaned and slanted his mouth over hers. Naomi felt his tongue probing against the crease of her lips. She recoiled at the sensation and pulled her head back, gasping for air.

"You move me deeply, my beautiful little filly." Mr. Hayward kept one arm tight around her waist while the other hand moved up her side and then between them to cover her breast.

"No!" Naomi gasped. She wriggled her hips, ineffectually trying to pry herself loose of his grasp. Panic clawed at her throat as his smile deepened into something dark and predatory. "Stop this immediately, sir!" She balled her hand into a fist and struck his shoulder with all her might.

Amazingly, he spun as she hit him, as though torn away by a great force. Then there was a sickening crack, and Mr. Hayward crumpled to the floor with a groan, revealing a grim-faced Lord Freese. He released his right hand from its tight fist then flicked his wrist, as though shaking off a bit of dust.

With his opponent on the floor, Jordan turned his sharp gaze on Naomi. "Are you all right?" he asked. "Did he hurt you?"

Naomi blinked and realized her mouth hung agape. She shut it with a snap of her teeth. "No," she said, shaking her head, "he didn't hurt me." A deep breath left her in a whoosh and she smiled weakly. "Thank you, my lord. I had no idea he would try anything like—"

A tug at her skirt caused her to gasp. Mr. Hayward moaned and flailed blindly. Both his eyes were swelling shut and blackening, and his nose was bulbously enlarged and skewed at an unnatural angle.

"Pardon me," Lord Freese said with a polite nod. He hauled the younger man to his feet and led him toward the library door. "Off you go, Hayward. And should you ever be so foolish as to breathe a word of this business to a living soul, I shall be forced to offer my eyewitness account of how Lady Naomi felled you with one strike of her mighty hand. Iron fist in a velvet glove, indeed. Am I right?"

He called to a passing footman and handed the groaning gentleman over to the servant. "Poor Mr. Hayward's face made the unfortunate acquaintance of His Grace's floor. The rugs in this house are downright perilous, bringing down the high and low alike. Do assist our young man to his conveyance. Thank you."

When Jordan swiveled back to her, his charming smile fell away. He stalked forward, lips pulled in a tight line. His unsettling eyes drove right into her.

Butterflies buffeted Naomi's stomach. "Thank you once again for your assistance, my lord," she said in a rush. "I am most obliged, but should be getting back now—"

Jordan snatched her upper arm in a tight grip. His blue irises flashed dangerously. "What the devil possessed you to behave so stupidly? You never should have left the party," he scolded. "Do you know what that boy could have done to you?"

Naomi flushed at his rebuke. "I believed he would act as a gentleman!" Tears threatened as the shock of Mr. Hayward's assault gave way to shame, but she blinked them back. "Can't a lady trust—"

"No," Jordan snapped. "You can't trust a man to keep his hands to himself, Naomi. Not when he's freely offered a sumptuous delight." His lips quirked, and she couldn't tell whether or not he mocked her.

Something stirring in his eyes made her breath catch in her throat. Heat flowed over her breasts and chest, all the way from her neck to her face. "I didn't offer him anything improper," she whispered.

"I saw you stop him." Amusement tinged his words. He smiled like the cat who'd caught the canary. "Moreover, I arrived here in time to watch you participate quite willingly in a round of rather amateurish kisses. My first hint that I'd have to step in, in fact, was when I began to fear Mr. Hayward might eat you."

Jordan's hand slid down her arm, arousing all sorts of discomfort in Naomi. Surprisingly, though, she discovered there was discomfort that was also pleasurable. His fingers tangled lightly with hers. Jordan leaned in, bringing his face closer to Naomi's than it had ever been. He was gorgeous, scarred cheek and all.

"If you wanted to indulge in some kissing lessons," he murmured, his breath ghosting against her cheek, "you ought to have asked someone who could teach you better—and shares your unconventional opinions."

"What unconventional opinions would those be, my lord?" she asked, bewildered.

Jordan tsked and shook his head. "Wayland Hayward is wife hunting, my sweet. You nearly fell into his trap."

Naomi bit back a growl of frustration. She'd *wanted* to fall into Wayland Hayward's marriage trap! She'd thought to be laying one of her own, in fact—until *Lord Interfering* here meddled. "What business is it of yours whom I choose to kiss?" she shot.

His eyes narrowed on hers. "I just paid fifteen hundred pounds for two pies," he seethed.

She shook her head, utterly lost. "Are you also drunk, my lord?"

His large, heavy hands covered her shoulders, and he leaned forward to put their eyes on the same level. "I paid fifteen *hundred* pounds, Naomi, for two pies. I don't even like blueberries! I'm going to give it to the first street sweep I see tonight. 'Here you are, lad, a seven hundred fifty-pound pie to take home to Mother, all because I had to get out of that room and save Naomi from her own foolishness.'"

She lifted her chin. "You can hardly lay that at my feet. Furthermore, you treated Mr. Hayward far more viciously than the situation warranted." Naomi paused to take a breath.

A thoughtful expression crossed Jordan's face as his gaze drifted somewhere past her left ear. Naomi was vexed he seemed not to be paying any attention to her words. "What you need, my lord, is—"

"Women." His lips parted as he drew a quick breath, and his eyes roved hers. "I need women," he whispered in amazement.

Naomi sputtered. "My lord! Pray do not include me in such lascivious confidence."

He squeezed her shoulders and grinned. "I need women, Naomi!" He kissed her forehead and straightened. "You're brilliant, sweeting." He winked and pinched her chin.

Before Naomi could collect herself out of the utter confusion into which he had tossed her, Jordan hurried out of the library.

She followed him out, just in time to see the butler open the front door for him. "He needs women," Naomi murmured, no less perplexed than she'd been a moment ago. Shaking her head, she turned in the opposite direction to rejoin the charity auction. She tried to put the upset of the last little while out of her mind. Her family needed her.

Chapter Three

Jordan turned his mount into Hyde Park and started toward Rotten Row. His eyes burned from lack of sleep. Despite the fact that the sun had just begun to blush the dew-kissed grass, he'd already been to see Lord Castlereagh, who approved his scheme. Notes had been hastily jotted off to his stepmother and the men on the list Jordan knew to have wives or other female relatives, but he still needed a few more ladies to round out his plan. He'd looked for Marshall at Monthwaite House, but the butler had informed him His Grace was out for a morning ride.

As he made his way through the park in search of his friend, Jordan's tired mind drifted to Naomi. Last night had been . . . an aberration. Jordan had no idea why he'd fixated on the young lady. In the end, though, he was glad for it, as he'd found her in time to pull that sleazy Hayward off of her before the scoundrel had done worse than paw her.

When he thought about what might have happened, Jordan's knuckles itched to plant another facer on the cur.

Naomi's reaction to Jordan had been something of a puzzle. She'd been glad enough for his assistance with Hayward but had turned testy when he'd suggested they shared similar opinions on matrimony. Perhaps it was as simple as a young lady not wanting word of her unusual views to get around. But, he thought with a frown, if she were going to dabble in peccadilloes in lieu of marriage, she would have to be far more circumspect.

He heard his name and glanced up to find he'd arrived at his destination. Marshall rode toward him at a trot on his white stallion, Amadeus. He pulled alongside Jordan, and the two men shook hands.

"A happy coincidence," Marshall said.

The easy smile on his face was a contrast to the brooding demeanor he'd worn during the years following his and Isabelle's divorce. Jordan could only credit their remarriage with the change in his friend. He was especially glad of his good mood this morning.

"Not a coincidence, Marsh. Might I have a word?" Jordan dug his heels into the sides of his own black beast, Phantom, and started off at a walk.

Marshall wheeled Amadeus about and caught up. "What is it, Freese?"

Jordan scowled beneath the brim of his tall hat before turning a smile on his friend. "I would like to host a party at Lintern Abbey—for grouse hunting. I have plenty of gentlemen guests but need some ladies to balance out the party. As you happen to have several delightful females in your household, I hoped you'd do me the very great favor of attending."

"Absolutely not," Marshall answered with a jerk of his chin. "It's out of the question, Jordan. I should have had Isabelle home to Helmsdale a month ago, but we stayed on in Town so she could throw last night's benefit. We leave tomorrow morning."

Jordan sighed heavily and pressed his thumb and forefinger to his aching eyes, suddenly more weary than he could remember being in years. "Of course. I'm sorry. It was foolish of me to even consider . . ."

His mind raced. This was the solution to his problem—he knew it was. He would not fail for lack of women at his party, even if he had to empty out a brothel and pay whores to act the part. But the ruse would be more convincing if there were known society ladies in attendance. The fingers of his dangling left hand drummed against the smooth leather of his tall riding boot.

"I don't suppose you know of any other ladies left in Town I might invite?" he ventured.

Marshall eyed him suspiciously. "Does this party have anything to do with Castlereagh commandeering my study last night?"

Jordan glanced up and down the Row. There were no other riders within earshot. "As a matter of fact, it does."

Marshall's lips pursed thoughtfully. "Let's see, here. A hunting party that I must now assume is not, in fact, a hunting party. Castlereagh provided you with your gentlemen guests, then?"

Jordan nodded. "Yes, exactly. I need women there to give the appearance of an ordinary house party."

"Why is the Foreign Office descending on Lintern Abbey? Why not the Home Office?"

"You know I can't tell you that, my friend."

For a while, they rode in silence. The rising sun began to burn away the cool mist hovering above the ground and dry the little droplets clinging to the dark green superfine of Jordan's coat.

"You haven't asked for my help in Foreign Office business since Spain," Marshall said.

Jordan glanced sidelong at the other man and could almost picture him as he'd looked on the Peninsula. His intense dark eyes had been large in his boy-slim face; he'd been much younger then. *God, we both were,* he mused. They'd looked like lads playing in their fathers' uniforms next to the seasoned officers, but they'd been called upon for some of the most important missions of the campaign. Marshall and Jordan were of an age, but sometimes Jordan felt as if he'd already lived enough for three lifetimes. He wondered if Marshall ever felt the same. "I never told you it was Foreign Office business."

"No, but you've just confirmed it," Marshall said wryly. "And we never spoke of it," he added. "It was like it never happened."

Jordan shrugged. "That's the nature of my job, I'm afraid. I never meant for you to take a bullet for me."

The duke grinned. "I never thought I'd be asked to stir up a peasant insurrection just to keep you, your man, and your Spanish informant safe in that village." His smile faltered. "I'm sorry I let you down. When I heard you and Ditman had been captured . . ."

Reaching the end of the Row, he pulled Amadeus to a halt. Gazing into the trees, he nodded slowly. "That was a low point, Jordan. I worried I'd let the government down, harmed the war effort—but worse, I failed you."

Jordan clapped his friend on the shoulder. "You didn't fail me, Marsh. You did a good thing, helping those people protect their village. The French would have plundered and raped their way through it, otherwise. Besides, we found our way home, only a little worse for wear."

Marshall gave a half smile. His eyes darted to the scar on Jordan's cheek. "A miracle in and of itself. The missing young lord escapes his French captors and returns home. You should've had a hero's welcome, but not a word was breathed publicly. That was how I knew I'd been tangled up in something of dire importance."

They started their steeds back in the opposite direction. "So," Marshall continued, "if you need ladies for your party, I assume you have good reason. Perhaps one of dire importance once again."

Jordan raised his brows but gave no answer.

Marshall held his gaze for a long moment, then looked away. "Isabelle and I can't come, but I might be persuaded to send Aunt Janine and Naomi."

Jordan breathed a little sigh of relief. If Ladies Janine and Naomi were to come to the Abbey, he could stop fretting about recruiting women. "That would be fantastic, Marshall. I don't know how to thank you."

He started to inquire after the duke's brother, whom he assumed would escort the ladies, but Marshall interrupted with a raise of his hand.

"I haven't agreed to anything yet. Will Lady Whithorn act as hostess?"

"I sent Clara an express this morning," Jordan answered. He smiled as he thought of his stepmother, a lovely woman only ten years his senior. "Nothing feeds her ego like knowing she's invaluable. I've no doubt she'll meet me at Lintern Abbey with bells on."

"Will Lady Kaitlin also come?" Marshall's question was simple on the surface and delivered in an even tone, but Jordan didn't miss the tightness around his friend's mouth. *Shrewd devil,* he thought. Marshall was really asking if Jordan believed the situation safe enough for his own younger half-sister's presence.

The answer was more complicated than a simple yes or no.

In truth, Jordan didn't know *what* he would find when he got home. If his plan worked—and he had every reason to believe it would—then the ladies in attendance would simply enjoy a country house party, never the wiser as to the true purpose of the armed men prowling the estate. Even so, some things were not suitable for children. There were no roles for babes in the staging of political stratagems, and so Jordan had not included Kate in his letter to Clara.

Saying so might decide Marshall against him, though, and Jordan needed the ladies to attend. "No, Kate won't come," he answered. "This is to be a house party in truth, Marshall; there will be entertainments in the evenings. As Kate's still in the schoolroom, it wouldn't do to bring her to the Abbey, only to keep her locked away."

Marshall frowned. His chin worked side to side as his lips twisted in thought. He fidgeted in the saddle and threw Jordan a scowl. "Can you ensure my sister's safety?"

Inside, Jordan squirmed, but he tossed off one of his devil-may-care smiles and chuckled. "I can't guarantee Lady Naomi won't meet any mishap whatsoever, my friend. There are stairs she might tumble down, needles upon which she might prick a finger—"

"Freese." Marshall's voice carried a warning tone. "Prevarication does not endear me to your cause."

Jordan scratched his chin. He pulled Phantom to a halt. Under his thighs, the stallion huffed and stomped the soft grass. The animal wanted a good run, and grew impatient with Jordan's sedate pace. Marshall brought his horse to a stop, as well. He lowered his head and stared at Jordan.

"Marsh," Jordan said in a more serious tone, "the ladies will be in no danger. If my ruse works as I anticipate, they'll spend a few pleasant weeks in the country—nothing more. Besides, with Lady Janine for her chaperone and Clara hostessing and Grant watching out for her—"

The duke's dark brows snapped together. "Who mentioned Grant?" Amadeus sidestepped, as though detecting his master's sudden change in demeanor. Marshall moved around him in a tight circle. Jordan stared straight ahead, accepting his friend's lambasting. "You asked me for women to sit in your parlor. You didn't request another man to take up arms for your mysterious cause, Freese."

Jordan started to protest, but Marshall forged on. "Despite your claims of safety for the women, I cannot imagine you could issue any such guarantee for my brother. If you will step out every day with firearms, it is because you face the possibility of meeting similarly armed enemies."

Damnation, the man had a point. Grant Lockwood was no agent of the Foreign Office. But if he came to Lintern Abbey to hunt, he might wind up exchanging fire with Frenchmen, instead of felling birds. In good conscience, Jordan could not enlist an unwitting combatant to his cause.

Bringing Amadeus nose to nose with Phantom, Marshall shook his head and spat. "This is lunacy. Forget it, Jordan—all of it. I'm not putting my family in harm's way for you."

So saying, he jerked his horse around.

Jordan's eyes squeezed shut while thoughts tumbled through his mind. By gad, he *needed* Naomi and Lady Janine. Time was too short to find more ladies. He should have already been pounding his way up the Great North Road.

"Marshall, stop," he called. His friend did so, but did not turn. Jordan cursed under his breath, disgusted with himself for the tactic he was about to employ, but necessity left him no choice. "Last night," he said, "I believe I was the only one who noticed that Lady Naomi was in some degree of distress."

Marshall wheeled Amadeus around. "What are you talking about?" he snapped.

"She was distracted, upset. I saw her slip out of the salon with Wayland Hayward." He arched a brow and asked in a blasé tone, "Did you notice when your sister went missing, Marshall?"

The duke frowned. "I was occupied with the auction."

Jordan returned his friend's frown with a bitter smile. "Too occupied to notice she'd vanished, I suppose. However, I *did* notice. I watched for her return, and when it didn't happen, I purchased two fruit pies for an inordinate sum and went searching. As it happens, she was in need of . . . assistance." Jordan didn't elaborate. He didn't need to.

He'd struck home with that remark, he saw, even as the bitter taste of bile burned the back of his tongue at divulging Naomi's predicament.

Shame and pain contorted Marshall's features. "Thank you for your service to my sister," he rasped, his jaw hardening. The muscle at his temple twitched, and Jordan thought Hayward would be lucky if he escaped from Marshall with nothing worse than a lashing.

Jordan met his vengeful expression. "I tell you this to illustrate I am already concerned for your sister's welfare. Not only is she your sibling, but she's also one of the finest ladies of my acquaintance. I would lay down my life before I let her come to harm, my friend." The odd thing was, as the words left his mouth, Jordan knew he spoke the truth. "She'll be perfectly safe at Lintern Abbey. Grant need not come, but please allow Naomi and Lady Janine to attend. You might not have been able to save my hide in Spain, but you can help me now by simply sending your ladies to my party."

The lump of Marshall's tongue moved behind his lips. He held Jordan in a fierce stare. "You will return my sister to me in the same condition in which I send her to you," he said in a low, dangerous tone. "Anything less will be your skin."

Jordan nodded once. "That I will, Marshall. I swear it."

Marshall turned Amadeus away without bidding Jordan farewell.

As Jordan watched the retreating view of Marshall's back, he had the sinking feeling he may have signed on for more than he was prepared to deal with. Though the French threat was undeniably the more important matter in the grand scheme of things, Jordan couldn't help feeling excited by the prospect of having Naomi Lockwood under his roof for a few weeks. He could take the opportunity to explore the attraction he'd sensed blossoming between them. After all, the French might miss Lintern Abbey altogether, giving him plenty of time to further their acquaintance.

Damnation! His mind was already wandering. With a vicious snarl, he pulled Phantom in the opposite direction and dug his heels into the horse's sides. He tore hell-for-leather down Rotten Row, attempting to pound his priorities back where they belonged.

Chapter Four

It occurred to Naomi—as she examined the illustration of an infant's head emerging from his mother's body—that she really was allowing her unfettered curiosity to get out of hand. But the books she read were so interesting, and the information she learned sometimes proved to be valuable, as it had when she'd rightly advised Isabelle to lie on her left side to stop her pains.

She sat in the window seat in her bedroom, a refuge from the household's bustle as preparations were made to decamp to the country. Turning a page, she inhaled at an illustration of the newborn infant, his umbilical cord trailing from his belly back into his mother. "Thank goodness for French obstetricians," she murmured. Continental sensibilities, being rather less restrained than English, proved to be quite a boon in matters such as medical texts. She doubted she could find such a frank examination of pregnancy and childbirth penned by an English doctor.

Just as well she'd held on to this book all these years, she reflected. She'd come into possession of it when she was just eight years old. Her mother, Caro, had suffered a mid-pregnancy stillbirth. Father was sitting in Parliament, Marshall at Oxford, and Grant at public school. Naomi was the only one Caro would allow to tend her. She'd stolen the book out of the midwife's bag, frightened and desperate to understand what was happening to her mother and how she could help. The text was beyond her rudimentary French skills, but with the help of a French dictionary she'd spent hours each night working her way through the book, increasing both her command of the language and her comprehension of Caro's plight.

While the experience had stripped away some of her innocence, it had been the moment when she'd first felt the satisfaction of being useful. It had also given her a taste of the power of information, of knowledge. She'd been hunting it ever since—in secret, of course. A genteel young lady was not supposed to know about placentas. But she did. A polite miss ought never to have read a brazenly sexual poem like Donne's "The Sun Rising." But she had.

And more. Much more.

But all in secret.

Aunt Janine already wore the brand of bluestocking for the Lockwood clan. An eccentric aunt was one thing. It lent the family an exotic flair. Being regarded as an eccentric oneself, however, was an entirely different matter. Naomi found herself in trouble enough with this Snow Angel business—she had no desire to add *Overly Educated* to her list of deficiencies.

She licked her finger, turned the page, and was thoughtfully absorbing the proper technique of clamping and cutting the umbilical cord when she was startled by a soft knock at the door. Naomi slammed the book shut and hastily stuffed it under the cushion as Brenna entered and curtsied.

"His Grace wishes to see you, milady," the maid said. "He awaits you in the library."

Naomi knit her fingers together in her lap. "Thank you." She maintained a placid countenance even though her right sitting bone perched painfully on the hard cover.

After Brenna left, Naomi retrieved the book. She passed a half-packed trunk standing at the foot of her bed and shoved the volume beneath a pile of shifts.

In the library, she found Marshall standing beside the fireplace—filled with a painted screen now, instead of a fire—and Aunt Janine seated on the sofa. Naomi's eyes flitted across the room to the spot where Jordan had put an end to Mr. Hayward's unwelcome advances. She flushed, remembering the kiss Lord Freese had spontaneously pressed to her forehead after issuing his baffling remark about needing women.

"I was going to go to Kew Gardens today," Aunt Janine said in an indignant tone, "to see this one's exhibit of Amazonian plants." She pointed an accusing finger at Marshall. "You'd best have a good reason for spoiling my morning, boy. And you owe me a private tour, too." She pursed her lips in a miffed fashion and nodded firmly, flapping the brim of her lace cap against graying hair.

Uneasiness stole over Naomi. "Is Isabelle all right?" Her sister-in-law was not present for what looked like a family meeting. Had something gone wrong during the night?

"Isabelle's fine," Marshall assured her. He waved absentmindedly at the sofa. Naomi sat beside her aunt, who was dressed in a typically unstylish frock. The drab flower print of her calico dress recalled a funerary arrangement. Aunt Janine's sharp eyes cut to Naomi. Suddenly self-conscious under the older lady's scrutiny, she jerked her gaze back to her brother.

"Are you all packed?" Marshall asked.

"Nearly so," Naomi answered. She prettily folded her hands on the muslin lap of her own fashionable morning dress. *Thank goodness I don't share Auntie's disdain for style, too,* she thought.

"Good." Marshall braced an arm against the mantel. He parted his lips and hesitated, then turned a heavy gaze on her. "There's been a change of plan, Naomi. You and Aunt Janine will travel to Lintern Abbey, rather than to Helmsdale."

Confusion shook her. "Lintern Abbey?" For a moment, she struggled to recall whose property bore the name. "Oh!" Her startled eyes flew wide. "That's Lord Freese's estate! Why ever would you send us there, Marshall?"

Aunt Janine straightened and lifted her chin. "I am not going to any such place, young man. I'm remaining right here in Town for another month, and *then* I shall come to Helmsdale in time for your child's birth, just as I said I would do."

"And I promised Isabelle I would help arrange the nursery," Naomi added. "Besides, why should Lord Freese want to host the two of us?"

Marshall looked from one to the other, his jaw working from side to side. "It's not just the two of you," he explained. "Lord Freese is hosting a house party and has graciously invited you to attend. Wouldn't you like to have fun with other young people? There won't be any excitement at Helmsdale for a while."

Naomi frowned. Despite his talk of fun and parties, it seemed like Marshall was trying to get rid of her. Her stomach knotted as she felt more than ever like an interloper. "I'd rather be at home with my family," she said unhappily.

Maybe Isabelle didn't want Naomi there, after all, and had asked Marshall to find her somewhere else to go. Had the incident the night of the auction vexed Isabelle more than she'd let on?

"And I should much rather be in Town." Aunt Janine stood and poked Marshall in the chest. "I'll not be bullied about by my own nephew."

Marshall took Aunt Janine's hand and gently lowered it. "Lord Freese tells me there will be dancing," he told Naomi. "And there is a ruin to explore, and gardens. Jordan's stepmother, Lady Whithorn, is hostessing. She and the earl don't come to Town much, so you haven't made her acquaintance. I believe you would get on with her very well, though."

The more Marshall talked, the more convinced Naomi became that she was unwanted at home. Her throat tightened and she blinked rapidly. "Please don't send me away." Her voice was thick with misery, scarcely more than a whimper.

While she was attracted to the handsome Jordan Atherton—intrigued by him, even—she scarcely knew him at all. The thought of spending weeks in the man's home made her uneasy.

Aunt Janine sniffed in disdain. "Nothing you've said has convinced me to agree to this scheme. I shan't take part."

Marshall huffed and his lips pressed together. "I'm sorry to hear that, Aunt," he said tersely, the cajoling tone evaporated from his voice. "Naomi is going, and that's an end to it. If you wish her properly chaperoned, you will go, too."

Aunt Janine's jaw snapped shut and she blinked in surprise. For a moment, she looked dumbstruck, an expression Naomi could not recall ever having seen on her face before now. Marshall's words chilled Naomi with their finality. He crossed his arms, obviously not intending to budge.

Aunt Janine turned to her niece. "And what say you, Naomi? Will you tolerate this . . . this . . . dictator's edict?"

Naomi glanced from her aunt's pleading gaze to her brother's steely one and then to her lap. Her clenched knuckles had gone white.

The times Naomi had defied her family were rare. Most notably, she had befriended Isabelle when Isabelle was the divorcée, Mrs. Lockwood, bearing the same name as Naomi but estranged from her family. It had never seemed right to Naomi how Isabelle was just . . . dismissed . . . like an unsatisfactory maid. To her mind, Isabelle's first marriage to Marshall had made her Naomi's sister, and no railing by her siblings or mother had been able to persuade her to see it otherwise. And so, she'd done the apparently unspeakable and treated Isabelle like her friend and sister because for the life of her, Naomi had been unable to see what the fuss was about. The real injustice had been in how the rest of the family had treated Isabelle so abominably.

Anyway, she reflected, that had all worked out for the best. Isabelle and Marshall were legally married once again, and no one held that *faux pas* against Naomi any longer. Indeed, Isabelle had often credited Naomi with helping to bring her and Marshall back together.

This situation was different, though. As much as Naomi wanted nothing more than to go home and spend the summer with her family, her family didn't want her there. She struggled against a feeling of betrayal. After Naomi had poised herself against her family's wishes for Isabelle's sake, this was how she was to be repaid—like a baby bird shoved from the nest.

"If Marshall says I must go, then I must," she said. Aunt Janine sputtered; Naomi threw a sharp look at her. "I know my duty, Aunt."

Marshall exhaled; his posture relaxed fractionally. The idea flickered across Naomi's mind that if she had held her ground, Marshall would not have forced her to go, but it vanished almost as soon as she'd thought it.

"Aunt Janine," Marshall said, "I suggest you follow Naomi's sensible lead and prepare to make your departure. You set out in the morning."

Aunt Janine's face drained of color. She nodded curtly and strode, stiff backed, from the library.

When their aunt had gone, Naomi lifted her eyes to Marshall. Her brother held himself awkwardly, as though uncomfortable in his own skin. Once again, Naomi wondered why he was doing this and how committed he truly was to the plan to send her away. By all appearances, he was no happier about it than Naomi.

She rose and stood before him, her arms stiff at her sides. "Must I really do this?"

A pained frown creased Marshall's brows. "I'm afraid so." Her lips parted, but Marshall held up a forestalling hand. "Promise me you'll be careful, Naomi."

His urgency confused her. "Careful of what?"

"Just . . ." He shook his head. "Please, just be careful. Steer clear of Lord Freese. I mean it, Naomi. Keep your distance from him." His jaw tightened as his eyes looked precisely to where Naomi had been accosted by Mr. Hayward.

Suddenly, Naomi wondered what Marshall knew about what had transpired. Judging by the tightness around his eyes and mouth, she was almost certain he knew the whole of it. Embarrassment brought a heated flush to her cheeks. "I shall do as you say."

She pressed a hand against her lips as she flew up the stairs, suffering an agony of shame at having her indiscretion found out. Lord Freese was the only person beside herself and Mr. Hayward who knew what had happened. Jordan must have told Marshall. *How could he?* A true gentleman would never compromise a lady so. All the more reason for her not to go to Lintern Abbey!

Naomi's slippered feet carried her to Isabelle's bedchamber. If Marshall didn't really want to send her away, then maybe his wife could convince him not to.

She found her sister-in-law in her dressing room, selecting clothes for the trip to Helmsdale.

Isabelle was laughing at something her maid had said when Naomi entered, but her laughter died in her throat when she saw the younger woman. She hurried past Naomi into the large, adjoining bedchamber. "Hello, dear," she said, tossing Naomi a nervous smile.

Anxiety roiled in Naomi's stomach. "Marshall says I must go away," she blurted.

Isabelle paused in front of her vanity. Her fingers slowly wrapped around the silver handle of her brush.

"He's sending me to a party at Lintern Abbey, even though I said I don't want to go, that I'd rather help you at home." Naomi approached her sister-in-law and touched her shoulder lightly. Beneath her fingertips, she felt tension in Isabelle's body. "Won't you please speak with him?"

Isabelle swiped hastily at her cheek before she shook her head and turned. Her blue eyes were bright, and color stained her cheeks, though the rest of her face had gone pale. She trained her eyes on her maid, packing the trunks. "I don't . . . No, Naomi, I don't think I shall speak to Marshall. I'm sorry. You must do as he says."

Naomi tilted her head. "Isabelle, please," she begged. Why wouldn't her friend and sister look her in the eyes? "The nursery, you said—"

Isabelle sucked in a breath. She lifted her chin and bestowed a withering look on Naomi. "I'll make do without you."

Naomi jerked back as though struck. They really didn't want her at Helmsdale, neither of them. She stammered an apology and returned to her room. There, she looked around with the sense of doing so for the last time. If Marshall and Isabelle were sending her away because they no longer desired her presence, then she could never return after the party at Lintern Abbey. Not really. Naomi now knew her days with her family were numbered, and she was a woman without a home.

*

As the door closed behind Naomi, Isabelle collapsed into a chair. She pressed cold, shaking hands against hot cheeks and squeezed her eyes shut. In her swollen belly, the babe moved slowly. A lump of . . . something—was it head or rump?—dug uncomfortably under a rib. Isabelle winced and massaged the spot, willing her child to settle. As though in defiance of her wishes, the infant only ground against her bone all the harder. "You think I've done wrong, too, don't you, my love?" Isabelle muttered. "Go on and punish me, then. I think your papa is wrong this time, little one."

After a moment, her babe's movements calmed. She heaved a tired sigh then pushed herself to her feet. In her mind's eye, Isabelle raced down the hall to run Marshall to ground. Reality held her back with a body she no longer recognized as her own. She stood as straight as her spine allowed but still felt as though there was no room inside to draw adequate breath. Aching hips and swollen ankles had transformed her usual, graceful gait to an ungainly, lumbering stride. She felt like an elephant tromping through the house—one that perspired in unseemly quantities, at that.

By the time she found her husband in his study, Isabelle was short of breath, unbearably hot, and cross. Marshall looked up from sorting papers with Perkins, his secretary. Though not a stick of furniture went anywhere, moving back to the country was still an enormous undertaking. Marshall's face lit at her entrance, and he stepped around the desk to greet her.

"I've just had to treat Naomi most cruelly," she announced before he'd come within arm's reach. "Why, Marshall? Why, why, *why* must she go away?" Isabelle stomped a foot and planted her hands on her lower back. She pinned Marshall with the fiercest glare she could summon.

Marshall glanced at Perkins. The secretary cut a bow and beat a hasty retreat. "Come sit down, Isa." He reached for her arm.

Isabelle scowled. "I don't want to sit. I'll get stuck in that little chair again, and you'll have to call Perkins back to tug it while you pull my arms. No, thank you, I'll stand."

A hint of laughter twitched across his lips, but Marshall wisely smoothed his features. "Darling, as I said before, I cannot tell you why. I'm terribly sorry everyone involved is so upset. Aunt Janine may never speak to me after this."

Isabelle pressed a hand to her chest. "And Naomi may never speak to me! If you'd seen the look on her face when I told her I don't need her . . ." She covered her eyes with her palms and once again saw Naomi's stricken expression. A fresh pang of guilt shot through her.

"I hurt her," she muttered miserably, "and I lied."

Marshall's arms wrapped around Isabelle; she sank against the support of his broad chest. "I *want* her to come home, Marshall. I've looked forward to her advice on decorating the nursery. I need another woman in the house besides your mother—" Isabelle groaned as she realized she now had no company to look forward to during her confinement other than her estranged mother-in-law. "Naomi would have helped keep Caro's claws in check, but now—"

Marshall pushed her back to look into her eyes. "She won't grieve you any more, Isa. I swear it. There's nothing Mother can say or do to cause you trouble ever again." He kissed her gently, and Isabelle's heart constricted. His warm hands cradled her face. "You and the baby are all that matter," Marshall said, his voice thick with emotion. "If she steps an inch out of line, I'll lock her in the dower house."

Isabelle drew a shaky breath and shook her head. Her fingers idly worked at fixing his perfectly good cravat knot. "But what of Naomi? Please say she can come home."

Marshall rested his forehead against hers. Isabelle sensed how this weighed on him. Something had convinced him sending Naomi off to a country party at Jordan Atherton's estate was more important than the wishes of Naomi, Aunt Janine, Isabelle, and even Marshall himself. "I wish I could tell you that," he said, squeezing her hips. "But Naomi must go to Lintern Abbey. It's important to all of us, though I don't suppose we'll ever know just how important."

With a confused and aching heart, Isabelle sighed. What could possibly be so crucial about Naomi's attendance at Jordan's party? She knew Marshall told the truth—at least as he saw it. She could only hope he'd based his decision on something truly extraordinary. "Whatever it is," she grumbled, "it had better be worth making us all so unhappy."

Chapter Five

Jordan rubbed ink-stained fingers across tired eyes. "Do any of you wish to contribute to this conversation, or am I as good as talking to myself?" The inn's taproom was deserted but for them. Jordan had paid handsomely to ensure their privacy.

With a heavy sigh, he looked down the table where five of his men sat. They glanced at one another, avoiding Jordan's gaze in the way of schoolboys loath to make eye contact with the headmaster.

"I think we should rotate the watch," John Bates said after a long silence. The heavy man leaned back in his chair; the rickety furniture creaked and popped. His right hand dabbled idly in a ring of moisture at the base of his tankard, while the left scratched at the scrap of beard planted beneath his bottom lip. With slicked-back hair, mustache, and the bristles on his chin, Bates looked like something from the age of Elizabeth. In that era, he'd have held a profession with -eer attached to it—privateer, balladeer, musketeer—something to complement his affected bravado. It remained to be seen whether the man could match action to appearance.

Jordan tapped his sheet of notes. "We've already decided to mix the groups every day."

Bates shook his head and waved a hand. "Not what I mean, Freese. I'm suggesting that, in addition to rotating through the groups, we spread ourselves thinner—keep a full watch going at night, as well."

"Ahem," interjected Ferguson Wood. Jordan glanced at the man sitting across from Bates. Wood blinked three times in quick succession. "Wouldn't that arouse, uh"—his fingers danced in the air, just above the table, like a conjurer working an incantation—"notice?" he blurted. He flashed a smile, offering a glimpse of overlarge teeth. Blinking several more times, he tilted his head. "If the whole object of this exercise is to allay the, the, the *suspicion* of"—*blink blink blink*—"our *friends*, as it were, surely sending out full *hunting groups* at night would be"—*blink blink*—"inadvisable."

Jordan's eyes watered in sympathy with the man's abused eyelids. "Good point," he agreed. "Maintaining a lighter watch at night should be sufficient—a few men stationed close to the house."

The house. His house. His once and future prison. As a youth, he'd escaped the place as fast as he could and had spent the bulk of his adulthood avoiding Lintern Abbey. Castlereagh's orders still felt like a bridle specially designed for Jordan. His nature bucked against the confines of it, resisting the call to home and all the drudgery it entailed. The muscle in his right cheek twitched around the scar. The ridge was numb, a streak of death embedded in his living flesh.

God, he did not want to go home.

The man seated on Jordan's left, Andrew, Lord Gray, loudly gulped ale and made a satisfied sound as he set down his tankard. "There's a cave not too far from here," he said. "S'posed to be a lovely outing for ladies. Easy path. Not far in, there's an underground pond full of blind fish. There's torches available for sale." The young man's hazel eyes lit hopefully. There wasn't a line on his face. Jordan doubted he shaved more than once a week.

"Are you quite sure you're supposed to be here?" Jordan inquired with a scowl. "You didn't open a letter meant for your father, by chance?"

Lord Gray's light brows drew together quizzically, and he laughed, a golden, boyish sound. "I should think not, sir. My sire's been dead these last five years." He nudged his neighbor, Mr. Elton, and laughed again. That gentleman gave Lord Gray a sidelong glance from close-set eyes and moved his chair slightly away.

Jordan caught a shadow of motion out of the corner of his eye. He felt a twist of alarm until the shadow broke away from the wall and materialized into the tall, lanky form of Solomon Perry. He'd divested himself of boots, Jordan saw, and now crept up in stocking feet behind Percival Young, who had quietly taken in the others' conversation from the far end of the table. Perry winked at Jordan and held a finger to his lips. From behind his back, he produced a long goose feather and tickled Young's ear.

Percy swatted as though shooing a fly; his wrist flicked effeminately. The man was delicate boned and skirted close to pretty, with his milky complexion, reddish hair, and petulant lips. All too often, Jordan had seen such males draw the undeserved contempt of their peers.

Mr. Perry grazed the feather against Percy's ear again. The gentleman brushed it away, visibly annoyed.

Percy Young was newly betrothed. Whether his impending marriage went with or against his natural inclinations was of no import to Jordan. He didn't waste time thinking about what people did in their own beds. However, the subject mattered a great deal to other men, who acted out—as though they were somehow threatened—against males who didn't fit their idea of how a man ought to look and act.

Solomon once more touched Mr. Young's ear. "Stop it," Jordan snapped.

At the same instant—before Jordan had finished uttering those two brief words—Percival Young was on his feet with a pistol aimed at Perry's chest. It was the quickest draw Jordan had ever witnessed.

"Percy, Percy!" Solomon held his hands wide, the offending feather pinched between his thumb and forefinger. "It was just a bit of fun. Where's your sense of humor, man?"

Percival's eyes narrowed. "In my line of work, men who creep behind my back don't get the chance to do it again." He was a slip of a man next to the towering Solomon Perry, but there was no doubt as to who dominated.

Solomon licked his lips and laughed nervously. "Lord Freese, there's a loose cannon on deck."

"Stand down, Mr. Young," Jordan ordered. Slowly, Percy lowered his weapon. Jordan's eyes flicked to the taller man. "Mr. Perry, if you pull a childish prank again, I won't stop Young from dealing with you as he sees fit. Sit. Now."

With a sulky air, Solomon pulled out a chair and folded himself into it.

A serving girl appeared, carrying a large, round tray loosely at her side. She hovered expectantly near the door, awaiting requests for more refreshments. The Foreign Office agents exchanged peevish glances with one another. Solomon Perry pouted at the table, and Mr. Elton exhaled a sigh of long suffering. When none of Jordan's men said anything, the girl darted out.

"I suppose this meeting is effectively over," Jordan snapped. His back and legs ached from two long days spent riding, and he longed to be free of these *children* Castlereagh had saddled him with. Six boys sulking at their father, another four to meet them at home, and ten females to entertain, too.

"In that case," Lord Gray said lightly, "how about an excursion to the cave I mentioned? My wife would enjoy the outing." He passed his smile around the table, blithely ignoring the dour mood that had descended upon the party.

Jordan shook his head once. "No. We've work to do."

Lord Gray's brows closed in a frown, his young skin folding as crisply as fresh linen. "Come now, Freese, have a heart. My lady and I have only been married a few weeks. Surely you wouldn't disappoint a new bride. Wouldn't it be all right if—"

The flat of Jordan's hand slapped against the table. "No," he said in a steely tone between clenched teeth, "it would *not* be all right." He leaned over the table until his nose was mere inches from Lord Gray's.

The young man swallowed. His lips went white around the edges, but he held his ground. "My lord, you just said the meeting is over."

"I spoke in haste," Jordan retorted. He stood up and crossed to the window, which overlooked the inn's stable yard. A coachman in dusty livery argued animatedly with one of the stable boys. Despite the driver's theatrical gesticulations, the boy shook his head, refusing to capitulate to the older man.

Abruptly, Jordan turned and swept a fierce scowl over his six men, these supposed agents of the British government, none of whom, if it were up to him, he would allow to wipe a baby's bottom, much less entrust with European peace and security.

"I want you—every one of you—to think about why we are here and what we're about. Spend a moment of introspection and consider your loyalties."

John Bates raised a skeptical brow. Jordan restrained the urge to wipe the smirk off the man's face. Instead, he circled the table at a slow, stalking pace. "An acquaintance of ours has given us a task," he said tersely. "It is our job to fulfill that task. Period." His eyes narrowed on Lord Gray. "It is not our job to take the ladies to outings at caves." A stony glare for Solomon Perry. "Nor is it our job to torment one another with idiotic pranks." Mr. Perry ducked his head, abashed. "My loyalty lies with king and country, gentlemen. What say you?"

"King and country." Percy Young lifted his tankard.

John Bates's tankard joined Percy's. "To king and country."

A muttered chorus echoed the sentiment. Lord Gray lifted his drink reluctantly and only after his lips pinched together while he seemed to weigh the merit of continuing the quarrel.

Jordan lifted his own glass. "To king and country." After the men had all joined in the toast, the tension in the air eased somewhat. Jordan returned to his seat and lifted a quill to resume the discussion of the upcoming operation. But before he could, a sharp rapping sounded from downstairs, followed by an irate, female voice. Only a few words were intelligible.

" . . . not my concern . . . mean to say . . . *ladies*, no less!"

A smile tugged Jordan's lips. "Don't move," he told his men. He went down the stairs, turning so his broad shoulders could pass through the narrow space.

In the common room, he saw just what he'd expected. Lady Janine Lockwood was in high dudgeon, giving the innkeeper what for. She punctuated her tirade with an occasional strike of her parasol handle against the polished expanse of countertop separating her from the harangued landlord. "Don't think you quite comprehend who my nephew is, you imbecilic nitwit!" *Thwack!*

Naomi stood to the side, watching her aunt's diatribe with an expression of horror and mortification. Her face was stained pink all the way from the bit of neck visible above her melon traveling costume to where her forehead vanished beneath the brim of her fashionable bonnet.

In spite of her obvious discomfiture, Jordan once again thought her utterly enchanting. He put a hand on the wall to halt himself; the strength of this newfound attraction to Naomi unnerved him. She hadn't spotted him yet, and he greedily took advantage of being unnoticed to drink her in.

"My—my lady," the innkeeper ventured, "I most certainly do know who your esteemed nephew is. It is most regrettable that I do not have a room available to offer you and your niece, but I am filled to capacity with—"

"A traveling party," Janine snapped. "So you said already, you redundant oaf."

Naomi winced at this last exclamation from her older relative. "Auntie, please," she murmured. Placing a hand on her aunt's elbow, Naomi attempted to draw her toward the door. "There will be another inn soon enough. There's still plenty of daylight to travel by."

Lady Janine ignored her niece's gentle persuasions. "What is the world coming to?" She gestured widely with the parasol; the innkeeper ducked behind the counter to avoid being clubbed. "When two ladies of quality are refused accommodation, society must surely be in sad decline. Sir, I would remind you of the fate that befalls all great civilizations when mannerly behavior goes by the wayside. If I may recall your notice to Babylon . . ."

Naomi shook her head. Suddenly, her gaze landed on him; her eyes widened.

When their eyes met, something stirred in Jordan. Two somethings, to be precise. Neither the physical awakening nor the more immaterial sensation in his chest were welcome at the moment. Yet he couldn't stop himself from smiling as he approached, looking away from Naomi only when Lady Janine drew his attention.

"Lord Freese!" the woman exclaimed. "A most welcome sight you are."

He carved a bow. "May I be of service, my lady?"

Lady Janine thrust her parasol handle menacingly toward the harried innkeeper. "*This* man," she said with a scowl, "tells me he has no room available for myself and Lady Naomi. *This* man says all the chambers are spoken for. In all my years, I have never yet seen a truly full inn. Surely there is a cupboard or loft into which he could shuffle some menfolk to make way for two ladies, but he will not do so!"

The innkeeper turned a pained expression on Jordan. "My lord, I told her that your party—"

"You did no such thing!" Lady Janine scolded. To Jordan, "He never once mentioned your name, Freese. Had I known it was your party ensconced within these unworthy walls, I would have asked for you straightaway."

Jordan pressed a hand to his chest. "My sincere apologies for taking up so many beds. Of course, we'll rearrange to make way for you and Lady Naomi."

Janine gave him a satisfied smile.

Jordan addressed the innkeeper. "I'll take the floor in Mr. Elton and Mr. Perry's room, and the ladies can have mine."

"My lord!" Naomi exclaimed. "You must not discommode yourself on our account."

Jordan smiled lightly, pleased by a soft inhale and parting of her lips.

Her gaze did something soft and ticklish to the inside of his throat. "I haven't," he said. "It's no trouble at all."

With all parties appeased, the innkeeper bustled off. Lady Janine stepped back outside to issue instructions to their servants and Naomi made to follow.

"Naomi."

She turned. Pink touched the apples of her cheeks. Jordan slowly closed the distance between them, unwilling to part ways with her just yet. "It's an unexpected pleasure to have you and Lady Janine stop at the very inn in which our party is already gathering."

"Unexpected, perhaps, but not altogether surprising." She tilted her head. "We *are* traveling to the same destination, my lord."

Their mutual destination . . . Lintern Abbey. Jordan didn't want to talk about it, didn't want to think about it, even. "So we are," he answered.

Soft afternoon light filtered through the sheer, white curtains, illuminating Naomi from behind. Loose tendrils glowed with pale reddish-gold translucency. He'd never before examined her eyes closely enough to see it, but the irises began blue around the edges, then transitioned to green near the pupils. In her left eye, a delicate ray of golden brown fanned upward from the center, like sunrise bursting over the horizon.

"My lord?" Her brow lifted quizzically.

Jordan snapped shut the jaw he hadn't realized he'd allowed to go slack. "Lady Naomi," he blurted, "would you be so kind as to wait here a moment?"

She nodded.

He bounded back up the stairs to the taproom. Six bored faces looked up at his entrance. "Oh, good, you're still here," he said.

"Where else would we be?" drawled Mr. Bates. "You ordered us to stay put."

"So I did," Jordan quipped. "Gentlemen, I've reconsidered the matter and believe a group outing to the cave Lord Gray mentioned sounds like just the thing. Gather up your ladies, and we'll set out in half an hour."

Lord Gray grumbled and flung his hands out in an exasperated gesture. "Are you always so indecisive, Freese? It would be best to know right off if we can't rely upon you for steady guidance."

Jordan sniffed. "This is to be a party, is it not? I thought the matter over and decided it would be good to begin the charade now. Besides," he said with a quick grin, "far be it from me to disappoint a new bride."

He left his men to hustle themselves and their female companions into a state of readiness while he hurried back to the common room. Naomi had taken a seat in the bay window overlooking the village's bustling high street.

"Our little party is making an excursion to a nearby cave," he announced.

She raised her face, and he suddenly found himself in unfamiliar waters, grasping for words like a tongue-tied boy. "I was hoping . . . That is . . . Would you like to come, too? And Lady Janine, of course. There's an underground pool, I've heard, filled with blind fish."

Her eyes lit from within. Jordan could see the suggestion intrigued her. Then the lights went dim and her face fell. "Thank you for your kind invitation, my lord," she said coolly, "but I'm afraid I must decline. We've had two hard days of traveling, and I could use some rest."

Jordan stiffened. He could see plain as day she was not fatigued. She was brushing him aside.

And he didn't like it.

"If you'll excuse me," she said in the same cool tone. Jordan bowed as she swept past him to the stairs leading to the guestrooms.

He couldn't help but stare at her hips swaying gently from side to side as she moved with the easy grace he'd come to recognize as her hallmark. "Snow Angel," he muttered under his breath. Beautiful but cold. Maybe there was something to the rumors, after all.

*

Midnight had come and gone. Jordan sat with his notes spread before him. Plans, tactics, stratagems . . . all drawn up for Lintern Abbey. It still seemed inconceivable that a sleepy, boring estate had suddenly become the epicenter of international intrigue. He and several men had returned to the taproom a couple hours ago to hammer out more details. Unfortunately, they'd no longer had exclusive use of the room; a stranger had sat ensconced at a table in the corner. His back faced them, and he hunched over his mug with the air of a man who wished to be left alone. Jordan couldn't risk speaking of their plans, for fear of being overheard.

Instead, he ordered round after round of ale, all the while talking and laughing with the others, like men enjoying an ordinary night amongst friends.

For an hour or so, they'd tried to wait the man out. But the stranger stayed, working his own way through a steady supply of ale.

When John Bates's eyes had gone glassy and his voice brash, Jordan had surrendered and sent him and the others off to bed, while he'd remained behind to review everything one more time. A heavy slash here, a circle around something there . . . Finally, Jordan stacked together his notes and capped a little bottle of ink. It was a good plan, he decided. Solid. It would work.

Behind him and to the left, the chair of the man in the corner scraped against the rough, wooden floor.

Odd that he should choose to leave now, Jordan thought—having been in the same damned spot all night—just as Jordan also prepared to retire.

The man stood and pushed his chair neatly back in place. Despite the quantity of alcohol he'd imbibed, he was as sober as Jordan.

French agent.

The words ripped through Jordan's mind, like lightning in the night sky. In one smooth motion, he drew his pistol and sprang to his feet to meet the enemy.

The thin man was several inches shorter than Jordan. Ginger hair fell in lank waves to his jaw. He raised an amused brow and smiled. The right cheek of his gaunt face twisted around a scar that twinned Jordan's.

"Fitz," Jordan breathed, slowly lowering his weapon.

"Settle down," Fitzhugh Ditman said. "You've gone pale. It's me, my friend, not a malevolent ghost." His voice tumbled in his throat, like gravel, a permanent reminder of the garroting that had partially crushed his windpipe. Jordan had avoided that particular torment while the two men were imprisoned together in Spain. He bore the matching scar on his cheek, but he'd escaped before their captors could take his voice.

Getting Fitz out of there alive had been a near thing. For days after their escape, Ditman gasped like a fish out of water. His lips went blue from the exertion of their flight, and more than once his partner urged Jordan to leave him behind. Jordan had declined to do so.

"Of course I'm glad to see you," Jordan said. He returned his gun to his coat, and the two men clasped forearms in greeting. "I thought you were still on the Continent."

"I was," Fitz rumbled. "Just got back a couple days ago. Checked in with our friend. He said you might need help."

Jordan frowned. "Why didn't he send me word?"

Fitz rasped a laugh. "Where would he send word, you sod? If he'd sent a note ahead to Lintern Abbey, I'd have been standing at your shoulder while you read it, anyway. I s'pose I could've brought a courier along with me and waited in the hall while—"

"All right, all right." Jordan held his hands out in surrender. "Point taken. What has Castlereagh told you?"

Fitz sniffed loudly and wiped his nose with the back of his hand. "We're dealing with a bunch of bastards, like I've been up to my ears with over there these last few years. I know a thing or two about how these men of Boney's operate."

Jordan felt a weight lift from his shoulders. "I'm glad to hear it," he said. "I've been given men of questionable value to work with. It'll be good to have your expertise on our side."

"That's what I'm here for," Fitz said, extending his hand.

Jordan grasped his old partner's hand. "It's good to work with you again, Fitz."

His friend's grip was firm and sure, confident, able. What a boon this was, to have Fitzhugh Ditman at his side once more.

Chapter Six

Aunt Janine poked Naomi's rib again. Naomi rolled over and moaned as though deep in sleep. Rain beat steadily against the diamond window-panes. Watery, gray light had dimly illuminated the room for the last hour and a half. It had become an effort to feign sleep, but Naomi was determined to have Lord Freese up, out, and well on the road before she so much as set foot outside her room.

It should not have startled her so, to find him at the same inn. The Swan Song was the last well-appointed inn before their journey took them off the Great North Road to strike into the Yorkshire moorlands. Nevertheless, when she'd seen him yesterday, her heart had jumped against her ribs. It had taken all of her willpower to mind her brother's caution and turn down the tempting cave outing.

Aunt Janine jostled her shoulder. "Come now, my girl. Stop lazing the day away."

Naomi squeezed her eyes and burrowed deeper into her pillow. Across the backs of her eyelids, she once again saw Lord Freese as he'd stood off to the side, observing Auntie's tirade against the poor innkeeper. Where Aunt Janine's bluster and bluff had gotten them no closer to lodging than they'd been when they first arrived, it had taken Lord Freese but a few words and a flash of his charming smile to set the situation to rights.

In spite of Marshall's warning, she found herself drawn to the man. All the more reason to mind her brother's instruction to keep her distance, hence her decision to lay abed well into the morning.

"Child, are you unwell?" Aunt Janine's voice held a note of genuine concern. Naomi guiltily cracked an eyelid. Auntie was already dressed in a charcoal-gray traveling costume. A dowdy bonnet framed her face, and worry lines creased the skin between her eyes.

"I'm not ill," Naomi answered as she swung her legs over the side of the bed. "I still have no great desire to spend the next several weeks at

Lintern Abbey." At Aunt Janine's sympathetic smile, she said in a small voice, "They don't want me at home anymore."

Janine hurried to take her hand. "Hush now. There's not a bit of truth to that."

Naomi's stomach twisted as she remembered her brother and sister-in-law's cold words. "To be honest, Aunt, I'm not sure what to think. It was so startling to hear Isabelle say she didn't need me, when just a week ago, we were making plans for the nursery at Helmsdale."

Scowling, Aunt Janine pulled Naomi to her feet. "There must be more to this than we know. I cannot believe Marshall and Isabelle have suddenly had done with us. But come, we've a long drive ahead of us. We'll fill the time trying to solve this mystery."

Downstairs, Aunt Janine settled with the innkeeper. Naomi looked around. The inn felt emptier than it had yesterday. She hoped that meant Lord Freese and the rest of the party had gone on ahead.

Their carriage was brought around. A footman wearing Marshall's livery held out a hand to assist Aunt Janine.

"Allow me."

Naomi sucked in her breath as Lord Freese strode from the stable yard to hand Aunt Janine up. He wore a dashing ensemble consisting of a tall hat, a tailed riding coat, and tight, buckskin breeches that revealed every curve of his muscled thighs and . . .

Oh, dear.

Inside her kid gloves, Naomi's palms began to sweat. "Why are you still here?" she blurted.

Lord Freese flashed her a roguish smile and touched the brim of his hat. Moisture was collected there, as though he'd been out in the weather a good deal already. "Good morning, Lady Naomi," he said affably, unperturbed by her tone. "Much to my dismay, I am here once more, rather than still. I set out bright and early this morning, but Phantom threw a shoe not two miles up the road. So back I came."

When he shrugged, the deep crimson superfine of his coat moved with his shoulders like a second skin.

"You're riding the entire distance from London to Lintern Abbey, my lord?" Naomi asked in wonder.

"I've never cared for the confinement of a closed carriage over long distances. Makes me feel like a caged bear." He waggled a brow, and Naomi couldn't help but giggle at the mental picture of the great Lord Freese prowling behind bars at a fair.

His answering wink shot right into her. Her breasts tingled, and delicious warmth crept through her. Naomi looked away from his shockingly blue eyes, discomfited by her body's response.

"Your steed is reshod, then?" Aunt Janine asked from inside the carriage.

"Not yet," Lord Freese replied. "The farrier is making calls at some farms this morning. I'm told he will be back by noon."

"Will you wait until tomorrow to complete your journey?" Naomi asked.

Lord Freese shook his head. "No, I'll set out the minute Phantom is back in form."

"My lord, you cannot!" Aunt Janine protested. "That would have you on the road well past dark. Highwaymen! It is most inadvisable."

"Then, I shall have to trust my wits and a brace of pistols to see me through." His wolfish grin and the glint in his eye made Naomi wonder whether he didn't relish just such a challenge.

What an odd man.

Aunt Janine snorted derisively. "Nonsense. You shall ride with us."

Naomi's eyes went wide. Hours and hours cooped up with Lord Freese? She shot her aunt a meaningful look.

The older lady frowned. "Are you certain you've not taken ill, Naomi? You've an air about you as if you're in pain. Does she not, my lord?"

"I'm perfectly well, thank you," Naomi said through clenched teeth.

"If you're sure it's not an inconvenience, I'd be most obliged," Lord Freese said with a bow. "My man can bring Phantom along later."

He took Naomi's hand to help her into the conveyance. She wondered whether he noticed how her fingers melted against his palm.

"Freese!"

Naomi and Lord Freese turned at the same instant. A man approached, slender of build, with a hat pulled low over his eyes. He moved confidently as he maneuvered on the wet cobbles to avoid luggage and crates. As he neared, Naomi was startled to see a scar on the man's right cheek, too like Lord Freese's to be a coincidence. But where Jordan's scar was a neat, slightly curved line running from ear to mouth, the newcomer's was jagged at the end near his lips, like a lightning bolt. His cheek puckered around the pinkish ridge in places, pulling his mouth into a permanent smirk.

Her fingers reflexively tightened around Lord Freese's. He squeezed back and held her hand when he addressed the man.

"Fitz, we agreed you'd ride on ahead with the others."

The man's light brown eyes narrowed on Naomi's face. His menacing demeanor intimidated her, but she met his stare and lifted her chin. Pursing his lips, he cut his gaze back to Lord Freese.

Jordan looked at Naomi as though surprised to find her still standing beside him; he dropped her hand. "Oh, forgive me. Lady Naomi Lockwood, please allow me to present Mr. Fitzhugh Ditman."

The introduction was acknowledged on each side with the barest degree of bowing and nodding civility allowed. There was something about the man Naomi did not like.

"Lady Naomi and her aunt have graciously offered me a place in their carriage," Lord Freese explained. "I won't be as late getting in tonight as I'd feared."

Mr. Ditman's lips twisted as he looked the carriage over. "You'd make better time walking," he rasped.

"Our carriage is in excellent repair," Naomi assured him. "Lord Freese will be delivered to his doorstep in time to change for supper."

Ditman's cheek twitched. He swiped at a strand of wet, reddish hair, ignoring her. "We need to talk," he said to Lord Freese in a low voice. "That's why I returned."

"We'll speak later," Jordan replied. He handed Naomi into the carriage and followed her up. Mr. Ditman said something Naomi couldn't make out, and Jordan's body filling the door blocked him from view. Pausing, Lord Freese turned. "We agreed you'd go on ahead, Fitz." His voice carried a warning tone. "We'll talk later. Safe travels, my friend."

Naomi and Aunt Janine exchanged a wondering look as Lord Freese settled into the opposite seat.

He removed his hat and ran a hand through his hair, loosing a riot of dark curls. "Once again, I thank you ladies for coming to my rescue."

"Have we rescued you, my lord," Naomi asked, "or merely caged you?"

His laughter filled the small space. "How could I be anything but grateful for confinement with two such dazzling ladies?"

Aunt Janine lowered her chin and looked over the rims of her spectacles. "Thrust out your tongue, young man. I'm curious to see the silvering."

Naomi spared her aunt a wry grin, and Jordan smiled amicably. "*Touché*, madam."

"My lord," Naomi ventured, "I could not help but notice your friend bears a scar similar to your own."

Jordan's expression fell blank. "War injuries. We fought side by side and bumped into the same saber. Bit of bad luck."

Poor Mr. Ditman had as bad a time of it in Spain as Lord Freese, then—worse, perhaps, if his unusual voice and gaunt, haunted face were any indication. No wonder the man glowered. Naomi resolved to think more kindly on him.

"And yet, my lord," Aunt Janine ventured, "if I may say so, your scar is not all bad luck. It's widely regarded as a badge of your courage—a testament to your sacrifice. The ladies find it rather dashing, you know."

Naomi's eyes widened. Never before had she heard her aunt compliment a gentleman's looks.

A small smile touched Lord Freese's lips. "You must forgive me, Lady Janine, if I'd prefer medals on my chest to commemorate my service."

Naomi winced inwardly at the pain she detected behind Lord Freese's words. Speaking of the war caused distress he could not entirely conceal with levity. She wondered how often she'd missed these moments of revelation by taking the man at face value. The temptation to discover more was alluring—but dangerous, if Marshall was to be believed.

For the next couple hours, Naomi kept to herself as much as the cramped dimensions allowed. She faced the window, her eyes riveted on the passing countryside. Aunt Janine and Lord Freese chatted quietly, occasionally lapsing into companionable silence.

No matter how hard she tried to ignore him, though, Naomi found herself listening closely, examining each of his words, his inflection, his turns of phrase, hoping to glean some further insight. Nothing informative surfaced, but she found herself drawn to the warm velvet of his voice. It crept down her back and wrapped around her like a secret embrace. The sound of his voice made it bearable to keep her eyes averted. He was still present, still near.

She decided to relish these hours in the carriage. Once at Lintern Abbey, she would have to resume her observation of Marshall's edict and stay away from her handsome host.

After a time, the angle of the sun and a discomfort in her middle told Naomi it was nearly time for luncheon. The innkeeper's wife at the Swan Song had packed them a picnic basket, now tucked behind the coachman's seat. The rain had stopped a short time ago, but the ground remained wet. It would probably be a while yet before the driver spotted a suitable location for the meal.

Aunt Janine's internal clock must have matched Naomi's. Out of her voluminous reticule, she produced a cloth-wrapped parcel, from which emerged two scones. "Oh, dear," Janine said, glancing guiltily at Lord Freese, "I only brought two."

"Lord Freese can share mine," Naomi suggested. The gentleman's blue eyes widened a fraction. Naomi felt herself blush. "That is, if you wish, my lord. I'm not very hungry."

"Thank you, that's very kind." He accepted the larger of the two pieces. It vanished in two bites before Naomi had begun to nibble hers.

As she lifted her morsel to her mouth, the coach hit a rut. Aunt Janine's scone plummeted from her hand and crumbled into bits on the dirty floor. Auntie looked longingly after the ruined bread then sat back with a heavy sigh.

With a wistful glance at her own treat, Naomi held it out to the older woman. "Have mine, Auntie. I'm really not hungry."

Her aunt took the offering with a smile of gratitude. "Thank you, dearest."

Naomi looked out the window again and tried not to think about food. The grass was drying. Perhaps they would stop soon.

Her stomach emitted an audible growl. Naomi clenched her muscles, willing her body to cease its dreadful row.

She felt *him* looking at her. Mortified, she turned her head the barest degree, fully expecting to witness his disgust at her indelicate digestive tract. Instead, his too-blue eyes were trained thoughtfully on her.

After the much-needed break for luncheon, they settled back into the coach for the final leg of the journey. The next few hours saw them through villages nestled in the Yorkshire hills and its rugged farmland. Despite her reluctance to spend the remainder of the summer at Lord Freese's home, Naomi began to feel excitement as she examined the unfamiliar countryside.

Lord Freese's head leaned back against the squabs, his hat tilted forward to cover his eyes. She thought him asleep, but then a slit of blue peeked from under the brim.

"Tell us what we shall find at Lintern Abbey, my lord."

He cleared his throat. "My stepmother will be there, Clara, Countess of Whithorn. She's a pleasant type, and I expect you'll get along famously." He nodded to Aunt Janine. "An uncle lives with me at Lintern Abbey. Sir Randell."

Aunt Janine sniffed. "I prefer the company of young people to tottering old men."

Jordan laughed. "You will find that Uncle Randell is neither particularly old nor tottering, my lady. But I would encourage you to tell him so, in any case. There's nothing he likes better than someone to trade barbs with."

Naomi's gaze slid to her aunt. "He sounds like you, Auntie."

Aunt Janine harrumphed. "Not a bit of it."

Smiling, Naomi looked back to Lord Freese. "How much longer before we arrive, my lord?"

"As I am riding backwards, it's hard to say for certain, but . . ." He leaned forward and craned his neck around to peer out the window. "Yes, that is Lintern Village, just ahead. We'll be on my land in a moment, though it's another two miles to the house."

Soon they rolled down a broad high street lined with neat shops and houses. Curious villagers stepped out of the way and watched them pass.

"Do they know you're coming home?" Naomi asked.

Jordan smiled ruefully. "Servants at the Abbey will have made sure of that."

"They're proud of you, I'm sure," she rejoined gently. "How long have you lived here, my lord?"

"All my life," he answered. "My father's seat moved to Crummock Grange when he was granted the earldom. Prior to that, Lintern Abbey had been the family heap for generations. There's been a Viscount Freese at the Abbey for two-and-a-half centuries. Father saw no reason to disrupt the tradition. He gave me use of the estate and its income when the title became mine."

Naomi breathed in at the thought of it. "You see, the people depend on you."

As they passed through the other side of the village, Jordan's brows drew together in a frown. "Lady Naomi, I feel it incumbent upon me to warn you: Lintern Abbey boasts little to amuse ladies. We gentlemen will be hunting every day."

"There will be entertainments at night, will there not?"

"There will," he assured her. "But you shall be left to your own devices during the day, and there isn't much to choose from."

His forecast of a grim party seemed out of place, especially as each turn of the road brought a vista more charming than the last. In the distance, heathered hills gently descended to meet green pastures marked with neat lines of stone walls. How could he claim nothing to offer with such splendid country ready to explore?

They passed through the gates and into a deer park where grass grew lush beneath a canopy of verdant trees. Woods gave way to manicured parkland. A stream ran the length of the park on one side, a shimmering silver ribbon in the late-afternoon light.

At last, they pulled up before the house, a stately Jacobean mansion. Its stone façade had an ethereal, golden gleam in the sunlight. Naomi loved it at once. She thought it the most enchanting house she'd ever seen.

For a moment after Jordan helped her down, she could only stare at it. She counted five stories, but the neat symmetry of the house's architecture kept its size from overwhelming the observer.

"Dreadful old heap, isn't it?"

Startled, she glanced up at Lord Freese, who took in the same view as she, but with an attitude of distaste. "Not at all, my lord. I think it's marvelous."

He raised a quizzical brow. "You musn't lie for my sake, Naomi. I know how sadly antiquated it is."

She was about to argue, but the great door opened. A lady came out on the arm of an older gentleman. They traversed the short walk in front of the door then descended the stairs coming down to the pebbled drive. Jordan introduced Naomi and Aunt Janine to his stepmother and uncle.

Lady Whithorn took Naomi's hands. "I'm so happy to meet you at last," she said kindly. "Jordan's told us all about your family over the years. I know we shall be friends."

"I'm sure we shall, my lady," Naomi said.

The handsome woman looked about forty. Her hazel eyes were wide and bright, and a dimple in her cheek lent her a youthful air. At a glance, Naomi saw that Lady Whithorn had good taste, but was no slave to fashion. Her floral-patterned, calico dress and the lace shawl tied around her shoulders would pass muster in all but the most prickly ladies' drawing rooms.

While Lady Whithorn gave the Monthwaite servants directions, Sir Randell and Aunt Janine eyed each other as warily as two cats circling in an alley. Jordan's uncle stood nearly as tall as his nephew. His hair was an impressive silver mane, and the spectacles on his nose did not diminish the impact of fierce, blue eyes. A family trait, Naomi observed.

"We expected you earlier," Lady Whithorn commented to Jordan as they went up the stairs to the house. "Your friends have settled into their rooms."

"A horseshoe delayed me," Lord Freese said. "Thankfully, the ladies accommodated me in their coach, else I'd have been even later."

"Tell me you aren't still gallivanting all over the countryside on poor Phantom!" Lady Whithorn exclaimed.

"You see?" Jordan grinned down at Naomi. "My step-mama does suffer so, on my account."

A squeal from the door caught Naomi's attention an instant before a bundle of lace and feet hurtled down the walk and straight into Lord Freese's middle.

Startled, he wrapped his arms around the entity, which, upon stopping, sorted itself out into a young lady. Her muffled voice prattled excitedly against his chest until he pushed her back.

". . . So happy to see you," the girl said. "It's been ever so long since you've come to the Grange. I *hoped* Mama and Papa would take me up to Town this spring, but Mama said I'll be there soon enough, and Papa wouldn't budge, even when I told him I only wanted to come see you."

Naomi was amused by the girl until she saw the shock on Jordan's face. His cheeks had drained of color. "Just . . . just a minute, my dear, let me introduce you to my guests." He seemed completely rattled. Who was this child, Naomi wondered, to cause Lord Freese such alarm?

"Oh!" The girl twirled around to Naomi and Aunt Janine. "I'm sorry. I've forgotten myself already." She was all coltish arms and legs. Her dark hair hung in a braid down her back. A liberal sprinkling of freckles dotted the bridge of her nose and the apples of her cheeks. Her smile was as yet overwide in her thin face, but Naomi could tell she'd bloom into a beauty in a few more years.

She nodded to the girl as Jordan made the introduction. "Lady Janine, Lady Naomi, allow me to present my sister, Lady Kaitlin. Who is not," he said, rounding on his stepmother, "supposed to be here."

Chapter Seven

In the entry hall, Jordan reined in his temper. "Kate," he said to his sister, "please escort Lady Janine and Lady Naomi to their rooms."

The young adolescent wore a stricken expression. She bit her lips nervously, and her hands tangled at her waist. Kate nodded rapidly, her eyes large and pleading on his.

Jordan sighed.

Naomi gently touched her arm. "Lady Kaitlin, if you'd be so kind? I'm beyond ready to change into something less travel worn."

Kate's huge eyes rolled toward Naomi, who smiled reassuringly. Thankfully, his sister took Naomi's gracious cue and led the ladies upstairs.

"Thank God for Naomi Lockwood," he muttered. "Clara, come with me."

"For shame!" his stepmother hissed, hurrying to keep pace beside him. "You should not have said what you did in front of Kate. The poor girl adores you, Jordan, and you proclaim her unwelcome!"

Jordan opened the door to his study and gestured her in. The room's air was stale from disuse.

"Why did you bring her?" he demanded. Clara's mouth pinched together. "When I wrote," he said, jabbing his right index finger demonstratively into his left palm, "I specifically instructed that Kate was *not* to attend. She should be home with her governess." He crossed to the other end of the room, unlatched a window, flung it wide, and inhaled deep breaths of the cleansing, fresh air.

"Miss Allen has scarlet fever," Clara explained. "Even you must agree it is better for Kate to be out of the house than cooped up with such an illness."

"Where is my father, then?"

"In Scotland," Clara declared with a note of triumph, "fishing." She raised a brow. "What choice did I have but to bring her with me?"

Jordan growled and ran both hands through his hair. What a fool he was to concoct this ridiculous house party! The whole scheme had already gone wrong with him being unable to perform the most basic function of keeping his sister out of harm's way.

"But she'll feel left out." He restlessly prowled the room, working the stiffness of his long, cramped confinement in the coach out of his legs. "She cannot participate in most of the evening entertainments—dancing, cards, and so forth. It would be quite beyond the pale. I won't allow it, and neither, I know, will you."

"Of course not!" Clara sounded scandalized at the merest suggestion that she might be less than assiduous in protecting her daughter's reputation. "I have already discussed the matter with Kate, and she understands. But there can be no harm in her mixing with the other ladies during the day. I shall watch her closely, of course. Your claims," she said, shaking her head, "about her feeling left out are entirely unfounded, and I dismiss them out of hand." She flicked her wrist as though physically waving away Jordan's arguments. "It can be nothing to you if she's here, in any event. You'll be outdoors while she's with the ladies, and she'll be in her room at night while you while away the hours downstairs. When would you even see her?"

Jordan couldn't help but feel a twinge of guilt at neglecting his sister. True, he could avoid her entirely if he wished. But that wasn't the point, and he said so.

Confusion clouded Clara's eyes. "What *is* the point, Jordan? I must confess I am utterly baffled by your objections. Believe you me, had I known what a fuss you would make over Kate, I would have told you to find yourself another hostess." Her arms crossed beneath her chest, and one toe peeking from beneath the hem of her dress tapped out an annoyed cadence.

God, this was getting worse and worse. Briefly, he wondered if he should tell Clara the truth—the real reason for the house party. He'd built a career lying and manipulating people. Never before had the lies hit so close to home. Never would he have thought the people he loved would become ensnared in his world of secrecy. But if he told her the truth, everything would fall to pieces.

"I'm sorry, but Kate cannot remain," he said sharply. "Surely, there's somewhere else you can send her. Your sister lives not twenty miles from here, I believe?"

Hurt filled Clara's eyes. "Jordan Atherton," she said quietly, "you and I have scarcely exchanged harsh words since the day I married your father. Despite the numerous scrapes you've gotten yourself into over the years, I have always spoken up for you. It grieves me deeply now to experience this . . ." Her lips curled in distaste. ". . . this *side* of you. And I pray never to witness it again. If you want Kate to go, then *you* shall tell her. I'll not be the villain in this farce."

Jordan stood with his feet braced wide and glared down into his stepmother's fierce expression. He closed his eyes and groaned, his resolve crumbling. He couldn't bear to disappoint Kate, not after he'd managed to hurt the child seconds after his arrival. And there really wouldn't be any danger, he supposed, not if he and his men performed their duties as they should.

"Fine." He flung his hands up in surrender. "She stays. But you *must* keep her with the other ladies, Clara," he said emphatically. "I mean it. Keep her close to the house. She cannot go rambling about the estate as she does at the Grange. It isn't—"

He started to say, *It isn't safe,* but was saved from revealing too much by a sharp knock at the door, followed immediately by the entrance of Fitzhugh Ditman with their harried butler, Weston, fast on his heels.

"My lord," Weston cried, "I told him you were busy, but he barged past!"

"A word, Freese." Ditman cut his eyes to Clara then back to Jordan. The mud splatters on his boots and cloak indicated he'd not taken the time to change since his arrival. "It's urgent."

Jordan nodded. "If you'll excuse us, Clara. I'll see you at supper."

Clara treated him to a mocking curtsy. "As you say, my lord." Her voice was treacly sweet, but he read annoyance in her eyes. He'd not been in the house ten minutes and already, his wounded-feelings tally was up to two.

When they were alone, Jordan took in the intense lines of his friend's posture. "What is it, Fitz?"

"I stopped at the tavern as I passed through Lintern Village," he said. "Thought I'd get a feel for where we stood."

Jordan frowned. "And?"

Ditman shook his head. "Bad news. Two Frenchmen were in the village yesterday, making inquiries about Lintern Abbey, wanting to know whether or not you were in residence. They're here."

*

After depositing Aunt Janine in her room, Lady Kaitlin led Naomi to the next room over. It was a very pleasant bedchamber. Ivy-patterned wallpaper and vases of late-summer blooms made the room feel like its own secluded garden. Naomi pulled aside the curtain. Her window overlooked the east garden, which featured pretty little puffs of lavender contained in a grid by a low hedge. Box cones stood at regular intervals along the walk, green sentinels at attention.

"Does the room suit, my lady?" Lady Kaitlin's voice was timid and still hovered in the timbre of girlhood.

Naomi turned around and smiled. "It suits me well, thank you. His lordship has a lovely home. I should very much like to see more of it."

Now, where had that sudden enthusiasm come from? Naomi frowned inwardly as she realized that it was true. The tiny portion of Lintern Abbey she had seen pleased her immensely. She could not understand Lord Freese's dismay at his own home.

Kaitlin smiled shyly. "I should like that, as well, my lady. I didn't grow up here, you see. This is my first visit to Lintern Abbey."

"What do you think of it so far?"

The younger girl's eyes lit up. "Oh, it's *marvelous!*" she declared. "Jordan is the very best of brothers, and I knew he must have the very best of homes. We only arrived yesterday, you see, so I haven't seen much, either. What I have seen is grand, though, just grand!"

Naomi found Kaitlin's zeal infectious. She grinned as the girl continued her animated praise of the estate and its master.

"There are ruins nearby," Kaitlin said, "of the abbey that used to be here. I suppose that's why the estate is still called Lintern Abbey. It's so very clever of Jordan to have his very own ruins. I can't think of anything more romantic."

Chuckling, Naomi wondered whether Kaitlin believed Jordan to have hung the moon in the sky as well. *Probably*, she thought. She'd once been a young girl, too, who'd worshiped her older brothers.

"That *is* exceedingly clever of Lord Freese," she agreed. "Perhaps we can explore the ruins together."

Kaitlin nodded her eager acceptance. Naomi liked the girl already. She was bright and well comported for a child of . . . what? Thirteen or fourteen, Naomi supposed. Just on the cusp of womanhood. She couldn't imagine what had sparked Jordan's earlier fury at finding this inoffensive girl in his house. Most peculiar.

In the corridor, a pair of ladies passing by stopped. "Oh, hello," said one. Her large figure filled most of the doorway. "You must be our late arrivals," the woman said. "I'm Gertrude Price."

Lady Kaitlin gestured. "This is Lady Naomi Lockwood."

Naomi nodded. "Pleased to make your acquaintance, Miss Price."

The woman bobbed a curtsy. "Likewise. Please call me Trudy. My friends do, and I'm sure we shall all be friends before long." She giggled and shrugged, a blush deepening her ruddy complexion. "I do so love a house party, don't you? Oh!" she exclaimed. "I nearly forgot Miss Elton."

She retrieved her companion, who was as frail and pale as Miss Price was robust and healthy. "Lady Naomi, this is Miss Elton."

"My lady," breathed Miss Elton. The young woman curtsied, and for a moment, Naomi worried she would collapse with exhaustion. Then she straightened. "It's so . . . diverting . . . I always say. To expand one's acquaintance." She spoke slowly, pausing every few words to draw a deep breath.

"It is indeed, Miss Elton," Naomi replied. "I am very glad to have made yours. I hope we shall have the opportunity to speak again soon."

Miss Price looped her arm through Miss Elton's. It looked as though the former's limb could snap the latter's in two with a minimal degree of effort. "We shall leave you to settle in, my lady," Miss Price said. "Until supper. Oh!" she exclaimed again. Naomi wondered if it wasn't just her habit to amend her statements with such enthusiastic addendums. "You must introduce us to your gentlemen as well. Don't forget!" With a waggle of her fingers, Miss Price led Miss Elton on down the corridor.

"Our gentlemen?" Naomi mused out loud.

"All the ladies have come with one gentleman," Lady Kaitlin explained. "Except for you and Lady Janine, that is."

Naomi frowned. "Pairs? Everyone? Are there no families?"

Lady Kaitlin bit her lip and furrowed her brow. "No, my lady, I don't believe so. There is Mr. Wood and Miss Wood, his sister. Mr. and Mrs. Richard. Lord Herrick brought his sister, Lady Griffiths. She's a widow. Well," she said, blushing, "you see what I mean."

Naomi did, and it was still in her mind when she and Aunt Janine went down to supper. The guests assembled in a parlor and mingled over glasses of claret.

She detected a current of unease cutting through the conversation. "I would like to introduce you to my cousin," said a Miss Hunt. "But Mr. Bates seems to have found some sudden business in the village." She frowned. "Oh, well," she said with a dismissive laugh. "Whatever it is must be quite urgent. Mr. Bates does important work for the government and is sometimes called away at a moment's notice."

The gentlemen surrounding them all fell silent and turned to look at Miss Hunt and then glanced at one another. Naomi was grossly uneasy, but Miss Hunt seemed oblivious to all the attention she'd attracted.

"How . . . unfortunate," Naomi said slowly, "that he's been called away so . . . suddenly." She was acutely aware that no fewer than five gentlemen she did not know were all honed in on her conversation. "What kind of work does your cousin do, Miss Hunt?"

One gentleman erupted into a fit of coughing, and another slapped him on the back and called for a glass of water.

During the disruption, a man stepped between Naomi and Miss Hunt. "Please permit me to introduce myself, my lady," he said, "Robert Elton, at your service." He pressed a hand to his chest and bowed deeply. Behind him, she saw Miss Hunt had been drawn away into another group's conversation.

"Are you, by any chance, related to Miss Elton?" Naomi asked the man.

He nodded and smiled self-consciously around overlarge front teeth. "Miss Elton is my sister. Have you met?"

"We have been introduced . . ." Naomi's voice trailed off as she caught sight of Lord Freese walking around the perimeter of the sitting room. Lady Whithorn moved beside him, speaking in a low voice, a vexed expression on her face.

She excused herself from Mr. Elton and hurried to her hostess. "Pardon me, Lady Whithorn."

Lord Freese and his stepmother paused. The large male raised a brow as he held Naomi's gaze. Awareness built between them until Naomi blushed, sure everyone in the room could see it pulsing in the air. She jerked her attention to Lady Whithorn. "My lady, is there anything I might do to be of service?"

The countess smiled and patted Naomi's hand. "Thank you, Lady Naomi, but I'm afraid not, unless you happen to have stowed away three gentlemen you can bring out for supper." She cast an annoyed glance at her stepson, whose face was a mask of innocence. "It seems three of our guests are indisposed for various reasons. Now there are not enough men to escort all the ladies in to supper."

"What about Mr. Ditman?" Naomi asked. "He was a late addition to the party, was he not? There's one spare gentleman for you."

"Mr. Ditman?" Lady Whithorn frowned and glanced around the parlor. "Is that the man who barged in earlier, Jordan? I don't recall seeing his name on the guest list."

Jordan's attention had wandered. He stared intently at the parlor door until his stepmother said his name. "Hmm? Yes, Ditman. Bumped into him by happy chance just yesterday and invited him to join the party. He's an old friend. From Spain. In fact . . . Fitz!" he called, waving the gentleman over.

Mr. Ditman bowed to Lady Whithorn while Lord Freese made the introduction. When he straightened, their hostess gasped. "Oh, sir!" she exclaimed, clearly startled by Mr. Ditman's scar. "Forgive my forwardness," she said, "but how can this be? I did not notice this earlier, but . . ." Her hand tentatively rose toward Mr. Ditman's face; she snatched it back.

"It was my great honor to fight alongside Lord Freese, my lady," Mr. Ditman said.

"And it was our equally great misfortune to run up against the same French bloke who had a dab hand with the bayonet," Lord Freese quipped.

"I thought it was a saber." Naomi didn't realize she'd voiced her musing aloud until the others looked her way. Flustered, she said, "This morning, my lord, you said your and Mr. Ditman's injuries came from a saber blade."

"Did I?" he said smoothly. "Perhaps I misspoke. It was a bayonet."

Mr. Ditman shook his head. "I recall it as being a saber, Freese. But then," he turned his hard eyes on Naomi, "one blade looks much the same as another at such close range. All you can make out is the gleaming point of steel whistling toward your head." He slashed a finger through the air near Naomi's cheek. She flinched and took an involuntary step closer to Jordan. "Uncertainty and chaos are the order of the day on the battlefield, Lady Naomi. Women love to hear tales of their gallant heroes' exploits, but truth is hard to come by where war is involved. Attempting to pin down details as inconsequential as the nature of the implement Lord Freese and I each met is an exercise in futility, so I suggest you desist."

A muscle in his temple twitched, jerking the upper end of his scar.

Cold tendrils slid down her chest and spread through her middle. She could not feel easy around this man; no matter he had fought as bravely as Lord Freese and thus deserved her approbation. "I beg your pardon, sir. I meant no impertinence."

His lips twisted in a mocking smile.

"Please think nothing of it, Lady Naomi," Lord Freese interjected. He fired a glance at his friend before looking back to her. "Of course, you meant no offense, and none is taken. By either of us," he added with a hint of finality.

Naomi was grateful for his intervention. He seemed to have a knack for coming to her aid just when she found herself in over her head.

The butler—Weston, she recalled—announced supper.

"Bosh! I still haven't sorted out who shall escort whom," Lady Whithorn despaired.

"I'm sure no one cares how we convey ourselves to the dining room," Lord Freese drawled, "so long as a meal awaits us when we arrive."

It was all finally sorted out, with a few gentlemen escorting two ladies. There was nothing to be done for the seating arrangement, however, leaving some ladies to sit side by side. Naomi sat at Lady Whithorn's left hand at the foot of the table.

At the head of the table, Lord Freese seemed distracted. He sawed his meat more than the tender cutlet required. He laughed when his immediate companions had made no jest. Though he wore his typical smile and spread it around liberally, there was a brittle quality to it this evening. He repeatedly glanced at the doors.

There was no window in the room, and Naomi remembered what he'd told her earlier about detesting the feeling of confinement. Was he confined here, she wondered, in his own home? By his own guests?

His eyes found hers, and a flicker of awareness passed between them. Naomi was unsettled by her body's immediate response—the quickening of her pulse, the knot in her belly. Yet she kept her head and nodded politely. Surely, it was nothing for a guest to turn her eyes upon her host from time to time?

"Lord Freese has always been more like a younger sibling to me than a stepson," the countess remarked. The lady looked sophisticated in a dark green evening gown and elegantly dressed hair. She leaned slightly toward Naomi, amusement crinkling the skin around her eyes.

Naomi realized her hostess had noticed the lingering gaze she and Lord Freese had shared, and blushed. "Perhaps you regard him so because you are nearly the same age," Naomi suggested.

The countess laughed. "Not quite. And please call me Clara. May I call you Naomi?" At her nod of assent, Clara smiled. "There are little more than ten years separating me and Jordan. I'm too young to be his mother, but closer in age to him than to my husband. It made for an interesting family dynamic in the early years of my marriage."

Clara's gaze slid over Naomi's shoulder, focusing on nothing in particular. "For a while, I tried to be his mother, but a spirited boy of fourteen was not about to have any of it. I finally contented myself just being his friend." Her eyes came back to Naomi's. "That arrangement has served us very well. Peace has reigned in our family for fifteen years. The earl and the viscount have a relationship founded on mutual respect. Jordan is a loving, if rather absent, brother to Kate, and he sometimes seeks my advice. Whether or not he listens to it is another matter." Her wry smile faded as her voice dropped. "But this party of his is something else. Only a moment after you all arrived, Jordan humiliated his sister and then berated me. Something here is upsetting my family's peace, and I do not care for it."

She held Naomi's gaze for a long moment. So long, in fact, that Naomi began to feel scrutinized. "I'm sorry, my lady—Clara—if I have in any way contributed—"

Clara shook her head. "You mistake me, Naomi. I lay no blame at your feet. Indeed, of the guests assembled here, I believe you may be the only one Jordan trusts."

Naomi's mind reeled. What was she to Lord Freese but the younger sister of a friend? "How can that be? My acquaintance with Lord Freese is scarcely more than . . . well, just that, an acquaintance."

"Because, Naomi, of all the names on the guest list Jordan sent me, only yours and your aunt's were known to me through Jordan's communications over the years. My stepson has never, to my knowledge, fraternized with anyone else at this table." Clara's eyes moved down the row of diners. "I suppose there must be truth to his association with Mr. Ditman, but this is the first I've heard of the man."

Feeling conspicuous at engaging in such a lengthy private conversation at the table, Naomi cut to the point. "Why do you tell me this, Clara?"

The older lady's eyes were full of concern and pleading. "Please help him. Whatever troubles Jordan is beyond me, and perhaps beyond you, as well. I do not like this party, and I do not trust the look of some of these men. Jordan is uneasy in a way I've never seen him. But I see how he looks at you." Her wry smile returned. "I probably shouldn't tell you, but he instructed me as to the particular rooms you and Lady Janine should have. He took no such pains for any of the others. Jordan has a connection to you he doesn't share with anyone else here, Naomi. I hope I do not misjudge your kind feelings toward him."

Naomi flushed. "No, of course not. I esteem Lord Freese greatly. I don't know what I can do for him, though."

"Just be his friend," the countess said. "I think that may be enough. Talk to him, put his mind at ease. Please, say you will."

Biting a lip, Naomi nodded. "I shall try." Clara seemed satisfied, so Naomi gave her attention to her other neighbor.

Only later, when the sweet course arrived, did Naomi realize the promise Clara had exacted from her ran in direct contradiction to the one she'd given Marshall. Lady Whithorn wanted her close to Lord Freese, whereas her brother wanted her to stay as far away from the man as possible.

Torn as to which promise she should honor—for surely she could only uphold one of them—she cast an anguished look up the table. Lord Freese's eyes were already on her, searching. Under his gaze, she felt as though little flames danced across her skin.

Naomi would have to break her word to someone. Never had she been disloyal to her family, even when she was accused of it for her friendship with Isabelle. In the end, it was seen she had been loyal to *all* of her family, including her then-disgraced sister-in-law. Her greater duty must lie with her family. But Clara was her hostess. While she remained in this house, did she not owe her some degree of loyalty, as well? She struggled with the unsavory choice, wishing she could somehow avoid this predicament without hurting anyone.

As Lord Freese continued to hold her gaze, Naomi realized that she, at least, would not escape unscathed.

*

After dinner, Clara led the ladies to the parlor while the gentlemen remained behind to enjoy their port. Aunt Janine claimed her for a turn about the room.

"What's in your head, girl?" Aunt Janine asked shrewdly. "You've scarcely said a word in twenty minutes."

Naomi gave her what she hoped was a reassuring smile. "I'm sorry, Auntie. I am rather distracted tonight. We've had a long day of traveling, and so many new faces—"

"Stuff and nonsense," Aunt Janine grumbled. "You're the only person I've ever known who is not fatigued by travel, and there's nothing you like better than meeting new people. You flourish in society, while I quite wither in it."

Naomi wondered whether she should confide Clara's concerns to her aunt. After all, Aunt Janine had already expressed her belief that there was more to their presence at Lintern Abbey than met the eye. Before she could say anything, however, Clara invited Janine to join her on the settee.

She was replaced at Naomi's side by a young woman of her own age with striking red hair and green eyes. "Lady Naomi, I wonder if you remember me." Her voice, like Naomi's, carried the smooth, even tones of a privileged upbringing.

Taking in the woman's appearance, a twinge of familiarity tickled the back of Naomi's mind. "Rochelle, isn't it?" Glancing at her companion's hand, she saw a band on the fourth finger. "Forgive me, but I don't recall your married name."

"I'm Lady Gray now." The elegant woman held her head proudly and took long, even steps to best display her purple silk dress, the very crack of fashion. "We were débutantes together last year, you and I."

Suddenly, Naomi mentally saw the woman at her side in a white dress at Almack's. "Oh, yes! I remember now. But I didn't see you in Town this spring."

Lady Gray shook her head. "No, I was already betrothed, of course." She stopped to pluck a chrysanthemum from an arrangement on a marble pillar. "I came up to arrange my trousseau and attend a few events then returned home to prepare for the wedding."

"Congratulations on your marriage," Naomi said. "Lord Gray is a fine gentleman."

Smiling, Lady Gray suddenly looked more girlish. "He arranged the excursion to the cave yesterday. It was extremely romantic, I must say. Cold and dark, with only torches to light the way. You should have joined us."

Naomi recalled how Lord Freese had invited her to do just that. Learning that it was a romantic excursion only confused her further. There had been no hint of romance in Lord Freese's description of the place—only blind fish. "We had just arrived at the inn," Naomi offered by way of explanation.

"Ah." Lady Gray turned Naomi to face the vase of flowers and touched them here and there, as though studying the arrangement. Leaning close to Naomi, she whispered, "Tell me, Lady Naomi, does anything about this gathering strike you as odd?"

A thrill coursed down Naomi's spine. The number of ladies who found something amiss about the party was growing. She glanced over her shoulder to make sure no one was listening. "Yes," she answered, "it does."

Lady Gray nodded sagely. "I knew you would have noticed," she said in a quiet voice. "It makes perfect sense for you and your aunt to have been invited. As well as Lord Gray and myself. Lord Herrick and Lady Griffiths." She nodded toward the widowed lady, who sat with Miss Price and Miss Elton. "The Perry siblings, as well," Lady Gray added, "though he is a younger son and she's decidedly on the shelf." Her lips pursed before she lowered her voice even more. "But these other people . . . Who *are* they? Where did they come from? Truly, I would not have consented to attend had Lord Gray told me there would be people here who are . . . *in trade.*" She shuddered as the words passed her lips.

Naomi groaned inwardly and sighed. Her own reasons for finding the party odd did not incorporate snobbery such as Lady Gray's. She cast the woman an incredulous look. "Please excuse me," she said at last. "The day's exertion is beginning to tell on me."

"We shall have to stick together," Lady Gray said with a nod.

Snapping open her fan, Naomi took advantage of the covering to blow her cheeks out. "Not likely," she muttered.

She sat on a vacant loveseat just as the gentlemen came in. Lord Gray went immediately to his wife and kissed her hand in a great display of gallantry. Mr. Ditman followed, deep in conversation with Mr. Richard.

When Lord Freese entered the parlor, Naomi felt as though half the oxygen vanished from the air. His dark curls shone elegantly, even as they fell in a haphazard fashion. He was every inch the perfect gentleman in his evening wear. The cut of his black coat was even closer than the one he'd worn earlier in the day, and his breeches clung to his muscled legs as though they'd grown in place. That veneer of civility, however, did little to conceal his overwhelming maleness. Primal virility rolled off of him in great waves, threatening to pull her under. Naomi wondered that all the women in the room did not faint on the spot. She, for one, was glad she'd already taken a seat.

His head was bent close to his uncle, Sir Randell, when he entered, the two engaged in intense conversation. Jordan frowned at something his older relative said, shook his head, and broke away from their exchange. At once, the frown vanished, replaced by a politely detached expression. She expected him to make his way around the room, speaking to each of his guests in turn. Instead, his eyes clapped onto her almost instantly. Lord Freese crossed the room as though no one else was in it. "May I join you?" he asked.

Naomi nodded, feeling lightheaded and breathless. The cushion listed his way when he sank onto the loveseat; she had to lean in the other direction to stop herself from tumbling against him. But, oh, how tempting was the desire to let herself tumble.

She studied him in her peripheral vision. He sat seemingly at ease, with one elbow casually propped onto the arm of the small sofa and his lips turned up in a light smile. Yet, every line held tension, every muscle was taut as though he was ready to spring into action in an instant. This inner turmoil of his was so near the surface, it seemed if she so much as reached out and touched him, his outer façade would shatter into pieces.

Clara caught her eyes and glanced meaningfully at Lord Freese. *She sees it, too.* And she was reminding Naomi of her promise.

Be his friend.

She plucked at a crease in her satin skirt, struggling to remember what she would say to a friend. Her capacity for language seemed to have abandoned her to a mute fate. At last, she summoned the wherewithal to speak. "Supper was excellent, my lord. Has your cook been in service here very long?"

Lord Freese shrugged. "I couldn't say. You'd have to ask the housekeeper."

"I see." Naomi tapped her closed fan absentmindedly against her thigh while she fumbled for something else to say. When she looked back at the man beside her, his eyes were trained on where her fan hit her leg. She stopped the activity at once. His eyes raked slowly over her torso on their way to her face. Banked heat smoldered behind the cold blue of his irises.

Naomi's stomach trembled. The bodice of her gown suddenly felt too tight. She remembered the feel of his hands on her arms in the library the night of the charity auction, how he'd teased her about kissing lessons. Her gaze dropped to his lips.

She inhaled sharply and averted her eyes. She was turning into a wanton, just as her mother had warned her happened to unmarried females. Rallying her virtue, she forced herself to summon the most unromantic subject she could think of. "Are you looking forward to the hunt, Lord Freese?" Bloodsport. There. The thought of killing animals by way of amusement made her stomach turn and went a long way toward squelching her wayward senses.

He leaned closer. "The hunt has already begun," he murmured.

Naomi's eyes widened. "My lord—"

"Don't do that," he said, frowning slightly and shaking his head. "How long have we known one another?"

She glanced at the other guests, who were all engaged in their own conversations and not paying attention to hers. Turning back to face him felt like plunging underwater. She couldn't stay this close to him for long; she would drown. "Forever," she answered.

A dark brow angled over an eye. "Ought you not call someone whom you have known forever by his name?"

"But you're my brother's friend, my lord. Though I've known you for years, I really don't know you at all."

He nodded thoughtfully. "I noticed that deficiency, too, especially when I realized we share common attitudes on certain subjects."

She puzzled over this for a moment. "What subjects would those be, my—"

"Jordan," he said firmly.

"Jordan." She smiled and ducked her head when his name crossed her lips.

"That's better." He sighed, and for a brief instant, he looked as though he carried the weight of the world on his shoulders.

Nerves buffeted her middle. *Be his friend.* "Jordan," she said quietly, "is there anything . . . ? You can talk to me." She blushed furiously and looked down at her hands clamped around her fan. What a fool she was making of herself!

"Would you play for me, Naomi?"

There was a haunted look about his eyes, his smile sad. His expression aroused her sympathy and the desire to indulge him. But a public performance when she wasn't prepared? She warily eyed the pianoforte in the corner. "This was not to be a musical evening. We've all just arrived. Everyone is fatigued—"

"Please," he whispered. He looked tired, Naomi thought. His cheeks were a little pale; the scar stood out more boldly tonight than it usually did.

She nodded hesitantly.

He rose and offered his hand to her. "Lady Naomi will favor us with a selection at the pianoforte," he announced to the group.

In the hush that immediately followed, she crossed to the instrument. Clara hurried to her side. "I haven't even looked through the music yet. I don't know what's here . . ."

"No matter." Naomi smiled nervously. "I have several pieces committed to memory."

She sat down at the instrument and glanced at the assembly. Aunt Janine's brows furrowed behind the frames of her spectacles. Jordan's Uncle Randell hovered slightly behind and to the side of where Auntie was seated. He scowled at the back of her head. Most of the other gentlemen wore looks of vague interest, but Mr. Ditman took no pains to conceal his boredom. Miss Price clapped encouragingly then nudged Miss Elton with an elbow; that frail lady contributed languid applause. Lady Gray leaned against her husband and whispered into his ear.

Well. She wasn't here to play for them, was she?

From her seat upon the tufted bench, she had a clear view of Jordan, isolated in the midst of the group. The strain of whatever troubled him wrapped about him like a cloak. His eyes fixed on her, drinking in every detail.

Drawing a deep breath, Naomi blocked out every other person in the parlor. In her mind's eye, she was alone with Jordan, playing just for him.

Her fingers touched the keys and danced their way through a selection from Mozart, a lively piece she hoped would raise his spirits. At the end, she acknowledged the others' applause with a gracious nod but looked to Jordan to measure the effect of her efforts. His shoulders had relaxed a bit. Some of the tension had eased around his eyes. He gestured with a hand.

Play another.

Nodding, she turned back to the keys and proceeded into a song without giving the matter any thought. Her fingers seemed to have chosen for themselves. After a few introductory bars, Naomi began to sing:

> *Come live with me, and be my love;*
> *And we will all the pleasures prove*
> *That hills and valleys, dales and fields,*
> *Woods or steepy mountain yields.*

Glancing at Aunt Janine, whose eyebrows had risen nearly to her hairline, she abruptly realized she was favoring Lord Freese with a *love ballad*, of all things, and quickly transitioned to the melody's final bars.

Another round of applause followed the song. "Bravo!" called Mr. Elton. He offered Naomi a hand up from her seat. "Only a prodigiously talented lady can play and sing at the same time. Beautifully done, my lady."

"One of my favorites," said Lady Griffiths, clasping Naomi's hand warmly. "I do wish you had played all the verses."

"Another time, perhaps," Naomi demurred.

She made her way back to the loveseat, accepting compliments along the way. What did Jordan think of the song? She felt exposed as she closed the distance between them. Jordan stood as she approached. She was relieved to see him far easier than he'd been before she'd played.

Humor brightened his face. "Marvelous, Naomi," he said with an appreciative grin. Bending his neck, he spoke in a voice for her ears only. "Don't think I missed your meaning in that second piece."

She flinched inwardly, and her knees trembled. "I really didn't mean anything by it, my lord. It's just a song I happen to know—"

A low chuckle escaped his throat. "Come now, Naomi. I know you meant it for me. 'Come live with me and be my love?' A song of domestic felicity set against the supposed pleasures of pastoral living?" He chucked her gently on the chin. "I do so appreciate a woman with a heightened sense of irony. Thank you for obliging my request." Bowing slightly, he bid her a good night and turned his attention to other guests.

Thankfully, he didn't seem to have taken the song as a confession of sentiment. Rather, he had gleaned something else entirely from the lyrics. What that meaning was, she had no idea. "Heightened sense of irony?" she muttered to herself, mystified.

Being Jordan Atherton's friend was shaping up to be one of the most frustrating endeavors she had ever undertaken.

Chapter Eight

The morning after her arrival at Lintern Abbey dawned fine, so Naomi set out with Clara and Kate to explore the abbey ruins. The gentlemen had left the house before dawn and weren't expected back until tea. Clara had issued a general invitation to the other ladies, but no one else had elected to join their excursion. Naomi had been surprised when Aunt Janine had declined to come, but her relative's eyes had sparkled when she'd told Naomi how she would spend her morning.

"Have you seen the library, child? The only private collection I've seen to best it is the one at Helmsdale. I'm going to hunt new selections to read while we're here." She'd cast Naomi a shrewd glance. "Would you like me to pick something out for you?"

Naomi had colored. "No, thank you. I brought a novel," she'd said, thinking of the birthing guide tucked into her trunk. They'd parted ways in the entrance hall, Auntie bound for the library, Naomi's party off to the abbey, and the other ladies left to entertain themselves.

She was glad to be keeping country hours once more. Drawing a deep breath of the bracing, morning air, Naomi's gaze swept across the manicured lawn. Remnants of dew clung to the grass, but their shoes and skirts were spared the damp by the well-maintained walk cutting through the park.

Yesterday evening had yielded no further enlightenment about the party. Besides herself, Aunt Janine, and Lady Whithorn, none of the other ladies seemed to detect anything amiss about the gathering. They were all content to enjoy several weeks of country idleness.

Naomi wished she could speak further with Clara, but Kate's presence restrained her. She contented herself in gleaning what intelligence she could about the estate, which, sadly, was not much.

"I'm afraid I know little about Lintern Abbey," Clara said. "My husband became Earl of Whithorn just before our marriage. This place has been without a mistress since the time of his first wife's death—more than twenty years now."

As she looked about, Naomi felt a little sad, not only for Jordan to have lost his mother at a young age, but also for the estate itself to have gone so long without a lady of the house. "And yet," she said while they paused at the edge of a reflecting pool, "Lintern does not seem to have suffered the lack of a mistress."

Clara tilted her head thoughtfully. "Not suffered, perhaps, but neither has there been any change or rejuvenation. The plantings are exactly the same as they've always been since the first time I visited here fifteen years ago. Beautiful, immaculately kept, but static." She glanced at Naomi as they continued along the path. "Lintern Abbey is not a true home."

Naomi shook her head. "I cannot believe that, Clara, not in my heart. This place *is* a home. It feels so welcoming and gracious."

"Jordan does not share your good opinion, I fear," Clara said. "Of course, he's never been one for home and hearth. Did you know he bought his own commission on his twenty-first birthday?"

Naomi stooped and plucked a weed growing in the retaining wall surrounding the pool. "No, I didn't."

The three ladies continued toward the abbey. The path carried them away from the house and up a wooded hillside.

"His father was furious, of course," Clara continued, a smile of reminiscence on her lips. "He tried to forbid Jordan from joining the army. I had to remind Lord Whithorn that his son had reached his majority and could do as he pleased."

"I remember him then," Naomi said as a memory sprang to mind. "He came to visit Marshall before reporting to his regiment."

All at once, Naomi was back at Helmsdale, eleven years old. Her eldest brother was home—a treat in and of itself. At that time, Marshall was such a rare presence in the house that he'd become a mythical figure to her—a grown-up man who lived in London and had been to Oxford and did all manner of adult things. Her heart had nearly burst with pride when she saw him because surely he must be the handsomest, most interesting brother anyone could have.

Thinking back, she now realized how she must have annoyed poor Marshall. During that visit, she'd dogged his heels, following him absolutely everywhere to see what fun or fascinating thing he would do next, hoping against hope he would include her in whatever it turned out to be. Then when his friend, a Lord Freese, had joined Marshall, he'd utterly intrigued Naomi, too. He was a grown-up, just like her brother, at first an object of fascination only because he offered a vicarious glimpse into Marshall's life away from Helmsdale.

When Lord Freese had arrived, she'd caught a brief look of his tall, masculine figure striding into the house from her window. All that day, she'd remained in the care of her governess, Miss Patterson, and ate in the nursery that night, listening as Nurse and Miss Patterson whispered about him. Naomi determined to see him for herself.

The following morning, directly after breakfast, she slipped out of the nursery and took the servants' stairs to evade Miss Patterson. She crouched outside the door to the breakfast room where Marshall and Lord Freese dined. Peeking around the door frame, Naomi spotted a head covered with black curls.

He was handsome but not as handsome as her brother, she decided with stout loyalty. Lord Freese laughed and smiled a lot. His voice was animated as he told Marshall about someone named Roger. This confused Naomi because he seemed to be talking about a lady, since he made mention of the light skirts she wore. Lord Freese must have been a very clumsy fellow. He kept tumbling Roger over this and that. Naomi wondered why poor Roger had anything to do with Lord Freese; *she* would not want anything more to do with an oaf who continually knocked her off *her* feet.

Marshall laughed at the story. Lord Freese reached for a slice of toast and spotted Naomi. For an instant, Naomi couldn't breathe. She had never seen such eyes. They looked like the sky in early autumn when the leaves change color and the sky has to be bluer than normal, just to catch anyone's notice.

Naomi was sure he would tattle on her. Marshall would be very cross because he'd warned her not to bother him while his guest was visiting. Instead, Lord Freese winked at her and offered to pour Marshall more coffee.

For the remainder of the week, she spied on the two men whenever she could slip away from Miss Patterson. Marshall never caught on, but Lord Freese knew what she was about. He left her two peppermint sticks to find in the hallway outside the billiard room. There was a daisy lying in the middle of the path the day Marshall took him to see the fruit orchard. By the week's end, Naomi was desperately in love with Lord Freese and despondent he was going away.

Knowing he was leaving, she had refused to begin her lessons, and for the first time, ran away from Miss Patterson right in front of her face. She hurtled out the door and sprinted as fast as her legs would carry her to where Lord Freese was already sitting tall in his saddle and bidding Marshall goodbye. Miss Patterson followed close behind, commanding her to stop *at once*.

"Wait!" Naomi cried, waving her arms madly. Her breath wheezed through a tight throat as she fought stinging tears.

Marshall looked vexed when he saw her flying toward him, but Lord Freese just took her in with those blue eyes of his and smiled.

He dismounted and turned just as Naomi skidded to a halt. Now that she stood face-to-face with him, Naomi's tongue tied in knots, and she couldn't think of anything to say.

Miss Patterson caught up and snatched her arm. "I beg your pardon, my lords," the governess said, pulling Naomi back toward the house.

Naomi's pained gaze was riveted to Lord Freese's face. He had perfectly smooth cheeks and a wonderful dimple in his chin. "Who is this?" He tossed the question over his shoulder to Marshall, all the while keeping an eye on Naomi. "Don't tell me you've been hiding this delightful creature from me all week, Marsh."

"A moment, Miss Patterson."

Naomi could tell by Marshall's voice that he *was* annoyed, but he would be polite, anyway. "Freese, this is my sister, Lady Naomi. Naomi, this is Lord Freese. Come and make your curtsy."

Naomi did so. It wasn't a very good curtsy because her knees knocked together under her skirt. "H-how do you do, my lord?" she said, belatedly recalling Miss Patterson's etiquette lessons.

"How do *you* do, my lady?" He took her hand, bowed, and kissed the air above her fingers.

Naomi smiled beatifically.

"You're a very clever girl, aren't you?" Lord Freese said kindly. "Try not to get into too much trouble, all right?" He winked. "I have a sister, too, you know. She's very small yet, only three years old."

"What is her name?" Naomi asked reverently, overcome that he would bestow any grain of information upon her.

"Kate," Lord Freese answered. "I shall be the proudest brother in the world if she grows up to be as pretty and clever as you."

Naomi was over the moon. Her feet didn't touch the ground once as Miss Patterson led her back to the schoolroom. She'd smiled serenely while her governess berated her shameful, hoydenish display. She'd daydreamed about the handsome Lord Freese while she stood with her nose in the corner for punishment.

It had been worth every word of scolding and every minute in that corner to have talked to and touched the lovely gentleman. Her young girl's heart had opened wide and let him in that week.

And he'd never left.

This realization came as quite a shock. Naomi gasped and stumbled over a stone step. Clara steadied her with a hand on her arm.

"I'm sorry," Naomi apologized. "I was remembering that visit when I first met Lord Freese. His cheek was not yet scarred. It's so much a part of him now, it was startling to recall his face without it."

"Indeed?" Clara's brows rose. There was something knowing in her eyes.

"He's very handsome," Kate announced. "Handsomer now with his scar. We have portraits from before."

The young woman's championing of her brother was reminiscent of Naomi's own girlish adulation of Marshall. "He certainly is very handsome. Not a lady in London would argue the point."

They rounded a bend in the path. Suddenly, the woods opened up, giving way to a breathtaking view of the abbey ruins, situated on several acres of green. Kate squealed and clapped with delight. Naomi felt herself awestruck and grinning at the impressive sight.

A heavy, square bell tower dominated the remains of the church. Arches flanked by columns marked the places where doors and windows had once been, reaching skyward to support a roof that no longer existed. "The stone is very similar to the house," Naomi observed.

"Not similar," Clara said, "the same. It was easier to take the stone from the abbey to build the house than to quarry new." She pointed a short distance away from the church to where the remnants of other structures stood. "There were other buildings, of course—a cellarium, a library. They were dismantled for the house. You can see there—" Clara indicated where the river that passed through the park below also washed past the abbey. "The infirmary was built over the water." All that remained of the building were vaulted tunnels spanning the river, supporting two crumbling walls.

"Astonishing," Naomi said. "How old is all of this?" she asked as she carefully picked her way down the stone steps set into the hillside.

"The abbey dates from the twelfth century, I believe," Clara answered. Soon the three companions wandered amongst the massive old ruins. They entered the nave from the west. Kate skipped down the aisle, touching each of the immense columns as she passed.

Approaching the altar area, Naomi was overcome by the grandeur. Even with no roof, no glass, and grass growing in the place of flagstones, the church was a humbling sight. The sun streamed in at an angle, casting long, cool shadows across the verdant floor.

"Jordan singles you out," Clara said softly. Naomi looked sharply at the other woman, who waved a reassuring hand. "I mean nothing by it, only that I believe I was correct in asking for your assistance. It was good of you to play last night. Did he ask you to do so?"

Naomi nodded.

"Just as I thought," Clara continued. "He seemed more himself afterward. Thank you."

"Clara," Naomi said, steering the conversation away from the person who had her emotions in a jumble, "I wondered if there would be any opportunity to do some charity work during my visit."

Clara tilted her head. "I don't see why not. The vicar at the village church would know where the need is in this area."

"If it's all right with you, then, I shall go speak to him, and perhaps organize a project for the ladies."

Kate had made her way up and down the nave and now returned to her mother and Naomi. Her cheeks bore roses dotted with her freckles. "Twenty-two columns in all," she reported. "Eleven on each side."

"What a feat it must have been to erect even one," Clara said, smiling at her daughter. Glancing back to Naomi, she nodded. "It's not my place to say what you may or may not do here, Naomi. I'm merely hostess, not mistress. If you want to organize some work, you're more than welcome to do so—but please don't become so busy helping others that you forget to enjoy yourself. This *is* a party, after all."

Kate tugged her mother's arm and led her into the tower. Naomi lingered behind, enjoying the solitude for a few minutes.

Strolling out of the church, she made her way toward the river, thinking to examine the infirmary. Before she got there, she was startled by the sound of a voice.

" 'Ave you seen zis? I found it some months back. *La porte* was weeds all over—not seen for many years, I think. What do you call zis . . . *petite cave?*"

Curious, Naomi peeked around a wall and spotted Jordan's uncle, Sir Randell, in the company of a boy. At a glance, she guessed him to be about fifteen. His dark hair fell in waves to his shoulders, and he wore finely tailored clothes.

"'Cellar' is the word you want," Sir Randell said.

"Une cave à vin, per'aps?" the boy suggested. His French was enunciated with clean tones, the universal mark of a good education.

"Perhaps wine, perhaps just a root cellar." Sir Randell crouched and grasped a heavy, iron ring on a dark wood door, flush with the ground. He tugged ineffectually at it. "Between the rust and the damp, I don't think we'll be getting in there. It's probably flooded. But good find, nevertheless, lad. I've lived here my whole life and never noticed that door."

The French boy turned around and spotted Naomi. His dark eyes flew open wide, and he tugged on his companion's sleeve.

Sir Randell looked up sharply at the lad, then turned to see what had him so alarmed. "Lady Naomi!" Wiping his palms down the front of his striped waistcoat, he glanced at the boy and pinched his lips together crossly.

Naomi stepped forward to greet the gentlemen. "Good morning, Sir Randell."

The older man cleared his throat and wiped his hands on his waistcoat again. He seemed agitated, Naomi thought. "Lady Naomi," he said, gesturing to his companion, "allow me to present Enrique Soto Vega."

The slender youth gave a crisp bow.

Naomi nodded in return. "Pleased to make your acquaintance, Master Soto Vega." The presence of a French boy with a Spanish name puzzled her immensely. "Are you also a visitor to Lintern Abbey?"

The youth opened his mouth then slammed it shut again. His large, dark eyes went to Sir Randell, as though asking permission.

"Permit me," Sir Randell said. "Enrique does not yet have command of the English language. You see, Lady Naomi, he is my nephew's ward." He gave a firm nod, as though closing the subject with that terse explanation.

Naomi shook her head, incredulous. "I'm all amazement, sir. Lord Freese has not mentioned a ward."

An alarming thought rattled her. Naomi peered closely at Enrique's face, searching for an Atherton family resemblance. It wasn't unheard of for the by-blows of the nobility to be passed off as wards or fosterlings. Could this child have been sired by Lord Whithorn, or even Jordan himself? He had dark hair, but so did a great many people. He'd not yet come into his full height, but he would not be as tall as the Atherton men. Not only were his eyes dark, they were a bit rounder than Jordan's and Sir Randell's, lacking the heavy lid. He was a beautiful boy, even frightened and bewildered as he appeared to be. Enrique was angelic, while Jordan's attractiveness was fiercer, more potent. *Perhaps not an illegitimate Atherton,* she thought.

Still, it was prodigiously odd Sir Randell claimed the boy could not speak English, when Naomi had heard him do so only a moment ago.

"Uncle!" Kate called. She and Clara crossed the green to join the others.

When Sir Randell introduced Enrique to the other ladies, Clara greeted him warmly. "So this is Enrique! At last. So nice to finally meet you, my dear."

The boy nodded, but bit his lips and said nothing.

Kate smiled shyly at him. Enrique's eyes slid to her then jerked away at once.

"We must take our leave," Sir Randell announced. "Come, Enrique; time for your lessons."

The gentlemen left the abbey ruins at a good pace. Naomi could think of no reason for it, but it seemed Sir Randell was eager to be away from them.

"You know of Enrique?" she asked Clara. At the older woman's affirming nod, she asked, "How long has he lived here? Lord Freese has never mentioned him in my hearing."

"Four or five years," Clara replied, "though Jordan only told us about Enrique a year ago. He was a war orphan Jordan found in Spain. He acted as Jordan's page, and soon after Jordan returned home, he sent for Enrique to join him here."

"What was a French orphan doing in Spain, I wonder?" Naomi mused. Clara tilted her head. "Oh, no, my dear, Enrique is Spanish."

Naomi stopped and frowned, perplexed. "I heard him speak French."

"Perhaps he is tutored in French as well as English," Clara suggested. "Jordan is providing the boy a gentleman's education." She wrapped her arm around Kate's shoulders and smiled warmly. "To tell you the truth, Naomi, I didn't know Jordan was capable of such a generous act. I'm very proud of him for taking the boy in. I daresay he's kept it quiet because bringing a Spanish orphan home like a stray puppy is not precisely good *ton.*"

"True," Naomi allowed. Still, what she had stumbled upon compelled her to seek out Jordan at the earliest opportunity. She knew what she had heard. Enrique spoke French with the fluidity of a mother tongue, and his English carried a French accent. If that child was Spanish, Naomi would eat her bonnet.

*

Drawn by the allure of new discovery, Janine went to the library again half an hour before supper. She had no purpose in mind beyond furthering her acquaintance with the splendid collection. What a joy it had been to discover such a marvelous bibliotheca tucked away in this rural corner of Yorkshire.

A wood fire crackled happily in the fireplace, providing light and warmth. Both were appreciated, as her eyes no longer cooperated as they used to, and her fingers grew stiff and ached in the cold. Breathing in the smell of gently warmed leather bindings and old paper, she made her way to a shelf.

"Aristotle, Locke, Plato, Spinoza . . . You're all here, my friends." As she perused the contents of the philosophy section, followed by religious texts and mythologies, her heart was soon as warm as the rest of her. There was nothing quite like being surrounded by so much knowledge to give one a feeling of gladness and security.

Janine had long felt she would like to devise a way to be interred in a library when her time came. She quite liked the idea of cremation as practiced by Hindus and other civilizations throughout time. In their heyday, the northern barbarians kept the ashes of their dead in clay urns.

"I shouldn't mind that," she mused aloud while she continued down the shelves. "I would look very dignified on a stand or mantel."

Like so many of her thoughts, however, that one was probably best kept to herself. Her nephew, Marshall, tolerated her eccentricities well enough, and Naomi rather doted on her. Grant, the middle child of the younger Lockwood generation, on the other hand, did not approve of her bookishness. And Caro, that odious beast, had scarcely had a word to say to her since the previous Duke of Monthwaite, Janine's brother, had died. Caro had kept the peace with Janine solely for the sake of appearances, but propriety notwithstanding, would no doubt have an apoplectic fit if she caught wind of this notion.

"Ah, here we are," Janine said upon finding the natural-sciences section near the front corner of the room. "Astronomy, physics . . . Oh, dear," she tut-tutted, "alchemy should be with the mythologies." Pulling the offending volume from the shelf, Janine turned and was startled by the sight of Sir Randell sitting in one of the two wingback chairs facing the fireplace. She let out a gasp and clutched the book to her chest. "Upon my word, sir, you gave me a fright! You should have made yourself known."

The gentleman's heavy brows crawled up his wide expanse of forehead. "And interrupt the conversation you were carrying on with yourself? That would have been frightfully rude, I daresay."

Janine's lips pinched together. "I do not talk to myself."

Sir Randell grasped the arms of the chair with long fingers that did not look as though they complained in the cold. Upon standing, he ran his hands down his waistcoat and looked about the room. "No? Where is your companion, madam? I should like to greet him."

He leveled a challenging look on her, and Janine felt heat rising in her face. Mercy, was she *blushing*? She had not done anything of the sort in . . . Well, she could not remember ever blushing. It must have only been a physiological response to the profound annoyance evoked by this ornery male. "If I were to talk to myself—which I do not—I should be with a pleasanter conversationalist than present company provides!" Her nostrils flared and she raised her chin.

"It is not my intention to force my unwelcome company upon you, dear lady." His tone was all politeness, but she could not help but feel he was laughing at her. "I must, however," he said, raising one enviably long, healthy index finger, "point out that 'twas not I who foisted myself upon you but the other way 'round." Gesturing toward a shelf on the far wall, he adopted the air of a concierge. "The novels are in this direction, if you are seeking a volume."

He plucked the alchemy book from her hands and returned it to its place on the shelf.

Janine's cheeks flamed with ire. Repellent man! "I have no desire for a novel," she snapped. "Rather, I'd hoped to find a geological survey of the country surrounding Lintern Abbey."

Sir Randell stalked to her. He was very tall with no hint of a stoop in his back, despite matching every one of her own fifty-three years and then some. His vivid blue eyes—almost identical to his nephew's—compounded the unsettling quality of his person. He smirked down at her with undisguised dislike. "There is no such volume in the collection," he said. "But if there were, I would not do you the disservice of turning it over to you."

Janine's eyes flashed defiance. "What I choose to read is no concern of yours."

He shook his head once. She noticed a streak of dark hair above his left ear; the rest was a dignified silver. "Not so," he stated. "The welfare of the weaker sex must concern all true gentlemen. It would not be a kindness to knowingly bewilder you with topics beyond your comprehension."

Janine's mouth dropped open, appalled at the affront. Her fingers clenched into fists at her side. The resulting dull pain throbbing up her arms only fueled her ire. "Sir, you did *not* just utter those foul words! Repent of them at once!"

"I cannot repent of that which I did not say," he rejoined. "You will have to decide whether I spoke foul words or not."

She fumed silently, shaking with the force of her vexation. Never had a human being gotten under her skin as quickly as this buffoon had.

He, however, remained perfectly composed. His lips twitched, seeming to enjoy her reaction. "I remember you, Jeannie Lockwood, as you looked as a girl."

Janine blinked and stepped back. No one had called her Jeannie in decades.

"Quite the antidote. Dowdy and overeducated by half." Sir Randell reached past her to pull a book from a shelf. His arm passed close enough to her head that she felt the warmth of him on her temple skin. "Still, as the daughter of a duke, you must have had suitors. I wonder that you never married," he mused, while examining the spine of his selection.

Dowdy? Unexpected self-consciousness crept over her and she glanced down at the loose bodice of her dress. Maybe she could have stood still a little longer for the seamstress, but it seemed such a waste of time. Clothes said nothing about the person she was where it mattered— in her mind. *There* resided her character and worth, not in the cut of her garments. "I never wished to marry," she said stiffly.

At that, he chuckled. "Which is what females say when there aren't any offers."

His jibe struck a little too close to the truth. There had been a few offers from old widowers, but none from the dashing, young gentlemen making their first trips to the altar. Janine pursed her lips and stared at a portrait of a pair of hounds, hanging on the opposite wall, while she drew a few breaths and struggled to regain her composure. One of the advantages of growing older, she'd found, was no longer suffering embarrassment during lapses in conversation. Her agile mind generally had a reply at the ready as soon as she required one, but she felt no compulsion to speak before she was prepared to do so.

At last, she looked back at the irksome creature standing before her. "I assure you, Sir Randell, I did not marry because I *chose* not to marry. The word 'spinster' is inscribed on my very soul. Old maid. On the shelf." She advanced toward him, propelled by a lifetime of witnessing injustice and prejudice against her sex. "I prefer any of those titles to 'wife,'" she sneered. "Every man of my generation is just like you— odious, overbearing—wishing only to dominate and dictate to women, keeping us ignorant to facilitate control over half the world's population. Well, I wouldn't have it, sir!" she proclaimed, gesturing sharply. "Thank you for reminding me why I preferred the company of books to men and for confirming that still to be the case."

Her chin lifted pertly and her eyes blazed in triumph as Sir Randell frowned.

The library door opened. Lord Freese entered, glancing over his shoulder at Naomi. "This should be a private place at this time of—oh! I beg your pardon."

Naomi's eyes went wide when she spotted her aunt across the room. She glanced at Lord Freese and colored. Janine wondered what the discomfort was. At last it occurred to her that she and Sir Randell had just been found alone and standing very close together.

Bother and bosh, she thought crossly. *I'm entirely too old to have aspersions cast in my direction. I don't need a chaperone—I am* the chaperone!

Naomi sidled away from Lord Freese.

Of course, Janine reflected, those two *should* have a chaperone. Why did they seek a private place for a *tête-à-tête?* Her niece was a sensible girl, though. Janine trusted her judgment as much as she'd trusted her own at that age—and her own sensibilities had never led her astray.

"There you are, Auntie!" Naomi blurted, a bright smile pasted to her lips. "We've been searching for you high and low, have we not, Lord Freese?"

"Indeed," the gentleman contributed. "It's nearly time for supper. You've been missed. In the parlor."

A moment passed wherein the four parties looked one at the other, electing by silent consent to accept this falsehood for the sake of appearances.

"Excellent!" Sir Randell broke the silence and offered Janine his arm. "Lady Janine and I were just wondering to one another what the time is. Now we know."

Lord Freese gave Naomi a meaningful look, and the two departed in the direction of the parlor.

Janine snorted. "Never mind the clock standing in the corner."

Sir Randell shot her a frown. "We wouldn't want to embarrass the children. Still," he said as they strolled toward the sounds of the assembled guests, "I wonder what they were about?"

"Some stones are best left unturned, sir."

"Now *that*," Sir Randell said, nodding sagely, "is a point upon which we are in perfect accord."

Chapter Nine

Throughout supper, Jordan could focus on neither the meal nor the company. Naomi had sent him a note while he prepared for the evening, begging a moment of his time. It had been an unexpected pleasure to hold words addressed to him, written in her hand. He'd urged his valet to hurry through dressing him, curious to know what prompted this unprecedented summons.

She awaited him in the entrance hall, looking every inch the fashionable lady in a green gown with a daring, square neckline. Yet something furtive shadowed her eyes, and she asked if they might not find somewhere more secluded to talk.

Intrigued, he led her to the library—where they found their respective uncle and aunt going at one another like sparring cocks. Naomi made a pretty excuse for their presence but abandoned the discussion she'd meant to have with him. He now cast significant looks in her direction, which she ignored.

Hosting was such a tedious chore. Jordan did not want to sit at the head of the table and separately engage Mr. and Mrs. Richard in conversation, since they could barely countenance looking at one another, much less speak civilly. What he really wanted to do was push back his chair, stalk the length of the table to where Naomi sat between Mr. Perry and Mr. Young, pull her onto the terrace, and—

His fork clattered onto his plate. Mrs. Richard pursed her lips and raised a disapproving brow. Jordan muttered an apology and swallowed half a glass of wine in one gulp.

What was *that* his brain had concocted?

This is Naomi, you degenerate, he scolded himself. The strain of this whole manhunt of a house party—the intrigue-riddled, international catastrophe of it—was already wearing him down, and it hadn't been a week. His mind was straying, turning things out of their proper place.

If Jordan did seek Naomi out every evening, if he'd hurried to answer her note, it was only because he'd been commissioned by her brother to take particular care of her. That was it.

He realized he was staring again, devouring her creamy throat with his eyes.

The ladies finally withdrew, and Naomi took her intoxicating innocence and sensuality out of the room. He could breathe again.

"I think we should set a night patrol," Mr. Richard said without preamble. His mean, little eyes peered at Jordan. "What good does it do us to tromp around the moor all day, if the Frenchies are free to come within a stone's throw of the front door at night?"

Lord Gray waved a hand in disagreement. "We settled this days ago. A few of our men close to the house at night is sufficient. Would you have us falling off mountainsides and breaking our necks, stumbling about in the dark? I guarantee you our French agents aren't that stupid."

"They're stupid enough to support a defeated madman," Solomon Perry sneered.

Ditman cast a contemptuous glance at Perry. "If Bonaparte was as soundly defeated as we'd like him to be, none of us would be here, would we?"

Jordan's temper rose in proportion to the volume of the squabble. "The watch remains as is," he declared crossly. "Who is out this evening?"

He glanced around the table, but for the life of him, he still couldn't recall all the men in his company. Forgettable faces were an asset to the Foreign Office, but Jordan's obliviousness was more than that. He didn't care enough about these men to become acquainted. He only cared to apprehend French agents. Beyond that, Jordan had no use for any of them except Fitzhugh Ditman, who had more than proved his worth in Spain.

Dispatching the remainder of his port, Jordan stood. "Let's join the ladies, shall we?"

"Ladies in the plural sense," Solomon Perry said with a smarmy smile, "or just the one? Lady Naomi might be the only female in existence, for all the notice you take of the others. You cling to her skirt like a devoted lapdog."

Jordan fixed the overgrown scarecrow in a wrathful gaze.

The man's Adam's apple bobbed up and down as he swallowed; his face blanched. "Not that I blame you," he said hurriedly. "She is, of course, without a protector, unlike the rest of our ladies."

Jordan pressed forward. Perry retreated until he stumbled against a chair and plopped onto it. Jordan snatched his lapels and brought his face within inches of the other man's. "Get out of my house," he sneered. "You have night watch for the rest of the week."

Nodding his hasty assent, Perry scrambled backward out of Jordan's grip.

Jordan was still out of sorts when he reached the parlor. He had half a mind to take the night watch himself. Whist, charades, and mindless gossip held no appeal. His gaze raked over the motley assortment of females, who all ceased their various activities when the men entered.

"Tea will be here in a trice," Clara announced while moving to Jordan. She took his elbow and steered him aside. "Is something the matter?" she inquired. To his blank stare, his stepmother made an exasperated sound. "You're going to frighten the ladies, scowling so fiercely at everyone."

With an effort, he schooled his features into a more decorous composition and gave her a toothy grin.

Clara frowned incredulously. "Worse. Now you look like a wolf come to devour the little lambs." She gave him an arch look as two maids entered with the tea trays. "Do try to be more domesticated, Jordan." She patted his arm and went to pour tea.

Jordan's attention lit upon Naomi, who chatted with Albertha Wood. Miss Wood shared her brother's unfortunate, overlarge teeth, but her smile was quite pleasant with lips closed.

He had only a glance to spare for Miss Wood, however, before his awareness returned to Naomi. Merely looking upon her was a balm to his agitated nerves—but also stirred up other, hungrier, sensations.

She must have felt his gaze, for Naomi caught his eye and favored him with a nod. Though an entirely different gesture than a crooked finger, that little bend of her neck beckoned to him all the same. "Deuce take it," he grumbled as he crossed the parlor.

"I beg your pardon," he said, interrupting Miss Wood in the middle of a sentence. "Lady Naomi, it has just come to my attention that Crawford, my head gardener, is having difficulties with a night-blooming primrose."

Naomi's brow arched in inquiry.

Hands clasped behind his back, Jordan continued. "It would appear the specimen in question has been flowering at noon, which is quite out of the question for a night bloom."

Miss Wood pressed a hand to her cheek. "My word! I wonder what could have caused such a curious deviation."

"Just so, Miss Wood. The answer has so far eluded poor Crawford. Even as we speak, he's in the hothouse with the primrose, seeking to unearth, as it were, the root of the mystery."

"Perhaps the cause is not in the roots," Naomi suggested, her face alight with mirth.

"You may be right, Lady Naomi," he said thoughtfully. "It occurs to me that your brother, His Grace the duke, is something of a botanist, is he not?"

Jordan perfectly well knew this to be the case, but Naomi caught where he was leading and played along.

"You remember right, my lord. It has been my pleasure to aid him in some of his research. As it happens," she said innocently, "last year I assisted his work with evening primrose."

"How fortunate!" Miss Wood proclaimed. She turned eagerly to Naomi. "I wonder if you might . . ." She covered her mouth. "Oh, but I speak out of turn. Forgive me for putting you forward, my lady."

Affecting surprise, Jordan looked from Miss Wood to Naomi. "Oh, well, I hadn't . . . That is, it never crossed my mind—"

"My lord," Naomi interjected, "might I see the specimen in question and offer my opinion?"

He waved his hands. "Only if it wouldn't be any trouble. Although," he said, adopting a tone of concern, "Crawford hasn't slept these last several days, as he's remained at the primrose's side, trying to set it to rights."

Miss Wood made a sound of dismay. "Oh, the poor man! What devotion! What care!" Shaking her head, she sighed. "You are fortunate to have him, my lord. Anything that might ease his burden should be considered."

Naomi's features fell into a convincing expression of pity. "Right you are, Miss Wood. I can think only of dear Mr. Crawford now, and I'm afraid I shall take no pleasure in the evening if I have not done my part." Nodding gravely, she said, "Please, my lord, take me to the primrose."

They slipped out of the parlor, leaving Miss Wood to explain their absence for reasons of botanical emergency.

Naomi did an admirable job maintaining her composure until they were outside, then she dropped Jordan's arm and laughed, silvery and musical. The sound delighted him, and he chuckled with her.

"Poor Mr. Crawford," she said, her voice thick with mirth. She dabbed her eyes with a finger until Jordan passed her a handkerchief. "You are shameless. No one besides Miss Wood will believe a word of it."

Jordan decided to take Naomi to the moon pond, located a fair distance across the park but still within sight of the house. "Perhaps they won't, but with you and I having begun the story, and Clara vouching for it, no one will dare suggest otherwise."

"Did you actually put the tale past Lady Whithorn before you approached me?" She seemed both amused and scandalized at the idea.

"No," he admitted, "but she's accustomed to my pell-mell ways and takes them in stride."

It was a cool night, and the path had them walking beside the stream running through the park. Naomi rubbed her arms, and Jordan mentally kicked himself for bringing her out-of-doors before she could retrieve so much as a shawl. Without a word, he removed his coat and draped it over her shoulders.

Naomi stopped. He felt her gaze and wondered if she'd ever seen a man disrobed beyond waistcoat and shirt. Before he could stop the insidious thoughts, blood pounded through his veins to the organ behind the fall of his breeches. He wanted to be the first man she saw undressed, the one to give her pleasure.

Stop, he chided himself. It had been too long since he'd bedded a woman. There had been one last tumble with Lady Evans before he ended their affair at the beginning of the Season, but no one since then had caught his eye.

Someone did *capture your notice,* whispered a voice inside. *She's standing in front of you.*

"Naomi." Speaking her name helped cool his lust, even if his mind was still a jumble. This was a girl he'd watched grow into a beautiful woman. He was attracted to her—he could admit as much to himself—but nothing could ever come of it. They were both disinclined to marry, and Jordan didn't dally with virgins.

"Yes, Jordan?" Her voice was scarcely more than a whisper.

He shook his head. They walked the rest of the way to the moon pond in silence. The water feature's name served descriptive double duty. The pond was placed in an open expanse of lawn to best reflect the heavens. It was also built in the shape of a half moon, with a statue of a water nymph in the center. The still, dark water mirrored the crescent and stars overhead.

"Beautiful," Naomi breathed. A dreamy smile touched her lips as she took in the celestial splendor at her feet. Jordan's coat slipped from her left shoulder; he gently replaced the garment. His hand lingered, and ever so slowly, his fingers brushed up her neck to cup her jaw. There was a reason he'd brought Naomi outside, but for the life of him, he couldn't remember what it was.

Her eyes closed, and for an instant, she pressed against his hand. Then she inhaled sharply and pulled away. But it was enough. That minuscule gesture confirmed she was attracted to him, too. It was a heady revelation.

Naomi took a step back and clutched the lapels of his coat closed at her throat. "I would still like to speak with you, Jordan. I'm sorry we couldn't do so earlier."

"I'm not." He closed the distance between them again, tight heat pulsating between his legs. He captured a wayward strand of her hair and brushed it against his lips. Its silky length carried a clean, lemony scent. He brought his other hand to her throat. Her pulse quickened beneath his touch and ordered his into unison.

"Aunt Janine and Sir Randell seem to have had a row, don't they?" There was a bewildered edge to her voice.

"I do believe they detest one another." He pressed closer against her soft torso and tilted her face up. Her lips were sinfully plump and inviting; the bottom one trembled.

"I met your ward," she blurted, "Enrique."

Oh. That put a damper on things.

She panted as though it had been a physical effort on her part to reengage her mind when he knew she'd been as caught up in the moment as he.

Blast it all, he thought crossly, she should not have met Enrique. She was not to have *known* about Enrique. None of them was. That way lay danger, and he was supposed to steer Naomi away from harm.

He chuckled softly, still cradling her head in his hands. "You wanted to talk about my ward?" He presented the question as though he found the idea silly.

Naomi shook her head. "Something isn't right. I was told he's Spanish, but I heard the boy speak French."

"He's Spanish," Jordan said flatly.

A frown creased her brow, and he saw a petulant look cross her face. She was going to argue. To question. There was only one thing to be done.

He kissed her.

Every thought flew from Naomi's mind when Jordan suddenly brought his mouth down on hers, warm and firm. She closed her eyes in shock then kept them closed because she suddenly experienced a new world of sensation that did not require vision. She felt breathless. A frisson of pleasure shot through her, settling low in her belly. The coat wrapped her in his scent, contributing another note of intimacy.

Jordan still held her face in his hands. He parted his lips. Instinctively, she opened hers, as well, relishing the closer contact. At the first, soft melding of tongues, he withdrew.

He lifted his face and regarded her with surprise. "Forgive me," he said softly. "I shouldn't have." His features still registering shock, Jordan led Naomi back toward the house at a brisk pace.

It took a moment for her mind to clear. The kiss had been brief, but Naomi's heart pounded in her chest, as though she'd run a long distance. The tall male beside her was all hard lines in the dim light, no sign of the sensuality she'd felt in his kiss. The contact had been such a surprise. Certainly, she'd never expected it when they'd come outside to talk about—

"Enrique," she said, pulling him to a stop. "I want to speak with you about him."

He huffed. "What is there to discuss? The boy is my ward; I provide him a home and education."

"How did you meet him?" Naomi asked, her eyes wide in the darkness.

Jordan made an exasperated sound and waved his hands. "My regiment was in Madrid, and I collared him trying to pick my pocket. Just a scruffy, little street brat. An orphan. I paid him to act as my page.

Took leave of my senses and offered him a home here." He started walking again.

"And that's it?" Naomi asked, incredulous at his perfunctory delivery and moving fast to keep pace. So quickly had his demeanor turned, she could hardly believe this was the same man who had kissed her only a moment ago.

"What more should there be?" His tone took on an icy edge that caused Naomi to wonder. Why did he bristle so on the subject of his ward?

"For one," she said, struggling to keep her own voice moderate, despite her frustration, "I wonder how a French boy came to be an urchin in Madrid."

"He's Spanish," Jordan insisted.

Naomi stopped again and scoffed. "I have been thoroughly schooled in the French language; I know a native speaker when I hear one."

She caught a hint of a sardonic smile. "I regret to inform you that you are sorely mistaken. You may know something of the French tongue, but your limited education seems not to have included the Basque region."

Naomi's cheeks burned as he heaped insults upon her head. Unfortunately, he had the best of her in this one particular, as she did not know anything about the Basque region, other than having seen the words on a map of Europe. "What has that to do with anything?"

They reached the house. Light from the torches out front lit Jordan's face. He turned his charming smile on her, but his eyes were cold. "Merely that the Basque people speak a hodgepodge of French, Spanish, and their own tongue, which is akin to the Slavic languages. If you heard Enrique speak French, it is because he grew up speaking it, in part. That does not, however, negate the fact that the child is a Spanish national."

She felt deflated. How could she have been so mistaken? "Perhaps," she said. Shaking her head, she frowned. "He sounds so very *French*, though."

"But he's not," Jordan said perfunctorily. He held the door for her as she slipped out of his coat. "You are mistaken on the matter. And Naomi . . ." He touched her elbow. Her stomach flipped. For an instant, she felt the same intense draw she'd experienced just before he kissed her. Then his lips hardened. "It would be best if you forget you saw the boy," he said flatly. "My ward is none of your concern."

Chapter Ten

The next morning found Naomi amongst a group of ladies headed to the village. She walked arm in arm with Aunt Janine who was unusually quiet. Ordinarily, Naomi's relative would have commented upon every interesting feature in the landscape. Ordinarily, Naomi would have commented upon her aunt's strange silence and inquired what the matter was. Today, though, she was distracted with last night's events.

Jordan had kissed her and then cut her down the very next minute. She could only conclude the kiss had been a diversion to stop her questions about Enrique. For the life of her, she could not imagine why Jordan had gone to such an extreme measure, merely to avoid discussing his ward. It was beyond mystifying.

Naomi reflected on her sadly brief catalog of kisses. There had been Mr. Hayward in the library the night of the auction and then Jordan last night. Of the two, only Mr. Hayward seemed to have kissed her because he felt anything. Jordan—the man she much preferred to Mr. Hayward—kissed her only to keep words from coming out of her mouth. How lowering! It was really too bad that kissing Jordan had been one of the most intense pleasures of her life, since he clearly did not share the sentiment.

"You're awfully quiet," Aunt Janine said. "What's rattling around in your head?"

Naomi raised a brow. "That should have been my question to you, Auntie. I was quiet because you were." She pointed to a mountain in the distance. "What do you make of the white streak cutting through the cliff face over there?"

Aunt Janine sighed impatiently. "Oh, I don't know, girl. Sir Randell has nothing at all to recommend him. That's what I know."

Up ahead, Kate walked beside her mother and trailed a hand through the tall grass growing alongside the road. Clara spoke with Lady Gray. At the front of the group, Trudy Price engaged in lively conversation, at least on her side, with the perennially frail-looking Miss Elton. Beside them, Miss Knight—engaged to marry Mr. Young, Naomi had learned—cast impatient glances in her companions' direction. Though her coloring differed from Lily's, Miss Knight's manner reminded Naomi of her good friend's no-nonsense attitude.

Gently leading Aunt Janine around a puddle in the path, Naomi asked in a neutral tone, "What was your disagreement with Sir Randell about?"

The older woman's cheeks colored. "What disa—oh!" She let out a strangled huff. "I knew he was making too much noise, the great brute!"

Naomi smiled to herself. She did not tell her aunt it was *her* raised voice that had greeted them when she and Jordan had entered the room, not Sir Randell's.

"I'll tell you what the disagreement was about," Aunt Janine stated. She proceeded to explain, word by word, just how the "insolent man" had wronged her.

Naomi tried to attend—something about a geologic survey—but she found herself thinking yet again about what had passed between her and Jordan last night. Had he really felt nothing when they'd kissed? Naomi had felt . . . well, quite a lot!

"Auntie," she said, cutting off Janine's diatribe, "perhaps you should try being more agreeable to people."

Aunt Janine sputtered. "I'm all agreeableness!" she protested.

"No, you're not," Naomi countered. "You're marvelous to those of whom you approve and rather cantankerous with everyone else, if you don't mind my saying."

A sniff from her aunt was the only reply.

They topped a rise and saw the village nestled in the valley a quarter mile away. Just outside the picturesque settlement, Naomi, Clara, and Kate called at the vicarage while the others continued to the shops. They met with the clergyman's wife, Mrs. Barton, who was delighted to hear Naomi's inquiry about local needs. She took them to a small outbuilding behind the house where she and the Reverend Mr. Barton were attempting to build up a store of foods to help sustain needy villagers through the coming winter. Two hams hung from the rafters and a few crocks of preserves stood in a row. Other than those, the shelves were bare.

Naomi sighed to herself and shook her head. These were Jordan's people. He should be aware of the need in the village; he should be the first and greatest contributor to this worthy endeavor. She and Clara assured the vicar's wife they would begin preserving some of Lintern Abbey's summer bounty the very next day.

"May I help, too?" Kate asked her mother as they walked into the village to rejoin the others.

"You have my permission," Clara said, "but must ask approval from Lady Naomi. This is her cause."

Naomi startled at her new friend's statement. "No, no!" she insisted. "This is our project—all of ours."

Unpersuaded by her words, Kate looked at her hopefully. "May I help, Lady Naomi? I could gather fruits, or stir the pot, or chop—"

"No chopping!" Clara interrupted. "I'll see you grown with your fingers intact, if it's all the same to you."

"Of course you may help," Naomi said. "I would never turn away willing hands."

The younger girl beamed.

"It's unlucky my sister-in-law, the Duchess of Monthwaite, is not here," Naomi said. "She's a wonder in the kitchen and would preserve everything in a three-mile radius in a single afternoon."

A smile split Kate's freckled face, and she laughed in delight. "Is that true? A duchess who works in a kitchen?"

Naomi nodded, and a smile tugged at her lips as she recalled her party last year, which Isabelle had saved from disaster by single-handedly preparing the massive supper for the guests. A more recent memory, however, of Isabelle telling Naomi she was not needed at Helmsdale, chilled her heart. She tried to cheer herself with the thought that she was with new friends now and amongst people who *did* need her.

Lintern Village was too small to truly bustle with activity, but the high street was nevertheless populated with a fair number of people going about their daily business. There was a butcher shop and a general store. The engraved brass plate on one door indicated the presence of a surgeon. A mail coach stood in front of the inn. A young woman, no older than Kate, in simple garb, clambered up to a seat on top of the coach and waved goodbye to her mother and siblings huddled together on the curb as the vehicle pulled away.

"Going into service somewhere," Clara murmured. A pained expression marked her face as she looked at the family the girl had just left behind.

"Why wasn't she given a place at the Abbey?" Naomi wondered.

Clara shook her head and sighed. "Nothing goes on at the Abbey. It's maintained by a skeletal staff who only has Sir Randell, young Enrique, and themselves to wait upon. If Jordan were married, if he did more entertaining, perhaps there would be need for more servants. But as it is . . ." She shook her head sadly again and crossed the street to offer a handkerchief and a sympathetic shoulder to the weeping mother who had just sent her daughter out into the world to fend for herself.

Even as she told herself she had no right to be, Naomi found herself perturbed at Jordan. If he were more attentive to his estate and its dependent village, that poor child might not have had to leave her family. The wages of one more maid would be nothing to him, while the money would mean everything to the girl's mother.

Kate waved her over to where she stood in front of a shop. "Will you go in with me?"

They entered the little business, an all-purpose women's clothier. Bolts of colorful fabrics were neatly stacked on tables on one side of the space, while the other side was dedicated to headwear. Behind the counter, spools of ribbon and bins of buttons and other trimmings occupied several shelves.

A pleasant, middle-aged woman emerged from a back room. "Good morning, ladies. May I be of assistance?"

Naomi glanced out the window and saw Clara still speaking with the village woman. A pang shot through her chest. "I require a new bonnet." She surprised herself with the declaration, as she'd had no intention of doing anything beyond settling on a charitable project this morning, but the brightening of the proprietress's face confirmed that her patronage was most welcome. Her eyes flicked to Kate. "My young friend requires a new bonnet as well."

Kate's cheeks went scarlet. "I haven't any pin money," she whispered.

"I didn't ask if you did," Naomi said with a fond smile. "I would like to make you a gift."

Jordan's sister grinned with surprised delight.

"Are you ladies from the Abbey?" the shopkeeper inquired.

"We are," Naomi confirmed.

The woman smiled apologetically. "I'm afraid I have little ready-made, such as what you must be used to find in London."

"Never mind," Naomi said kindly, "I prefer to begin with a form. Shall we?"

The woman—Miss Scrimshire, as she identified herself—gestured Naomi to a little chair before a vanity. There followed a parade of bonnet forms and discussion of fabrics and trims, with Naomi consistently choosing more costly materials.

Then came Kate's turn in the chair. Given the girl's age, Naomi began by choosing a closer-cut form and directed Miss Scrimshire to the cottons and muslins rather than the silks and satins Naomi had drawn from. Beyond that, however, she gave Kate free rein to choose what she pleased.

Kate quickly settled on a cream fabric for the exterior and said she wanted a green lining. When offered fabrics in various shades of green, Kate bit her bottom lip and looked from one to the other. Finally she turned in her chair. "Which should I choose, Lady Naomi?"

"Whichever you like, dear."

A worry line creased the skin between her brows. "But which will look *best?*"

Naomi looked over the choices laid on the vanity. "They are all very fine," she said. "Each will complement the cream muslin."

"I'll choose the sage," Kate decided with a nod. "Jordan would like it better than the others."

Naomi's heart gave a lopsided thump. "This isn't your brother's bonnet," she said in a lightly teasing tone, "it's yours, Kate."

"I know, but . . ." Kate shrugged awkwardly. "I want him to like it."

Naomi smiled wanly. "I'm sure he'll like it very much." She stood by while Kate and Miss Scrimshire chose trimmings.

Poor child. Kate wanted so much to catch her brother's notice, to win his love and approval. *And she'll have it, too,* she acknowledged to herself. *For a time, at least.* But in the end, even the most doting brother could decide that his unmarried sister is in the way of his own little family.

Underfoot. Unwanted.

Jordan is not Marshall, she reminded herself. But if Lord Freese couldn't be bothered to pay attention to his estate and his ward, what chance did his sister have in the long run?

When Kate finished making her selections, Miss Scrimshire drew up a bill for the two bonnets. Naomi insisted on paying in full right away. With profuse thanks and a promise to have the work complete in a few days, Miss Scrimshire curtsied the ladies out the door.

Kate drew a deep breath and turned her face to the sky. Sighing happily, she linked her arm through Naomi's. The familiar gesture caught Naomi off guard, but she accepted it with good grace. She truly liked Kate very much and was happy the girl returned her regard.

They strolled together to meet Lady Clara who stood outside the general store with Aunt Janine and Lady Gray.

"Kate," Naomi said in a low voice before they'd reached the others, "may I ask you something?"

"Of course."

"When we met Sir Randell and Enrique yesterday morning, did you hear Enrique speak at all?"

Kate's lips screwed up in thought. "No. I don't think he speaks much English. He's Spanish, you know."

"Yes, but—" Naomi bit her tongue. Kate was not the person with whom to discuss Enrique. Basque, Spanish, French . . . Whatever the boy's nationality, it confounded all reason that he should have lived in England the last several years, received a gentleman's education, yet not speak English.

Everything Naomi had encountered in the last week since coming to Lintern Abbey made her feel as though she was slamming against a wall. It was clear to her Jordan should be more attentive to his estate, to the village, to the people living there . . . yet he was not. It was clear to her that Enrique was a French child . . . yet he was not. It was abundantly clear that Jordan Atherton should be nothing to her—he was thoughtless, negligent, high-handed—and yet he was not nothing to her. Far from it, much to her chagrin.

Lady Gray drew close to Naomi's side. "What a horrid little backwater," she murmured. "Some . . . person . . . in the general store actually suggested we attend a dance at the *assembly rooms.*" She hissed these last words with her lips curled in contempt.

Naomi shot an arch look at the other lady. "Lintern Village is just as pleasant and hospitable a place as anyone could hope for. The people are welcoming and good-hearted," she said, thinking of the food pantry at the vicarage. "You couldn't ask for a lovelier village."

Lady Gray wrinkled her small nose. "I defer to your judgment in the matter, as there is no such thing as a pleasant or lovely village to my mind. Only unsophisticated provincials and boredom everywhere the eye falls."

The woman's unrepentant criticism of the village dismayed Naomi. Why couldn't Lady Gray acknowledge the small community's charms? Naomi already thought Lintern Village one of the most amiable she'd come across. There was something exceedingly comfortable about the neighborhood, which felt like slipping into a favorite pair of gloves.

The sound of pounding hooves immediately preceded the appearance of three horsemen barreling down the high street. Villagers scattered before the fast-approaching beasts. When the three drew to a sharp halt in front of their small group, Naomi recognized gentlemen from the Abbey party.

"Ladies," called Mr. Young, "here you are!" His eyes swept over the five present; his face blanched. "But where are the others? Where is Miss Knight?" He turned his horse in a tight circle. His hand disappeared inside his coat, reaching for something. The hairs on Naomi's neck stood on end.

Just then, his fiancée stepped out of the general store, followed by Miss Price and Miss Elton. "Percy!" she exclaimed. "Whatever has happened? You look a fright."

Mr. Young's alarm drained away at the sight of his intended. "Nothing, Lucy. We only—"

"We didn't know you ladies were coming to the village this morning," cut in Lord Sidney. He was slight of build, like Mr. Young, but his features could not have been more different. While Mr. Young's delicate face could almost be called pretty, Lord Sidney's bone structure was all sharp angles and hard lines.

The third gentleman, Mr. Richard, looked at each of them in turn, as though mentally performing a head count.

Clara stepped forward. "What is the problem, gentlemen? It is not my habit to inform the whole world of my goings and comings, nor do

I see any reason for these ladies to do so. We were perfectly aware of our own whereabouts at all times." Her words carried a hard edge.

Mr. Richard flashed a questioning look at Mr. Young. Lord Sidney's dark eyes met Clara's; his face was expressionless. "There is no problem, my lady. We've only come to offer our escort back to the Abbey now."

Aunt Janine leaned close to Naomi. "No one said we were returning to the Abbey now," she whispered.

"No," Naomi murmured. The sudden arrival of the gentlemen was curious, and she didn't know what to make of Lord Sidney's explanation. When they'd first arrived, Mr. Young hadn't possessed the look of a man who'd simply come to escort his fiancée—he'd been worried, if not fully frightened.

"Come along, ladies," said Mr. Richard.

The men dismounted and walked their horses as they accompanied the women to Lintern Abbey, but there wasn't anything sociable about their escort. Naomi rather felt as though they were cattle being herded back to the barn.

Chapter Eleven

Jordan dismounted and handed Phantom's reins to a waiting groom. The great stallion snorted and pawed with a heavy hoof, cutting a dark furrow in the ground. "Come now, old man," Jordan said, patting the animal's neck, "I didn't drag you out that early."

The sky gave lie to his claim. The first hints of purple and gray were just beginning to touch the horizon.

John Bates drew up alongside Phantom. He glared, bleary-eyed, from beneath the rim of his tall hat. The collar of his great coat was turned up against the early chill. "You've brought us on a fool's errand, Freese," he complained. "Even if we trip over a brace of grouse, it's too dark to see a blasted thing." He sniffed loudly and wiped his nose with the back of his gloved hand. "Don't see why we must do this. We're not here to hunt. Our time would be better spent on security."

A short distance away, Lord Gray lithely hopped down from his horse then retrieved his gun from where it was lashed behind the saddle. "Give over, Bates. You've heard the ladies ask why we haven't brought down any birds. Even your own cousin thinks you're a lousy shot." His unlined face showed amusement. "Let's have her believe that's the worst of it and not suspect anything else."

Bates glowered at the young aristocrat before finally giving up his saddle and gathering his hunting gear. His fingers tightened around the stock and barrel of his weapon, then he turned on a heel and strode through the dew-wet heather to stand apart from the others.

The fourth and final man of the group, Dylan Price, stared after Bates, his full lips slack. Suddenly, his mouth snapped closed and he turned to Jordan. "Well, I think you have the right of it, m'lord. It's jus' not good policy to have the ladies askin' uncomfortable questions, if you want my opinion. Which I 'spect is the same as yours. Which I 'spect is why we're out here right now, idnit?" He tapped the side of his thick nose and nodded once, knowingly.

Jordan picked up his fowling piece and drew a deep breath of the brisk, Yorkshire air. The ladies *were* growing suspicious. One, in particular, was already too curious for her own good.

With a jerk of his head, he collected the other men and started up the hillside.

When he'd invited Naomi Lockwood to Lintern Abbey, Jordan never imagined she would be the source of his greatest aggravation. She didn't strike him as the type to nose and pry, but last night she'd asked questions about Enrique and pressured Jordan for answers he couldn't give—even after he'd kissed her to distract her.

Kissed her!

The wet undergrowth bested the brown fabric of Jordan's breeches; cold dew seeped through to his legs. He shivered.

That kiss overrode all other thoughts in his mind. Wanting unlike any he'd ever known had galloped through his body, shaking him to the core. Instinctively, he sought to deepen the kiss: to taste, to explore. Her scent intoxicated him. Holding her face in his hands wasn't enough—wasn't nearly enough. His arms hungered to wrap around her. His hands itched to feel her skin. Naomi's skin.

Ah, Naomi.

Innocent, untouchable Naomi.

Only the painful recollection that this was a woman he could not have—*must* not have—had allowed him to pull his lips away from hers. But, oh, how loath he'd been to do it.

He still hadn't collected his wits when he'd done the only thing he could do—flee. Jordan hadn't trusted himself to remain alone with her. He wanted her too much.

His mind had been trained only on getting them back to the safe confines of polite company, when she'd started in again about Enrique. Naomi, he decided, must have far greater fortitude than he. She'd showed dogged determination in pursuing the subject.

That kiss had been for nothing, then, since he'd failed to divert her attention. It was *worse* than nothing. His attempt at manipulating her had fallen flat, but *he* was entirely discombobulated. Lust had still saturated every fiber of his being when she'd stopped him to talk about blasted Enrique. He'd wanted to touch her again, to quiet her with his mouth once more.

It made him angry with himself to feel so out of control—and a little upset at Naomi, too. Who was she to unexpectedly become the most desirable female he'd ever known—to have been benignly on the periphery of his life for the better part of a decade and then suddenly occupy center stage? He felt duped, somehow. Taken in.

His withering lecture about the Basque region and language *had* been a tad overboard. Her feelings had been bruised, he could see. But, deuce take it, she had no business poking her nose into Jordan's affairs and tripping into harm's way. It was better if she thought him loutish and kept her distance since he could not trust himself to do so.

Off to his right and in front of the others, Bates stumbled over some unseen obstruction. His arms wheeled as he took several staggering steps. Steadying himself, he clenched his teeth and growled. "Dash it, Freese, we're going to do the French's job for them. We've no call bumbling around, breaking our necks in the dark."

"The sun is nearly up." Lord Gray pointed with his fowling gun to where the sky behind the hills transitioned from purple-gray to pink. "This is the best time of day to hunt." He nodded to Jordan in a show of solidarity.

Jordan appreciated the young man's loyalty, but he made an awful racket stomping through the heather. "Why don't you take the lead, Gray?" he said to the fellow. "Act as beater for us; flush the grouse out."

The young lord strode to the fore, casting a cool stare at Bates as he passed the angry man. Bates muttered something only Lord Gray could hear. The younger male scoffed. "Your cousin had no such complaints last night."

Bates's lips drew together in a tight line. "Come a little closer and say that again," he challenged.

Gray slowly turned, disdain marking every line of his posture as he approached Bates. Stopping toe-to-toe with the other, Gray's boyish face turned jeering. "Your cousin had no such complaints last night," he repeated.

"If you have laid a single finger on Prudence . . ." Bates growled through clenched teeth.

"Andrew, that's enough," Jordan snapped before the altercation dissolved into a brawl. "We're not here for pistols at dawn."

Lord Gray's eyes narrowed, and his lips drew down in a petulant frown.

"Bates," Jordan said, "stop provoking him. You brought that on yourself. I'm certain there's no reason to fear for Miss Hunt's honor."

With a final, silent, hate-filled exchange, the two men separated. Gray turned to lead while Bates stalked to a distance away from the group.

Behind Gray, the others formed a line. Bates took the far right, Dylan Price the center, and Jordan the left. Mr. Price soon drifted closer to Jordan. "You handled that just right, m'lord," he said in his peculiar, fast mumble. He chuffed a white cloud of breath into the morning chill. "Although," he continued, "if I might say so, sir, there doesn't seem to be much in the way of *esprit de corps* amongst the men. Why," he said, pointing the butt of his shotgun toward Lord Gray, "take these two for example. If not for you, they'd've torn each other to bits and been happy to do so."

It took a great deal of concentration on Jordan's part to distinguish one word from the next in the man's speech, but the trace of censure was clear.

Price sighed. "It's like they don't take the job seriously. What don't they understand about the danger? Why can't they stop arguing long enough to focus on finding the Bonapartists? What would they say if—"

"That will do, Mr. Price." Jordan cut a glance at the man. "We're on a hunt. Please let Lord Gray make the noise for us."

Price blinked. "Right, sorry." He drifted back to his center position in the line, leaving Jordan to stew over his observations.

It was true that the band of Foreign Office men lacked any sense of cohesion. In part, Jordan blamed this on the nature of their work. Agents were accustomed to working singly or in pairs, establishing their own networks of contacts and informants. Espionage was quiet, secretive work. Openly discussing a mission with a large group did not sit well with the men. They distrusted one another because they had learned to trust no one.

Yet Jordan could not exonerate himself of responsibility in this mess. The men didn't have to become friends; their loathing for one another shouldn't matter. It was his duty to force them to work together and successfully complete Castlereagh's assignment.

In the beginning, he had allowed his distaste for Lintern Abbey to color his perception of the task. He simply didn't care enough to exert the kind of authority the men would respond to. His efforts up to now had been sporadic, at best. The men didn't know whether they could count on him to lead the operation.

Beyond that, Jordan had become distracted from his work. His ever-intensifying attraction to Naomi Lockwood was more than a trifle inconvenient.

Even now, the yellow light bursting over the horizon and mingling with the pale rose sunrise reminded him of her hair. The strand he'd tucked behind her ear last night had been silk between his fingers, delicate and warm. He couldn't have *her*, but perhaps she would grant him a lock of hair—as a token of friendship, he would have to say. Although, *drat it all*, he thought with a sharp frown, it wouldn't be at all the thing for him to request a lock. Only a besotted oaf would pull such a blunder. No, she would have to volunteer the favor, a most unlikely event. But if he gave her something first, he thought, his eyebrows raising at the possibility, she would feel obligated to give him something in return. And, being as she was currently separated from most of her own belongings and familiar surroundings, what would she have available to gift him, other than a lock of hair?

He was congratulating his unassailable reasoning when a dark shape suddenly rose up from the ground off to his left and ran toward them. A fraction of a second later, the mass broke apart, resolving into the forms of several brace of grouse skimming above the heather, their wings flapping madly to lift them into the air.

Without thought, his mind still mostly on Naomi, Jordan raised his fowling piece, tracked the birds for half an instant, and fired.

Directly at Lord Gray.

Birds tumbled to the ground just as Andrew bellowed.

Shock numbed Jordan's chest as his comrade spun and fell to his knees, his face frozen in a rictus of pain. Jordan dropped the gun and bounded to where Lord Gray had doubled over on himself. "Gray!" he yelled, pulling the man upright.

Jordan sucked air through his teeth when he saw the damage—numerous holes made lace out of the back of Lord Gray's heretofore immaculate wool coat. Blood welled in the small holes and wept hot tears down the fabric.

Lord Gray groaned. "Goddammit, man! What the hell is wrong with you?"

Jordan swallowed hard. "I'm sorry, Andrew. I'm so terribly sorry."

Guilt made room for humiliation as Bates and Price hurried to join them. Dylan Price took a look at Andrew's back and let out a low whistle. Then he straightened and walked to where Gray's hat lay several yards away amongst the felled grouse.

Bates hissed. "I'll see you strung up for this, Freese. Your incompetence is going to get us all killed."

"Did you get the grouse, at least?" the wounded Gray asked weakly.

"It was an accident," Jordan told Bates. "I certainly didn't mean to harm Gray."

"But you have," Bates shot, jabbing a finger toward the injured man. "Castlereagh will know about this as soon as I can get an express to London."

"How many did you bag?" Gray's eyes were pleading on Jordan.

"Four or five," Jordan told him curtly. His lips tightened as he returned his attention to Bates. "Fine. Fire off an express to Castlereagh if it will make you feel better. Tell our superior that there was a hunting accident, just as there are all over Great Britain, numerous times each year."

Bates's mouth twisted in a frown.

"Before you can report me, though, we have to get Gray back to the house. Can you walk, Andrew?"

Jordan and Bates helped Andrew to his feet. The young man grimaced. "I'd rather not." He smiled wanly at Jordan, who was impressed with his attempt at humor at a time like this. Lord Gray took several halting steps forward, braced on each side by Jordan and Bates.

"Gentlemen!" Price's voice rang clear for once.

Jordan turned awkwardly, his left arm still around Andrew's waist and the injured man's right arm around his shoulders. "What is it?"

Mr. Price trotted to his side. The length of twine he'd used to string the grouse together was wrapped around his hand, leaving his fingers free. In them, he held Lord Gray's hat. Jordan winced when he saw two holes in it. Thank goodness he'd missed the man's scalp. How could he have made such an idiotic mistake?

The answer held no comfort. Shooting a man because he was distracted thinking about a woman's hair had to rank as one of the most horrifyingly negligent errors he could imagine.

"You should see this." Price extended his other hand, which held a half-burned and soggy piece of paper.

Jordan took the scrap in his free hand. He turned slightly to allow the sunlight to fall across the ruined page. The paper's straight left side had remained intact. Jordan made out the following:

Les age
Free
Sidn
Woo
Herr
Elto
Rich
Gray
Pric
Youn

Below the last item, the paper had been torn, but Jordan had no doubt it originally continued on with five more entries. "*Les age . . .* agents. It's us," he whispered harshly. "They have our names. *They have all our names.*"

Panting, Lord Gray lifted his head to see the paper. His face blanched further; his eyes wildly wheeled around the moor. "Are we safe? For God's sake, Freese, get us out of here."

Jordan nodded grimly. "Let's move," he ordered. Dylan Price took Lord Gray's legs, and together, the three carried him to the waiting grooms and horses. Halfway there, the man passed out from pain. Jordan couldn't help but envy him. He suddenly wished very much he could escape from the terrible truth they'd just discovered. The French knew their names—which meant there was a traitor in their midst.

Chapter Twelve

The clock had not yet chimed eight when Naomi quickly donned a morning dress. She left her hair in its nighttime braid, coiled it at her nape, and pinned it in place. There was nothing to be done for the wisps near her scalp making a bid for freedom, so she covered them up with a bandeau. Finally, she selected a favorite cashmere shawl and wrapped it around her shoulders.

With a deep breath and a wipe of cold palms against her skirt, Naomi tiptoed to her door. Frowning, she realized the pointlessness of doing so. "You'll never make it down the hall, acting this way," she scolded herself.

She opened the door a crack and glanced into the corridor. As she suspected, the long row of female guestrooms lay silent, their occupants still abed. Holding her breath, she drew handfuls of muslin into tight fists and raised the hem to her ankles. She darted to the end of the corridor and peeked around the corner. Two housemaids dusted mirrors and sconces. Not wishing to be seen, even by servants, she waited until they moved out of her line of sight then dashed to the central stairwell.

Her back felt exposed as she quietly jogged up the stairs. The tension between her shoulders eased a bit as she rounded the landing.

"Lady Naomi?"

Naomi choked on a gasp as she came face-to-face with the housekeeper coming down the stairs. She hoped she betrayed none of the anxiety hammering her ribs. Behind her shawl, damp fingers twisted together in knots. "Good morning . . . Mrs. Walker, is it not?"

The upper servant glided down the stairs, her eyes never once leaving Naomi's. She was swathed from chin to toes in austere, charcoal bombazine, her graying hair neatly styled in a knot. The large, brass key ring hanging conspicuously from a loop at her right hip marked her position in the household.

Mrs. Walker's shoulders squared, blocking Naomi's progress. "May I help you, my lady?" Her tone was harassed, as though she had somewhere else to be.

Naomi's mind whirled. She detested lying and had never been any good at it, but the truth would see her marched straight back to her own room.

"I—I—" she stammered. Her face flushed under the housekeeper's intense scrutiny. "I'm looking for some . . . *cloths*," she finally whispered.

At once, Mrs. Walker's demeanor changed from exasperation to understanding. "Oh," she breathed. Then she frowned. "Why isn't your maid on this errand?" she asked softly.

Agony washed over Naomi and her eyes squeezed shut. *Please don't make me lie any more,* she silently pleaded. She could think of no good reason to give Mrs. Walker and knew her scheme was about to fall apart.

Mrs. Walker, however, seemed to take her silence for embarrassment. "Never you mind, dear," she said in a maternal tone. "There's been an injury I must see to, but I'll have one of the maids fetch some to your room."

Relieved, Naomi smiled gratefully. "Thank you so much, Mrs. Walker. You're too good." The older woman gave her a brisk nod then bustled off.

When she'd gone out of sight, Naomi's smile fell, and she raced up the stairs, slowing to catch her breath only when she'd reached the very top. Dreading to stop for fear of being caught again, she continued until she came to the nursery door. It stood slightly ajar. Biting her lip at the gross breach of etiquette, Naomi pushed open the door.

The "nursery" was a marvel to behold. Her lips parted in amazement as she took in the finely furnished front room of the suite. A stylish sofa and chairs made up a seating area on one end while an elegant round table occupied the other side of the room.

Enrique sat alone at the table—in a chair as delicately carved and expensively upholstered as those in Jordan's dining room—partaking in a generous breakfast spread. The young man looked up at her entrance. His shoulders stiffened and his eyes widened in alarm.

Naomi closed the door softly. "Hello, Enrique."

He held his peace, his lips drawing back into his mouth. The boy looked quite the young gentleman in a green coat and white cravat, with his hair neatly queued at his nape. The silver fork in his right hand trembled and clinked against the china plate. Enrique set down the utensil and placed his hands in his lap, his eyes following them.

"I'm glad to have caught you before you're busy with your day." Naomi approached slowly and sat at the table, leaving an empty chair between Enrique and herself. A long moment of awkward silence hung between them. Glancing at the boy, Naomi thought he looked sad. Frown lines furrowed his brow, and his lips seemed naturally inclined to droop. There was no sound anywhere in the apartment. Behind the door leading to the next room, she heard the muffled sound of a clock chiming the hour.

The chime faded, once again leaving a heavy silence in the nursery. *How lonely he must be,* she suddenly thought. Enrique had no one but his tutors and Jordan's uncle, Sir Randell, for company. The young man had no companions his own age, and Lord Freese didn't seem to pay any attention to his ward. *He might've been happier on the streets in Spain.*

Sighing, Naomi felt her relentless curiosity about the young man drain away. It didn't matter if he was French or Spanish or Basque—or Mongolian, for that matter. What he *was*, was a lonely boy starved for company.

"Would you like to take a walk with me tomorrow?" she asked.

Enrique's eyes lit. A small smile brightened his face, but the frown lines returned. "I don't . . ." His eyes pinched closed, and his face screwed up in concentration. *"Yo no entiendo,"* he blurted.

Lord, but Jordan was taking this "Spanish orphan" charade to great lengths, wasn't he? Not that there was any objection to the child learning Spanish—indeed, Naomi approved of multiple linguistic fluencies—but the reason behind this particular education was mystifying.

"Enrique," she said patiently, "I know you speak English. I heard you talking with Sir Randell." His dark eyes widened again. She shook her head and shrugged one shoulder. "I don't know why you must pretend you can't speak English, but you can trust me with your secret. I only want to be your friend. I think you could use one." Tilting her head slightly, she smiled. "Am I right?"

The boy of ambiguous nationality exhaled audibly. His shoulders relaxed a bit as he regarded her. "Yes," he finally said. "I would like to 'ave a friend."

Her smile deepened. "So would I," she said. "So, that walk tomorrow?"

He nodded his happy agreement. They arranged to meet at the moon pond at eight o'clock the following morning. Though the words weren't spoken, they both understood the need for circumspection.

Naomi slipped out to return to her own room, only to encounter someone topping the stairs—Jordan, this time.

At once, his eyes cut to the nursery door. "What are you doing?" he demanded.

"Oh, well . . ." Naomi cleared her throat. "I had a thought about bonnet trimmings," she said, gesturing near her temple with her left hand. "Did Kate tell you about the new bonnets we ordered?" At Jordan's puzzled expression, she continued, the lies coming a little more easily. "Anyway, I came looking for Kate to discuss trimmings. I thought she'd be in the schoolroom, but she wasn't." When Jordan quirked a brow, she added, "I didn't see anyone. Actually."

Jordan's face darkened. "Not even Master Soto Vega?" He strained forward, leaning in the direction of the nursery.

"Oh, yes!" Naomi blurted, surprised by Jordan's alarm. "Yes, I saw

Enrique. He was having breakfast. He didn't say anything to me, of course. That's . . . that's all I meant." She smiled ruefully. "I should have said I *spoke* to no one."

Which is a wretched lie, she chastised herself.

Jordan looked rather bedraggled. His brown breeches sported water-dark blotches, his damp boots had bits of vegetation stuck to them, and his cravat hung hopelessly limp. His face was flush and a sheen of perspiration caused several curls to cling to his forehead.

"Have you been hunting this morning?" she asked.

"I have," he replied. "I brought down several brace of game." He clasped his hands behind his back. Jordan's restless eyes moved from her to the nursery door and back again.

"Congratulations," Naomi said. "Well, don't let me detain you. Good morning, my lord."

"Jordan," he corrected sharply.

For an instant, a cloud of turmoil crossed his features. Frowning, he absentmindedly lifted a loose tendril of her hair and rubbed it between his thumb and fingers. The gesture startled Naomi. Even when he'd released the lock and once more met her gaze, he didn't seem to realize what he'd done.

"I must check on Enrique," he said. "After that, would you accompany me to the gallery? I thought we could begin the tour you unaccountably desire." His crooked smile was devastatingly charming. Naomi doubted she could refuse him anything when he smiled at her so.

"Of course," she readily agreed. "I should like that very much."

She waited at the top of the stairs while he went to his ward's apartment. When he'd vanished behind the nursery door, Naomi exhaled heavily and slumped against the wall. Her stomach roiled. Lying did not sit well with her. Her heart felt especially sick about misleading Jordan.

At the sound of the nursery door opening, Naomi straightened. Jordan reappeared and offered his arm. The formal gesture juxtaposed against his rumpled, damp state was endearing. As she hooked her hand into the crook of his elbow, she felt more strongly drawn to him than ever.

Nevertheless, she would lie to him again, if she must. His determination to keep poor Enrique cloistered away in friendless solitude was nonsensical and bordered on cruel. Jordan was not a cruel man, but she sensed it would be best to circumvent him on this topic.

They entered at one end of the gallery, a long, airy room running the length of the back of the house. The sun poured through the many windows at a low angle, creating puddles of buttery light on the marble floor. The illuminated spots were stepping-stones for Naomi's eyes, leading her attention from one piece of art to the next.

Jordan seemed distracted. His lips twisted to the right, drawing up the end of his scar so that it mirrored the perturbed set of his mouth. His dark brows pulled down hard over intense eyes, which roved the room without appearing to notice anything.

Naomi had not been convincing enough in peddling untruths, she realized with a sickening start. He was probably attempting to riddle out the real reason she'd been near the nursery—or perhaps Enrique had volunteered the information. She flushed hot and cold in turns; her back prickled an instant before a bead of sweat rolled down her spine.

"Tell me about this one." She pointed to a small picture on the wall.

For a few seconds, Jordan seemed not to have heard. The middle finger of his left hand tapped against the front of his thigh while his eyes continued to flit back and forth, seeing something Naomi could not.

Suddenly, he stilled. Jordan looked down at Naomi. The furrow between his brows deepened, as though he was puzzled by her presence on his arm.

Blood pooled in Naomi's cheeks under his scrutiny; her heart gave a lopsided thump.

Abruptly, Jordan's features cleared, the lines smoothed away. "Which do you mean?" he asked.

She again indicated a small square painting on the near end of the wall, framed in heavy, dark wood. When she strolled to stand just in front of it, the image clarified into an assortment of buildings that, at first, Naomi took to be a village. A massive, stone church dominated the center of the scene, surrounded by smaller buildings. A river was glimpsed in the background. The structure spanning its width sparked a flash of recognition: It was the infirmary she'd seen the day she, Clara, and Kate visited the ruins on the estate grounds.

"Lintern Abbey," she said, delighted. She leaned closer to the painting and made out the figures of several Cistercian monks standing in the shadow of the church. The black scapulars over their white habits gave them a spectral appearance of white heads and arms huddled against the cold stones.

Naomi recognized the perspective; it was the same scene she'd taken in while standing on the stone steps set into the hillside. It awed her to think that hundreds of years earlier, an artist had stood in the same spot to capture his subject. She turned her inquisitive eyes on Jordan. "Do you know from when this dates?"

"Hmm?" He scowled at the painting as if to spot some obvious answer to her question. "No, I don't."

"It must be very old," she reasoned.

"I suppose it could be." The expression on Jordan's face communicated that he neither knew nor cared about the painting's history.

Naomi looked at him askance, but he didn't notice that, either. Pursing her lips, she moved on to the family portraits, her hands clasped behind her back.

The face in one of the paintings captured her attention. The gentleman had to be a direct ancestor of Jordan's—the family resemblance was too strong to allow otherwise. The artist had captured a man who exuded authority. Everything about his upright posture proclaimed it, from the firm set of his mouth to the strong lines of his shoulders. The man had the Atherton blue eyes, which stared out of the gilded frame with a hint of amusement, suggested by the slight creasing at the corners. The gentleman's costume of a century or more ago—a long, curled wig and satin clothes adorned with lace and other fripperies—detracted nothing from his essential masculinity.

"Who is this?" Naomi breathed. "Was he a Viscount Freese, as well?"

"I don't know."

When she turned toward his bored drawl, Jordan was standing by a window overlooking the back garden. He'd not so much as glanced at the portrait.

Naomi made an annoyed sound and crossed her arms beneath her breasts. "Jordan Atherton, what is wrong with you?"

He turned, clearly startled by her use of his full name—not to mention the testy tone with which she had said it. "I beg your pardon?"

She gestured toward the long wall of paintings. "Why did you begin a tour here, in this room, if you can't tell me anything about the pieces?"

There was something of a lost boy about his expression. Suddenly, Naomi wished she could scoop him into her arms and tell him everything would be all right. "House tours often begin in galleries," he said with a shrug. "It seemed as good a place as any."

"You seem to know so little about your home, your history."

Jordan scoffed. "What is there to know? These people lived, they died, they gave me a name and a family heap." He pointed to the far end of the line of portraits. "Those are my grandparents there," he said, as if that morsel of information made up for his general ignorance.

"And you don't know anything about the painting of the abbey?"

His lips tightened. "No, I don't. I imagine there's a book lying about somewhere which will tell you everything you want to know."

She quirked a brow. "You imagine? You don't know that for certain, either, do you?"

He stared at her impassively.

Naomi shook her head, saddened by Jordan's lack of interest in Lintern Abbey and its previous inhabitants. Already, she thought it one of the finest estates she'd ever seen, nestled as it was in the wild Yorkshire hills, surrounded by natural beauty—both raw and tamed. She thought of the abbey, which lay in ruins, still secluded as the cloistered monks had intended. It held ancient secrets—centuries of history. How could Jordan not be awed?

"You don't know what you have," she said quietly.

"I know what I have," he insisted, his voice flat. Despite his words, a shadow of doubt flitted across his face, pinching his brows together.

"No, you don't," she said with a soft chuckle. "What's happened to you, Jordan? You used to be the kind of person who noticed things. You noticed other people, and you cared." She swallowed hard. "Even about a young girl caught spying on her brother and his friend."

He rubbed the bridge of his nose and breathed a laugh. "A girl with a long braid and big eyes and an uncanny aptitude for sneaking away from her governess. I remember that young lady. I wonder whatever became of her?"

Their eyes met, and Naomi's breath left her in a hot *whoosh*. All vestiges of disinterest fell away as Jordan took three long strides to close the distance between them. Her heart fluttered wildly at his sudden closeness. She drank in the clean smells of heather and wood that attested to his morning hunt.

"What do you see, Naomi?" He spoke urgently, imploring, his gaze searching her face. "Tell me what you see when you look about my place. For the life of me, all I've ever seen—all I've ever felt—is dreary *sameness*, day after day and year after year. How could it not drive you mad?" He grasped her upper arms and shook her lightly, as though to jar something loose. "Since I notice nothing, you must notice for me. What do you see that I don't?"

Jordan's fingers clasped her tightly, and Naomi's blood quickened in response.

For a moment, she couldn't recall the topic of conversation. She couldn't think of anything but the marvelous warmth of his strong hands on her arms, of the answering heat sliding into her lower belly.

Unthinkingly, her hand drifted to his face. Her fingertips traced the scar on his cheek. It was tougher than the flesh surrounding it and interrupted the growth of facial hair along his jaw. Fascinated with the unique topography of his features, her fingers splayed wide, cupping the side of his face. His hands slid down her sides and came to rest on her waist. As he squeezed his eyes shut, a fringe of dark lashes came together like a fan snapping closed.

What had caused this change in Jordan? Oh, he still possessed keen powers of observation. She'd seen him employ them in ballrooms, snatching details overlooked by others to compliment ladies or entertain his friends. But it was all superficial. The kind, young officer she'd developed a girlhood *tendre* for was gone, replaced by this distant man. Maybe, if she treated him like a friend, as Clara wished, she could find out what had happened.

Naomi dropped her hand and gently turned out of his grasp; Jordan made no move to restrain her. She tightened her shawl around her shoulders, struggling to regain control of her thrumming heartbeat. "I see a wonderful home," she said, finally answering his request. "Come look again at this one." She took his hand and led him toward the abbey painting.

A smile of tolerant amusement played at the corners of his mouth as he allowed her to steer him.

"See the brothers in their robes?" Naomi pointed out the shadowy monks she'd spotted earlier. "And the intricate architectural details?" Her fingers danced lightly over the canvas, indicating the soaring Gothic arches of the church and the hints of carving around the infirmary door. "This was painted by a first-hand observer, Jordan—probably one of the monastery's residents."

"And?"

"And," she replied, "we know that Catholic lands—including, presumably, Lintern Abbey—were seized during the dissolution of the monasteries. So, this painting was produced, at the latest, in the sixteenth century." A wondering smile lit her face as she turned excited eyes on him. "It's at least three hundred years old, Jordan. This painting survived the seizure of the abbey, the confiscation of its valuables, the dismantling of the buildings . . . Isn't that amazing?"

He looked at the painting again. "I never considered that, but it is a little bit amazing," he said, nodding thoughtfully.

Jordan's hand curled around her elbow as he guided her down the row of artwork again, this time pausing to discuss each with her. When Naomi pointed out the pug dog peeking out from under the hem of a very dignified lady's skirt, Jordan laughed and clapped his hands once, delighted with the discovery.

He touched the small of her back lightly. "Perhaps *you* should give *me* a tour," he teased. "It seems you could teach me a few things."

"I'm sure that's not the case," she demurred. "Maybe you could start the tour over. This time, show me the parts of your home you enjoy."

His hand exerted a small pressure on her back, turning her to face him.

Naomi's breath stuttered in her throat. It had only been a few days ago that Jordan was a handsome man she admired from a safe distance. Now he touched her comfortably, more frequently than his escort necessitated.

Her eyes swept over a sturdy shoulder and neck—their firm lines softened by the hopelessly rumpled cravat—to his face. The smile he gave her now was unlike any Naomi had ever seen on Jordan's face. She was well acquainted with the devastatingly charming, flirtatious smile that caused women to suffer heart palpitations, but this was something else entirely. The curve of his lips was secondary to the *feeling* of a smile that exuded from every part of him, as though he was really seeing her.

Naomi could only stare while her bones turned soft, melting at his touch. His gaze flicked to her lips, and she shivered with anticipation, wondering if he would kiss her again.

Jordan's smile faltered. "Are you cold?" He tugged her shawl back up over her shoulders. "There," he said. "So, I'm to show you something I enjoy?"

A wry twitch of his lips sent another jolt of awareness through Naomi. "If it isn't any trouble—" she started.

From another room came the muffled sound of a clock striking the hour, pulling Naomi out of the magic of their stolen hour. The day's obligations awaited. "Another time," she told him regretfully. "I must go."

Jordan breathed a laugh. "Turn into a pumpkin at the strike of nine in the morning, do you?"

"Nothing so enthralling," she teased back. "Lady Clara, Lady Kate, and some of the others have agreed to help me make jam this morning."

"Let them make it without you."

The note of persuasion in his voice could tempt the dead to rise, but Naomi shook her head. "I promised," she explained. "I don't want to let the others down."

"Of course not."

His tone was all politeness, but as she nodded and bid him a good morning, Naomi wondered about the slight frown puckering his forehead and the way his eyes drifted back to the painting of the abbey.

Chapter Thirteen

This was the first morning Jordan had not ridden out before dawn with the patrol since his return to Lintern Abbey. Sitting at the breakfast table while guests slowly trickled in left him feeling more tightly leashed than ever. He should be out there doing something, by Jove, not sipping coffee. However, there had been a consensus among the men that Jordan was a tad high-strung and ought to take a day off from wielding weaponry in the vicinity of other human beings.

By luncheon yesterday, news of the hunting accident had spread through the party, like flame on tinder. He'd spent the rest of the day checking in on Lord Gray, consulting with the village surgeon, and withstanding withering glares from Lady Gray.

Fortunately, the shot had all been retrieved, and there was every expectation that Lord Gray would heal fully and quickly. Unfortunately, the surgeon insisted the young man remain abed, on his stomach, until the wounds healed over. Jordan was now a man short—a hefty loss when he'd only had twelve to begin.

Compounding his problems was Naomi Lockwood. *Who else?* he thought, frowning into his coffee cup. In all the years he had known her, the youngest Lockwood had never struck him as a nuisance. Yet that assessment had been made before he'd brought her to his home, where she could nose into things she ought not.

He shouldn't have been surprised to find her outside of Enrique's apartment yesterday morning. Naomi possessed a dogged determination to pry into the boy's history, despite Jordan's insistence that she mind her own business when it came to his ward.

He glanced up at the arrival of another guest.

Lady Janine paused, the dark wood of the entryway surrounding her like a picture frame while her restless eyes skimmed the several diners taking their meal. Her lips puckered slightly, deepening the lines around her mouth. She stepped hesitantly into the breakfast room, greeting no one on her way to the sideboard.

Jordan watched Naomi's aunt while she helped herself to toast and a poached egg. Her rheumatic fingers could not fully close around the serving utensils, and only his knowledge of her prickly, independent nature kept him from offering to serve her himself.

Janine's usually indomitable mood seemed off this morning . . . melancholy. There was something else. He appraised her with an analytical eye. Her steel-gray hair, pinned in a knot on the crown of her head, was unremarkable except for the absence of the frumpy cap she usually wore. Her dress was faded calico, the color palette ten years out of fashion.

Janine added a few apple slices from the fruit bowl to her plate. As she turned to the table, her eyes met Jordan's. Color rose under her lined cheeks, which made no sense whatsoever. Lady Janine was much too fierce to *blush*, for heaven's sake.

He rose to offer the seat next to his own. He tucked the chair securely beneath her before returning to his place. "I trust you slept well, my lady?"

"Not particularly," Janine grumbled while she scraped butter across her toast. She glanced at Jordan over the rims of her spectacles. "When you get to my age, the body plays cruel tricks at night. By the time your mind finally stops tormenting you with a lifetime of regrets and missed opportunities, one ache after another takes over the watch to ensure you will toss and turn. Old age is a plague—I don't recommend you ever acquaint yourself with the condition." She jabbed a triangle of toast into the egg yolk, sending a thick, golden puddle oozing across her plate.

Jordan watched her mop the yolk with bread while he puzzled over her desolate words. What did she mean by "a lifetime of regrets"? *No matter,* he told himself. He had enough on his mind without adding the woes of a brooding, female intellectual to the list.

Both their heads rose at the sound of more arrivals. He thought he heard a little, wistful sigh escape Janine as Clara entered, Kate following close on her heels. He felt, but did not voice, a sigh of his own. Neither was the face he wished to see.

He seated his stepmother and sister on his other side. Lady Janine returned Clara's greeting then retreated back into her bubble of gloom, still dragging circles in her egg with the now-soggy toast.

Kate kept her eyes on her food, occasionally casting shy, furtive glances at the other guests, never interjecting herself into any of the conversations. The eating utensils looked overlarge in her spindly fingers, and she moved them with awkward self-awareness. There was a charming, unconscious grace about her when she didn't overthink things and get in her own way. Once she bloomed, he would have a devil of a time keeping suitors at bay. The light pink of her morning dress didn't suit her milky complexion, but he supposed there was nothing to be done about that until she was *Out* and at liberty to wear bolder shades.

She jabbed a grape with her fork. The purple-red orb shot off her plate and landed in a nearby butter crock. Jordan stifled a chuckle while Kate, her face burning, tried to cover the mishap. She grabbed the crock and tipped it over her plate; the wayward fruit rolled onto her ham. Though no one else noticed the incident, his sister looked at him with anguished eyes.

Jordan gave her a reassuring smile then realized with a start that he'd hardly spoken five words to his half sister the entire time he'd been here. Despite his efforts to keep her away, she was in his home, and he was neglecting her woefully. He remembered the Duke of Monthwaite's brotherly attention and concern for Naomi—how he'd hovered over her during her first Season and interrogated Jordan to make sure she'd be safe at Lintern Abbey. By comparison, Jordan was a sorry excuse for a sibling, indeed. Well, he would just have to remedy that.

"Lady Kaitlin," he ventured, "are you enjoying your stay?" Ordinarily, he would not address her so formally, but it was time for her to learn how to carry on in company.

Clara caught his eye and gave a tiny nod of approval.

The embarrassed red in Kate's cheeks deepened when his question drew the attention of several onlookers. "Yes," she finally answered in a timid voice, "thank you, I am. The ladies are all very kind. Miss Barker is teaching me an oyster stitch, and Lady Naomi lets me help with her food-pantry project."

Food-pantry project? Jordan stopped himself from asking. Kate had given him the perfect opening to inquire after the absent lady's dubious excuse for her presence at the nursery. Best not to get sidetracked. "Lady Naomi mentioned the two of you ordered new bonnets."

Kate's guileless face vacillated between pleasure and disappointment. "Yes, but—oh, I'd hoped it would be a secret. I wanted to surprise you."

Jordan breathed a laugh. "Surprise me with a bonnet?" he said, incredulous. Surely his little sister didn't expect him to don women's headgear. The very idea set him to laughing again.

Bafflingly, Kate's face crumpled. Her cheeks paled, and her slender shoulders stooped.

Clara stared at him in pinch-mouthed fury, eyes flashing fire and nostrils flaring.

What did I do? Somehow, his attempt to behave like the older brother he was supposed to be had severely misfired. "Kate—" he started in a quiet voice.

His stepmother shot him a warning look that stopped the apology in his throat.

To his right, Lady Janine scoffed. Jordan didn't know whether the derisive sound was aimed at him, as the older woman still glared balefully at her breakfast. "Men don't know anything about anything," she muttered to the sad remains of her abused egg.

Every female under his roof had taken leave of her senses!

"Good morning," said a soft, musical voice—the one he'd been waiting to hear.

Naomi's cheeks gleamed with a healthy glow; a light sheen of moisture glistened at her temples.

Jordan tensed with suspicion. As Naomi filled her plate, he scrutinized her. At first glance, everything seemed in order. Her locks were neatly curled and pinned, not a hair out of place. Likewise, there was nothing to criticize about her attire. The high-waisted, light blue dress was impeccable. He followed the garment's clean lines over her breasts and down her waist and legs, not entirely sure what he was looking for. *Something*, some indication . . .

There. There it was.

As Naomi turned to choose a scone, her skirt swung, following her movement, and in so doing, betrayed her. At the hemline on the back, just above her right heel, a small patch of fabric was dark with moisture. Had the spot been anywhere on the front of the dress, Jordan might be forced to allow for a stray splash from a washbasin or a clumsy drink of water. Being on the back, however, he could only conclude the wet came from below, rather than above. The dew-damp ground was the most likely culprit. She'd already been out-of-doors. The evidence of her flushed face and moist hemline convinced him.

The only question remaining was: With whom had she been? To Jordan's mind, the answer was all too obvious.

Enrique.

In the handful of seconds it had taken him to uncover her duplicity, everything changed. *And she accuses me of not noticing anything.* Jordan had the queasy feeling that events were starting to spiral out of his control, if, in fact, they'd ever been *in* his control, which he now rather doubted. Naomi had always seemed most reasonable. Never once had she given Marshall a moment of grief. Why did she have to choose now—while she was *his* responsibility—to behave willfully? He only wanted keep her safe, to shelter her, protect her, to take care . . . Alarmingly, that train of thought had no end in sight. In any event, she was making his job damnably difficult.

Naomi finished filling her plate and came to sit beside Lady Janine. She murmured to her relative then greeted Clara and Kate. When her smiling face at last turned to Jordan, it encountered the glacial stare he'd trained on her. Her brows slanted over blinking eyes; her full bottom lip pushed out in a tiny pout he was tempted to kiss away. Jordan scowled all the harder, fighting to rid himself of the wayward urge.

"Kate and I will be ready to go after breakfast, Naomi," Clara said across the table.

Naomi pulled her large eyes away from Jordan to respond to his stepmother, a smile once again in place. "So shall I. I'll only be a moment to fetch my bonnet, and we can be off."

"Would that be your new bonnet?" Jordan asked.

The ladies all regarded him quizzically.

"You did purchase new bonnets, did you not?" A note of accusation colored his words.

"We ordered them," Naomi said slowly, as though explaining the obvious to a simpleton. "It will be a few days before they are finished."

Lady Janine snorted.

Returning her attention to Clara, Naomi effectively shut Jordan out as if he wasn't there. "I sent a note 'round to Mrs. Barton yesterday; she's expecting us."

Clara nodded. "Be sure to wear your sturdy boots," she instructed Kate. "It looks like rain."

"You mean to walk to the village?" Jordan demanded. Uneasiness tickled between his shoulder blades.

"Yes, of course," Clara responded. "We're to deliver the preserves we made yesterday, for Mrs. Barton's food pantry."

There was that pantry again! He huffed an exasperated breath. "And why would you do such a thing? The good reverend earns more than most anyone else in Lintern Village, I'd wager. Why should you fill their pantry when they are perfectly capable of filling their own?" A thought crossed his mind and he added, a touch more moderately, "Unless you mean to make her a gift. That would be a neighborly gesture."

Once again, the females regarded him as an unwelcome interloper in their conversation, despite carrying it on right under his nose.

Whatever small hurt he may have caused Naomi with his disapproving expression turned to sour annoyance as she fixed him with a quelling look. "It isn't *Mrs. Barton's* pantry we wish to fill, Jordan, but the charity pantry she keeps for the neighborhood." One light brown brow arched scornfully. "Surely you know of and contribute to this endeavor?"

This was the first he'd heard of any such thing, but Naomi's attitude suggested he should know of it and she found him lacking for not. Her accusations of him not noticing, of not caring, rang in his ears.

"I'll accompany you," he announced.

"It isn't necessary," Clara said. "We can carry the baskets ourselves. It's but two miles to the village."

Marvelous! he thought. Three unescorted females with their hands full of preserves, tromping two miles down a country road. They'd be plum targets for the French, or a highwayman, or a deranged billy goat, for that matter.

"Necessary or no, I'm coming," he said with finality. "We'll take the barouche."

Clara's mouth tightened. She leaned close and pitched her voice for his ears alone. "I would have a word with you. Now, if you please."

Jordan pushed back from the table and gestured for Clara to lead the way. He felt Naomi's wondering gaze on his back as his stepmother stalked from the room, her spine ramrod straight. She said nothing more until she closed the door of his study. Her jeweled fingers lingered on the knob.

"You've behaved abominably to Kate since the moment you arrived." Her thinning lips twisted into a hurt scowl. "After what you just did at the table, I wonder that you can think to press your company upon her. Pray do not cause my daughter further grief. Leave us to our morning, and we'll leave you to yours. We do not need your escort to the village, and frankly, Jordan, I do not *want* your escort."

"What did I do?" Bewildered, he flung his hands wide. "I know I hurt the chit's feelings, but I couldn't tell you how. Clara, you must believe it was not my intention to upset Kate. I should hope no man of nine-and-twenty makes sport of a young girl."

Clara planted hands on her hips, her splayed fingers digging into the ivory fabric of her morning dress. "Are you truly so daft? What you did, Jordan, was squash Kate's poor little heart. That girl thinks you hung the moon in the sky, and you behave like she's an unwanted mongrel. When she said she wanted to surprise you with her new bonnet, she meant that she hoped you'd find her pretty in it—that you would approve." Deep lines appeared between her eyes. "Naomi told me that she chose the colors with you in mind, hoping for your admiration."

With a heavy sigh, Jordan pinched the bridge of his nose. He didn't have time to coddle a child. Bonaparte's men were on his land—the list they'd found yesterday proved it. And yet, he couldn't help but feel like the world's greatest cad for hurting Kate.

"I'll make it up to her," he assured Clara. "But I *will* drive you to the village. I'll have the barouche brought around."

Clara's eyes narrowed in a treasonous glare, and Jordan prepared to deal the low blows. If he must, he would remind her that his father was out of the country, leaving Jordan to serve as head of the family and Clara obligated to do as he said.

Fortunately, his stepmother must have caught a hint of how deadly serious he was about this because she did not voice any further objections. "I'll tell Kate to finish her meal," she said before turning on her heel.

Thirty minutes later, Jordan strode out to the waiting carriage, found Clara and Kate already inside, and Naomi issuing directions to two footmen. In the half hour since he'd seen her, she had donned a pelisse and bonnet, both a darker blue than the dress beneath. Several fluffy white feathers adorned the hat, while the pelisse featured a scalloped hem and flowers worked in white piping, making Naomi look like a particularly delectable *petit four*. Under her watchful eye, the servants loaded baskets of preserves, hams, several parcels wrapped in butcher's paper, two wheels of cheese, and bushels of carrots, onions, potatoes, and apples into the vehicle.

"You planned to carry all this?" he asked her, incredulous.

Her rosebud mouth pursed, and once more the desire to kiss her caught him unawares.

Briefly, he thought what a shame it was she had decided against marriage. Naomi might carry on affairs undetected for some time, but if she were ever found out, she would be banished from society. Not even Marshall's considerable influence could shield her from public scorn. The thought of never seeing her pretty face at the same dinner table again, never again dancing on the same floor as she felt . . . wrong. Jordan and every other man of the *ton* was free to do as he pleased sexually, to keep mistresses and paramours. Right or wrong, women were held to different standards than their male counterparts. He wondered if he ought not have a word with her, offer some advice for maintaining discretion, but that, too, sat uneasy with him.

"Of course we weren't going to carry all this," Naomi said, "just the preserves. But since you graciously offered the carriage, I decided to take some more."

"You mean you raided my larder and root cellar." The footmen packed the last of the stores into the carriage with Clara and Kate. His sister's feet perched on top of the cheeses. There was no seat for Naomi. "Is there any food left for my household?"

Naomi dismissed his question with a flick of her wrist. "Oh, bosh. You have plenty to spare and then some. I spoke with the cook and this"—she nodded to the pile of food—"is only a small portion of your excess." She turned a dazzling smile on him. Two dimples appeared on either side of her chin, and her eyes danced merrily. "Your generous support is most appreciated, my lord."

He stifled a groan. As he took her hand to help her to the driver's bench, he bent down to speak in her ear. A strand of her silken hair tickled his nose; he inhaled her gentle scent. "You're a danger to yourself and everyone around you when you're charming, Naomi. The Haywards of the world won't be dissuaded forever."

"Perhaps I wish they wouldn't be," she replied with a shrug and a smile. Grasping his hand harder, she stepped up into the carriage.

For an instant, Jordan was stunned into silence. Even though he had an idea of her course, to hear her say it aloud—and so blithely, without a scrap of shame—was something of a shock.

He pulled himself up and settled beside Naomi on the driver's seat. He gave her a long look. She smiled back, utterly guileless, looking every inch the polite lady.

He had to admire her frank attitude toward sex—what else could she have meant about not wanting to dissuade Hayward? If Jordan hadn't intervened that night, the man would've had Naomi's virginity before much longer. At the time, Jordan thought he'd done her a service, but maybe not. Perhaps Naomi had chosen Hayward as her first lover, and Jordan had interrupted not an assault but a rendezvous.

Then he remembered how that oafish, drunken ass had handled her so roughly. In excruciating detail, Jordan recalled Hayward's hands nipping into Naomi's arms, her soft flesh reddening between his fingers. The way his mouth had possessed hers, lips peeled back, teeth and tongue wet and scraping. His hand moving from arm to breast, taking what was not his . . .

Jordan's vision went red at the edges, and suddenly he wished Wayland Hayward stood in the middle of the drive so Jordan could run him down with the pair of horses. And then, just for good measure, Jordan would run over him again. And kick him in the ribs. Twice.

"I believe we're all quite settled."

Naomi's soft voice cut into his vengeful daydream. The white lining of her bonnet and lace ruff of her pelisse reflected light back onto her face, lending her skin a pearlescent glow. Combined with the coppery curls swaying around her cheeks, she was a heartbreaking angel—or a goddess. *Aphrodite*, he thought. *Destined to take lovers and shatter men.* Other men. Not he, of course. Jordan did not dally with virgins.

He gritted his teeth and repeated it to himself like a mantra as he snapped the reins.

Soon enough, Kate twisted around in the rear-facing seat to perch with her head hovering over Jordan and Naomi's shoulders. She pointed out a beech tree in the distance, its immense canopy a green dome. Starlings perched in a row on a roadside fence next caught her attention, and then she wanted to know what was Jordan's favorite bird.

"I've never considered it," he said. He was still brooding about Naomi and her as-yet anonymous, future lovers, but because he'd vowed to do better by Kate, he returned the question to her. "What bird do you like best?"

She gave the matter some thought. A line creased the skin between her brows in a manner that looked just like Clara. She turned to look at him. The brim of her bonnet clipped him on the cheek. "Oh, sorry!" she exclaimed.

"It's all right." He glanced at her and smiled. "That's very fetching, by the by. It becomes you. If one must be dashed with a hat, it might as well be a pretty one."

Kate's face broke into a wide grin; a flush of pleasure colored her freckled cheeks.

"Turn around, Kaitlin," Clara scolded. "We can't have the neighborhood thinking Lord Freese's sister a hoyden."

The girl obeyed at once.

When he glanced Naomi's way, she gave him an approving smile, her eyes soft and warm.

Soon enough, they pulled in front of the vicarage, a pretty situation on the edge of the village. Geese floated lazily on a small pond behind the house, while a trio of apple trees hung heavy with fruit.

"You didn't need to steal my fruit, after all," he teased Naomi, nodding to the trees.

As Jordan disembarked and handed the ladies down, the front door opened. The cottage's inhabitants spilled out—Mrs. Barton, a maid, and two black spaniels excitedly yapping and jumping. The maid swatted the dogs with a rag. They twisted out of her reach and ran toward Jordan's party, barking with great enthusiasm.

One of the beasts jumped straight for Jordan's buff breeches, its slobbery tongue flapping like a banner in the breeze. Jordan caught the dog mid-leap by the scruff of the neck, swung it about and plopped it onto the ground. "No," he said in an authoritative baritone. "Down."

The animal sank to its haunches at once. The other dog, which had been making a beeline for Naomi, also sat. Jordan fixed a quelling look on his captive before releasing its fur.

"Gracious, me!" Mrs. Barton exclaimed. She dropped a hasty curtsy. "This is quite a surprise, my lord. A pleasant one, of course. Dolly," she called over her shoulder to the maid—all the while waving her hand rapidly by her skirt —"set out a few more cakes."

The servant shooed the dogs back into the house and scurried in behind them.

Mrs. Barton greeted the ladies before once more addressing Jordan. "Mr. Barton is with Mr. Gillows—the carpenter, you know. I fear he took a nasty fall from a ladder."

"Is he all right?" Naomi asked.

"He suffered a dislocated shoulder," the vicar's wife said. "The surgeon expects he'll do right enough. In the meantime, Gillows can't so much as lift a spoon to his mouth. No wife to help him, poor fellow, so my husband and our manservant have gone to offer some assistance."

"How dreadful," Clara said, her face etched with concern. To Naomi, "Fortuitous you thought to bring all you did—it sounds as though Mr. Gillows will need some of this right away. With no income now that he's abed . . ."

Naomi made a sound of agreement while Mrs. Barton looked past them to the food heaped inside the carriage. She gasped in amazement and went to examine the bounty.

Jordan frowned. Should he have been informed of the carpenter's injury sooner? He would have liked to have known. He could have . . . what? What had Jordan ever done for these people—his people?

"Dolly!" Mrs. Barton called. "Where has that girl gotten off to?" she muttered. "Dolly, come here and carry these things!"

"No need," Jordan said as the maid appeared at the cottage door. He returned to the carriage to load his arms with provisions. "Point me in the right direction, and I shall take care of moving this."

"My lord, are you sure?" Mrs. Barton fretted. She gestured frantically to the maid to come out.

Jordan shifted his burden so that a ham balanced securely on top of a cheese. "It's no trouble, I assure you. Your girl need not be bothered."

Dolly reached the little bower over the front walk just in time for Mrs. Barton to wave her back inside again. The maid glowered at the back of her mistress's head before complying.

Once the food was tucked away in the shed, Mrs. Barton admired her stocked shelves. "Lady Naomi, how can I thank you?" She took Naomi's hand and then reached for Clara. "And you, Lady Whithorn."

While the women shared a moment of sorority, Jordan stepped out of the cramped food pantry. Ought he not to have known about this charity? Shouldn't he have spearheaded something of the sort? He slapped his driving gloves against his thigh as he considered. The sound of his name drifting out of the pantry brought his attention back to the ladies.

"—Lord Freese's own stores," Naomi was saying.

Mrs. Barton hustled across the short distance to clasp his hand. "Thank you so much, my lord. Your donation will make all the difference. Once word of your largesse makes its way around the village—which will be accomplished before tea, I've no doubt—I'm certain the rest of the community will feel inspired to do their share."

Shame twisted his middle. " 'Twas not my thoughtfulness that brought this to pass," he said with a gesture to the pantry, "but that of the ladies ensconced at the Abbey. Especially Lady Naomi."

"As you say, my lord," Mrs. Barton demurred. "Such modesty is becoming in a gentleman. Now then, tea?" She led the group toward the house where the pesky dogs could be heard pawing at the door.

Settled in the drawing room with refreshments, the vicar's wife returned to the object of their visit. "Lady Naomi, I must pick your mind on the subject of soliciting donations. How best to go about it?"

The women discussed the matter for the remainder of the call. Jordan watched the older women nod at Naomi's suggestions. Her gentle voice was the one that commanded attention. Pity, he thought, that Naomi would not be on hand to offer her continued support to Mrs. Barton's pantry.

During the ride home, the ladies all sat in the open carriage while Jordan drove. The solitude gave him ample opportunity for reflection.

He still felt a great deal of self-recrimination. Jordan had spent so long trying to escape Lintern Abbey and its boring responsibilities that he'd neglected the greatest of those responsibilities—the people. Estate business wasn't all crop rotations and grazing patterns, though those were the kinds of issues he had always associated with his home. The village depended on the success of Jordan's lands.

In a few weeks, Naomi would leave Lintern Abbey. Jordan vowed to himself to pick up where she left off and become a more conscientious landlord and patron of the community.

Idly, he wondered what Naomi would do with herself once she left. Marshall and Isabelle's child would be born soon. Naomi would undoubtedly make herself useful to Isabelle and the babe but then what?

Clara murmured something that set Kate and Naomi off in laughter. Jordan scowled. Mentally, he ran through an inventory of his memories of Naomi. In almost all of them, she was doing for others. When was Naomi ever on the receiving end of someone's kind efforts?

He truly liked and admired Naomi Lockwood. She'd turned out to be a fine specimen of woman—beautiful and accomplished in all the ways society deemed necessary. If it were ended there, Jordan would not feel one tenth the admiration he did. Such conventional beauties were a dime a dozen on the Marriage Mart.

Naomi, he decided, was a walking contradiction. On the surface, she was everything typical in terms of propriety. Beneath that cultivated exterior, Jordan had found a rare treasure. She was thoughtful and generous, kind and witty. But tenacious, too, he thought ruefully, recalling her determination in interrogating him about Enrique. She was virginal and guileless, yet possessed a downright shocking open-mindedness about sex and marriage.

As he pulled the horses to a stop in front of his own house, inspiration struck. *He* could do something for Naomi, something pleasurable and indulgent and—all right—more than a little bit indulgent for himself, as well.

Since Naomi had chosen an unmarried life, the least Jordan could do was help her on the path to a fulfilling, yet discreet, life of pleasure. He could give her some lessons in physical delights. Not too many lessons, of course—Jordan didn't dally with virgins. He'd once teased Naomi about kissing lessons, but it really wasn't a bad idea.

Not that she needed much help in the kissing department. The kiss they'd shared had been laced with her sweet, unschooled innocence, more intoxicating than the machinations of a practiced lover.

But there were other sensual indulgences he could help her experience without breaking his own rule. He'd wager she knew nothing yet of the sweet torture of teeth and tongue on an earlobe or how the lightest caress along the ribs sent a shiver down the spine . . . Thoroughly pleased with his imagination's work, Jordan helped the ladies step from the carriage. He handed Naomi down last and held back while Kate and Clara mounted the steps to the door.

"Come with me," he said, tugging her by the hand as he started across the lawn.

Naomi's feet obeyed, her steps quick beside his long strides. "Where are we going?"

He forced himself to slow, surprised at his own eagerness. Having decided that some degree of love play between him and Naomi was permissible, his body thrummed with anticipation. Where *were* they going? Jordan hadn't thought further than getting Naomi alone. "I want to talk to you about something . . . important," he finished lamely.

As they rounded the east side of the house, Jordan scanned their surroundings as carefully as if he was scouting a battlefield. Rather than hunting defensible terrain, however, he searched for a secluded place to conduct his lesson.

On the far side of the walled east garden, he spotted the ideal spot: a small shed, which hugged the wall on one side and was not visible from the house. "There," he said, nodding toward the structure.

The door creaked when he opened it. Jordan winced, even though no one in the house could possibly have heard. Naomi followed him through the entrance. The space under the door allowed a breeze to cool their ankles, while the still air about their heads smelled of soil and wood. Sunlight streamed through the one, dusty window, lighting motes in the air. Gardening implements—clippers, scythes, trowels, shovels, and the like—neatly lined the walls on sturdy iron hooks driven into the wood.

Naomi looked around then turned to him. "I don't see your irksome primrose. The greenhouse is some distance from here, is it not?"

Jordan reached out, palm up. Naomi looked from his hand to his eyes. He gazed down at her with steady intensity.

She regarded him cautiously. Then her gloved fingers gently lighted on his palm. The delicate touch added another thread to the coil of wanting that had Jordan bound tight.

With one fluid movement, he drew her close and pulled open her bonnet ties. He nudged the hat off her head and hung it from an available hook.

Naomi frowned. "Jordan, what—?"

He covered her lips with a finger. "To begin, find an out-of-the-way venue. Libraries are too easily stumbled into, yes?" he teased.

A line formed above her nose. Jordan massaged it away with a thumb. His fingers traced lightly over her brows, down the bridge of her nose, and over the bow of her lips. A soft sigh touched his fingertips.

At the small of his back, that coil of desire twisted its way up his spine. Heavy blood thudded through his veins. He must move slowly, he reminded himself, and then only so far. "Close your eyes," he whispered.

Naomi's features were soft, dazed. Her lids fluttered shut.

His hands shook with the force of his lust. Trembling fingers closed around her neck. He tilted her head to the side, exposing her ear and throat. His lips brushed the velvety petal of her earlobe. She inhaled sharply, pressing her soft torso more closely against his. Lightly, he nipped and flicked his tongue around the whorl of her ear, murmuring encouragement as he went.

"That's it, sweetheart," he said when she moaned and her hands fell limp to her side. "Just feel me."

He pressed kisses along her jaw to her chin, then her eager lips caught his, offering her sweet mouth to his exploration. Jordan's tongue swept over hers and across the sensitive palate. Naomi suddenly went heavier, as though her knees had given a little. Jordan's arms clamped tighter in response. He pressed her against the wall, eliminating every shred of space between them.

His hard ridge pressed into her soft belly while he made love to her mouth, recreating with his tongue the motions he wished he could do with the rest of his body. Jordan grabbed her hips and ground against her.

She broke away, gasping. At once, he dipped to her neck, giving the tender flesh there the same treatment he'd given her mouth. Her hands went to his shoulders where fingers clenched into his flesh.

He released her just long enough to work the buttons on her pelisse. Then he pushed the blue garment down her arms and tugged the neck of her gown to bare more of her neck. When he closed over the place where neck and shoulder meet, she cried out softly. Raw need tore through Jordan in response.

"What are you doing?" she asked, panting between words. "Jordan?"

At the sound of his name, he raised his head. Her delectable lips were red and swollen from his kisses. Her previously neat hair had fallen in several places, setting loose a few curls to drape down her damp temples and cheeks. Her hazel eyes were twin pools of trust and longing.

Suddenly, a fierce protective impulse arose, every bit as strong as his lust. He took her face in his hands.

"There's so much you deserve." His voice came out raspy, his throat choked with unfulfilled desire and emotion. "Any man lucky enough to touch you should worship you forever. Never let anyone close to you who is not worthy, Naomi."

Her gaze clouded. She shook her head; damp copper curls clung to her neck. "*Any* man? What man? I don't understand."

A sharp crack sounded not far from the shed. *Gunfire.* The thought had barely registered before another shot sounded. A split second later, the window shattered. Pain tore through Jordan, and then he hit the floor.

Chapter Fourteen

Naomi's eyes flew wide in shock as something slammed into her. Not quite a second ago, there had been two sharp cracks outside. The glass broke and then—

Her head swam as she tried to make sense of what happened. Jordan would know, but when she opened her mouth to ask, an unfamiliar croak came out. Dimly, she became aware of twin pains blooming in her chest and across the back of her head.

Air. I need air. But struggle as they might, her lungs would draw no breath. It felt as though a boulder pressed on her ribs. *I've been shot,* she thought. *Oh, God, I'm dying.*

Vaguely, she wondered what prayers one should offer up at the moment of mortal expiration, but intense regret swept away all concern for her soul. If she died now, she would never see her family again. Never meet Isabelle and Marshall's baby. Even they were granted only an instant of sorrow before their images were supplanted in her mind by the face she wished she could see one last time.

Jordan. Jordan. Jordan.

His name thumped through her in time with the painful beats of her heart. She should have told him that she loved him while there was time. But the last thing he'd said to her had been something about her being with other men, as though kissing her was just an afternoon's entertainment. Another pain—immaterial but just as sharp as the ache in her skull—lanced through her middle.

All at once, the boulder on her chest was gone. In its absence, she felt weightless, unbound. Ribs creaked as her lungs abruptly inflated. She wheezed and coughed.

"Are you all right?" Jordan's voice was urgent, afraid.

Her eyes opened. His face swam above hers as her vision cleared. Concern etched deep lines between his eyes. The beautiful, intense blue eyes she'd feared she would never see again. Giddy with the sudden rush of oxygen, she reached for his cheek. His scar pressed into her palm.

"There were shots and the window . . ." Her eyes flicked to where a single, wicked shard clung in the otherwise vacant frame. "You knocked me to the floor. You protected me," she realized. "The only threat to my life was you, you great ox. You nearly suffocated me." For good measure, she poked his shoulder.

A strangled sound gargled in his throat, and his hand clamped on to his shoulder. His mouth pinched, his lips tinged white around the edges.

"Oh, God!" Naomi cried, scooting out from under him and pushing up to her knees. "*You're* shot!"

"I'm not shot," he ground out between clenched teeth. "Not much, anyway. Only grazed."

She pulled at his wrist. "Let me see."

A ragged tear marred the navy blue material, the edges darkened by seeping blood. Before she could more closely inspect the wound, Jordan waved her back. "Be quiet," he hissed.

Naomi plopped onto her bottom. Her head still hurt from its impact with the hard floor, but the pain was forgotten when she recalled the gunshots that had precipitated all this. Who had shot at them?

Jordan rose smoothly and pressed to the wall beside the window. He leaned just enough to peek outside. He whistled a sound like a nightingale. The tension evident in his neck made Naomi uneasy. After several seconds, a nightingale answered. In the distance, a crow called.

Signals, she realized with a start. She pressed her hands against her suddenly churning stomach. Something was very wrong.

Jordan pulled back from the window and crouch-walked to the door, carefully avoiding the shattered glass. He flattened against that wall; then his right hand vanished inside his coat and reemerged holding a small pistol. Casually, he checked the priming.

Naomi gaped at the firearm. "Why do you have that?" she demanded.
"Hush!" he rasped.

His left arm pressed tight against his side, recalling her to his injury.
Other than the way he held that side of his body slightly hunched, he
gave no indication of discomfort. She remembered how he'd reacted
when she'd touched him, and wondered what it cost him now to put his
hurt out of mind and remain on guard.

Another bird call sounded from just outside the shed. Instinctively,
Naomi curled tight against a pile of burlap tarps in the far corner. With
the flat of his hand, Jordan eased the door open a crack. It swung open
farther as a man stepped in—Mr. Price.

"M'lord." He nodded. "I had one of 'em right in my sights, sir." He
huffed in frustration. "Saw 'im laying on the rise behind the kitchen
garden, watching the house through a spyglass. I don' know what tipped
him off, but 'e turned and looked right at me and—"

Jordan made a sharp sound, startling Mr. Price into silence.

The man's gaze took in the shed's interior, and he spotted her in the
corner. His mouth worked silently, full lips opening and shutting, like a
fish. "Then, ah, the uh, the grouse . . . flew away."

Jordan shoved the man outside and followed him through the door.
From her corner, Naomi heard their voices murmuring back and forth.
She picked nervously at her skirt as she ineffectually attempted to make
out the conversation. Conjecture followed speculation as she tried to
decipher what Mr. Price had said.

Facts: Someone had been spying on the house. Mr. Price and that
unnamed someone exchanged gunfire, and one of those shots had
demolished the shed window. There were likely multiple "someones"
lurking around. Naomi based this conclusion on Mr. Price's words,
"one of 'em." Finally—and perhaps most alarming—Naomi had heard
Jordan, Mr. Price, and perhaps someone else signal to one another with
bird calls.

Normal men engaged in normal hunting did not behave this way.

Ergo, Naomi was not engaged in a normal, country party. There had been small hints here and there that something was odd—the way each male guest had brought a lone female companion. There were no families, no children. Except for Kate, of course, and Jordan had been surprised and angered by her appearance. And there were other things . . .

She squeezed her eyes and pressed fingers to her temples, as though to force greater efficiency from her brain. Naomi felt she knew almost *what* was happening, but not *why*. Aunt Janine would be able to make sense of this, she thought. Putting their heads together, perhaps she and her relative could solve this puzzle.

The door swung open and Jordan strode across the small space. He took her hand and hauled her to her feet. "Let's get you back to the house now."

Her mind still in a whirl, Naomi took several faltering steps.

Behind her, Jordan cleared his throat. She turned to see her forgotten bonnet dangling from his finger. "Rule number two," he said as he replaced it on her head and tied a bow as neat as her maid's, "never return looking disheveled. It gives people cause to gossip."

"Just what are these rules you're going on about?" she asked as she buttoned her pelisse.

"Quiet now."

He raised a finger to his lips and held her elbow tightly as he led her from the shed. His own hat had been abandoned in the shed's wreckage, she noted with annoyance. Black curls now softened the hard plane of his forehead.

Rather than take her to the front entrance, Jordan hustled Naomi through the east garden and up a flight of limestone stairs to the balustraded terrace off the parlor. This time of day, the formal room stood empty. The ladies would be in sitting rooms or their own chambers. She reached for the French door, but he snatched her hands before she could open it.

"Rule number three," he said in a low, urgent tone, "you must never, *never* let on in public that anything has happened. Do you understand me, Naomi? *Nothing happened.*"

His words were a slap across the cheek. Would he, to her face, deny what had passed between them? An echo of the pain she felt in the shed reverberated through her, the knowledge that he had only kissed her as a diversion.

But his eyes continued boring into hers, communicating something more.

"Oh," she whispered as understanding dawned. "I see."

He squeezed her hands. "Good girl. I'm counting on you." His fingers traced over one cheekbone and then he strode back the way they'd come, leaving a stunned Naomi alone on the terrace.

*

The evening meal came as close to disaster as it could without the dining room bursting into flame. Before dinner, Miss Price made a circuit of the parlor, asking in her overloud way whether anyone had seen her cousin. When she approached Naomi, it was all she could do not to keep a bubble of hysterical laughter from bursting out.

Aunt Janine arrived wearing a new dress. The taupe fabric actually complemented her skin tones, and the scoop neck was lower than Naomi had ever beheld on her aunt, displaying the barest hint of pillowy bosom. Smartly pleated ribbon adorned the cuffs and hem. Altogether, the frock approached fashionable. Naomi hoped her aunt had not suffered an apoplexy to bring on such a change. Janine moved awkwardly in the garment. Her face colored every time a man's eye settled on her, and while the others took a glass of claret, Janine slipped behind a screen in the corner.

When they finally made it to dinner, a full half of the gentlemen were absent from the table, Jordan among them, leaving Clara in a lurch over where to seat everyone.

Though she didn't know precisely what was going on, Naomi had Jordan's vote of confidence. He needed her to . . . Well, she wasn't quite sure, but she recalled his words: *Nothing happened.* She should carry on, then, as if nothing was amiss.

Giving herself a little shake of resolve, Naomi strode to the head of the table, organza skirts swishing, and seated herself in Jordan's spot. Clara blinked then nodded gratefully. Naomi gestured to the butler to begin serving. They passed a tense meal, despite Naomi's best efforts at conversation. No one mentioned the vacant chairs, but the gaping holes drew gazes. During the meat course, Miss Elton burst into tears and ran from the room.

Judging everyone's nerves to be sufficiently tried, Naomi skipped the sweet course and called for the gentlemen's port.

She led the ladies to the parlor and was startled to see Kate spring to her feet from a sofa. Normally, the girl kept to her own room in the evening rather than mingle in adult company. "Lady Kaitlin," Naomi said. "What a lovely surprise."

Turning a questioning look on Clara, the older woman answered in a quiet voice. "I thought it would be . . . more prudent . . . to have her nearby."

"Of course," Naomi said, attempting to walk a line between polite agreement and confirmation of fears.

The women settled into their accustomed places. Miss Price looked strangely adrift without the slight figure of Miss Elton at her side. Miss Barker and Lady Griffiths sat side-by-side on a settee. Lady Griffiths's fan blocked their faces from the others. No one remarked upon this rude behavior. Kate stood uncertainly to one side until Naomi gestured her to the loveseat beside her. Aunt Janine sat with an open book in her lap, but her eyes kept darting to the door.

A maid entered and hovered near Clara, who stared blankly into the fireplace. The servant cast a helpless look in Naomi's direction. Naomi took charge of ordering tea and refreshments.

As she'd done at dinner, Naomi attempted to ignite conversation, but no one seemed in the spirit for idle chatter.

Finally, after several moments of silence, Lucy Knight stood. "Where are the men?" she asked the room at large. "What is happening here? I haven't seen my Mr. Young since last night, and no one will tell me where he is!"

As though her words had broken a dam, a flood of worries and questions spilled from the other ladies. Their fears fed Naomi's. She suspected she had more actual cause for alarm than the others after what she'd witnessed this afternoon. "Now, now." Her voice rose above the din. "We must remain calm, ladies. I'm sure we are all perfectly safe."

"Yes, but are our men?" Miss Knight demanded. Naomi had no answer.

When the small group of men entered a short time later, the women were once more subdued. Naomi's stomach sank when she realized Jordan was still absent. Sir Randell moved toward Aunt Janine, who threw up her book in front of her scarcely exposed chest, like a shield. He sat beside her without an invitation. Janine gave him a look over her book, and Naomi wondered whether the two would start bickering again. Sir Randell ignored Janine's glower, and she settled back in peaceable—if not affable—silence.

The other men spread themselves around the room, none of them seated. They looked all too much like sentries for Naomi's comfort. She remembered the gun Jordan had tucked into his coat and wondered how many here were likewise armed.

Striving to reclaim a sense of normalcy for the evening, Naomi poured tea while Kate handed it around. Jordan's friend, Mr. Ditman, took his cup from the girl. His eyes continued to follow her as she moved about the room. Naomi watched him uneasily. The men would not be drawn into conversation. Pretty Miss Barker took tea to her betrothed, Lord Sidney. He thanked her for the beverage and immediately lapsed back into silence.

The ladies spoke to one another in low tones under the watchful gaze of the five men standing around the parlor. Beside her, Kate squirmed in her seat. Naomi patted her hand reassuringly.

The girl lifted her other hand to block her mouth and leaned close. "Mr. Ditman keeps staring at me," Kate whispered.

Naomi glanced at the man and hissed under her breath. He was always glowering and looking disapprovingly at people. Though Naomi had tried to think better of him for Jordan's sake, she did not trust him, and his sudden interest in Kate disturbed her. "A moment," she murmured.

Then she rose and crossed the room to where Clara sat beside Lady Gray. Naomi touched Clara's arm to get her attention. "Kate is tired. I'll see her to her room now, if that's all right with you."

"I'll escort the girl," Ditman interrupted. As he stood several feet away, his announcement drew the attention of other guests. Poor Kate's face drained of color.

Naomi straightened and rounded on him. "What a highly irregular suggestion," she said, trying to keep her voice light, though her face felt as rigid as ice. How dare he ogle Kate and then propose something so indecent!

The muscles in his jaw clenched, but he voiced no further objection as Naomi gathered Kate and swept her from the parlor.

Once in the corridor, Naomi hesitated. Her distrust of Mr. Ditman stayed her from taking Kate straight to her own room. Besides, after what she'd seen this afternoon, she didn't like the thought of leaving Kate alone.

"Come," she said as an idea struck her. "Let's pay a visit." She tugged the girl's hand and led her to the nursery apartment. At her knock, the door opened on an unfamiliar face. The man was on the short side and slightly stooped of posture. His hair was a middling brown and receding from the front. He stared at Naomi and Kate.

Behind him, a familiar voice spoke in French, asking who was there. The man responded in Spanish, too rapidly for Naomi to understand. There seemed to be something deliberate about the man's tone, emphasizing the change in language.

Another signal, she thought. Another secret. Another lie. She was hip deep in them and suspected she didn't know the half of it.

Enrique made an exasperated sound. His face appeared over the shoulder of the man blocking the door. "Eet's Lady Naomi and the young miss," he said in his heavily accented English. He rattled off something in French and swatted the other man on the back. He frowned and stepped aside to admit Naomi and Kate, then retreated to another room in the apartment.

"That is Bertrand, my tutor. Do not mind 'im," Enrique said, gesturing them to the small seating area. The young man wore black pants, white shirt, and black waistcoat. The matching coat was probably in his dressing room. With another year or two on him, she'd think he was headed out for the evening. "He is not normally 'ere so late," Enrique continued. "Bertrand goes to his 'ouse on the grounds before supper, but not tonight. My Lord Freese asked him to stay." Enrique shrugged in a thoroughly Gallic fashion.

As she sank into a luxuriously soft seat, Naomi could not help but wonder at the room's fine appointments. Though he was strangely strict about his ward's social life, Jordan clearly doted on the boy. "We're all under a bit of strain this evening," Naomi said. "I thought you might enjoy some company. I know I'm glad to see a friendly face."

Enrique flashed a roguish smile and bowed. "And glad I am to see you both. Eet is rare for two such beautiful ladies to grace my doorstep." His dark hair flopped over a brow. With a casual flick, he brushed it aside. Naomi could have sworn Kate sighed.

"Lady Kaitlin," Enrique said as he took a seat across from them, "I've 'eard much about you from your brother and your uncle and also from the fair Naomi. But I long to hear from *you*. I'm wild to know all about you. Tell me, which is your favorite bird?"

The girl radiated delight. "Why, I asked Jordan the very same question earlier today. How did you know?"

The French lad clapped his hands. "I did not know! But you see, we have this interest in common. What a fun discovery."

Naomi sat back and sighed contentedly as she watched Kate and Enrique chatter about this and that. They both flourished in the company of another young person.

Despite Jordan's order to stay away from his ward, she was glad she'd brought Kate here. Enrique was clearly starved for companionship; how could she ignore him? And Kate needed to forget the fears voiced in the parlor and Mr. Ditman's alarming behavior. A friendship between the youngsters was just what they both needed.

Twenty minutes later, Clara found them and collected Kate. The ladies all bid Enrique a good night. He gave Kate a florid bow and winked at Naomi.

Out of the apartment's friendly warmth, unease began to seep through Naomi's bones once more. "Clara," she said.

The older woman met her gaze. A look of understanding passed between them.

"Kate," Clara said, wrapping an arm about her daughter's shoulders. "I'd like for you to stay with me tonight."

"Why, Mama?"

"Because my dear," Clara said as she sedately led the small group toward their bedchambers, "sometimes mothers are taken with strange fancies and want their children close. You'll have to forgive an old lady's whim."

Kate giggled. "You're not old, Mama. But if it will make you feel better, I'll stay in your room."

As they rounded a corner, Clara caught Naomi's eye. "It will make me feel better, sweet love. It will."

Chapter Fifteen

She awoke to the soft voice of her maid. "My lady? Are you awake?"

Naomi extended her arms and legs in a languorous stretch and opened her eyes. Brenna stood beside the bed, arranging a tray with Naomi's chocolate and toast. A small parcel beside the cup caught her notice.

"What's that?" she inquired in a sleepy voice.

The maid handed her the rectangular item. "From his lordship. He wanted you to have it first thing."

The plain, white-paper wrapping gave no clue to its contents. She gave it a gentle shake. A soft rattle inside intrigued her. "Thank you," Naomi said.

After Brenna left, Naomi untied the bit of twine holding the paper closed, revealing a small box. She opened it and found a note.

> *Clara told me what you did at dinner last night. Thank you.*
> *Please enjoy these with my compliments. Do not leave your bed until*
> *you have eaten each one. If you're still interested, I'd like to show you*
> *the parts of my home I enjoy. Join me later for a walk?*
> *J*

Beneath the note were three cubes of caramel dusted with cocoa powder. A slow grin spread over her face. Naomi rarely ate candy and never first thing in the morning. What a rare indulgence. As she bit into the first sweet, she glanced at the note again. *Do not leave your bed . . .*

Under her night rail, heat slid over her skin and settled in her breasts. It was improper of Jordan to mention her in bed, wasn't it? Knowing he'd ordered her to stay there and enjoy the buttery, chewy treats did strange things to her. Was he thinking about her right now like she was thinking about him?

Did Jordan eat sweets in bed? What else did he do in bed? Her body continued to heat while her imagination supplied a number of possibilities: Jordan reading in bed, having a cup of tea in bed. Why did the piece of furniture make even mundane activities seem forbidden? Then she thought about Jordan kissing her, and her mind relocated the action—to bed.

In her core, a dull ache throbbed. She squeezed her thighs together. The ache suddenly wasn't dull anymore. Her belly tensed.

She took a whole caramel into her mouth and tried to concentrate on the melting sweetness sliding down her throat. No good. The candy was silk against her tongue. What was this man doing to her? Naomi squirmed.

Her hands fisted into her night rail and rucked it up around her thighs. She reached down and touched her swollen, needy flesh. A finger slipped easily between the folds, its passage eased by the hot wetness she found there. Gliding up the cleft, she lightly circled the pearl at its apex and let out a hiss.

A knock at the door startled her. Naomi lurched to a sitting position, sending the box with its last seductive treat tumbling to the floor.

Brenna peeked around the door. "Ready to dress now, milady?"

"Yes, of course." Naomi clambered out of bed and covered her legs before her maid could discover her state.

The process of readying for the day helped calm her, and by the time Naomi went downstairs, she felt once more in control of her body. Still, this morning's unexpected madness alarmed her enough to send her looking for Aunt Janine.

She found her in the library, naturally. The woman was sitting at a table with a large book open before her; rubbings of hieroglyphics spanned the pages. Sir Randell stood at her shoulder.

"I tell you, that cartouche is the name of a goddess," Aunt Janine said.

"Nonsense, woman," replied Sir Randell. "That is not a cartouche at all, but part of a larger rumination on pharaohs in general—not the name of a particular king and certainly not the name of a female deity."

"This figure is clearly a seated woman."

"It's a man. Look, there's a beard coming from the chin!"

"I suppose you would know," Janine said tartly. "You were probably there when it was chiseled into the stone."

"Oh-ho! Is that the way of it, madam? With no academic rejoinder, you resort to juvenile insults. Not very becoming for someone who wants to be taken as a serious intellectual."

"Auntie?" Naomi ventured. The two combatants looked at her. Behind her spectacles, Aunt Janine's eyes gleamed. "I'm sorry to interrupt, but I wondered if you might like to take a walk with Lord Freese and me."

As if speaking his name had summoned him, she was suddenly aware of Jordan's presence at her back. Her breath hitched in her throat.

"What sort of a walk?" Aunt Janine inquired.

"I thought I'd take Lady Naomi on the nature walk," Jordan answered. He moved to stand beside her. Today he wore a dark green coat, buff breeches, and Hessian boots. The waves of his raven hair were damp at the ends. "You're both welcome," he informed their elders. "There's an old stone circle to see."

Aunt Janine's brows rose. "Hmm. I was working on some translations, but that sounds fascinating. I'll just go change into my walking boots."

Sir Randell smirked. "So you forfeit the debate, do you?"

She made an indignant noise. "Certainly not!"

"I shall take your departure as proof that you concede the point about the male figure." Sir Randell tapped the page.

"That is a *woman*, you stubborn old mule!" Aunt Janine shoved her chair back and strode to a bookshelf. As she scanned the volumes, she continued her tirade. "Your eyes fail you, sir, if you do not recognize a simple crack in the stone revealed by the rubbing. But leave it to a man to see a phallus in anything. Ah-ha!" She plucked a book from the shelf and waggled it at her adversary. "Now you shall see I have the right of it."

She flipped through pages as she resumed her seat. Sir Randell sank onto the chair beside her. Their heads bent over the text while their argument continued at full steam.

Jordan glanced at Naomi. "I believe we've been forgotten."

"That's Auntie's way," Naomi confirmed. "When she's interested in a subject, there's almost no pulling her out of it before she's satisfied her curiosity. Woe unto any who try. I fear Sir Randell has gotten himself into a debate that could last all day."

"I suppose it's just us, then. Shall we?" Jordan gestured for Naomi to precede him into the corridor. Nerves buffeted her middle as they made their way outside and across the park.

Jordan strolled easily at her side, his hands clasped behind his back. He looked relaxed, with only a slight tightness around his eyes betraying any anxiety.

"Is it safe to be out-of-doors?" Naomi asked. "After what happened yesterday . . ."

"Nothing happened yesterday."

Oh, he was so frustrating sometimes! Why must he always speak around things, she wondered. "Jordan, you know what I mean. I won't say anything to the ladies, but—"

Jordan abruptly stopped. "Yes, you're safe, Naomi." He caressed her jaw with a warm hand. "I would never expose you to unnecessary risk."

She stared into his eyes, weighing the sincerity of his words. Her gaze traveled to the scar on his cheek. A tiny, red line, a shaving nick, stood out on the white ridge of flesh. A wound atop a wound. She brushed it with a fingertip. "And what about you, Jordan? Are you safe?"

His gaze darkened for an instant. Then he stepped back and tossed her his devil-may-care grin. "Safe from everything but your fatal charms, my dear," he said as he offered his arm and continued toward the tree line. "Is that your new bonnet? It complements your complexion to an astonishing degree."

Naomi's mouth pulled to the side as she raised a brow at him, thoroughly unimpressed with his parlor tricks. He might be able to distract other women with his outlandish flirtations and compliments, but she knew him too well now. What was he hiding?

But experience with her father and two brothers had taught her that men usually thought females were better left in ignorance of a great many things. She would not get to the bottom of Jordan's secrets now that he'd dug in. Since he had his guard up about one thing, though, she might as well discuss another.

"You need to spend more time with Enrique," she ventured. "He's a very lonely boy. You should have seen the way he lit up last night when he had the opportunity to chat with Kate."

They were surrounded by trees now. A pathway, narrow but well tended, wended through the woods. The air was filled with the smell of rich earth and the occasional sweet or spicy aroma wafting from a plant.

"Yes, don't think I'm not perturbed about you taking Kate there," Jordan said. "I asked you to stay away from Enrique, Naomi. I have my reasons."

She scoffed. "Whatever they are, they can't be worth making the poor fellow miserable. I've already caught you out in your 'Basque urchin' lie. Enrique is as French as a *crêpe*. You might as well—"

His hand clamped around her forearm. Gone was the jovial, flirtatious man of a moment ago. His lips drew into a hard line, and every inch of his large frame tensed as though to pounce on an enemy. "Enrique is not a subject I will discuss with you, Naomi. He is absolutely none of your concern. None. Do not raise the matter with me again."

She wrenched out of his grasp. "Fine. I just don't understand, Jordan. I don't know what's happening here. I don't know why people were shooting at each other yesterday. I don't know why you were whistling signals. I don't know why you pretend Enrique is someone he isn't. It's all so confusing, and you won't explain anything! How should I know what to say or do when everything you say or do could be a lie? I don't know what's really important, or what's true or—"

His Adam's apple bobbed as he swallowed hard. "I'm sorry it must be this way, Naomi, but I cannot answer your questions. I never meant for you to get caught up in this."

In what? she wanted to ask. But she didn't. She knew he wouldn't answer.

For a while, they strolled through the woods in silence. Sudden breaks in the trees opened onto stunning vistas. There was a picturesque meadow where two rabbits nibbled clover. High clouds gathered in the sky. They weren't threatening, but the gloomy atmosphere reflected her state of mind.

"Was it the stone circle you wanted to show me?" she finally asked. "Is that the part of your home you like best? Is it much farther?"

Jordan laughed. "Questions abound, about everything. I begin to see more and more similarities between yourself and your worthy aunt."

She lifted her skirt to step over a log. "Well, you won't address the questions I really want answered. I'll take what I can."

"As it happens," he replied with a playful tone creeping back into his voice, "the stone circle is not what I had in mind. I said that on the spot to conceal our true destination. The place I mean to take you is just ahead."

A clap of thunder caused Naomi to yelp in surprise. With no further warning, the sky opened, and rain fell fast and heavy. They'd walked nearly a mile. There was no escaping the deluge.

Naomi started to head back the way they'd come. Jordan grabbed her hand. "This way," he said, tugging her deeper into the woods. Her protest was swallowed by another rumble of thunder.

For several minutes, Naomi kept her head down and let Jordan lead her. There must be a gamekeeper's cottage nearby, she reasoned. Cold water poured off the brim of her bonnet until it seeped through the straw and lining and into her hair. It ran down her nape, into her dress, and on down her back. In short order, the hem of her walking dress was a sodden, muddy mess.

"Here."

Jordan pulled her to a stop and she looked up. And up. And up.

"Gracious," was all she could think to say.

Before them loomed an enormous pine tree. The lowest branch was ten feet above Naomi's head. She forgot the rain washing over her face as she tried to take in the entirety of the huge tree. It towered over everything else in the forest.

Jordan pulled her off the path and around the massive trunk. On the opposite side, an opening yawned wide, revealing a hollow place inside the tree. They stooped to enter.

Naomi blinked in the enveloping gloom. Eventually, she made out a small, needle-strewn space that was just big enough for the two of them. Fortunately, the rain hadn't blown into the hollow. The pungent aroma of pine resin permeated the area.

"This is what you wanted to show me?" she asked, incredulous.

"Yes."

"A tree?"

Jordan wrapped his arms around his knees. "Yes."

Naomi folded her legs beneath her and tried to arrange her sodden skirts, but they were hopeless. "Why is this place special to you?"

He stared at the curtain of rain and ran a hand through his wet hair. "When I was a boy, this was my secret spot. I could stay in here for hours, playing with my tin soldiers. Or I'd imagine I was an Indian in America, and this was my wigwam." He smiled ruefully. "Once, I was pretending to be a hunter stalking through the forest. I was seven, I think, and it must have been late afternoon because I came upon a badger emerging from its burrow. I don't know what I thought I was going to do with the thing, but I managed to sneak up behind it. Suddenly, it spun and hissed at me. Oh, how I screamed. I ran the whole way home and didn't stop until my face was buried in my governess's skirts."

Naomi laughed at the charming mental picture he'd sketched for her. "I'm sure the badger ran home, too." Their eyes met, and Naomi's laughter died in her throat.

"You shouldn't have a cold, wet hat on your head." Jordan reached over and loosened the ribbons of her soggy bonnet. "There now," he said, tossing it to the floor where it fell in a limp heap. He surveyed the rest of her ensemble with a gimlet eye as well. His hand extended, palm up, fingers flapping. "Pelisse."

A jolt of nervousness shot through her as she rose onto her knees and started to remove the garment. She must have been colder than she realized; shivering fingers fumbled the buttons.

Jordan twisted to face her and gently swatted her hands away. "Let me."

He started at her waist. At his light touch, Naomi's belly clenched. If he noticed her body's response, he didn't let on. Steadily, he worked up her torso. Every brush of his fingers was a torment. Beneath her wet clothes, her nipples puckered.

The silence was becoming charged. "Thank you for the caramels," she said to break the tension. "They were delicious." Blood rushed to her face as she recalled her seduction-by-confection.

"You're welcome." His hands stilled. There was only the top button remaining. Intense blue eyes lifted, watching her from beneath a fringe of sooty lashes. "Did you do as I asked?"

Her cheeks flamed. "You mean, did I have them—"

"In bed." His sensuous lips spread in a lazy smile that made her insides melt.

"Yes," she whispered. "But why?"

"After the day you had yesterday, you deserved a little something special."

Oh, he'd given her a little something, all right. More than he knew. "It was quite indulgent. Such treatment will spoil me, my lord."

With a flick of his wrist, he loosened the last button. "Good," he said as he peeled the garment off her shoulders and rolled it down her arms. "You need spoiling."

His lips brushed the corner of her mouth, traced the contour of her bottom lip. Just a whisper of a kiss. Naomi trembled.

"You think I don't pay attention to people, but I do. How could I not be aware of you, always?" he murmured, taking tiny sips at her mouth between words. "You're there, quietly supporting everyone, always doing for someone else."

He was always aware of her? Naomi's heart soared. Could it be he reciprocated the feelings she'd had for so long?

When he reached the opposite corner of her mouth, his lips parted slightly and swung back in the other direction. She felt his warm breath as he followed the line of her chin and jaw to her ear. He nuzzled against her earlobe. "Soft as a peach," he murmured. A tiny nip caused her to inhale sharply. "But sweeter." His voice softened her brain, reducing her mental faculties to porridge.

Then his featherlight kisses crossed her cheekbones while his slightly rough fingertips caressed her forehead, her temples, and traveled down her neck. One hand cupped the base of her skull, while the other tilted her chin, handling her with exquisite delicacy.

"Yours is the kindest heart I've ever encountered," he said. Dark brows furrowed over his blue eyes.

This time, when his mouth returned to hers, she was eager, wanting. She tried to reach for him, but the wet pelisse, which had only gotten as far down as her elbows, snared her arms. At her whimper of protest, Jordan rested their foreheads together. "Shh, let me spoil you."

His lips covered hers; his tongue teased back and forth along the seam of her mouth. Naomi's lips parted on a sigh, seduced by his tender words and exquisite kisses. His tongue swept into her mouth. Slowly, he deepened the kiss, exploring her at leisure.

Naomi wrestled against the confines of her pelisse bindings, yearning to touch him. Between her thighs, the throbbing ache she'd felt this morning returned, every beat of her heart drumming through that hidden flesh. His hands roved her face, her throat, her shoulders. Always moving. Learning her. Branding her with his touch. She wanted to learn him, too.

He responded to her struggles by firmly holding her arms to her sides.

"Please," she moaned. "Oh, please, I want . . ."

His teeth teased her collarbone. His tongue swirled into the hollow at the base of her throat. He buried his nose in the soft swell of her breasts and inhaled deeply. "What do you want, sweetheart?"

She brushed her cheek over his hair. He smelled of rain and warm male. Intoxicating. "I want to touch you," she confessed in a rush. "Let my arms out."

A groan rumbled deep in his chest. "I can't, Naomi." His hands covered her breasts. She arched her back, pressing into his palms. Thumbs and fingers found her nipples. Sharp pleasure shot to her core. She let out a choked sob. "If you touch me, I won't be able to stop myself," he crooned. "I want to give you pleasure, but I can't take mine."

Her breathing changed to short pants. "You can, you can. Just, please."

With his teeth, he pulled the sad, soggy ruin of her fichu from her neckline. Jordan tugged at the sprig muslin of her bodice until first one, and then the other breast spilled free. Hot palms met chilled flesh. His fingers worked mercilessly, pulling and kneading her nipples to stiff peaks. And then his mouth replaced a hand, and every suck caused an answering tug low in her belly.

She couldn't take any more of this passive torture. Using her knees for leverage, Naomi hurtled against Jordan's chest, taking him off guard and knocking him to the soft floor of their little sanctuary. His hands clamped around her waist as she sprawled atop him, steadying her.

Naomi thrashed wildly until she got one hand free of a sleeve. With a desperation unlike anything she'd ever felt before, she yanked the pelisse off her other arm. She was mindless, almost feral. All she knew was need. Her body needed Jordan like it needed air. She would die if she couldn't touch him.

Straddling his waist, she pried open the buttons of his coat and waistcoat and clawed his shirt free of his breeches. Her hands slipped under the hem to the flat plain of his stomach. She felt a fine tremor in his muscles as she moved to his sides, her nails dragging. She fell forward to kiss him, her open mouth gorging on his. Her bare nipples grated across the lawn of his shirt, tormenting that already-sensitized flesh. "What do we do?" she asked breathlessly. "I don't know what to do. Help me, please."

Jordan's eyes squeezed shut and he groaned in defeat. When they opened again, the irises were nearly obliterated by dilated pupils. "Dammit, woman," he growled. He snatched her wet skirts and worked them up her legs. Those large hands clamped around the backs of her thighs and pulled her down. Her intimate flesh came into hard contact with the erection straining inside his breeches.

She cried out at the jolt of pleasure. Under her ruined dress, his arm clamped around her waist, while the other propped him up. He took her breast in his mouth. Naomi cradled his head close. Her hips rocked over his.

"God, you're so hot," he ground out. "I can feel your heat through my clothes." His hand shifted to splay over her bottom and squeezed.

Outside, the rain continued. The ongoing droning sound of falling water cut them off from the rest of the world. There was only she and her man in their primitive shelter.

Something was building deep inside Naomi. She didn't know just what it was, but it had to do with the parts of Jordan still covered. "Still. Not. Right." She scrabbled at the fall of his breeches.

Just then, his fingers eased her folds apart. A keening mewl escaped her lips at the same instant he let out a hum of approval. "So wet for me." His voice was guttural, savage. "I want you so much."

She thrilled at his words. She had done this. She'd taken this beautiful, urbane man and reduced him to a lust-crazed beast. The last button gave way and he sprang free.

His penis looked so long and thick. She knew it was supposed to go inside her, but how? She took it in her fist to better judge its size. The lines of his veins were smooth ridges beneath the velvet skin. She pulled toward the tip, fascinated by the hard member. He thrust into her hand. "Christ, Naomi. What are you doing?"

The smell of musk undercut the sharp tang of pine resin. It was their smell, she knew—the perfume their bodies were creating together.

Her thumb swept over the tip of his penis. The bead of moisture she found there was slick, like the wetness between her legs. "Trying to see how it works. Am I doing it wrong?"

His eyelids drooped. "No, pet, exactly right."

His hips bucked again. She braced a hand on the hard muscles of his chest, and rearranged, replacing her hand with her swollen flesh.

She mimicked his motions and rocked her hips, nestling her nether lips around his hard length. Soon, his shaft was wet with her slickness, and she slipped back and forth along his ridge. The pleasure was astonishing. She tilted a little, bringing her tight bud into contact with him. She cried wordlessly while the thing building inside her continued its relentless demands. It still wasn't quite right. Her wet flesh clenched and released, as if grabbing for him. That's what she needed. Him. Inside her. Now. She rocked faster. Harder. Her breasts jounced in time with her movement.

"Oh, God." Jordan grabbed her hips. His fingers dug into her flesh, forcing more from her. "Not inside, Naomi. Finish like this. Christ. No, Naomi, not—"

She impaled herself on his staff. Something pinched deep inside just as she was consumed by the most exquisite pleasure-pain. "Jordan!" she called. Wave after orgasmic wave rolled through her. *Yes.* This was how it worked.

Jordan thrust hard, setting off another spasm. Her thighs clamped around his middle while she rode the peaks bombarding her senses. "God, you feel so good," he growled through clenched teeth. He drove into her over and over, wrenching pleasure from her body until she was mindless with it.

"Off off off," he said.

Before she had time to decipher his strangled order, he quickly pulled out. He held her tight and let out a guttural yell. Wet heat spread between them while his shaft pulsed and twitched against her abdomen. The hot stream seemed to go on and on. She clung to his shoulders, stunned by his body's reaction to hers. Something fiercely protective unfurled in her bones. Even as his climax faded, she wanted to cradle him with her body, keep him close to her.

For a few minutes, she could do nothing more than lay on top of him, gasping for breath, waiting for her heart to slow its frantic pace. She nestled under his chin and drank in his heady scent. His skin was covered in a thin sheen of sweat. Reveling in their intimate contact, she kissed his neck and savored the salty tang.

Jordan flung an arm across his eyes. His other hand combed through her hair, which had come loose at some point in the proceedings. She felt utterly relaxed and sated.

"Naomi?"

She raised her head. "Hmm?"

"I have to say something." He licked his lips and exhaled a heavy sigh. "But you're going to hate me for it."

*

A tiny frown puckered her brow. "Hate you? What a peculiar notion."

She wouldn't think so when she heard what he had to say.

Jordan was uncomfortable. The most powerful orgasm of his life had left him a mite woozy. A stick dug into his shoulder blade. The top of his head was jammed against the rough, interior wall of the hollow. And there was a soft bundle of femininity on top of him, all loose limbs and silky hair, perfectly content to use him for a cot.

Worst of all was the feeling of his spilled seed pressed between their bodies. It wasn't a physical discomfort, but it seemed ominously portentous. The drying puddle glued them together. He was stuck.

There was nothing for it, so he manfully plowed ahead. "Will you marry me, Naomi?"

Naomi's kiss-swollen lips fell open in surprise. Her deliciously pert breasts were still exposed, and her damp notch rubbed against his cock. It twitched, roused again to half-mast; she inhaled sharply and shifted her hips from side to side.

She was so responsive, artlessly so. Jordan grabbed her thighs, meaning to put a stop to her arousing maneuvers. His fingers dug into her creamy flesh. His bollocks tightened while he continued to harden. He'd have thought himself already wrung of every drop, but he wanted her again. So much. This was madness. "Naomi." Was it a warning? A benediction? He wasn't sure. All he knew was that their fate was sealed. She must be made to see reason.

Naomi's eyelids fluttered. "Is this when I'm meant to begin hating you?" His hands slid up her thighs, fingers spreading to cover her firm buttocks. She pressed against his hands, filling them with silky skin. She bit her lower lip while her mouth spread in a sleepy, seductive smile. "Because you proposed?"

Who knew the Snow Angel had such raw carnality simmering behind her decorous façade? Having known her since she was a girl, he was acquainted with her kindness, her selflessness, her loyalty. But this passionate side of her was a surprise. Even her eager response to his kisses hadn't prepared him for the soul-jarring experience of coupling with her.

He quickly flipped, pinning her beneath him.

Her hair, the color of a gentle sunrise, spread over the dark earth. Her legs wrapped around his hips, drawing him closer even as he tried to pull away, locking them in a sensual stalemate.

"I know this isn't what you want." Jordan's throat was tight with regret and leashed desire.

"It isn't?"

Naomi reached between them. Her hand brushed against his cock as it passed. Lust surged through his groin, and he muffled a groan. Muscles worked as her fingers reached her folds. She winced and sucked air between her teeth.

"A little sore," she murmured, "but I'm wet here again." Her hazel eyes loomed huge in his vision, drawing him in. "Doesn't that mean I want it? I read in a book—"

Oh, sweet Christ. Her innocent eroticism was going to be the death of him. He wanted to plunge into her, make her scream his name again and again. Instead, he wrenched away and rolled up to his knees.

"I mean marriage, Naomi. You don't want it and neither do I." His words were harsher than he intended. Restraining his sexual need was all he could handle right now; he couldn't manage guarding his tongue, as well. She looked stunned. "Don't worry," he said, softening a little. "I don't think you strange for it. In fact," he said with a lopsided smile, "it's one of the things I like about you."

Naomi struggled to sit. She hauled her bodice over her breasts and gazed at him thoughtfully as she reached into her dress to manipulate them back into place.

He forced his eyes elsewhere and drew a deep breath. Outside, the rain slowed to a drizzle.

"Please make sure I understand you, Jordan," she said.

When he looked, she was tucking her fichu back into the neckline of her dress.

"You don't want to marry."

"No," he confirmed.

She tilted her chin. "And . . . *I* don't want to marry? How do you know this?"

He raked a hand through his hair and dislodged some forest debris. "It's obvious to me, Naomi, though you play your role in society flawlessly. I'm sure no one else suspects. But you haven't entertained any suits for two years." Her befuddled expression made him chuckle. Gently, he extracted a leaf from her hair. "You haven't married or struck a betrothal. For a woman like you to remain unattached . . . It must be your choice to stay unwed."

"I'm not sure whether to take that as a compliment or set-down."

"Definitely a compliment," he assured her. "If it weren't for the fact that I don't dally with virgins—"

"You just did."

"—we wouldn't have to do this. Alas." He gave her his self-deprecating smile, the one that never failed to win a lady's admiration.

"Oh," she said with dawning comprehension. "That's why you found my ballad so amusing. Because of our shared views on the topic of matrimony. I understand now."

"I knew then we were kindred spirits." He shook his head ruefully. "I didn't expect it to turn out like this."

She scowled. "Jordan, if you don't want to marry me, then I don't think we should." She glanced outside. "The rain is letting up. Let's go back to the house."

Jordan grabbed her arm. "Just a minute now."

Naomi's hair hung in a curtain of damp tendrils and pine needles. She looked wild. A dangerous glint flashed in her eyes. "There's nothing further to discuss, my lord. As neither of us *wishes to marry*," she said, her voice becoming thick, "we shall not. I won't be ruined by rain."

What on earth was wrong with the woman? Surely, she knew the score. "Your virgin's blood is all over me!" He gestured to his groin, where a slick of red colored his cock and matted his hair. If he were any sort of gentleman, this blood would have spilled on the sheets of her marriage bed, not the fall of his breeches. Hastily, he fastened up his clothes, hiding the evidence. "We must marry. When Marshall finds out—"

"Why should he find out?" she snapped. "Are you about to go running to him with this tale? I'm not." Her chin trembled. Naomi turned her face away and sniffed.

Jordan's heart lurched. He hated knowing his inability to keep his hands off her had forced her into a life she didn't want. "Listen," he said, "marriage might not have been in either of our plans, but it won't be so bad." When her face crumpled into a mask of sorrow, Jordan took her into his arms. "We get along so well," he said as he rocked her from side to side. "You're already a remarkable mistress for Lintern Abbey. You know more about the goings-on in the village than I ever have. What you did for the pantry . . ."

She lifted her pretty, tear-stained face to meet his. "These are good people, Jordan. I c-can't believe how badly you neglect them."

The barb struck home. "I do. It's true. I don't deserve them, Naomi, but they deserve you." A flicker of doubt crossed her face. "They need you," he pressed. And then he whispered, "I need you."

Her eyes softened in a melting pool of tenderness. "Do you mean that? Please, do not play with me now."

Raising her hand to his lips, he kissed her fingers gently. "I do mean it." He hadn't realized it until just this moment, but the truth was clear.

Since she'd come to Lintern Abbey, Jordan had depended upon her in any number of ways. With the strain of their mission testing the limits of Jordan and his men, Naomi had become the calm center of his home. She saw to the ladies' entertainment. She'd taken Kate under her wing and become a friend to Clara. Her presence was something he now took for granted. He looked for her whenever he walked into a room. The thought of losing her as a fixture in his life sent an unexpected pain through his chest.

"You make me better than I am," he said. "If I'm to marry anyone, Naomi, it must only be you."

Naomi's chin trembled. "Oh, Jordan."

He was already on his knees. So was she, but the tight confines of the hollow didn't permit otherwise. "You are my friend, Naomi, and now you're my lover. Please do me the very great honor of becoming my wife."

Suddenly, her arms were around his neck. She shook in his arms, trembling with something that was half laughter, half tears. "I will," she said against his throat. "Yes, Jordan, I will."

Relief swamped him. He took her face and kissed her soundly. The beatific smile she graced him with provoked one of his own. "You look mightily pleased for a woman who didn't want to marry."

She giggled as she collected her bonnet and pelisse, preparing to head back outside.

He followed her out and took her wet things to carry for her. His other hand took hers. Their fingers twined together easily. A natural fit.

Naomi leaned her head against his arm as they strolled back through the forest. Jordan kissed the damp crown of her head. Now that everything was settled, he felt enormously pleased. Maybe even happy. He found himself thinking forward to a life with Naomi. She would make Lintern Abbey a home he'd happily return to after his Foreign Office assignments.

"Jordan?" she ventured.

"Hmm?"

"I don't know why you thought I didn't want to marry. The truth is, I want a home and family of my own more than anything."

The confession startled him. Had he been so very wrong? "But that night in the library. Wayland Hayward. You seemed angry with me for disrupting. When I thought about it later, I realized it must have been an assignation. That you wanted him for a lover." The thought of that fool having Naomi in the way Jordan just had made him ill. Now that he'd claimed her for his own, he most assuredly could not send her on her way to a life of discreet affairs with other men.

She lifted her head and met his gaze with a horrified expression. "You believed that of me? That I could share myself with someone in that way without the surety of marriage?"

Jordan pulled her to a stop. "Did you want to marry Mr. Hayward? You said to me that you wished I hadn't interrupted." God, they'd been talking at cross purposes for weeks. Had he botched things up worse than he already knew he had?

Vivid red spots bloomed on her cheeks and her hands wrung together at her waist. "I didn't particularly want to marry him, no. But I knew he felt favorably inclined, and I thought he might be the only option remaining."

Now he was getting angry. For two years, he'd heard all the moaning and groaning from men whose hopes she'd dashed. And he'd silently toasted her every time, admiring her for leading them all a merry chase. "How could you think such a thing? Don't you know you could have had anyone you wanted—anyone at all?"

Her pretty eyes welled. *"Snow Angel,"* she said miserably. "They all think me cold and arrogant. No one wants me. Not even my family!"

Jordan wiped her tears with a thumb. "That moniker is the result of bruised egos, pet. Believe me, if you'd picked any one of those dolts, he would have crowed his good fortune to his dying day. And you are your family's very treasure. Your brothers, Lady Janine, your sister-in-law . . . They all adore you. Your mother, too, I'm sure, in her own, twisted way."

The mention of the officious Caro Lockwood brought a wry twist to Naomi's lips. Then she sighed and resumed their walk. She made a sorry figure with her head drooped and her heavy skirts trailing over muddy terrain. "Whatever my family felt before is a thing of the past. Marshall and Isabelle don't want me in their home any longer, now they're starting a family. They said so when they sent me away."

"Sent you a— Oh, blast." He hadn't thought. *Why* hadn't he thought? He hadn't thought beyond securing Naomi and Lady Janine's presence for his *faux* house party. Not once had he wondered what Marshall had to do to convince Naomi to leave her family. Just as he'd made Kate feel unwelcome in his bid to keep her safe, Marshall must have done the same to drive Naomi from the nest. Jordan cursed himself for a heartless cad and vowed to make it up to her.

A distant rumble reminded Jordan of the touchy weather. He put a hand on the small of his fiancée's back to nudge her into a quicker pace.

The rumbling sound did not let up. It grew louder until a horse burst over the rise from the direction of the stables. Two more followed close behind.

He recognized Ditman on the lead horse. The trio pulled to a stop. Fitzhugh Ditman's eyes darted between Jordan and Naomi. "You're needed at once, Freese. Urgently."

The hairs on the back of Jordan's neck stood on end. What had happened? "Of course. But first, I must escort Lady Naomi to the house."

Ditman snorted in obvious annoyance and slid from the saddle. "I'll go," he rasped. "Take my mount."

Naomi's eyes widened in alarm. She shook her head. "Jordan, please don't."

"I must go." He returned her wet articles. "Go take a warm bath. I'll see you soon."

She shied away from Ditman's offered hand. "Please," she pleaded in a panicked whisper, "not him."

Jordan didn't have time for feminine hysterics. "You're made of sterner stuff, my dear." A brush of his lips at her temple was all the comfort he could offer just now. He swung up onto the horse. "Take care of the ladies, Naomi. I'm relying on you."

A true clap of thunder seemed to startle her out of her horror. She nodded stiffly as he wheeled his mount and ordered his men to a gallop.

Chapter Sixteen

An insistent tug on her elbow drew Naomi's anguished gaze away from the swiftly retreating forms of Jordan and the other men.

"Come along, Lady Naomi," said the harsh voice. "There's no time for dallying."

She removed her arm from Mr. Ditman's hand.

His ruined face held no warmth. Every harsh line suggested potential cruelty. His eyes gleamed meanly like two little coals smoldering in deep sockets. Mud spatters on his boots and great coat bore witness to the wild ride that had brought him here.

There was something dark and barely contained about this man. Naomi could not like him, not after he'd tried to press his escort on Kate. What reason a grown man might have for attempting to get a young girl alone, Naomi didn't care to dwell upon.

Without a word, she started to the house. They weren't far now, maybe a quarter of a mile. She wouldn't have to suffer the loathsome man's presence for long.

Before she'd taken five steps, his hands were yet again upon her person. "This way," he said, veering her to the northeast, away from the house, toward the ha-ha separating the park from a grazing pasture.

"Let me be," she protested when she saw he meant to force her into the ravine.

A snarl erupted from his twisted lips. "I got no time for brainless chits. If you know what's good for you, you'll do as I say." He snatched her bonnet and pelisse from her hands and threw them into the ditch. "Down. Now."

She clambered down the steep side, struggling to find purchase on the slick grass. The tiny dot pattern of her dress was quite obliterated by green-and-brown stains. She spared a rueful thought for Brenna, who would despair of ever getting the frock clean.

Mr. Ditman offered her no assistance. His eyes roved their surroundings until she'd made it to the bottom. Then he leaned forward and stepped onto the slope, easily sliding down upright, with one hand trailing behind for balance. In a few seconds, he was once again towing her behind him.

Cold rainwater had collected in the bottom of the ha-ha. In short order, Naomi's shoes and stockings were saturated, to say nothing of the water weight dragging down her skirts and petticoat. Getting caught in the rain with Jordan had left her soggy. This was an entirely different, unpleasant experience.

Her toe caught, sending her reeling. She only just retained her footing. "Please slow down," she gasped.

Astonishingly, the forbidding man paused to allow her to catch her breath.

Naomi's lungs heaved air in and out. She turned her face up to the sky, eyes closed, welcoming the cold drizzle on her flushed skin.

"Have you seen a French lad about the place?" Mr. Ditman asked.

For the space of two beats, Naomi's heart stopped. What did he want with Enrique? If Jordan hadn't seen fit to reveal the boy's presence to Mr. Ditman, she certainly wasn't about to—especially after the way he'd frightened Kate.

Struggling to maintain a calm visage, she met his impassive gaze with one of her own. "No, Mr. Ditman, I have not." She arched a brow. "Do we expect such an addition to our party?"

A muscle just beneath his right eye twitched, making the top end of his scar jump. He turned in a swirl of wet, black wool, flinging even more droplets onto Naomi. As he slogged through the muck, his voice rolled back to her like rough stone tumbling downhill. "You stick your nose where it don't belong, and it's likely to get bit off. Freese isn't the only one watching you, and you ain't the only one poking about."

A shiver that had nothing to do with the cold, miserable conditions shook down her spine. Apprehension for Enrique's safety prompted her to push herself faster.

The next few minutes passed with no words between them. Naomi kept a wary eye on the taut line of her escort's shoulders. He stopped and raised a hand to halt her. Ditman's head tilted. Naomi held her breath, wondering what he was listening for.

She supposed he must have been satisfied, for he grunted and climbed the ravine. At the top, he poked his head up to make a visual inspection then motioned for Naomi to follow. As before, he left her to her own devices.

"I'll scramble right up," she muttered as she fought against her clothes and nature to reach the crest. "Don't trouble yourself on my account." She saw they stood about fifty yards from the corner of the house.

Ditman crouched, the skirt of his great coat billowed around his bent legs. "Go," he rasped, waving her forward. "I'll cover your approach."

For a second, Naomi was paralyzed. The manicured park was no longer a luxurious expanse of lawn but exposed ground. A prickling between her shoulder blades made her wonder what hidden eyes were watching.

She hauled up her ruined skirts and ran. Her pumping legs burned from trudging and climbing and—God forgive her—from her intimate exercise with Jordan. A sob caught in her throat. Then she was at the door, pounding. "Let me in," she cried, her voice almost as hoarse as Mr. Ditman's.

A footman opened the door. His cross expression turned to shock as he took in her bedraggled appearance. "My lady!"

She shoved past the servant and ran to the stairs, determined to check on Enrique. If Ditman was curious about him, then the boy must be in danger. Of this she was certain. Water streamed from her as she climbed. She was creating so much work for the maids, but she couldn't spare them more than the briefest regret.

Three flights later, Naomi was gasping like a fish on dry land. Her legs trembled, threatening to collapse. She gritted her teeth. The door to Enrique's apartments was slightly ajar. Her shoulder hit the door, flinging it open. "Enrique!" she called.

Silence answered her.

*

The only sound was her own harsh breathing as Naomi turned in a circle. The room looked just as it should, not a stick of furniture out of place. Something felt off, though.

She crossed the room and opened the door to a short corridor lined with several doors. The first door she opened revealed a bedroom fit for a lord. The next door was narrow and locked. Closet, she surmised. Her anxiety mounting with every step she took, Naomi finally reached for the last door. She turned the knob and flung it open.

It was a schoolroom. Enrique and his tutor sat at a table covered with papers, holding a heated conversation in French.

At her entry, their faces turned as one. Enrique sprang to his feet. "My dear Lady Naomi!" he said. He hooked his hair behind an ear and smoothed a hand down his waistcoat. His smile seemed tight, forced.

Behind him, Bertrand, his tutor, hastily swept the papers together in a pile.

After a quick bow, Enrique touched her elbow and gestured with his other hand to the door. "*Quelle suprise!* Come, let us adjourn to the sitting room. Shall I ring for tea?"

Did he not see the puddle collecting at their feet? "No, thank you," she answered. She resisted his gentle nudge and looked past him to where the tutor was now clearing the papers off the table altogether. "I just wanted to make sure you're all right."

His laugh was as tight and false as his smile. "But of course! Why should I not be? Although, Bertrand and I were just discussing the finer points of Saint Thomas Aquinas. *Mon dieu*, the man was a bore. Per'aps I was in danger of expiring of tedium."

"Well, all right, then," she said dubiously. "By the way, Enrique, have you met Lord Freese's friend, Mr. Ditman?"

"I have not 'ad the pleasure," the boy replied.

"If you do encounter him, be careful."

Enrique nodded once, his cheeks pushed out in a quizzical expression. He escorted Naomi to the door of his apartments and bid her a cheerful *au revoir*.

As she trudged to her own room for a bath and change of clothes, Naomi's anxiety refused to relent. She had seen Enrique with her own eyes, hale and whole. Why did she still fear for him?

Soaking in the tub a short while later, she wondered if her focus on Enrique's safety wasn't just a way of getting her mind off of Jordan. After all, her new fiancé—she still couldn't believe they were actually engaged!—had ridden off hell-for-leather into what was almost certainly a dangerous situation.

She tried to think about what had happened between them. She had given her virginity to, and accepted a marriage proposal from, a man who thought she was only interested in tawdry liaisons. *Given* might be a bit generous, she allowed. She'd more chucked her virginity at him than anything so refined as *given*.

Their lovemaking had been unlike anything Naomi's furtive reading had prepared her for. They had been inside a tree, for pity's sake! And she'd been atop him, riding him like a stallion on the hunt. She hadn't expected it to feel so earthy. There had been no romance, no gentle words. Only desperate, searing need.

And yet, her heart had been fully invested in the act. The love she'd harbored for Jordan all these years had made it possible. He was the only man who had ever interested her on this primal level. Even though he had some misguided ideas about her morals, Naomi couldn't regret what had happened or the result.

She was going to get married. Finally! At last, Naomi would have a family and home of her own. A wellspring of joy spilled from her heart and suffused her body all the way to her fingertips.

If only her betrothed would return home safely, perhaps she could truly relax and enjoy being newly engaged. In the meantime, she must see to the ladies. And look in on Lord Gray, she reminded herself. The poor man might be in need of something.

As the hours ticked by, Naomi kept herself busy. She accompanied Miss Knight on the pianoforte while that lady practiced a piece to sing after supper. Clara sought her advice on the matter of a damaged chair requiring reupholstering. She visited the Grays and commiserated with Lady Gray over her husband's piteous state.

None of these activities could wholly alleviate the worry prickling the back of her head. Thinking of Jordan out there in the cold rain, more than once drove her to a window, peering into the mist for any sign of him or his companions.

At last, when the ladies were sitting down to tea, the sounds of the great front door closing and male voices laughing filled the parlor. An unacknowledged tension in the room eased.

He's safe. She restrained the urge to leap to her feet and find him. If there had been any symptom of distress in what she'd heard of the gentlemen's arrival, nothing in the world could have stopped her from dashing to his side. But he was safe, and she had to play her part.

As soon as she could reasonably extract herself from the company, however, she excused herself to rest before supper. Up the stairs she went at a sedate pace, exchanging pleasantries with the guests she passed.

When she reached the correct corridor and found it clear of witnesses, she dashed on tiptoe toward what had to be the master bedchamber. The portal began to swing open. Naomi ducked into the neighboring room, which was open.

Her back pressed to the wall, she waited while a man passed. She peeked out to see the back of a man, shorter, slighter, and browner of hair than Jordan. His valet, she supposed.

"What are you doing?"

Naomi yelped and spun, her hands clapped to her throat.

Jordan leaned against a doorframe on the other side of the room. His face looked freshly scrubbed, and he'd already changed for supper.

"I was looking for you," she said quietly, not wanting her voice to carry into the corridor. A quick look around told her she was in a lady's sitting room. "I wanted to make sure you were all right. You left in such a hurry earlier."

His heavy-lidded eyes took on a heated look as he pushed away from the door and sauntered to where she stood. He stopped just inches away from her. Their gazes held while he closed the door. "Perfectly well, thank you for asking."

The proximity of so much large, solid male made her skin feel sensitized. "Does Mr. Ditman know about Enrique?"

A shadow crossed Jordan's face. "No, no one—" His lips pressed together. "No, he doesn't."

"Well, he asked me earlier if I'd seen a French boy. And he frightened Kate the other night. He tried to make her go off with him alone. Jordan, I don't trust him. How well do you know this man?"

His palms grazed along the curve of her hips and his eyes settled on her chest. "Fitzhugh Ditman and I were taken prisoner together in Spain. Our captors tortured us, but Fitz got the worst of it. That's where these came from," he said, turning his head to display the scar on his cheek. "We worked together to escape. He's not a man of graces and airs, but I trust him."

Capture. Torture. My God. He said it so casually, so matter-of-factly. She knew something of being held against one's will, thanks to the actions of a vengeful madwoman last year. She knew what it was to fear for her life, to suddenly feel the need to look over her shoulder, even now, a year after she had been taken hostage. No wonder Jordan struggled with connecting to people.

She had no evidence against Mr. Ditman, only the uneasy feeling he aroused whenever she was near him. And maybe that was the result of the torture he'd endured. It was so hard to be certain of anything anymore.

Trying to put the gruff man out of her mind, she glanced about the room then flicked her eyes to Jordan. "What were you doing in here?"

His half smile tugged at the lower end of his scar. Naomi liked how it seemed to smile at her whenever Jordan did, so different from Mr. Ditman's forbidding wound.

"I was thinking about you occupying this suite," he said lightly, "and here you are."

"This is the lady's boudoir, I take it?"

A warm hand cupped her jaw and tilted her face. "*You* are the lady, pet. These are *your* rooms." Their lips brushed and clung together for just a few seconds. "Would you like to see?"

At her nod, he held her hand while they took a turn about the boudoir. Sage-green silk covered the walls. An ecru chaise lounge waited beside the fireplace for a lady to recline upon it. Polished silver accents—frames, a tea service, a plant stand—glittered, like jewels strewn about the room.

"These were all my mother's things," he said. "You must have whatever you like. Redecorate any way you please."

She squeezed his hand as a flush of pleasure swept through her. At last, everything she'd yearned for would soon be hers. It wasn't the sumptuous room that made her happy, but the knowledge that it was *hers*. Her place, where she belonged, with a man who cared for her. "Thank you," she murmured. "Your mother had exquisite taste. For the time being, I think I shall leave this room just the way it is."

"As you like."

He led her into the adjoining room, the bedchamber. The color scheme was watery shades of blue with touches of rose gold. The bed was made of pale maple; each of its four posts was intricately carved with vines and leaves climbing up to the canopy.

Naomi lightly ran her fingers along the elaborate design. "It's beautiful."

Jordan's arms wrapped around her from behind. "It will look better with you in it." The tip of his tongue flicked the sensitive skin behind her ear then followed the curve of her neck. "And you will look better with me in you."

Naomi gasped. Her face flamed at his outrageous remark, but she couldn't deny its effect. Her breasts grew heavy. The flesh at the juncture of her thighs ached for his touch. She turned in his arms and pulled his face down. Tiny laps at the seam of his lips convinced him to open. A groan rumbled in his chest. The kiss deepened as their tongues danced.

There was a sudden sensation of vertigo, until she realized he had maneuvered her onto the bed. For a moment, his weight pressed her into the satin duvet. The feeling of his hard length cradled against her brought all the feminine parts of her body flaring to life. Instinctively, her hips rocked up to receive him, only to encounter layers of clothes in the way.

A low chuckle raised gooseflesh on her arms. "So eager." He drew the words out, until they were as sweet and seductive as the caramels she'd had that morning.

"It feels right," she whispered in breathless explanation.

"Shh," he soothed, stroking down her ribs with the back of his hand. "I can't have you again, Naomi. Not like this morning."

She made a whimpering sound of protest. Her body assured her that he could and very well *should* have her again. And perhaps again after that.

"There isn't enough time right now," he answered her wordless question. His shadow beard raked across her collarbone while his hand covered her breast. "The next time I'm inside you, I won't leave for hours. But I want to watch you come again. I didn't properly savor the moment this morning."

Even as the pulsing heat began building down low, part of her mind tucked away the new vocabulary word for later contemplation. *Come.* He didn't use it the usual way; the new implications excited her.

She explored the broad expanse of his back, feeling the play of hard muscles as he smoothly moved over her. If only he were bare. She longed to explore his body until she knew it as well as her own.

Jordan knelt back and grasped her ankles. A sharp thrill shot through Naomi's core, causing her to moan and lift her hips again. Slowly, his hands followed her legs, nudging them apart and pushing her skirt as he went, until it piled around her waist.

"So beautiful," he let out on a sigh. His head dipped and he kissed the inside of her knee, then laid a trail of teasing nips and kisses up her inner thigh. When he'd almost reached her apex, Naomi held her breath, wondering what he was going to do. Surely, he didn't mean to kiss her *there*, as well!

No. His tongue instead traced the rise of her hipbone then dipped into the hollow beside her belly. Her abdomen trembled; her hands raked through his hair and over his scalp, holding him close. His fingers covered her sex and she felt herself plump in his hand. Deftly, he parted her folds and spread the slickness up and around her tight bead. She bit her lip to keep from crying out and exhaled a strangled moan instead.

"I love how wet you are." His eyes regarded her from beneath a fringe of dark lashes, the blue irises bright with wicked intent. "Is this for me, sweetheart?"

"Oh, yes," she breathed.

"Just for me?" A finger pressed into her and withdrew.

She mewled. "Just you." Her heart pounded in her ears. "Never felt this way before."

Two fingers plunged inside, stretching skin still a little sore from this morning's inaugural breach. His hand slowly pumped between her legs. Her thighs tensed as the pressure mounted.

"You feel so good," he said. "I want to bury my cock here and feel you wring every drop from me."

The forbidden words seduced her as much as his touch. Her head thrashed to the side. Her knees drew up, flagrantly offering him more. Everything.

His teeth closed over her hipbone, then his mouth dragged to her navel, where his tongue swirled. "I want to spend myself in you until you're too sore to walk. I want to know what you taste like."

That wicked tongue found its way to the taut bundle of nerves and gently lapped it. Naomi's spine arched. Her shoulder blades dug into the satin duvet; her fingers twisted into his hair. "Oh, that feels so . . ." There wasn't a word to describe it.

Jordan's mouth moved lower. He parted her nether lips and held them open, completely vulnerable to his erotic onslaught. He licked the length of her swollen flesh and dipped his tongue into her entrance, over and over, while his thumb worked deftly at her tender bud. The pleasure was an entity unto itself, taking over her, possessing her. "Yes, Jordan, yes. Don't stop. Oh, please!"

A throaty laugh vibrated against her sensitized tissues. "Don't stop what, pet?"

She let out a keening sound. So close. So close.

Suddenly he was over her; his hand now driving her toward the brink. She clung to his neck and lifted her face. He pushed her down again with his weight, delivering a bruising kiss flavored with her own essence. "Taste," he whispered. "You're sweeter than wine." His tongue speared into her mouth with the same rhythm as his hand, pinning her to the bed, like a butterfly specimen.

He ruthlessly broke the kiss. Hot, moist breath covered her throat. "Naomi," he growled in her ear, "I want to fuck you."

And she was gone. Over the edge, falling through a chasm of ecstasy. Jordan took her cries in his mouth, moaning his approval as her climax went on and on.

As she began to return to earth, he cupped her sex in his hand. She twitched against his palm, and a shudder racked her body. "You are magnificent," he said reverently. "And you are mine."

Her heart swelled with joy. It wasn't a declaration of love, not yet. But it would be.

When he kissed her this time, it was slow and tender. She caressed his face, wishing she could give him pleasure like he'd just given her.

She said so, and his eyes blazed. He held her gaze as he very deliberately lifted his hand and put his fingers in his mouth. His lids drooped and he made a satisfied sound. Naomi gasped when she realized what he was doing. "You have given me pleasure, sweetheart," he said. "Watching you writhe in ecstasy is the image I'll be taking with me to bed tonight."

He laid down and gathered her into his arms. Nestled against Jordan, Naomi couldn't imagine life feeling any better than it did right now. But it would, after they were married. They would be free to take their pleasure whenever they wished. Lintern Abbey would be her proper home. Jordan would be her husband.

Still floating in a drowsy afterglow, she asked, "Will you go see Marshall now?" They would want the banns read as soon as possible, of course.

His arms tensed. "Not at once. I'm hosting a large group of people."

She wiggled out of his grasp and lifted her face. "Write him, then. I'm sure he'd come."

"No," he said, sounding exasperated. "He won't leave Isabelle. Would you want him to do that? To leave her alone in her condition?"

"Of course not." All the warm feelings inside her started to cool and congeal. "But you must speak to him as soon as possible."

He moved off the bed and gave her a hand to assist her to her feet. "I will speak to him—*when* it's possible. It isn't right now, my dear."

Where was her fiery, generous lover of just moments ago? Every line in his posture was taut, every muscle locked in stubbornness. There was no point wasting another breath.

If he really thought they should marry, wouldn't he reach out to Marshall at once? Why delay, when they'd already anticipated their wedding night? Hurt and confusion clouded her mind. Without another word, Naomi abandoned the sumptuous chambers of the Viscountesses Freese, wondering if she'd made a terrible mistake.

Chapter Seventeen

Sleeplessness did strange things to the mind and body.

Naomi felt as if she was falling ill. Her cheeks were hot; her hands were cold. What she needed was a quiet morning in bed, but it wasn't to be. While her eyes burned for rest, her mind whirred with activity. A ball of nervous energy settled in her middle and sent tentacles through her limbs. She could scarcely sit still, much less relax in bed.

As soon as a pink blush limned the horizon, Naomi called for Brenna. With her maid's help, she dressed and headed for the dining room, hoping to meet Jordan. She considered looking for him in his own room, but after yesterday's events, the thought of finding him in bed was too upsetting.

Twice yesterday, she'd given herself to him. The first time was an error. She'd been swept up in the moment. Jordan hadn't intended to take her maidenhead. It had just . . . happened. One indiscretion might be understandable, but last night's interlude in the lady's apartments quite obliterated any illusion that Naomi was anything but fallen.

Jordan had done the honorable thing and proposed, albeit with obvious reluctance and suffering delusions of Naomi's unwillingness. She had accepted him, as was only right after the intimacies they'd shared. Marshall loomed large in Naomi's conscience. Without a doubt, she knew her brother would want her to marry at once. He'd sworn never to force her into marriage, but in this situation, he would encourage her in the strongest possible terms to do so. Being one of his closest friends, Jordan must know this, too. Why, then, did he refuse to go speak to Marshall—or even to write?

It was this that had kept her awake all night. She simply could not imagine a reason sufficient to justify a delay. And so she must have it out with her erstwhile fiancé.

In the dining room, she did not find Jordan, but a footman gathering up used plates.

"Has his lordship already eaten?" she asked the servant.

"Yes, milady. You've missed him by about ten minutes. He and his friends have already gone out hunting. Would you care for a cup of tea?"

"No, thank you."

Naomi tapped her hands together as she strolled back the way she came. Perhaps Clara could offer her some guidance. Jordan's stepmother possessed valuable insight into his personality, after all.

"Brenna," she said as she walked back into her chamber, "would you please inquire when I might have a word with Lady Whithorn?"

Her maid paused in plumping the pillows on Naomi's bed to answer. "Lady Whithorn isn't here, milady. She's gone."

"How can that be? I just saw her last night at supper."

Brenna shook her head. "She and Lady Kaitlin left during the night. Downstairs is all abuzz, wondering whether she's had a row with Lord Freese."

"I hope not," Naomi murmured. She drifted to a chair and sat, staring hard at the rug while she tried to make sense of things. It didn't seem likely for Clara and Jordan to have argued to such a degree, especially since they had been cordial with one another last night. When would there have even been time to fight between then and when Clara had left in the middle of the night?

All the oddities since Naomi's arrival at Lintern Abbey swirled through her head. The precise pairs of one gentleman and one lady, excepting Aunt Janine and herself. The propensity for several gentlemen to miss supper every night. The shooting at the shed, which Jordan claimed was a misfired hunting piece. The signals. Enrique—gracious, she could write a whole list on the topic of Jordan's ward alone. And now this, Clara and Kate's sudden departure.

Fear trickled down the back of her neck. She had to speak to Jordan as soon as possible. Briefly, she considered going out and finding his hunting group, but she discarded the idea almost at once. After she'd been escorted back to the house by way of the flooding ha-ha, she knew Jordan didn't want her getting in the way of whatever was happening. He'd asked her to look after the ladies. She had to keep her promise.

The next few hours passed in a daze as Naomi forced down a few bites of food at breakfast. Conversation flowed around her. She responded automatically to questions. Later, she blinked, suddenly aware she was in the sitting room with a group of ladies, embroidery hoop in hand. When had this happened? The strawberry fruit and flowers she'd been working on for a week now looked as though an elephant had trampled them.

She was trying to pick out the damage she'd done when the sitting room door burst open. The ladies all looked up at the intrusion. Naomi recognized the footman she'd seen this morning.

"Lady Naomi, come with me, please. Lord Freese requires your presence at once."

Ignoring the quizzical looks from the other women, Naomi set aside her work and followed, fighting to master the knot of dread that was threatening to choke her.

The servant led her to the study and opened the door. Jordan was in an armchair, bent nearly double with elbows on knees and his hands fisted behind his head. Mud spatters marked his Hessian boots and buckskin breeches.

Nothing good began this way. She took a tentative step inside. "Jordan?"

Grim lines etched the face that turned to her. "Thank you for coming so quickly." His voice reminded her of Mr. Ditman's—harsh and empty.

"What's happened?" Naomi took his hands. The fingers of one loosely responded to her squeeze. The other remained fisted.

"Two of my men are dead." His eyes were shards of ice, stark against his wan face. "Mr. Elton and Mr. Young. They're dead."

"Oh, God." Naomi swayed. Her head swam. She clenched her jaw and drew a deep breath. Poor Miss Knight! To lose her betrothed. And Miss Elton! Naomi pictured the frail creature, just a wisp of a woman, now lacking a brother. "How . . . ? What . . . ?"

"You have to help me, Naomi. Please. I need you." His one hand gripped hers almost painfully. The other squeezed harder into its white-knuckled fist.

Tears stung her eyes, and her throat started to constrict. "Have you told them yet? Miss Elton and Miss Knight?"

He sniffed loudly and swiped his sleeve across his brow. Twin splotches of color spread over his cheeks. "The women must leave. All of them. You, too, but you have to organize things for me. One hour. I cannot give you more than that. Faster, if you can manage it."

A strange numbness consumed her. Her thoughts felt slow, clumsy. She took his fist in both of her hands and pried at his fingers. Jordan needed to relax, she thought. If only he would calm down a bit and stop making that whimpering sound, she could concentrate on what needed doing.

He grabbed her arms and shook her. Something dropped from his hand and hit the floor with a heavy thud. "Naomi!" he snapped. It was then she realized the noise was coming from her, not Jordan. "You must see to the women for me. I have to gather the men and head back out before—"

The object on the floor caught the sunlight and glinted gold. Naomi stooped and picked it up. A ring.

At first glance, she thought it a signet ring, perhaps belonging to Mr. Elton or Mr. Young. Closer inspection revealed an eagle worked into the face of the ring, wings spread, beak open in a defiant scream.

"The French Imperial Eagle," she said. "Bonaparte's device." She looked up to see Jordan looming over her, wary and guarded. "For the love of everything holy, what is this doing in Yorkshire?"

*

Having been summarily evicted from the study with no answer but an ill-tempered snarl, Naomi set about evacuating the ladies. That wasn't the word Jordan used, but clearly this was, in fact, an evacuation. Two men were dead, by what means Naomi still did not know. Jordan must suspect an imminent threat to all of Lintern Abbey's occupants to order them out of the house.

Instead of sharing the news directly with the ladies, Naomi flew belowstairs and called for help. The housekeeper, Mrs. Walker, appeared.

"What is it, my lady?" she asked, clearly startled by Naomi's alarm.

"Muster every servant," Naomi said, panting from her race through the house. "Lord Freese has ordered all female guests from the house immediately."

"My gracious!" the woman exclaimed. "Why?"

Naomi made a sharp gesture. "I don't know, and it doesn't matter. The ladies cannot take more than a few essentials. There isn't time for anyone to pack properly. Have the maids help. The footmen and hallboys can help ready carriages. Once the ladies are off, you and the other servants must all go, too."

Mrs. Walker inhaled deeply, puffing her bosom like a hen defending her nest. "Of course, we shall do as his lordship says. But I'll not abandon Lintern Abbey. I've served here for twenty-eight years. If Lord Freese wishes me gone, he and I will exchange words on the matter." Her tone made clear Jordan would have an uphill battle convincing Mrs. Walker to go.

"Then stay," Naomi replied. "But we must see the ladies gone at once."

She left things in Mrs. Walker's very competent hands and dashed up the stairs. Naomi's lungs were beginning to ache from all the running about.

Getting Aunt Janine prepared for departure was her priority now. It would take both her and Brenna working together to convince Auntie to leave behind her academic accoutrements and take only her toiletries and a change of clothes.

Around Naomi, the house pulsed with fearful anticipation, as though a monstrous wave was about to break on the roof. The news made its way faster than she could. From the direction of the sitting room, she heard cries of alarm and the footfalls of half a dozen women running for their rooms.

Naomi made for the library, which had been her aunt's haunt since the day they'd arrived. The room was quiet and still. The table that had been the site of Auntie and Sir Randell's fierce debates was vacant, without so much as a single volume littering the top.

Upstairs, she rapped on Aunt Janine's door and opened it. "Auntie?" she called. Behind her, the corridor buzzed with frantic activity and voices. A clatter outside drew Naomi to the window. Several carriages, their teams led by grooms and footmen, were making their way toward the front of the house.

A cold fist squeezed around her heart. She pivoted on her toe. "Aunt Janine!" she called as she stepped into the corridor.

Naomi struggled against the stream of women and maids flowing to the stairs. In her own room, Brenna was flying about, grabbing needful articles and thrusting them into a valise.

"Do you know where my aunt is?" she demanded.

The maid spared her but a glance from her work. "She went for a walk this morning, to see some standing stones, she said. But that was hours ago. I couldn't say where she is now."

"Oh, no," Naomi whispered. The thought of her dear, distracted aunt outside, with danger circling her like wolves, was more than Naomi could bear. "*Nonononono.* We have to find her, Brenna. I can't leave without her."

Chapter Eighteen

Goddamn the Foreign Office straight to the infernal pits of hell. And damn Castlereagh, too, Jordan thought crossly. Now that things had finally gotten interesting, Jordan wanted no part of his work.

Right now, all he wanted was to grab Naomi and take her far away from Lintern Abbey as fast as he could. He hated that he'd put her in harm's way. He cursed the day he'd ever concocted this house-party scheme. As a front, it had failed miserably. It had, however, succeeded beyond all expectations in killing two men and endangering a dozen innocent women.

The closed study door did little to muffle the sounds of frantic leave-taking. His men could scarcely hear his orders over the din. "Perry, Richard, and Herrick, take the drive. Make sure the carriages all make it safely through the gate. If there's any trouble, shoot. Don't bother trying to apprehend them, just kill the bastards."

A wild gleam flared in Mr. Richard's eyes. He nodded once and led the other two out.

Thank God he'd convinced Clara to take Kate and depart during the night. It might take months to repair the damage he'd done to his friendship with Clara, but at least two women he loved were safe. If only the one he loved most would hurry away as well.

"Bates." The man Jordan addressed looked up from checking the priming on his pistol. "You, Wood, Price, and Sidney take positions around the house."

Mr. Wood raised a hand. Nervous blinking had his eyelids beating like hummingbird wings. "Sir, four of us aren't nearly enough—"

"Fair point," Jordan interrupted. "Too bad some of us are dead. Go."

And the devil take Napoleon Bonaparte and prance about on his entrails for depriving Jordan of the chance to consider the fact that he'd just realized he was in love for the first time in his misbegotten life. It might be nice to ruminate on that discovery for a moment, but no. International catastrophe was beating down his bloody door.

Oh, how he wanted to beat it back. Rage pumped through his veins, screaming for an outlet. How dare those Frenchmen skulk about his estate, ambush his men, threaten his family—Enrique and Uncle Randell, Lady Janine and Naomi.

Naomi was already lumped in with his primitive concept of family, he thought abstractedly.

She was his. His family. His to protect. To hold. His to love.

Unbidden, he pictured Naomi carrying his child, a beautiful, fertile goddess, with a rounded belly and heavy breasts. Some primeval bit of his brain snarled in lustful appreciation at the image. He would do his level best to make that fantasy a reality as soon as possible. But he had to get her to safety before he could think about the spring planting.

After dismissing the others, Jordan's eyes narrowed in steely determination on the silent man brooding in the corner. "That leaves you and me, Ditman."

The man with the scar so like his own stepped out of the shadows. "Where's the Frenchie, Freese?" His jaw clenched and released. "I don't know what tale you've spun for the toddlers," he said, jerking his head to the door, "and I haven't nosed about nearly so much as I'd like to've, but you must confide in me now. If we're to succeed, I must know what, exactly, we're guarding."

"I should like to know, as well."

Jordan squeezed his eyes shut and lowered his head at that angelic voice. *No, God, not now.* "Why haven't you gone?"

"Aunt Janine is missing." Then she was shaking his arm. Her eyes were wide with fear. "What have you done to us? Aunt Janine is missing, Jordan. I can't leave."

Oh no. The news was a punch to his chest. *Not Lady Janine.* "You will."

Her hands balled into bloodless fists at her side. "I won't." The stubborn set of her mouth told him she wasn't about to be budged.

He wondered whether to club her over the head and stuff her into a carriage, or if she'd kindly hold still and allow him to bind her up and toss her into same. There was no time to argue.

"There's no time to argue," she announced, her arms crossing beneath her breasts, fluffing them up, just over the edge of her neckline. "So you might as well tell me what's happening. The charade is over."

Fitz glided up behind her. Jordan knew an instant of unease in which he thought his old friend might do one of the things he'd just considered himself. He drew her against his side.

Ditman's eyes clouded with confusion. "I think you should tell her. I think you should tell us both the whole of it."

His teeth gritted. For four years, Jordan had carried this secret. Not even Uncle Randell, who lived in this house, knew the whole truth. Divulging it now went against every instinct he possessed, but Naomi and Fritz deserved to know.

Jordan drew a breath and exhaled deeply. "Naomi, you've met my ward, Enrique Sota Vega."

"Who is French," she interjected. "If you lie to me again, I swear I shall . . ." Her brow wrinkled. "I haven't decided yet what I'll do, but it shan't be pleasant."

He smirked. "Fitz," he directed to his old comrade, "you seem to know more than I thought you did, but you haven't met the lad?"

"I've tried to respect your assignment," came the graveled reply. "I figure if Castlereagh wanted me to know, he'd have told me. Doesn't mean I can't piece a few things together."

The man was good. There was a reason Jordan was glad to have him for an ally.

"As you so astutely observed, Naomi, Enrique is, in fact, French."

He paused to allow her a moment of victory. She merely raised an impatient brow.

"The boy is French," Jordan continued, "and his true name is Henri, Duc d'Artagne. He is third in line to the throne of France."

Naomi gasped. "But what . . . ? What is he . . . ? This is *Yorkshire*."

Fitzhugh Ditman wore a blank expression. Mentally recording the information, Jordan knew, filing it neatly away in his mind. "We're preserving the royal line, then."

"Precisely," Jordan confirmed. "I'm the young duke's guardian. Where better than the backwaters of England to hide a potential king of France? The first seven in line are scattered around Europe, likewise protected by other governments."

"A clear line of succession," Naomi said. "But with Bonaparte defeated and the monarchy restored—"

Ditman barked a laugh. "But Boney's not as defeated as we'd like. I'd wager most Frenchmen liked him better than all those Lewies."

Jordan crossed to retrieve a brace of pistols from his desk. "Bonaparte's men are clearing the way for his return. If they can pick off the Bourbon line, it would strike a fatal blow to royalist resistance. A little regicide and *ffi*—" He swiped his fingers across his neck. "There would be nothing impeding his return to power.

"The night of your sister-in-law's auction," he said, nodding to Naomi as he carefully settled the guns into his waistband, "Lord Castlereagh gave me an intelligence report, which indicated Boney's men were narrowing in on Lintern Abbey as a hiding place for a French royal. I had to establish a patrol at once, to try to bring in the agents. With no time to think of a better solution, I settled on the house party and invited all you ladies to come, to give the whole thing a legitimate air."

"Castlereagh?" Naomi frowned. "The Foreign Secretary? Do you work for the Foreign Office, Jordan?"

He gave her a level look; his lips remained sealed.

Naomi straightened. "I want to help."

Jordan huffed. "Oh, for God's sake, Naomi, you can't help."

"Enough talk," Ditman said. "I'm going to find the bastards and bring them down." His grim smile chilled Jordan's blood. "I've got some favors to return." He departed in a swirl of woolen frock coat.

Jordan opened his mouth to order Naomi away, but before he could get a word out, she had her arms around his neck and pulled his face to hers.

It was a greedy kiss, demanding his response. Jordan drew her into his arms, crushing her sweet body against his, forging a memory to carry with him into the uncertainty of the next hours.

She broke the kiss and tilted her head back. Jordan dipped to bite and tongue the length of her neck. His hands covered her breasts then sculpted her back. Naomi clutched his nape and arched against him.

"You have to be careful," she said desperately. "Stay safe for me, Jordan. If anything happened to you . . ."

He nuzzled her shoulder and drew her scent deep into his lungs. "I'll be fine," he assured her. The next words were hard to voice, but he did need her help. He'd never wanted Naomi involved, but she was. And, by Jove, her keen intelligence would be an asset. "Go to Enrique's apartment. It's the center of our protective ring. The safest place. I need you to keep an eye on him for me. He doesn't know anything about the assassins coming for him, and I don't want you to tell him. But if something goes wrong, get him out of the house. Get away as fast as you can, and hide."

He pulled one of the pistols from his waistband and held it out to her.

Naomi looked at the gun for a long moment.

"You can do this," he whispered. "I love you."

Her startled eyes flew to his face. A quiet smile pushed away the day's fear for one, brilliant second. "I love you, too," she murmured. "So much."

She raised up on her toes and pressed a kiss to his lips. Her hand closed over the pistol and pushed it back to him. "We'll be fine without it," she said.

A final kiss and she dashed off to fulfill her duty.

Jordan had never been so awed by a woman. His heart swelled with pride and love. What an amazing, brave creature.

Forget kings and countries and megalomaniacal despots. The world could burn to the ground around his ears, and he wouldn't bat an eye. In that instant, only one thing mattered. Jordan knew there was nothing he wouldn't do to protect Naomi.

Nothing.

*

She met Enrique—Henri, she reminded herself—on the landing one flight down from his apartment.

"Naomi, what ees 'appening?" he demanded. His eyes were wide. "I 'ear much noise and—" He flapped his hands. In the confusion, his command of English was deteriorating.

"Come with me," she said, taking a firm grip of his hand and leading him back to his rooms. "We're to sit tight and wait for Lord Freese."

Just inside his door, the young man yanked his hand free. In French he snapped, "Waiting is not an answer! Tell me what's causing the commotion."

Naomi cast a look around the place. "Where is Bertrand?"

"Not here!"

She huffed. "All right, Enrique. Just sit down, please." She gestured to the couch.

He stared at her in stony silence and refused to budge.

Two older brothers had taught her how to deal with obstinate males. She turned his glare right back on him and pursed her lips.

A moment later, he let out an exasperated sound and plopped into a chair. "Now, then. Please."

She lowered onto a seat and stared at a landscape in an elaborate gilt frame on the wall. How to tell him his very life was in peril?

At last, she started. "Enrique . . . Or rather, Henri, I should say."
His eyes widened.

"It's all right," she rushed to assure him. "Your secret is safe with me."

"'Ow do you know?"

"Lord Freese told me," she confessed. "Henri, there are men coming
here. Supporters of Napoleon Bonaparte. They've already killed two of
Lord Freese's guests, and he thinks they're trying to get to you."

For a long moment, his face was inscrutable. His gaze fixed, unseeing,
on the carved rug. When he lifted his face, she read determination on
his young features. "I must go."

Her hand darted to cover his forearm. "Lord Freese wants you to stay
here. He will keep you safe." She gave him a smile she hoped relayed a
sense of confidence. "Everything will be all right, Henri."

The young man dragged his fingers through his dark hair then
slumped back onto his chair. He closed his eyes. Every once in a while,
she saw his lips moving silently. She supposed he was praying. Taking
her cue from Henri, she clasped her hands together in her lap and
offered up her own pleas for Henri's safety and the welfare of Jordan
and his men.

A quarter of an hour later, Henri sprang to his feet with a growl.
"How long are we meant to stay like this—trapped, not knowing what
is 'appening out there?"

Naomi rose to place a soothing hand on his shoulder. "Henri, it's
been very little time. It could be hours before everything is done with.
Do you have any cards? We could play a game—"

A heavy *boom* reverberated through the house.

Henri's eyes locked onto hers. "Was that a gunshot?"

She shook her head. "No, I believe it was the door crashing open.
Lord Freese will be here any second with news."

The air erupted with the sounds of shouting and thunderous
rapports. Naomi clapped her hands over her ears while her stomach

almost heaved from fear. Only the thought of keeping Henri safe allowed her to maintain any semblance of composure.

"*That* is gunfire," she shouted over the din. She grabbed the young duke's hand. "Time for us to go."

Chapter Nineteen

She opened the door just enough to make sure there were no miscreants bearing down upon them. "All right," she said, waving Henri forward. "Follow me."

Naomi dashed to the end of the corridor and located the door for the servants' stairs, which cleverly blended in with the paneling. After Henri stepped into the stairway, she quietly closed the door behind them, although, given the ruckus taking place on the ground floor, they were in little danger of being overheard.

Oil lamps hung at intervals from iron wall sconces, providing light for their flight down stairs hewn from the same stone that made up the exterior of the house.

"Where are we going?" Henri asked.

A reasonable inquiry, but Naomi hadn't the foggiest idea. Her impulse was to hide in the tree where Jordan had taken her. It had provided shelter, safety, and love when she'd been there. But that was absurd. She couldn't risk crossing the grounds to an unsecured hole in a tree.

"We have to get out of the house," she answered. "It's not safe here."

"Yes, but—"

"The abbey," she said, bursting through a door into the belowstairs portion of the house. She paused for a few seconds to catch her breath. "You know the old ruins better than I, Henri. Do you think there's a place there we might hide?"

Henri planted his hands on his slender hips while he panted. His dark, winged brows drew together over his troubled eyes. "I think, maybe. We'll need . . ." His face screwed up while he obviously struggled to think of the word. In frustration, he held his fists together and swung them downward. "For wood?"

"An axe?"

"Yes! An axe!"

Frantically, Naomi's mind ran through the likely contents of this area of the house. "I don't . . . Oh! This way."

She grabbed his hand and started off again. Belowstairs, usually bustling with activity, was eerily silent. Their running footsteps slapped loudly against the gray stone floor.

In the kitchen, Naomi ran straight to the cord of wood neatly stacked between the hearth and enclosed range. "Ah-ha!" she exclaimed in victory as she spotted a small hand axe. "Will this do?" she asked her young friend.

"Bigger would be better, but yes, this should work." Henri snatched the tool then strode toward the door. "*Mon dieu*," he said, stuttering to a halt. "We should take some food, in case we're hiding a long time."

Leave it to an adolescent boy to let his stomach do his thinking for him. "All right, but hurry," she snapped. "The cold larder should have some cheese, and there's bread over there." She pointed out the food then dashed to the door. Once again, she peered outside and waited a moment to ensure their safe passage.

Henri tapped her shoulder. She glanced back and spotted a sack dangling at his side. Provisions enough to last several days, from the look of it.

"*Allons-y,*" he said.

Naomi was terrified of the open ground they crossed as they hurtled for the tree line. And she resented feeling unsafe in this place she'd come to love as her own home. She was mad as fire at the French assassins who threatened her young friend and endangered everyone at Lintern Abbey. How *dare* they?

Henri's longer legs plunged him into the cover of the trees a few seconds before Naomi got there. Her skirts tangled around her ankles, tripping her. Henri's hand clamped around her arm, preventing the fall. "All right?" he asked.

Naomi nodded. "Come on," she gasped. Her chest ached from

physical exertion and fear. They had to keep going. If Naomi stopped, she might curl into a ball and surrender to the terror.

They ran down the path leading to the abbey ruins. She hoped to see Aunt Janine around every curve, but there was no sign of her. In the distance behind them, Naomi heard the beating of horse hooves.

"Faster, Naomi!" Henri tugged her hand. Together, they crested the rise overlooking the old abbey. The tops of the church columns came into view. They dashed down the stairs built into the hillside. Naomi started for the nave, but Henri veered off to the side.

Naomi's legs felt like lead. She had never run so far, so fast in her life. She knew now where Henri was headed, and she made the remembered target the focus of her concentration.

A few moments later, they reached it—the overgrown cellar door Henri had been showing Sir Randell when Naomi first met him. She remembered, too, what the older man had said that day.

"It might be flooded," she wailed. "And it's not going to open." She gestured to the square portal, constructed of thick, sturdy wood, blacked with age, and she suspected, pitch. How else could it have resisted the elements all these years?

Henri gripped the heavy, iron ring set near one edge and tugged. The door didn't budge. "'Elp me," he insisted.

Naomi fitted her hands around the ring. She counted to three, and they strained against the ancient door's weight. It still refused to move.

"Good thing we brought the axe," Henri said, his mouth fixed in a grim line. He retrieved the blade from his sack and fitted his hands around the handle.

"What do you mean to do?" she asked.

"Break through the lock, of course," he said. Without further explanation, he lifted the axe over his head and brought it crashing down into the wood beside the ring.

He wiggled the blade free and lifted it again.

"There's no lock, Henri," Naomi pointed out. "It's just the ring."

Henri's eyes were wild. "Then, why won't it open?" he bellowed.

"It's sealed shut from all the soil and plants grown up around it. Help me clear it."

Determined to put his tool to use, Henri used the axe to hack at the grass and other weeds encroaching on the wood while Naomi clawed at the soil. In no time, her nails were black.

"There," she said after they'd managed to remove the bulk of the debris. "Let's try again."

They grabbed the rusted, old ring and heaved. They pulled until her hands burned from the friction of the metal against her skin. Beneath them, Naomi felt the smallest response.

"It's moving!" Henri's voice was jubilant.

Slowly, the door gave way. Inch by inch, the wood creaked its way into the air. A cold breeze whooshed out of the cellar. Henri gripped the door itself while Naomi continued to pull on the ring.

The sound of hoofbeats drew her attention. A horse whinnied. Naomi squinted and exhaled a sigh of relief when she recognized the dismounting rider. "It's Mr. Ditman," she said. For once, she was glad to see the man. She raised her hand high and waved to catch his attention.

That's when Fitzhugh Ditman lifted his arm, trained a pistol on them, and fired.

*

The shot might as well have gone through Jordan's heart. Naomi didn't have a gun, which meant someone had fired *at* her. Someone was trying to kill her. He dug his heels into Phantom's sides, urging the great stallion to speeds reckless on the narrow, woodland path. In the damp earth, he'd spotted the fresh prints of a lady's and a man's boots—Naomi and Enrique.

After the fighting in the entry hall, he knew they'd run. Obviously, he wasn't the only one looking for them.

He rounded the bend and saw the gunman hastily reloading. Jordan's blood ran cold at the sickening betrayal. Before Phantom had stopped, Jordan was out of the saddle and barreling down on Fitzhugh Ditman.

With a guttural roar, he tackled the man around the middle, sending them both flying down the hillside stairs. As they fell, Jordan grasped the front of his onetime-friend's coat and maneuvered so he landed on top. The impact stunned him for only a fraction of a second, and then his fist struck his foe across the jaw.

"You son of a bitch!" he bellowed. Naomi hadn't trusted the man, but Jordan had insisted on his value to the mission. He should have listened to her. "I'll kill you myself, you worthless traitor."

He glanced up, dreading the vision awaiting him. She wasn't there. Oh, God, had the bullet struck home?

Fitz's eyes were dazed. He made no move to fight back. Instead, he lifted his hands in surrender. "Pocket," he groaned.

Turning around, Jordan knelt on Ditman's arms to pin them while he searched the man's coat. He fished out a document, which he unfolded and read. Reading was slower going, as it was written in French. As the meaning became clear, Jordan's stomach plummeted.

"No," he said, shaking his head in disbelief. "This can't be right."

"Came off their courier," Ditman said. "He tried to tell me he was just a tutor."

"Is he . . ."

"I killed him."

"Good," Jordan said. He scrambled up and gave Fitz a hand to his feet. "Where did they go?"

Blood dripped from his split bottom lip. He swiped it with the back of his hand, spat, then pointed to a spot twenty yards from the old chapel. "Down a hole, like a couple of rats."

Jordan started forward, his only thought on getting Naomi out of there safely.

"Wait." Fitz Ditman's small eyes burned with malice. "That girl of yours. You know she's one of them. As much time as she spent snooping around, she must be."

Naomi? A traitor? Jordan's mind recoiled. "That's not possible." He gestured emphatically. "There's not a duplicitous bone in her body."

"Well, that's just what she'd want you to think, isn't it?" His scar puckered at his mirthless smile. "Just be ready, Freese. Be ready for anything."

*

"I knew it!" Naomi sputtered dirt out of her mouth as she picked herself up off the floor of a very old, and amazingly dry, cellar. "I knew that man was a snake in the grass." She made a frustrated sound. "I told Jordan, but would he listen to me? Of course not."

Henri was likewise brushing dust from his clothes as they examined the small chamber.

The only illumination came from the overhead door. Thank goodness it was daytime, Naomi thought. A shaft of light showed the narrow, stone steps they'd tumbled down when they'd dived into the cellar to escape Mr. Ditman's assassination attempt. The walls were lined with shelves carved into the bedrock. There were some stoneware basins stacked beside the stairs and a pail in the far corner.

"I suppose we have to close the door," Naomi said. She was loath to do so, as they'd be plunged into blackness. "There's another handle on the underside of the door. Maybe we can put something through it, so the door can't be opened again."

"What's going on out there?" The nobleman's voice wavered as he spoke.

Naomi looked at him over her shoulder and gave a sympathetic smile. "It will be all right, Henri."

She crept up the stairs and peeked across the grass. Mr. Ditman's horse still stood at the top of the hill and had been joined by another horse. "Phantom?" she murmured. Jordan must have been nearby. But where?

Finally, she spotted the two men conversing in the shadow of one of the church pillars. Jordan didn't know Mr. Ditman was a traitor. Otherwise, he would have taken him down by now. "Henri," she hissed to her companion, "help me close the door."

"Come 'ere first," he said in a low voice. "I found something that might 'elp."

Turning back into the gloomy interior robbed Naomi of her sight. She held a hand in front of her as she ducked down the stairs. Suddenly, Henri grabbed her hand and pulled her close. In his other hand, he held a knife. The dim light glinted off the long, wicked blade. She shivered. That thing could do some serious harm. "Did you find that here?" she asked.

Henri's chin trembled. "I brought it from the kitchen."

"Good thinking," she commended, "but I don't think it will do for barring the door. Maybe the axe handle."

Naomi tried to tug her hand free so she could retrieve the tool, but Henri would not relinquish his grip. His hold was surprisingly strong. "I'm sorry," he said regretfully. "I really did like 'aving you for a friend."

"What are you talking about?"

He swung her around, so her back was pressed against his front. She yelped. "Henri! What are you doing?"

The sharp edge of the knife touched her throat. "I really am sorry."

Naomi's mind froze. It was last summer, and she was in her brother's greenhouse, with a gun pressed to her temple by a madwoman. *This is not happening,* she insisted to herself. *It's a waking nightmare. Marshall warned there might be bad experiences after such a trauma, and I'm finally having one.* Why her brain had chosen to cast Henri in the villainous role, she had no idea. It was, however, patently absurd, which helped her keep a grip on reality. *Not. Happening.*

That was, until Jordan and Mr. Ditman appeared.

The stark look of horror in Jordan's eyes was something she'd never seen, nor could she have imagined it. Jordan wasn't afraid of anything . . . but he was afraid of this.

God help me, she thought as a sob welled in her throat. *It's happening again.*

*

Even though the letter Ditman had showed him had prepared Jordan for something like this, actually seeing the Duc d'Artagne holding a knife to Naomi's ivory throat peeled years off his life. Her eyes were wide and wild with fear. Her loose hair covered her captor's forearm. Her plaintive cry galvanized him to action. He reached for a pistol.

"My dear Lord Freese, please do not do that," Henri pleaded.

The young duke had attained a man's height. His shoulders were broad. He wore the finest apparel, befitting a nobleman of his station. Yet, a hint of childish roundness still clung to the apples of his cheeks—cheeks he'd only begun shaving in the last six months. In many ways, Henri was still just a child.

Slowly, Jordan raised his hands and waved at Ditman to do the same. He eased forward a step. "Henri, put the knife down. Lady Naomi has been your friend. This is no way to treat a friend."

"I know," the boy whined. "But this is the only way you'll let me go."

"Why do you want to leave?" Jordan asked. "You're protected at Lintern Abbey. Your uncle, His Majesty, wants you to remain here until it's safe for you to return to France."

Henri straightened. The knife pressed harder to Naomi's neck. A thin, red line welled along the blade's edge. "And when will that be?" he demanded. "I hate it here! I hate this stupid country. I 'ave to pretend to be Spanish. You won't let me do anything. I'm *bored.*"

If the situation weren't so dire, Jordan might have laughed at hearing his own sentiments echoed in this young man. He, too, had found life at Lintern Abbey debilitatingly dull—until Naomi had made it the only place he wanted to be.

Above ground, the sound of horses thundered toward the open, cellar door. Gunshots popped. Henri's gaze flicked to the square of space.

"There's nothing for you to gain by leaving," Ditman contributed. "You're putting yourself in Bonaparte's hands. At best, you'll be his hostage. More likely, he'll have you killed."

Henri blew his lips out in a juvenile scoff. "The Emperor needs me, I'll 'ave you know. When the people see his royal supporters, they will fight to bring him back. I will never sit upon the throne of France, but in exchange for my support, His Imperial Majesty 'as promised me the crown of Prussia."

The shouts and sounds of fighting were loud. Jordan heard more French than English, which worried him. "You're a fool if you believe Bonaparte will give you a crown! He's using you, Henri. All of my men up there came to defend you," Jordan said. "Englishmen have died protecting *you.* Does that mean nothing?"

A Gallic shrug dismissed the matter like so much piffle. "They shouldn't 'ave come. Better if you had just let me go with my friends."

He felt Naomi's eyes on him. He met her gaze and understood her wordless plea. She had been held hostage once before. He couldn't imagine how terrified she must be right now. And he was impotent to do anything about it.

There was a joyous whoop, and then a man called down into the cellar—in French.

"I must go now. After you, *s'il vous plait.*" Henri jerked his chin to the door.

Jordan turned to see two pistols pointed at him from above. He kept his hands raised at his sides while he ascended the stairs.

The scene that met him on the surface was grim. He counted five bodies strewn around the abbey and recognized three of them as his own men. The remainder of his force was on their knees in a line, hands clasped behind their heads. They were surrounded by armed Frenchmen.

He was prodded to join his men. Rough hands patted his body and removed his pistols. Ditman received the same treatment. It was a cold comfort knowing Fitz hadn't been a traitor, after all, although Jordan could happily strangle the bastard for shooting at Naomi.

Henri emerged from the cellar. Naomi still had a knife to her throat, and pistols now augmented that threat.

Jordan watched helplessly as her wrists were bound behind her back. When a Frenchman in a blue frock coat touched her ankles to tie them and made a crass remark, Jordan snarled.

"No, please," Naomi begged her captors. "Please, don't do this to me. Jordan!"

He tensed to lunge.

"Don't do it, man," Ditman warned. "Wait."

It took everything in Jordan to watch while the woman he loved called for him. While she was trussed up and tossed over the back of a horse, her eyes stayed on his. Her loose hair fell down the side of the horse and dangled past the stirrup.

Henri swung up onto the saddle behind her. "I'm not ready to part ways with my Lady Naomi just yet," he said jovially. Now that he had his gang of thugs keeping him safe, the boy was full of bravado. "I thank you for your 'ospitality all these years, Lord Freese. Now I bid you a fond *adieu.*"

With that, he wheeled his mount around and carried Naomi up the hillside and out of his sight.

"Do you s'pose they're going to kill us now?" Mr. Perry asked.

One of the French soldiers snorted and spit phlegm in Perry's face. "Not all of them," he said in heavily accented English. "Just you."

The rapport of the gun was accompanied by a spray of hot blood and shards of Perry's skull.

Shocked by the fluids splashed on his cheek, Jordan gaped at the Frenchman. The guard sneered. He pulled another pistol from his waistband and leveled it in Jordan's face. "Per'aps you as well, *monsieur*."

Chapter Twenty

Oddly, when she was tossed across the horse's withers in front of the saddle, Naomi's first concern was for the animal's welfare. Would she put too much weight on the roan creature's shoulders and cause it pain?

When Henri mounted, her next concern was her hair. "Ow!" she yelped as his boot yanked on a lock that had fallen into the stirrup.

"I do not wish to hurt you, Naomi," Henri said as the horse carried them up the hillside. "You must remember the knife. My men are also armed."

"What's happening to Jordan and the others?" she demanded over her shoulder. "Please don't let your men hurt them."

The adolescent kicked the horse into a trot. "Lord Freese was not very good to me, but his uncle was. For Sir Randell's sake, I 'ave spared Freese. I make no promise for the others."

Sir Randell! In the chaos of evacuating the women and servants, Naomi hadn't realized she'd not seen Jordan's uncle. In fact, she hadn't seen him since the previous day. Had something bad befallen him, as well as Aunt Janine?

Frightening images plagued her, and the jouncing of the horse against her ribs made it difficult to breathe, much less to think. She pictured her aunt's exuberant intellect, snuffed out by men serving a selfish little boy. Tears welled, making her view of the ground beneath her face even more blurred. There were so many people to worry over, so many to mourn. All those men killed to protect someone who didn't want protection.

Behind her and Henri came the pounding of more horses. Hope flashed through her, only to be quickly extinguished when she saw all of the riders were French soldiers. What had become of Jordan and the others? Queasiness rolled through her.

On the road headed toward Lintern Village, they paused. The soldiers fell into formation surrounding Henri.

Henri called out in French, "Is the ship ready?"

"It will be; don't worry," answered one of the men. "Didier went ahead to alert the captain."

"What of the woman?" asked another.

"We take her to the ship," replied the first. "Then maybe toss her over the rail once we're at sea."

"That seems a terrible waste of a pretty girl. I'm sure we can think of a more entertaining way to toss her."

"*Silence!*" Henri yelled. His hand pressed firmly into the small of Naomi's back. "None of you touch her."

Another man snorted. "*Le duc* keeps her for himself. She might be gentle enough to train the pup."

Conversation stopped as the group picked up speed.

Trees and rocks passed in a blur. Naomi's neck ached from the strain of holding her head upright. Below her torso, the horse's powerful muscles bunched and pulled, propelling them forward at a dizzying speed.

Her teeth clattered and her temples soon throbbed. Her arms ached from being tied behind her back. Naomi had no control of her body, trussed up as she was, but she had to escape. Being on a ship with this bunch simply was not a version of reality she was willing to entertain.

Thinking became increasingly difficult by the moment. Her head swam from being inverted as well as from the physical pain of the horse's gallop. Her vision started to go dark around the edges.

No, Naomi screamed to herself. If she lost consciousness, she'd lose any hope of escape. She squeezed her eyes shut and concentrated on something that didn't hurt—Henri's hand on her back. It was warm and broad and held her firmly in place to keep her from tumbling off the mount. Setting aside her desire to throttle the boy for his evil duplicity, Naomi concentrated on that single touch, the one point of her immediate experience that was not torturous. Forcing that small sensation to overwhelm every nerve-shattering pain kept the darkness at bay.

Had she not been intently focused on his hand, she might not have noticed when it began to move. The warm pressure slowly traveled from her back to the slope of her rump.

Delightful, she thought crossly. *Not only am I captive to an adolescent with delusions of grandeur, I'm now his first touch of derriere as well.*

This was intolerable. She would not be held at risk of mortal peril and suffer abuse at the hands of a randy youth. Lintern Village loomed ahead. Going through the village must have been the fastest route to achieve their destination. Would any of the community's inhabitants see her in time to help? Anger churned her mind into action, and a dangerous idea floated to the surface. They were approaching the vicarage now, wherein dwelt two obnoxious dogs. Henri was distracted by her rump. And he only had one hand on the reins.

Before she could talk herself out of it, Naomi pressed her rear hard against Henri's hand. She felt, rather than heard, his sharp intake of breath. Gripping her legs and waist around the horse and using Henri's wandering hand for leverage, Naomi lurched her torso to the front, grabbed a rein in her teeth, and yanked it to the right, as hard as she could.

The galloping horse veered sharply, aiming for the edge of the road and the fence marking the Bartons' garden.

Henri shouted in surprise and released Naomi to regain control of the horse.

Naomi went limp. When Henri jerked the reins back to the left, momentum allowed Naomi to slide off the barreling horse.

She met the road with her face. Something crunched, and pain erupted around her eyes. Her back hit a fence post, reminding her to do something very important.

She screamed.

Naomi screamed as she'd never done in her life. Blood ran into her mouth and down her throat. She kept screaming. It was a full-body scream, as her entire being cried out for help.

"*Zut alors!*" Henri shouted. He wheeled his horse around while his men slowed to a stop. A few trotted back to where she lay on the ground.

"Get her!" she heard Henri yell to one of the men. "Hurry!"

The man dismounted just as the front door of the vicarage opened, and those two obnoxious, marvelous beasts shot out, barking as though they were the hounds of hell, not spoiled spaniels.

"No time," shouted one of the Frenchies. "Leave her, just leave her."

Blood stung her eyes and clouded her vision, but beneath the bottom slat of the whitewashed fence, Naomi saw two pairs of booted feet emerge from the house. Mr. Barton and his manservant. Grateful tears slid down her face.

"But I want—" Henri protested.

What Henri wanted was never to be known. Seemingly out of nowhere, a horse flew past at a dead gallop. An arm shot out and hit Henri across the chest, like a jousting lance.

The young duke tumbled from the saddle and hit the ground.

More horses approached. Mr. Ditman vaulted from the back of his and landed on Henri. A gunshot felled one surprised Bonapartist, while another was shoved from his horse. The other men from the Abbey gave chase to the routed French.

Naomi's erstwhile knight pulled Phantom to a halt. He slid down, grimacing in pain and clutching his arm.

Jordan's pain reminded Naomi that she was in quite a lot of it herself.

Their eyes met and held. She offered a wavering, bloody smile before slipping into the welcoming abyss.

Chapter Twenty-One

The door to Naomi's room opened.

Jordan, sitting on the floor in the hallway across from her door, lifted his head. The surgeon's grave expression sent his heart into convulsions. He jumped to his feet. For the last hour, he'd felt as though his own life hung in the balance. He couldn't stop picturing her as he'd found her, jammed against the fence post, twisted like a broken doll. And so much blood. It had poured from more sources than he'd been able to identify. Her glorious sunrise hair had been matted with it. Her beloved features had been obliterated by rivulets running down her face. "Well?"

"Lady Naomi suffered a broken nose, multiple contusions on her face and scalp, a dislocated elbow, and probably a concussion, as well."

A shudder rocked his body. So many injuries. "Will she live?"

The doctor patted his arm. "Of course, she will. Despite the number of injuries, none of them put her life in danger. She's fortunate not to have broken her neck."

Once more, he saw her broken body on the road, and this time pictured it with her neck at an unnatural angle. It could have been that. So. Bloody. Close.

"Can I see her now?" he rasped. The surgeon gave his assent and promised to check in on her in the morning.

In Naomi's room, her maid, Brenna, had her mistress's head propped over a basin to wash the blood from her hair.

"Let me help." He cradled her head while Brenna gently worked fragrant soap over her scalp. Shouldn't such activity rouse her? "Why is she still unconscious?" he demanded.

"She woke up in a great deal of pain," the maid explained. "Sawbones had to stitch, too, and needed her still. He gave her some medicine for the pain and to help her sleep."

His eyes roved her face, assessing the damage.

The bridge of Naomi's nose was swollen. Bruising seeped onto her cheeks and ringed both her eyes as if she'd been given the one-two by a prizefighter. Her lips, usually delectably plump and eager for his kisses, were gruesomely distended. Tiny cuts and scrapes marred her forehead and cheekbones. A gash on her chin had been sewn shut. That would leave a scar.

He stroked her cheek softly with the back of a finger. "Don't worry over the mark, pet," he murmured. "It will only make your face even more interesting. And it'll be a wonderful conversation piece at parties."

Brenna removed the basin and towel dried Naomi's hair. She combed through the worst of the snarls then quietly departed, leaving Jordan alone with her.

He took her hand and knelt beside the bed. For a minute, he just breathed in her lemon-blossom scent. His nose found her neck. The warmth there reassured him of her vitality. Naomi was alive.

But it could have been different. It could have been worse. She could have died.

Seeing her like this, injured, hurting, and stilled by a drugged sleep, nearly unmanned him. If he lost her, he didn't know how he would have gone on.

And that was a problem.

Jordan's work demanded he go on. Even now, Henri, Duc d'Artagne, his former ward and traitor to the king of France, was bound and locked in his old rooms. Two armed men guarded the door, awaiting Jordan's imminent presence to transport Henri to London, where the boy would be dealt with by Castlereagh and French authorities.

Becoming physically involved with Naomi Lockwood was foolish. Falling in love with her was disastrous. He hadn't been as focused on the mission as he should have been. He'd been too wrapped up in his budding romance with Naomi to see what was happening inside his own house. He couldn't devote enough attention to his work or to Naomi to properly see to them both. Whatever Jordan did, he had to do with his whole self. Anything less was unacceptable.

"I'm so sorry this happened." His voice was thick, his throat tight. His fingers worked through her damp hair, smoothing it across her satin pillowcase. "I told them to look for Lady Janine," he informed the sleeping woman. "I told them not to stop until they have her, even if they have to turn over every pebble in the county." He sniffed loudly. "She's a remarkable old battleaxe, isn't she? Now I know why you're all so devoted to her. I'd grown to like the idea of having her for my own aunt. I never had one, you see. Father only had brothers, and my mother was an only child. I wish—"

Teeth clamped over his tongue. No sense wishing for things that could not be.

"I love you." Half-expecting her to reply, he paused. With no response forthcoming, he pressed a tender kiss to the corner of her mouth, one of the only places on her face not marked by cuts or bruises. "No other woman could ever compare. After being loved by you, I don't want it from anyone else. It would be like settling for the stars after seeing the sun. But you have to understand—" His voice cracked. Ruthlessly, he fisted moisture away from his eyes. "You have to understand that I can't do this to you. If I stay, you'll always be in danger, again and again. This can't be, my love. *We* can't be."

One last touch of her hair. One last kiss. And then he was gone.

*

In her dream, she was falling. The sickening sensation of air rushing past her body, of weighing nothing and too much all at once. The certainty of pain at the terminal point.

She fell from windows, down stairs, from rooftops, out of a chair. Once, she even fell from her mother's arms as a fully grown adult. When she hit the ground, she cried out.

There was always someone on the periphery of her dreams. Often, someone malevolent. Sometimes it was someone she loved, who she couldn't reach or who couldn't reach her. Those people were shadows, insubstantial as a wisp of smoke.

Blue eyes peered at her as she fell. Cold but warm. She knew those eyes. If only she could fall to him, she'd be safe. But she couldn't. She didn't. She just fell and fell and fell. Over and over.

Until the time she smashed against a frozen lake and woke up.

There was no question of her location. She didn't have any of those foggy "Where am I?" moments the heroines in those overwrought Gothic novels she loved so well experienced. This was the room she'd been staying in at Lintern Abbey. She was in Jordan's house. Safe, warm, and feeling as if she'd been hit by a boulder.

"You're awake!"

The excited gasp drew her attention, but turning her head was slow going.

Aunt Janine stared at her from a chair beside her bed, a book open in her lap. Tight worry lines bracketed her eyes and mouth. She leaned forward and laid a cool hand on Naomi's forehead. "How do you feel, dear?"

"Auntie," Naomi moaned. "Oh, Auntie." Tears slipped down her cheeks, and she sobbed softly.

Kind arms enveloped her in a loving embrace. "Shh. There, there, child. It's all right."

A good, healing cry banished much of the lingering fear brought on by her nightmares, but she worried they would return. Aunt Janine offered her a glass of water. Naomi took a long drink and hiccupped.

"I expect you'll want to get up and stretch your legs," Auntie said. Her demeanor was returning to her usual no-nonsense attitude. Naomi took it for a good sign. "You've been in bed for the better part of four days."

"That would be lovely," Naomi said. "But how is it you're here? Are *you* all right? I was so worried when the ladies had to leave, and I couldn't find you. We couldn't find you anywhere."

Aunt Janine fidgeted in her seat. Her eyes were downcast and she cleared her throat. "Well, what happened was . . ." Her arthritic fingers patted at her hair. Aunt Janine *never* fussed with her hair.

"If I didn't know better," Naomi said coolly, "I'd think you felt guilty about something."

That did it. Aunt Janine's nostrils flared. "I feel guilty only for having worried you, not for my behavior. Not that it's any of your business, but the fact is, Sir Randell and I have embarked on an affair."

There was a terrible moment when Naomi was certain her hearing had been damaged during her recent ordeal. Perhaps too much blood had pooled in her head while she was observing the world from a bat's perspective, causing her to hear her aunt incorrectly. Maybe a tiny pebble had jammed in her ear when she'd rolled across the road. Brain damage was a possibility as well.

Aunt Janine blinked owlishly and pursed her lips. Her chest puffed on a deep inhalation, drawing Naomi's attention to her attire. Wide, horizontal pleats of—good heavens, was that silk?—encased Auntie's torso, giving definition to her shape and emphasizing her bosom. The neckline of the aubergine dress dipped demurely, revealing just a hint of cleavage. The dress was downright fashionable. Her hair was still an unruly pile of silvery tresses atop her head, but it was a fetching counterpoint to the dress's strong lines.

She looked lovely. Radiant, even.

A bubble of mirth rose in Naomi's chest and she struggled to restrain it. She let out an undignified squeak.

Aunt Janine's cheeks flushed. "I suppose you think I'm too old to go trolloping about?"

Naomi shook her head, failing to contain a stream of giggles. "You're so academic about it! *Embarked on an affair.* What does that mean? Are you going to marry Sir Randell?"

Aunt Janine snorted. Rising, she crossed to the window, pulled back the curtain, and opened the pane, allowing fresh, cool air to fill the room.

"Four days ago, we were on our way to Gretna Green, eloping, like a couple of young nincompoops."

"Aw, I think it's romantic, Auntie." Naomi turned on her side and rested her cheek on her hands. "So you're already married?"

"Ha! Thankfully, I snapped out of the sexual thrall Randell had cast over me and came to my senses before we crossed the border."

It was Naomi's turn to blush fiercely. Usually, she loved Aunt Janine's plain speaking, but really. There were limits to what a niece wished to hear.

Janine picked up Naomi's brush and turned it in her hands. "All my life, I've spoken against marriage. The institution was made by men, for men. Inequity is inherent to the married condition, and I refuse to put myself in such an unfavorable situation."

Naomi thought about Jordan, of course. He was bossy at times. He'd expected her to fall in line and obey his edicts about his ward. Then she remembered him beneath her in the forest, helpless against her feminine power. There had been plenty of times of balance, too, such as when they conspired together to spin a ridiculous tale about an ailing primrose.

"There can be equality in a marriage, Auntie," she pointed out. "Look at Marshall and Isabelle." A dull pain thumped in her chest when she thought about her brother and sister-in-law. Being ousted from her home wasn't as bitter anymore, though, not now that she had Lintern Abbey, a new home to call her own.

Aunt Janine set down the brush. "As much as I dislike Caro, it was inevitable that her sons grew up with a healthy respect for women and for you to expect the same from a man. But most men don't feel that way." With a sigh, she sat down again. "Anyway, I told Randell I wouldn't marry him. He shall be my companion but never my husband. We shall set up house somewhere, I suppose. Neither of us thinks tramping back and forth across the countryside for assignations has any long-term appeal."

"Oh. All right." Naomi couldn't think of another thing to say. It would be worthless to point out the impropriety of Auntie's plan. Janine had never cared about society's opinion. "Congratulations?"

Auntie's sudden laugh was sharp. "As good as anything. I'll take it."

Naomi's gaze went to the door. She didn't expect Jordan to have sat at her bedside the entire duration of her crisis, but it would be nice if he made an appearance. "Will you ring for Brenna, please?" she asked. "I'd like to freshen up a bit before I see Jordan."

"Take your time freshening up," Janine said as she crossed to the bell pull. "Freese is in London."

Naomi frowned. "Why?"

"Something to do with that awful French brat, I expect," Janine replied. "Here, he left this for you." She handed Naomi a letter with her name scrawled in a strong, dark hand.

Disappointment sank her spirits somewhat. She wanted to see her soon-to-be husband, to feel the comfort of his strong arms around her, keeping her safe.

Remembering how he'd appeared like her own champion atop a destrier and brought a swift and decisive end to Henri's torment helped her feel a little better. She turned the note over in her hands. A love letter, perhaps?

Brenna appeared and Aunt Janine slipped out. While her maid went to fetch water for washing, Naomi broke the seal on Jordan's letter.

There wasn't much to it. Only a couple dozen words. Just a few lines to shatter her heart.

Chapter Twenty-Two

It was a heavy-hearted Isabelle who slipped into the master bedchamber. Well, she tried to slip in. Her enormous belly clipped the door and flung it wide open.

Marshall, wrapped in a dressing gown, sat before the fire in his favorite chair, a glass of brandy dangling from his fingertips. Lean, bare legs stretched toward the warmth of the hearth. Firelight danced across his features, highlighting his striking profile. Strong cheekbones and a straight nose revealed his aristocratic blood. A finger absently traced the bottom of his sensual lips.

Despite the night's sorrows, Isabelle felt a flutter in her chest at the sight of her beautiful husband.

As she crossed the room, he set his glass aside. Without an exchange of words, he knew she needed the comfort of his arms. "How is she?" he asked as he settled her into his lap.

Nestling her head beneath his chin, Isabelle took a few seconds to breathe in his warm, musky scent. Strong, slender fingers worked into her hair and lightly grazed her scalp. She melted into his touch, content to let him hold the weight of her ungainly body.

"Caro is with her now, but I don't think she'll succeed where we have not. Naomi didn't tell me anything you don't already know."

Marshall grunted. "It was the same when I brought her home. She slept most of the way and held Aunt Janine's hand whenever she was awake. The letter Jordan sent me was harrowing enough. Living through the ordeal was certainly far more traumatic. Given that this is the second time she's endured something like this . . ."

A shudder racked his body. Isabelle knew he was fearful for his sister's health. In time, the shocking bruises and cuts marring her body would heal. It was her spirit Isabelle was worried about. She hoped this experience hadn't damaged the sweet nature that made Naomi the bright heart of their family.

A certain someone kicked her spleen; Isabelle winced. "Maybe the baby will help cheer Naomi. I, for one, can't wait to hold this little one in my arms rather than in my torso. I look forward to letting the rest of you share the burden, too."

Marshall's lips twitched. His broad hand spread over her belly. For a few minutes, they were quiet and still, both of them marveling at the movement of the infant in her womb. For the larger part, the shine had worn off of pregnancy. Isabelle was tired and achy all the time. She couldn't have a cup of tea without running for the privy, to say nothing of how every sip or bite of food set off blazing dyspepsia. Still, moments like these helped her remember the magic of new life. Everything else was relegated to background noise as she was washed in love for her husband and child. It was truly humbling, and she prayed Naomi might find the same healing peace in her life.

*

By her reckoning, Naomi had been home a week. It took some figuring to arrive at that conclusion, as days and nights blurred together in the haze surrounding her. Marshall had come for her the morning after she'd awakened. It felt to her that it had been only a week since the *Incident*, but then she had to figure back in the four days she'd lost in a drugged sleep.

Eleven days, then.

In the grand scheme of things, eleven days was no time at all, but it felt as though her heart had been broken forever.

Eleven days ago, Jordan had put words to paper calling off their blip of an engagement. He'd left her while she slept, oblivious to the pain that would make all her injuries put together seem like a stubbed toe by comparison. Part of Naomi wished she could return to that blissful place of unknowing. She would gladly relive every one of her hellish nightmares, if only her heart could feel whole again.

This has been a terrible mistake. I cannot marry you. You won't believe me, but this is for the best. Please do not argue the point. I'm so sorry for everything that transpired.

Within a minute of opening the note, she'd committed it to memory. Inside an hour, it was branded onto her heart, pulsing anguish into her bloodstream with every beat.

It was all she could do to keep the darkness from overwhelming her. She tried to fortify herself against the pain, attempted to build a wall around her heart. Sometimes, she felt blissfully numb. Other times, like now, despair found chinks in the mortar and flooded her until she almost choked on it.

A harsh inhalation dragged down her throat to inflate unwilling lungs.

Isabelle's fork clattered on her plate. A hand shot out to grasp Naomi's arm. "Are you all right?"

Naomi blinked slowly and looked around the breakfast table. The anxious eyes of her family took in her untouched food and the dark circles beneath her eyes. She knew they were worried.

Most of her bruises had faded to a yellowish-green, and the bridge of her nose was just a bit swollen. Her melancholy was their primary concern now. They all believed the Incident to be the source of her depression, and she let them continue in that misapprehension. She hadn't told anyone what had transpired between Jordan and herself, and she wouldn't.

Nothing happened. She recalled his forceful insistence that she deny the garden shed shooting, couched in the guise of lessons for carrying on a liaison. Part of such an affair was, evidently, denial. To act as if it had never happened. To deny him. To deny *them.*

Could she deny her love? He was all too ready to deny his, if, in fact, he'd ever actually felt anything for her. How could she be sure, when he so easily threw her over after she'd given him her virginity?

After he'd promised her marriage? A true gentleman never broke off an engagement. Never.

She prodded listlessly at the fried potatoes on her plate. Naomi had no appetite for food, or anything else.

"There you are!" Isabelle said, rising from her seat. "Did you sleep well?"

Naomi followed her sister-in-law's progress across the morning room as she greeted two newcomers. The Viscount and Viscountess Thorburn stopped just inside the door to accept Isabelle's welcome. Marshall, Aunt Janine, Sir Randell, and Caro all stood, as well.

Naomi frowned. "Lily?" She rose and drifted to the congregated friends. Lily took Naomi's hands and kissed her cheeks.

The viscountess looked lovely in a morning dress of rich ivory patterned with crimson roses. Her chestnut hair fell in loose waves to just beneath her ample bosom, with the top portion held back by combs.

"What are you doing here?" Naomi asked. "When did you arrive?"

Isabelle stepped back from accepting handsome Ethan Helling's warm greetings and touched Naomi's shoulder. "They arrived late last night. I told you several days ago that Lily and Ethan would be joining us. Remember?"

The too-bright smile told Naomi she *should* remember. But she didn't. Every day was a blank slate. Naomi awoke remembering nothing past the letter.

Lily put her arm around Naomi and hugged her shoulders. "Never mind that. We're all together now. Naomi, you and I will have our hands full with a nephew or niece to spoil senseless." The tall lady led Naomi toward the buffet. "What's good for breakfast? Let's see . . . bacon, kidneys, porridge, e—*hurr*." Lily made a heaving sound. She clapped her hand over her mouth and ran from the room.

Ethan Helling, Viscount Thorburn, spread a cat-that-got-the-cream grin around the room. "Surprise!" he exclaimed, his slate-blue eyes dancing with delight. "We're expecting, too." A second of silence was followed by exclamations of congratulations.

Naomi mouthed the right words, but she couldn't put any real heart behind her felicitations. While her dearest friends were happily married and expanding their families, Naomi felt lonelier than she ever had before. If she couldn't have marriage and children with Jordan, then she simply would never have them at all.

*

Several days later, a fire crackled in the drawing-room hearth. Naomi stared into the flames, her eyes parched from the heat. Still, she kept her lids open, forcing her vision to offer up a glimpse of the only face she cared to see. If a hot tear slid down her cheek, dry eyes were certainly the culprit.

Elsewhere in the room, someone sighed heavily.

"The rest of you may act like there's been a death in the family," Lily said testily, "but there hasn't been, and I won't. Out with it, Naomi."

Isabelle waved a hand at her best friend. "Hush, Lily. She doesn't have to talk about it unless she wants to."

Lily snorted. "Being a good hostage is old hat to our Naomi by now. If any of us is equipped to handle such a situation with aplomb, it's your sister. No, I don't think that's the trouble."

Naomi scowled even more fiercely at the fireplace. Lily was just an irritating noise in the background. No words could touch the fortification around her heart.

"Of course, the trouble is a man," Lily continued. "They instigate most of the world's ills, so I always look to that sex first when seeking to determine the source of any particular problem."

Traitorously, Naomi's lips twitched.

"Ah-ha!" Lily exclaimed in triumph. "I knew it." She wiggled in her seat. "Now, then, as Jordan Atherton was by far the most intriguing gentleman at this house party, I'd wager that's where we can lay the blame for the tormented state of the soul before us, Isabelle." Lily paused. "How have I done, Naomi?" she asked coolly. "Are you in love with Lord Freese?"

At last, Naomi blinked. Balls of light slid across the backs of her eyelids. "Yes," she confirmed in a hollow voice.

There was a long silence in the drawing room. Naomi let her eyes rehydrate and tried not to think about what was coming next.

A gentle hand touched her elbow. Naomi's eyelids fluttered open to see Isabelle crouching at her side, golden wisps framing a face etched with concern. "You can tell us anything, dear," Isabelle said. "We love you and only want to help you however we can."

Naomi flinched away from the compassion dripping from Isabelle's words. Usually, her sister-in-law's soft heart was one of the things Naomi loved best about her. But she couldn't stand it right now. Not when she felt as raw as a flayed corpse.

Lily appeared in front of Naomi, her arms crossed beneath her breasts. The firelight behind her licked her hair with flashes of bronze, like a slightly tarnished halo. "Am I correct in assuming he does not return your regard?"

In her mind, she saw the look in his eyes when he'd asked her to marry him. She heard him say he loved her. She'd believed it all. But that letter . . ." I'm sorry, Lily, I'm not sure how to answer you."

Lily pursed her lips. "I don't mean to be crass, but— Well, yes, I suppose I do mean to be crass. Were you intimate with Lord Freese?"

Naomi felt something. Finally. A spark of defiance shot through her, hot and bright. She met Lily's sardonic expression with a fierce one of her own. "That's none of your business, Lily Bachman," she seethed.

Lily smirked. "Good for you, dear," she drawled. "He'll come around any moment now."

Isabelle gasped. "I swear, Lily, the things that come out of your mouth! Can you not guard your tongue for five minutes?"

Shaking her head, Lily cocked her hip and draped a hand against her collarbone. "I really cannot," she said, totally unrepentant. "My unguarded tongue has brought me more good fortune than misery, so I feel no incentive to curtail myself. Besides," she said, her brows shifting sinuously above chocolate eyes, "my lord husband has a great fondness for my tongue."

Naomi chuckled. It was the first time she'd laughed since the Incident. The sound felt wrong in her throat and came out a little too guttural.

Isabelle rolled her eyes at Lily. Turning back to Naomi, she squeezed her hands. "Naomi, if you've been with Lord Freese, then you must marry him."

Naomi's chin jutted out mulishly. "I've confirmed nothing."

"You haven't denied it, either," Isabelle gently pointed out. "We don't judge you; we're only trying to help. Dearest, is there any chance you might be . . . increasing?"

The question slammed into Naomi and left her lips curiously numb. With child? Her? "My courses haven't come yet, but they're just a few days late. I've been under such strain since . . . It's natural for things to be a little out of sorts at a time like this."

Isabelle and Lily exchanged a worried glance.

*

The Right Honorable Robert Stewart, Viscount Castlereagh was becoming a right honorable pain in Jordan's arse. Once again, the Foreign Secretary was not to be found in his office. With his scheduled departure date for the Vienna Congress fast approaching, Jordan knew the man had buckets of official work to do, but Jordan hadn't been able to see him in a week.

He pulled on his black calfskin gloves and turned his greatcoat collar up against the fine mist as he walked down the bustling London street, all the while fuming over the treatment he'd received—or not—from his superior.

For so long, he'd wanted to be relieved of his assignment, but he'd never imagined it would end as it had. The young duke had been entrusted to Jordan's care at the tender age of eleven, a slender boy with wide, trusting eyes and the plump, rosy cheeks of a porcelain figurine. He'd provided the boy with his own, small household to tend his apartment. Uncle Randell, without the benefit of knowing Henri's true identity, had happily taken him under his wing. Had the arrangement held a few years longer, Jordan had even planned to bring Henri (in the guise of Enrique, of course) to London for a closely supervised introduction to society. He knew Henri had been lonely, but his safety had had to come first. No matter that keeping a young nobleman in a gilded cage was hell for all involved, it was Jordan's duty.

The fatal error, of course, had been allowing Henri's tutor to accompany him to Lintern Abbey. Jordan had argued for a clean break from anyone who knew him, but Castlereagh had insisted that keeping his own tutor would allow Henri an easier transition into his new life. It might have worked out, had Bertrand not been a secret supporter of a regicidal faction dedicated to reinstalling a miniature Corsican as Emperor of France. But he had been.

And so Jordan had spent a harrowing three days transporting the boy he'd watched grow from a child to a young man to London, under armed guard.

Jordan had failed. He'd successfully brought down the ring of Bonapartists, but doing so had uncovered his abject failure to see what had been happening under his own roof. Naomi was right. Jordan should have given Henri more time. He should have been more involved. Had he been, he might have realized Bertrand had been leading his pupil down the primrose path to high treason.

Given the strain this had put on Jordan, he'd hoped for more from the Foreign Secretary than a sniff and a nod at his report. A pat on the back and a distracted, "I'll be in touch," had sent Jordan on his way. Fitzhugh Ditman had been asked to stay behind, Jordan recalled with a twinge of rancor. He didn't doubt but that Fitz was packing his bags for another plum assignment on distant shores, while Jordan was left hanging in the breeze.

Even as he traversed Pall Mall on his way to St. James's Street, the normal, teeming morass of Londoners made the corner of Jordan's eye twitch. He couldn't get images out of his mind of foreign combatants on his own estate. French and English blood mingled on Yorkshire soil. Anyone could be an enemy. That man on the corner hawking pies might have baked a coded missive into one of the crusts, to be handed off to another seemingly innocuous individual. Any whore might be collecting state secrets between the sheets.

St. James's Street was a little less chaotic, and he drew a deep breath. The cool brick and stone façades of elegant shops and clubs bespoke an orderliness his life lacked. He stopped beneath the coffee-mill sign outside Berry Bros. and Rudd. Just how long could he continue like this, floating from party to party, making merry with people he could never let get too close, waiting on the whim of a man who seemed to take sadistic pleasure in making Jordan dance to his tune?

Everything was better at home, he found himself thinking. There had been enemy agents crawling around his property. He'd shot his own man. Others had died. It had been the most intense few weeks of his life and, oddly, the happiest.

Because of Naomi.

Sucking in a sharp breath of cold, damp air, Jordan hurried on to his club. The faster he was there, the sooner he could find someone to lose a few hours with in drink, conversation, and cards. The sooner he was losing time, the more hastily he could dull the ache throbbing in his chest. It hadn't relented, not once, since he'd penned that letter. But sometimes he could dampen his awareness of it.

"Good afternoon, Lord Freese," welcomed the doorman at White's. The knot in his chest eased a tiny bit. It wouldn't be long now. In a matter of moments, he'd be imbibing or gaming. He wouldn't have so much room in his head to think about all the ways he'd failed her or how being away from her left him feeling empty and somehow more trapped than any carriage ever had. He could, perhaps for an hour or so, set aside the guilt he felt for taking her innocence, as well as his pounding need for her sweet body. Every night, he relived their all-consuming encounters and dreamed of making slow, erotic love to his woman, of tasting every inch of her creamy skin and holding her in his arms while they slept. Every morning, he woke up hard and wanting and lonely.

A greeting called out from old Lord Bantam prompted Jordan to peel back his lips in a semblance of a smile. The wizened Tory firebrand was nearly swallowed by the soft cushions of his armchair. Though seated, he somehow managed to look down his impressive scythe of a nose at Jordan while he waggled the end of his walking stick. "There's no deference for your elders anymore. Snarl at me all you like, young man, but I'll go to sleep knowing I've put forth an honest effort for king and country this day. While I was advising the prime minister on matters of taxation this morning, you likely did nothing more strenuous than extend your leg for your tailor's consideration."

Jordan gritted his teeth in annoyance. Bantam's haughty disapproval of anyone he suspected of harboring sentiments of reform was renowned. He could have given the man a lecture on all Jordan had done in service to the crown in the last month, but everything he did for the Foreign Office was held in strict confidence. Besides, he thought, his consternation melting to grudging appreciation, Bantam had distracted Jordan from his woes, if only for a moment.

"Right you are, my lord," he said with a nod. "Although I must protest that my exertions were more strenuous than you imagine. Not only did I extend my leg, I pointed my toe, as well."

He spotted a group forming up for what looked to be a game of hazard. Jordan took his leave of the aged Tory. Plucking a glass of whiskey from a silver tray, he wove through chairs and tables, intent on losing time—if not too much money.

"Freese." It was a voice that knew it need not rise in volume to carry the tone of authority.

Jordan stuttered to a halt and whipped around. There sat Castlereagh, sipping a brandy and looking through the broadsheets, as casual as you please.

"Robert!" Jordan exclaimed. "I've just come from your office, where I learned that you were, yet again, away."

The Foreign Secretary's eyes sparked with amusement, but Jordan dared not laugh. "Here I am," he said, spreading his hands wide, "waiting for you, in fact."

A groan rolled up Jordan's throat. "Really, Castlereagh, this is beyond enough. You know I've been trying to see you. Why the devil didn't you just meet me at your office?"

There was something of the mischievous boy about Lord Castlereagh. His lips pouted just a bit, and his clipped hair tended toward a cowlick— albeit a steel-gray cowlick. "Try as I might, I cannot induce Whitehall to serve a decent beefsteak. Have a seat."

Jordan took the indicated chair adjoining Castlereagh's and dove straight to the salient points. "What's become of Henri?"

Castlereagh took a sip of his brandy and rolled it around his mouth. "The treasonous little duke has been shipped to his royal cousin, who shall decide his fate. Given his tender age, I suspect Louis will show mercy, although he'd be perfectly within his rights to have the lad hanged and quartered."

Jordan flinched inwardly at the picture those words painted. "He was just a youth without any companions but my uncle and his tutor. Exiled from home and reeled in with promises of power. It would be hard for any boy his age to resist."

The Foreign Secretary nodded. "I suspect that will be the king's view of events, as well. He knows his own hold on the throne is precarious. Can you imagine the public outcry if he had his young nephew executed? No, the boy will live to grow older and, hopefully, a little wiser." Castlereagh shifted in his seat. "Now, then. I suppose you know what this meeting is about."

Massaging the bridge of his nose, Jordan heard himself saying, "I don't suppose you're releasing me from service?"

Castlereagh chuckled. "You shan't be drummed out today. I'm pleased with how you handled the situation up north. Brought the bastards down with time to spare." His lips carved a cold smile. "But you're totally exposed now. You're spoiled for domestic work and probably anything on the Continent. I'd have to ship you across an ocean for fieldwork, which isn't beyond the realm of possibility. The last four years have been hard for you. I know you want to get into the field again."

Jordan gaped at his superior. "My lord—"

"Oh, one thing," the Foreign Secretary interjected. "Before you cast off for South America or Asia or wherever we decide to send you, I'd like you to accompany me to Vienna." When the man smiled this time, it touched his eyes. "The Congress should hear from you. This most recent incident will give them an idea of what Bonaparte is still capable of, and help steer the Allies' course."

Vienna. Not as a page and not even to collect intelligence, but as part of the official British delegation. And fieldwork abroad. To travel again, to immerse himself in a new culture . . . It was everything he wanted.

Almost.

Castlereagh clapped him on the shoulder. "You'll want to see about packing. We leave in three days."

For one crazed moment, Jordan considered going for Naomi. If she'd still have him, he'd marry her at once. She could accompany him to Vienna and then . . . And then . . .

Foreign fieldwork was for loners, like Fitzhugh Ditman. Like Jordan. A wife couldn't travel with a Foreign Office agent. She'd be a distraction at best. At worst . . . He remembered the sight of Naomi with a knife pressed to her throat, the paralyzing fear in his gut. There was no way he could expose her to that kind of risk. Never again.

With grim resolve, he stood and shook the Secretary's hand. "Thank you for the opportunity, my lord. I shall make my preparations at once."

Chapter Twenty-Three

Stepping into the Helmsdale nursery was like walking into a dollhouse, Naomi thought wistfully. All the furniture was scaled down in size to accommodate the diminutive stature of a young child. A dining table rested on short legs but was as finely crafted as the one downstairs in the dining room. Six Grecian-style chairs with squab cushions surrounded the table. She envisioned a sweet-faced girl hosting tea with her playmates. Or a full complement of Lockwood siblings squabbling over breakfast.

"The child isn't born yet, and he's already spoilt." Naomi's mother, the dowager duchess, stepped into the room and cast a gimlet eye at her surroundings. She sniffed in disapproval at small, plush chairs and ottomans arranged in a sitting area, but Naomi caught the softening of lines around her eyes and mouth. Caro was looking forward to finally becoming a grandmother. "I certainly never would have reduced myself to utilizing a chair of such absurd dimensions."

Naomi recalled how this room had looked when it was her nursery, all adult-sized furnishings to remind her she was small and out of place. The world did not bend to fit a child; rather, it was her duty to learn to fit into a grown-up world.

This nursery, though, was centered around a child's comfort. In this room, it was adults who would feel like outsiders. The only concession to the fully grown was a rocking chair near the fireplace. It was a bit too big for Isabelle and a bit too small for Marshall. A true compromise, then—a solution in which neither party was satisfied.

Soft voices in the corridor announced the arrival of Lily and Isabelle. "Isn't this darling?" Lily stepped around Naomi and Caro to coo over a toy rabbit with a velvet body and satin ears. "And the furnishings are all exquisite. Did you send away for them?"

"Most everything was made right here in the village." Isabelle sat in the rocking chair with a sigh of relief. Her hands cradled her belly. "I'm afraid we've been monopolizing the carpenter, Mr. Hardy, and both of his apprentices for the last two months."

While Isabelle showed Lily all the nursery's amenities, Naomi's mind drifted to Mr. Gillows, the carpenter in Lintern Village, who had been the first beneficiary of the charity pantry. She wondered whether he'd recovered from his injury. She couldn't help but imagine herself placing an order to outfit the Lintern Abbey nursery.

"But where is the cradle?" Lily's question cut into Naomi's daydream.

Isabelle looked radiant when she answered, "In our room. We want to keep the baby with us for a while, until we hire on a nurse. And we're not in any rush to do so."

"Won't you be using a wet nurse?" Lily inquired.

Shaking her head, the duchess pressed her toes into a soft, lambskin rug to continue rocking. "I want to feed the baby myself."

Caro strolled to the window, its casement freshly painted crisp white. "I never nursed any of my infants. Quite base, if you ask me, not to mention noblewomen tend toward thin milk. I suppose your low breeding is a boon in this one instance."

Behind Caro's back, Isabelle rolled her eyes at Naomi and Lily.

The tall brunette's mouth carved a mysterious smile. "I wonder if it's occurred to Ethan that he'll have to share my breasts with someone else."

The dowager duchess made a horrified sound. "I never!" she proclaimed in a scandalized tone. "Naomi," she said, "let us leave the common to their vulgar ruminations." She swept from the nursery without waiting to see if Naomi followed. Which, of course, she did not.

Naomi truly did love her mother, but even she could not deny how the very air in the room palpably relaxed once Caro quit the apartment.

"Isa," Lily said, pulling out one of the small dining chairs and perching precariously upon it, "do you suppose you might be a dear and have that baby today? We leave in the morning to return to Town.

Michaelmas term begins next week." She crossed her legs at the ankle and hooked them behind one leg of the chair.

"I'm quite willing," Isabelle assured her. "I'm not at all sure babies consider our preferences in deciding when to make their entrances. However, I shall have a word with the young lord or lady on your behalf."

"Your efforts are appreciated," Lily said with a laugh. She tossed a glance Naomi's way. "Are you to join our maternal ranks? Have your courses arrived yet?"

"Not yet," Naomi answered. "I don't believe there's anything to worry about, though." She'd awoken this morning with abdominal cramps, which always preceded the onset of her courses by about a day.

"That's good," Isabelle said. "You'll have lots of babies when the time is right."

Lily agreed, but Naomi only stared wistfully at a small, silver rattle on a shelf. The only man she cared to have children with had left her weeks ago, without so much as a word since. Jordan was gone. Naomi had to accept the fact, gather up the tattered remains of her life, and carry on.

*

In the end, it was all so simple. Jordan spent several days tying up business in London, and at the appointed time his carriage bore him away. Nerves had his toes tapping in the coach's chilly interior. His thumbnail worried at his cuticles. New adventures always made him anxious, and this surely qualified.

Once beyond the capital's sprawl, the coach picked up a little speed. Jordan tried without success to relax against the burgundy upholstery. His agitation was more of a surface disturbance, however. Deep down, he knew he had chosen the right course.

When he thought back over that final, dreadful day at Lintern Abbey, Jordan couldn't remember fighting for political stability. Duty never once crossed his mind. Earning accolades from the Foreign Secretary or serving the greater good were concepts which might have dwelt in a different universe.

That day, Jordan had fought for Naomi. He'd fought to protect her. He'd battled his way through the Frenchmen set to guard him and his men at the abbey ruins and pursued the fleeing agents to get Naomi back from her captors. Everything had been so clear. He'd known there was nothing he wouldn't do for her.

Later, he'd gotten fuddled up with ideas of keeping her safe, of fulfilling his duty to the Foreign Office, but he hadn't been thinking clearly. How was Naomi best served by Jordan staying away from her? How could he keep her safe if he wasn't actually with her? And besides, he'd realized, with a gnawing sense of dread, if he didn't marry that woman, someone else would. Jordan hated the thought of causing Naomi grief, but he'd damned well turn her into a widow before he let another man touch her.

The only home for Jordan would be with Naomi. The only children for him would be borne by her. The only bed he could sleep in would be the one he would share with his wife. He had to have her.

Castlereagh had offered Jordan everything he wanted. But Naomi Lockwood was everything he needed.

The journey lasted a small eternity of two days, but eventually he found himself in the parlor at Helmsdale, awaiting the entrance of his beloved. A large window granted him a view of distant, rolling hills and trees adorned with fall colors. The morning sky was leaden with dark, blue-gray clouds. Inside, a cozy fire and two oil lamps created a snug atmosphere. Jordan enjoyed the scenery, as well as the hot tea provided by the hospitable butler.

Noon was marked by the chiming of a clock on the mantel. On a base of black marble, a pretty shepherdess figurine lounged against the clock's movement with a lamb at her feet, gazing up adoringly. Jordan frowned at the insipid sheep. He'd already been waiting nearly half an hour.

Setting aside his teacup, he reached into his coat pocket to make sure he had his papers in order. Yes, there they were. He took them out just to double-check they were the correct ones. Of course they were. Christ, but he felt more nervous now than he had before his first tup.

"Jordan." It was Marshall's voice.

He turned with a smile in place to greet his old friend, only to meet thunderous fury in the duke's dark eyes. Then he was treated to the less pleasant sight of that same duke's fist flying at his face. The bone-jarring strike landed on his jaw. He tasted blood from a cut on the inside of his cheek. Jordan clapped a hand to his face and let out a strangled sound.

He fished out his handkerchief and released his bloody saliva into it. "Fair enough. I deserved that."

Marshall's younger brother, Lord Grant, had appeared at some point in the last five seconds while Jordan's head was ringing. Standing at about six feet tall, several inches shorter and a fair bit leaner than his brother and Jordan, Grant Lockwood still cut an imposing figure. Especially in his current, enraged state.

The younger man's shoulders rounded forward, his hands balled into fists the size of grapefruit. When he drew one back, Jordan couldn't help flinching, anticipating the blow. Hard as a stone, Grant's fist drove into his stomach, forcing out his breath. A sharp pain accompanied by a wave of nausea had Jordan doubled over, gasping for air.

"Goddamn you, Freese!" Marshall shouted. "*Keep her safe*, I said. *Just keep my sister safe.* You promised you would. You swore to defend her life with your own." Jordan propped his forearms on his knees and managed to raise his head enough to see his friend shaking and white-lipped. "Not only was she beaten and bloodied during your stupid mission, but you . . . *You.*" The word ripped from his throat and somehow managed to summarize all of Jordan's wrongdoings.

The duke flung his head back and dug his hands into his hair. "And now I have to call you out."

"Let me do it, Marshall." Grant cast Jordan a contemptuous glare. "Allow me to spare you the distasteful task of killing a friend."

The elder brother turned in a tight circle, hands on his hips. His chest rose and fell like a bellows. "Thank you, Grant, but I shall see to this myself. I would appreciate you acting as my second."

"Naturally."

All right, this had gone far enough. They were entitled to knock him around a bit for sullying Naomi's virtue, but he was here, damn it all. He'd come. "I'm not dueling either of you." He aimed for a moderate tone but went a bit wide of the mark, owing to his aching jaw and throbbing middle.

Grant stepped toe-to-toe with him. "We will have satisfaction," he seethed. "You have insulted our sister and *will* meet one of us on the field of honor."

Restraining the urge to roll his eyes at the hotheaded younger man, Jordan tried for reason. "Would you make a widow of Lady Naomi? I'm here to make things right, gentlemen."

Marshall paced around Jordan and Grant, circling, like a shark scenting blood. "My sister shall not be a widow for she is not married to you, nor shall she be, if she does not wish it." The deep baritone of his voice was clipped, each syllable undercut with indignation. "Years ago, I determined Naomi would be free to marry as she would, up to and including never marrying at all. Even if she had a child out of wedlock—or a dozen—she would be afforded my home and my protection. Always."

A surge of something primal pumped through Jordan's veins. He felt his grip on cool reason slipping. "Marshall, you could not deny me my child. If Naomi is increasing . . ." With a growl, he shoved Grant aside and pulled Marshall around to face him. "Is she, Marshall? Is Naomi pregnant?"

Marshall's nostrils flared, and he looked ready to plant another facer on Jordan.

Over the duke's shoulder, Jordan glimpsed a head of disarrayed, bronze hair appear in the doorway. Ethan Helling strolled in, took in the tense scene, and grinned. "Hello, Freese. I must say, the sight before me leaves me positively awash with . . ." He drummed his steepled fingers together beneath his chin. "*Schadenfreude*," he said with a snap. "I knew the Germans would come through for me." He sauntered over to a chair and sat, his long limbs lazily arranged, like a cheetah at rest. It wouldn't do to dismiss him, Jordan knew. Like the great cat, Thorburn could spring to action in the blink of an eye.

Jordan did not wish to fight all three men, but he would do it. He would tear this house apart brick by brick if anyone tried to keep him from his love, from Naomi. The thought that she might, even now, be pregnant with his son or daughter made him wild. He hadn't spilled inside her, but sometimes that wasn't precaution enough. He took a hasty, mental inventory of the parlor, looking for improvised weapons with which he could debilitate his adversaries—beginning with smashing that blasted clock into Thorburn's smug face. Just then, Ethan pointed to the floor at Jordan's feet.

"There's a paper on the rug. Did one of you drop it?"

Jordan snapped it up and shook it under Marshall's nose. "Special license, you idiot. Will you please give over this dueling nonsense and let me speak to Naomi? She wouldn't like it if your face is a wreck for the wedding."

Marshall snatched the slightly tattered document from his hand and smoothed it out. Some of the ire in his face drained away as he read it. "You're not good enough for her," he said without much heat.

"No," Jordan agreed. "But then again, neither is anyone else."

At that, Marshall's lips curved to one side. He clasped Jordan's hand for a firm shake. "I'll call off the hounds and let you speak to Naomi."

His grip tightened to a painful degree, while his smile remained in place. "If she won't have you, old man, I still may have to kill you."

*

Opening the parlor door, Naomi stopped in her tracks. Marshall hovered near the entrance, like a guard. Across the room, Jordan.

Just . . . Jordan.

There might have been descriptors to mark his dress or demeanor, but Naomi only registered his presence. In the weeks since she'd seen him, she must have forgotten the precise angle of his jaw and the contrast of his scar against his bronzed cheek, for neither were just as she remembered. He was gorgeous, always. But had his eyes always held such heat when he looked at her?

She pressed a hand to her middle, trying to calm the sudden onslaught of butterflies buffeting her from the inside.

Jordan likewise just stared, seeming to drink her in from a distance. Neither of them was ready to do more than revel in the nearness of the other.

Marshall cleared his throat. Naomi heard him, but her eyes could not leave Jordan. "Naomi," her brother said, "Lord Freese is here to speak with you." Her brother stepped in front of her, cutting off her visual access to Jordan. She huffed in annoyance and tried to step around, but his large hands on her arms put an end to her fidgeting. "Look at me, please."

Her gaze slid up his front to a face filled with love and concern.

"You know you're always welcome here," Marshall said.

Naomi's brow puckered. "No, I didn't know that. You said—"

"I said some things I wish I hadn't," her eldest sibling cut in. "But you *are* always welcome. This is your home, for as long as you want it to be. No matter what. Never think you must make a choice based on what you perceive to be my desires. I only desire what is best for you—and you're the best judge of that." Marshall squeezed her hands and kissed her cheek. Then he left the parlor and closed the door, leaving her alone with Jordan.

She felt unaccountably nervous. What if he rejected her again? Her heart wasn't strong enough to bear it.

"Would it help . . . ?" he started, his voice thick with emotion. He cleared his throat and began again. "Does knowing it was an international emergency help at all?"

Naomi shook her head.

Jordan took a step toward her. "What if I told you I've retired my position with the government? Would that make it better?"

She shook her head again and gasped a quiet cry.

"How about knowing I've been missing you all the time, wanting you to the point of physical pain?" Raw emotion marked every tense line of his tall, muscled physique as he stalked straight for her. "That I've been useless for anything because my heart will give me no peace, and I've had to stop myself on a dozen different occasions from abandoning my duty and coming to you? Does that alleviate your suffering?"

He stopped in front of her. A mere inch separated them. His warmth caressed her, while his scent of clean linen and sandalwood suffused her senses.

"No," Naomi murmured, tipping her head back to look at him.

A muscle in his jaw twitched. "What do you want from me, my love?"

"A kiss."

Before the words were well out of the gates, his lips were on hers.

What started tender and welcoming quickly intensified. Jordan wrapped an arm around her waist and pulled her against him. His mouth slanted, and his thumb tugged her chin, urging her lips apart. Naomi clung to his shoulders as velvet tongues slipped past each other, caressing and exploring.

Oh, he felt so good. His hard muscles tensing and straining for her. His arms and hands holding her so close.

Jordan kissed her jaw and down her neck, his mouth trailing fire on her skin.

"I missed you," she whispered breathlessly. "Every day, I felt like I was dying."

His answering groan was agonized. "I'm so sorry." His big hands gripped her hips, and he rested his forehead on hers. "Please believe I only did it to keep you safe. I hated that you'd been hurt. I couldn't stand the thought of you ever being in harm's way again, even if it meant I couldn't have you."

"Shh." Naomi hushed him with a soft kiss.

Beginning at her face, Jordan's hands traced Naomi's body. His fingertips glided over her throat and shoulders, down to her hands, then back up the underside of her arms. Pleasurable sparks danced across Naomi's skin. When he reached her underarms, Jordan rolled his hands to palm her breasts, squeezing them in turn and teasing her taut nipples through her clothes. Her back arched, wordlessly requesting more of the same. But he wasn't done yet. After giving her breasts their due, he spread his fingers wide and ran down her ribcage. His hands spanned the distance from hip to breast.

His nose dipped to trace her throat, her collarbone. Slowly, he sank, bending his knees to follow with his nose the path of his hands. At last, he knelt at her feet, with his arms wrapped around her, his hands flowing over the curves of her thighs and calves. His nose pressed into the juncture of her legs.

She gasped; he moaned. Naomi's fingers threaded into his hair for support.

"I love you, Naomi." His scorching eyes raked up her front to settle on hers. "I want to take you back to Lintern Abbey and make you my viscountess. I want to make a home with you. I want to make children with you. I want to worship your body with mine every day. And every night." He playfully nipped at her hip. "I want to give you Clara for a mother-in-law and Kate for a sister-in-law, and I want to warn off my father when the hugs he'll give you last too long. I want Lady Janine for my aunt. I want your brothers for my own, and God help me, I even want Caro, because having her for my mother-in-law means I've succeeded in making you my wife, and nothing could make me happier."

Joyous tears slid unheeded down Naomi's cheeks. She held Jordan's face in her hands and felt such love washing over her. He hadn't offered her jewels or dresses or his place in society. He'd offered her everything she ever wanted—love and a home and family of her own.

There was only The Question remaining.

"Oh!" A surprised yelp came from just outside the parlor, followed by a plaintive, "Naomi? Can you hear me in there? I could use some assistance."

Sniffing and wiping a hand across her cheeks, Naomi's head turned to the door. "That's Isabelle. I must see . . . ," she said apologetically.

She opened the parlor door. At first, she wasn't sure what she was seeing. Isabelle stood just about five feet down the corridor with a shocked expression on her face. She was hunched over a bit, her arms wrapped across her abdomen. She met Naomi's questioning expression, then her eyes drifted down.

Naomi followed the direction of her gaze. Isabelle's pale pink slippers were splashed with liquid. In fact, the duchess was standing in a puddle.

"Oh!" Naomi gasped, echoing Isabelle's surprise from a moment ago. She took Isabelle's arm and led her toward the stairs. "Jordan!" she called behind her.

"Is everything all right?" he asked, looking from her to Isabelle, to the puddle, and back again.

"Everything is wonderful," Naomi said. A broad grin spread on her face. "I need you to find Marshall. Tell him he's about to become a father."

*

Edwin Alexander Trevelyan Grantham Lockwood, Marquess Keighdon, future Duke of Monthwaite, and adorable infant, attempted to straighten his legs in the confines of his swaddling blanket. He yawned, displaying a shell-pink tongue and bitty gums. The little squeak he emitted had every female in the room cooing.

His Aunt Naomi touched her nose to his forehead and inhaled deeply. Little Edwin was warm and soft and perfect, and emitted that mysterious baby smell that made every maternal instinct in her body leap to attention.

"Are you sure you don't want me to hold him in here?" she asked her brother and sister-in-law.

In the bed a short distance away, illuminated by several candelabras and oil lamps, Isabelle's sweat-damp face beamed at her son. Her nigh trail was unselfconsciously open at the top, rumpled linen parted to reveal pale skin. Marshall, foregoing all claims to dignity, had shucked his boots and coat and sat on the bed beside his wife, clutching her hand and wiping her hair back from her brow. His face was taut with worry.

As these things went, Isabelle's labor hadn't been too bad. Naomi had felt privileged when Isabelle had asked her to stay. She'd done whatever she could to assist the midwife and comfort Isabelle, from making compresses, to ordering more hot water from the kitchen, to holding Isabelle's hand and encouraging her while she pushed. Seven hours after Isabelle's bag of waters ruptured, the tiny marquess had made his squalling appearance.

Everything was joy and smiles until the afterbirth. When the placenta came, it brought along a frightening quantity of blood. And the blood had kept coming. A few minutes later, Isabelle had gone ghastly white and her eyes rolled back in her head.

Marshall, who had come in to meet his son only ten minutes before, now saw his wife slipping away before his very eyes. "No! Isabelle, please

God, no!" He scooped her head and shoulders up, cradling her to his chest while he pleaded with her to stay with him.

"Put her head down!" Naomi snapped. "You'll make it worse." Bewildered and clearly in shock, Marshall did as she said, although his stream of endearments and curses and prayers continued unabated.

The midwife ordered Naomi to hold linen between Isabelle's legs while she ran for her bag of herbs. She produced a tincture of shepherd's purse and coaxed some of it down Isabelle's throat.

"Roll her to her left side," the midwife had instructed Marshall.

"And put the baby to breast," Naomi had added, recalling the chapter in her French book that dealt with post-natal emergencies.

Now, an hour later, Marshall did not seem inclined to leave his recovering wife's side for even a minute. "No, let Edwin meet the others." Marshall's eyes still looked haunted. "Oh, and please have something brought for Isabelle to eat. She can eat now, yes?" he inquired of the midwife.

"Aye," the midwife said from the foot of the bed, where she was washing her hands in yet another basin of hot water, "some blood pudding, if you have it, or a rare beefsteak." The older woman regarded Naomi. "You've a knack for midwifing, my lady. We make a fine team."

"We do, indeed," Naomi agreed with a smile.

"Naomi," Isabelle called in a tired voice. *Thank you*, her sister-in-law mouthed.

In the parlor, where Jordan's proposal had been interrupted, everyone gathered together, waiting for news. As one, when Naomi walked into the room, the group surged to their feet and formed a semicircle around her.

While they aww'ed and cooed over Edwin and asked after Isabelle, Naomi looked at the faces of the people she loved. Caro and Grant. Lily and Ethan. Aunt Janine and Sir Randell. They were a cobbled-together bunch, but they were family. Her family.

Behind the group stood Jordan, who hadn't eyes for the infant in her arms, only for Naomi. Quiet pride and love illuminated his entire being. This man, whose devastating smile and witty charm could seduce a ballroom full of women, now had no words. His eyes said everything Naomi needed to hear.

Gently, she passed her nephew to his grandmama. Then she took Jordan's hand and led him upstairs.

*

On such a night as this, Naomi thought as her lover slowly removed her clothes, layer by layer, she couldn't ask for another thing in the world. The baby was safely arrived. Isabelle would recover with some rest and good food, and the house was full of love.

Best of all, she had Jordan. This morning, she hadn't dared hope he would come back. It had hurt too much to dream. But here he was, standing shirtless behind her, tilting her head to the side so he could kiss the hollow where neck and shoulder meet, as though they'd never parted.

Jordan worked the fine muslin of her chemise back and forth across her nipples. The friction was exquisite on those sensitized nubs. His hands slipped beneath the material on her shoulders and pushed the chemise down her arms. It fell in a soft heap at her feet.

"My God, you're beautiful." His voice rumbled in his chest, sending a shiver up her spine. She leaned back against his chest, loving the feel of his warm arms wrapping around her, of his hands sliding over her skin. Those big hands cupped her bottom. He grunted appreciatively. "You have an arse to make men weep, my love. And these hips, lush. Just right for holding." The stiff bar of his erection strained against his breeches and pressed against the cleft between her buttocks. "Just right for . . ."

Suddenly, he went still. His hands slid around to her belly and gently, reverently cradled her flesh.

Naomi's heart constricted at his unspoken question. "Maybe," she confessed. "It's still too early to be sure." Those cramps had come to nothing, and her courses were a week late.

Jordan's fingers curled. He hugged her tight from behind then turned her around and pulled her against his chest. "I hope so," he murmured against the top of her head. "Is it wrong for me to hope for it, when we aren't married? If so, bollocks to that. I'm hoping, anyway."

Her nails grazed over his chest. She admired the muscles rippling beneath her fingers. "But we will be married." Fascinated with his body, she played with the crisp hair sprinkled across his chest, and followed a trail down through the cleft between his abdominal muscles. Her finger dipped into his navel and resumed traveling the road until it disappeared into his breeches.

Jordan was nearly purring under her caresses. "You're damn right, we'll be married. I brought a special license. Did I get around to telling you that?" His breathing kicked into a faster tempo.

Naomi worked the buttons on the fall of his breeches. "No," she said, beginning to feel pressure mounting between her thighs. "You neglected to mention it." She pushed his breeches down his lean hips, letting her fingers splay over his steely buttocks and then to his heavily muscled thighs.

He kicked out of his clothes and put his hands on her hips, walking her backward to the bed. His mouth claimed hers in an open, hungry kiss. His tongue pressed deep into her mouth, thrusting and withdrawing, just as he thrust against her lower belly.

Naomi fell back onto the mattress, and he fell with her. She scooted back and he crawled forward, never once breaking their kiss. When they arrived at the bank of pillows by the headboard, she sank down and started to wrap her legs around his hips. She needed to feel him inside her. Needed to express her love in this timeless dance.

"Not yet, love," he whispered, his breath hot against her ear. "Remember I said I want to worship your body every day and every night?" He latched on to a nipple and drew it deep into his mouth, rolling it between his tongue and palate. She arched into his ministrations. Her fingers threaded in his black curls, holding him close. "I'm starting now," he rasped. His tongue dipped in the hollow between her breasts. "Right now." He flashed her an erotic smile touched with mischief. "This is going to take a while, Naomi. I hope you have a while to give me."

She did.

More from This Author

A SNEAK PEEK FROM CRIMSON ROMANCE

From *Once an Heiress* by Elizabeth Boyce

Once an *Heiress*

Elizabeth Boyce

Author of *Once a Duchess* and *Once an Innocent*

Chapter One

Lily Bachman squared her shoulders, lifted her chin, and drew a deep breath. Behind the study door was another dragon to slay—or perhaps this one would be more like a pesky dog to shoo off. Whatever the case, one thing was certain; in that room, she'd find a man after her money. He was the fourth this Season, and it was only the end of March.

She smoothed the front of her muslin dress with a quick gesture, and then opened the door.

The Leech, as she dubbed all of them, halted whatever nonsense he was blathering on about and turned at the sound of the door opening, his jaw hanging slack, paused in the action of speaking. Her father sat on the sofa, situated at a right angle to the chair inhabited by the would-be suitor.

"Darling." Mr. Bachman rose. "You're just in time. This is Mr. Faircloth."

Lily pressed her cheek to his. "Good morning, Father."

Mr. Bachman and Lily were close in height. He was of a bit more than average height for a man, while Lily was practically a giantess amongst the dainty aristocratic ladies. She stuck out like a sore thumb at parties, towering over every other female in the room—just another reason she detested such functions.

The man, Mr. Faircloth, also stood. He was shorter than Lily and lacked a chin. The smooth slope marking the transition from jaw to neck was unsettling to look upon. He wore mutton-chop sideburns, presumably an attempt to emphasize his jawline. They failed miserably in that regard, serving rather to point out the vacant place between them where a facial feature should have been.

"My . . ." Mr. Faircloth wrung his hands together and cleared his throat. "My dear Miss Bachman," he started again. "How lovely you look this morning."

Lily inclined her head coolly. She settled onto the sofa and folded her hands in her lap. Mr. Bachman sat beside her and gestured Mr. Faircloth to his chair.

Mr. Faircloth cast an apprehensive look between Lily and her father. "I'd thought, sir, that you and I would speak first. Then, if all was agreeable, I would speak to Miss . . ." He lowered his eyes and cleared his throat again.

Good, Lily thought viciously. He was already thrown off balance. She knew from experience that when dealing with fortune hunters and younger sons, one had to establish and maintain the upper hand.

"When it comes to my daughter's future," Mr. Bachman said in a rich baritone, "there is no such thing as a private interview. Miss Bachman is a grown woman; she's entitled to have a say in her own future. Would you not agree?"

Mr. Faircloth squirmed beneath the intense gazes of father and daughter. "Well, it's not how these things are usually handled, sir, but I suppose there's no real harm in bucking convention just this—"

"Mr. Faircloth," Lily interrupted.

The man swallowed. "Yes?"

"I don't recognize you at all." She raised her brows and narrowed her eyes, as though examining a distasteful insect. "Have we met?"

"I, well, that is . . . yes, we've met." Mr. Faircloth's head bobbed up and down. "We were introduced at the Shervingtons' ball last week. I asked you to dance."

As he spoke, Lily stood and crossed the room to her father's desk. She retrieved a sheaf of paper and a pen, and then returned to her seat. She allowed the silence to stretch while she jotted down notes: name, physical description, and first impression. *Younger son,* she decided, *a novice to fortune hunting.* She glanced up with the pen poised above the paper. "And did I accept your invitation?"

Mr. Faircloth gave a nervous smile. "Ah, no, actually. You were already spoken for the next set and every one thereafter." He pointed weakly toward her notes. "What are you writing there?"

She leveled her most withering gaze on him. "Are you or are you not applying for my hand in matrimony?"

His jaw worked without sound, and then his face flushed a deep pink. "I, yes. That is why I've come, I suppose you could say."

"You suppose?" Lily scoffed. "You're not sure?"

"Yes." Mr. Faircloth drew himself up, rallying. "Yes, I'm sure. That's why I've come."

So there is a bit of spine in this one, after all, Lily thought. "That being the case," she replied, giving no quarter in her attack, "it is reasonable for me to keep a record of these proceedings, is it not? You are not the first gentleman to present himself."

Mr. Faircloth sank back into himself. "I see."

"Tell me, what prompted your call today?" Lily tilted her head at an inquisitive angle, as though she were actually interested in the man's answer.

Mr. Faircloth cast a desperate look at Mr. Bachman.

"That's a fair question," her father said. Lily loved many things about her father, but the one she appreciated more than anything was the way he treated her like a competent adult. Most females were bartered off to the man who made the highest offer, either through wealth or connections. When he spoke up for her, supporting her line of questioning, Lily wanted to throw her arms around his neck and hug him. Later, she would. Right now, they had to eject the newest swain from their home.

Mr. Faircloth grew more and more agitated with every passing second. He fidgeted in his seat and finally blurted, "I love you!"

Lily drew back, surprised by the tactic her opponent employed. She waved a dismissive hand. "Don't be ridiculous."

"It's true," Mr. Faircloth insisted. "From the moment I saw you, I thought you were the most beautiful woman at the ball. Your gown was the most flattering blue—"

"I wore red," Lily corrected.

Mr. Faircloth blinked. "Oh." He rested his elbows on his knees, and his head drooped between his shoulders.

He was crumbling. Time to finish him off.

"Let's talk about why you've really come, shall we?" Lily's tone was pleasant, like a governess explaining something to a young child with limited comprehension. "You're here because of my dowry, just like the other men who have suddenly found themselves stricken with love for me."

"A gentleman does not discuss such matters with a lady," Mr. Faircloth informed his toes.

"A *gentleman*," Lily said archly, "does not concoct fantastical tales of undying affection in the hopes of duping an unwitting female into marriage. Tell me, sir, which son are you?"

"I have two older brothers," he said in a defeated tone.

Lily duly made note of this fact on her paper. "And sisters?"

"Two."

"Ah." Lily raised a finger. "Already an heir and a spare, and two dowries besides. That doesn't leave much for you, does it?" She tutted and allowed a sympathetic smile.

Mr. Faircloth shook his head once and resumed his glum inspection of his footwear.

"I understand your predicament," Lily said. "And how attractive the idea of marrying money must be to a man in your situation." She tilted her head and took on a thoughtful expression. "Have you considered a different approach?"

The gentleman raised his face, his features guarded. "What do you mean?"

She furrowed her brows together. "What I mean is this: Have you considered, perhaps, a profession?"

Mr. Faircloth's mouth hung agape. He looked from Lily to Mr. Bachman, who sat back, passively observing the interview.

"It must rankle," Lily pressed, "to see your eldest brother's future secured by accident of birth and to see your sisters provided for by virtue of their sex. But do consider, my dear Mr. Faircloth, that younger sons the Empire 'round have bought commissions and taken orders, studied law or medicine, accepted government appointments. The time has come," she said, pinning him beneath her fierce gaze, "for you to accept the fact that yours is not to be a life of dissipated leisure. Instead of hoping for a fortune to fall into your lap, your days would be better spent pursuing a profession."

Mr. Faircloth wiped his palms down his thighs. "Miss Bachman, you've quite convinced me."

She blinked. "Have I?"

"Yes," he said. "I am well and truly convinced that marriage to you would be a nightmare from which I should never awake until I die. Sir," he turned his attention to Mr. Bachman, "I see now why you offer such a large dowry for your daughter." He stood. "It would take an astronomical sum to make the proposition of marriage to such a controlling, unpleasant female the slightest bit appealing."

Lily's mouth fell open. "Why, you—"

Her father laid a restraining hand on her arm. Lily exhaled loudly and pinched her lips together.

"Thank you for your time, Mr. Bachman." Mr. Faircloth inclined his head. "Miss Bachman." He hurried from the parlor. A moment later, the front door closed behind him.

"Well!" Lily exclaimed. "Of all the sniveling, puffed up—"

"You wore blue," Mr. Bachman cut in.

"I beg your pardon?"

"The Shervingtons' ball. You wore blue, just as Mr. Faircloth said." He stood and crossed to his desk where he poured himself a brandy from a decanter.

"Did I?" Lily murmured. "I could have sworn I wore red." She tapped a finger against her lips.

"No, darling," Mr. Bachman said with a sigh, "you wore blue. I'm quite certain, because your mother fretted that the color washed you out and no gentleman would notice you."

"Ah, well," Lily said. She rose and briskly rubbed her palms together. "It doesn't signify. One more Leech gone."

Mr. Bachman's chest heaved and heavy, graying brows furrowed over his dark eyes. "My dear, you cannot continue in this fashion. You know I'll not force you to marry against your will. But marry you must, and it *is* my desire that your marriage elevate this family's status."

Lily straightened a pile of papers on the desk as he spoke; her hands paused at this last remark. Indignation mingled with hurt slammed into her like a physical blow. She idly slid a paper back and forth across the polished desk and kept her eyes studiously upon it as she recovered, hiding the force of her emotions behind a casual demeanor. However, she could not fully suppress the bitterness in her voice when she spoke. "Fortunate, then, that Charles died. A mere ensign and son of a country squire would not have provided the upward mobility you crave."

Mr. Bachman's glass boomed against the desk. "Young lady, guard your tongue!" Her eyes snapped to his mottled face. His own dark eyes flashed rage, and his nostrils flared. "Had poor Charles returned from Spain, I would have proudly and happily given you in wedlock. Indeed, it was my fondest wish to unite our family with the Handfords."

A humorless laugh burst from Lily's lips. Turning, she twitched her skirts in a sharp gesture. "A fact you made sure to educate me upon from the earliest. I spent the whole of my life with the name of my groom and date of my wedding drilled into my head."

It was an unfair accusation, she knew, even as it flew from her mouth. Yes, she had been betrothed to Charles Handford since time out of mind, but for most of her life, it was simply a fact she'd memorized, along with the color of the sky and the sum of two and two.

There'd been plenty of visits with their neighbors, the Handfords, but Charles was ten years her senior and rarely present. Her earliest memories of him were his visits home from Eton and Oxford, and later, leaves from his lancer regiment.

Their betrothal only became more relevant as her twentieth birthday neared, bringing the planned summer wedding that was to follow on its heels—an event postponed when Charles's regiment could not spare him, and which was never to be after he died that autumn.

The silence stretched while her father regained his composure. Gradually, the angry red drained from his face. "Now, Lily," he said in a more moderate tone, "I'll not be portrayed as some chattel dealer, looking to hoist you off without a care for your feelings. Since last year was your first Season—and you just out of mourning—I did not push the issue. I still wish you to make your own match. The only stipulation I have placed is that the gentleman be titled—either in his own right or set to inherit. Surely, that is not too onerous? There are scores of eligible gentlemen to choose from."

"I don't wish to marry an *aristocrat*." She dripped disdain all over the word. "They're a lot of lazy social parasites with a collective sense of entitlement, just like that last one—"

Mr. Bachman's brows shot up his forehead. "Lily!"

She ducked her head. "I'm sorry," she muttered, abashed. "My mouth does run ahead of me—"

"And it's going to run you right into spinsterhood, if you don't mind yourself."

Heat crept up Lily's neck and over her cheeks.

"Now, dear," Mr. Bachman continued, "poor Mr. Faircloth certainly *was* here because of your dowry. It's big on purpose, and no doubt about it. But he also knew what color gown you wore to a ball last week. Do you know the last time I noticed a woman's gown?"

Lily shrugged.

"Thirty years or more," Mr. Bachman proclaimed, "if, in fact, I ever noticed to begin with." He lifted her chin with a finger. Lily raised her eyes to meet her father's softened expression. "You are an exceedingly pretty girl—"

"Oh, Papa . . ."

"You *are*. The way society works, however, renders it almost out of the question for the right kind of man to come calling, even if he thinks your dress *is* the most becoming shade of blue. Your dowry clears a few of those obstacles." He took her hand and patted it. "Now, let us be done quarreling and speak of pleasanter things."

Lily nodded hastily.

She happened to disagree with her father on the issue of her dowry. To Lily's mind, the "right kind of man" would want to be with her, fortune or no. She thought of her dearest friend, Isabelle, Duchess of Monthwaite. Even though she and her husband, Marshall, went through a horrible divorce—reducing Isabelle to the lowest possible social status—they still found their way back together. Marshall didn't allow Isabelle's reduced circumstances to keep them apart once they came to terms with their past.

For the thousandth time, Lily wished Isabelle were here. But she and His Grace were in South America on a botanical expedition-cum-honeymoon. They'd be home in a couple of months, but oh, how time dragged when Lily so needed her friend's advice.

Fortunately, Isabelle's sister-in-law, Lady Naomi Lockwood, would soon be in town. She'd written to Lily that her mother, Caro, would be sitting out the Season to remain in the country—a singularly odd choice, Lily thought, considering the dowager duchess' responsibility to see Naomi wed. Instead of her mother, Naomi would be chaperoned by her spinster aunt, Lady Janine.

Lily would be glad to see their friendly faces. She didn't get on well with *tonnish* young women, and there was always the suspicion that men were only interested in her money. Lily often found herself lonely in the middle of a glittering crush.

"Are you attending?" Mr. Bachman said.

Lily blinked. "I'm sorry, Papa, what was that?"

"I asked," he repeated patiently, "if you've decided on a project."

Lily's mood brightened. *This* was something she would enjoy discussing. "I have."

"Excellent!" Mr. Bachman sat in the large armchair behind his desk, the throne from which he ruled his ever-expanding empire of industry. He moved the chair opposite the desk around to his side. "Have a seat, dear."

Despite the tempest that had just flared between them, Lily felt a rush of affection for her dear father. Since she was a girl, he'd shared his desk with her. When she was young, he'd held her on his lap while he spoke to her about things she didn't understand then—coal veins and shipping ventures; members of Parliament and government contracts.

At the time, it all blurred together into papa's *work*, but as she grew, she began to make sense of it all.

She understood now that all her life he'd treated her as the son he never had, the heir apparent to the name and fortune he'd made for himself. Never had he indicated any doubt in her capability or intelligence on account of her sex. He took pride in his daughter's education and emphasized mathematics and politics, in addition to feminine accomplishments such as drawing and dancing.

Just before they'd come to town this Season, Mr. Bachman presented Lily with a unique opportunity. He desired her to develop a sizable charity project. He would fund her endeavor, but Lily had to do the work to bring her plans to fruition. She jumped on the proposal, glad for an occupation beside the *ton's* vapid entertainments.

Mr. Bachman rummaged through a drawer and withdrew a sheet of paper covered with Lily's neat writing.

"So, here is the list of ideas you began with. What have you settled upon?"

Lily pointed to an item halfway down the page. "The school for disadvantaged young women," she said. "I should like to keep it small for now. Girls would receive a sound education, plus some accomplishments that would enable them to take positions as governesses, ladies' maids, companions, things of that nature."

Mr. Bachman cupped his chin in his hand and listened with a thoughtful expression while Lily enumerated her ideas for the school. When she finished, he slapped his fingers on the desk. "Marvelous, my dear."

Lily swelled with pride at her father's approval.

He took a fresh sheet of paper and jotted a note. "I'm putting my solicitor at your disposal. The two of you can select an appropriate property for purchase. Meanwhile, you also need to secure a headmistress, who can, in turn, hire the staff. You'll need tutors, a cook, maids . . ."

As the plan came together, Lily's confidence in the project soared. There was nothing she could not accomplish once she knew how to approach a problem.

She kissed her father's cheek at the conclusion of their meeting.

"Just think, m'dear," he said on their parting.

"What's that?"

"When you marry one of those lazy aristocrats, he'll have scads of free time to help with your work." He winked and patted her arm.

Lily scowled at his back. He seemed to think a man in need of her dowry would also, in turn, look kindly upon her efforts to care for those less fortunate than themselves. She snorted. Such a man did not exist.

Find out more about *Once an Heiress* when you visit
www.crimsonromance.com/once-an-heiress/.

In the mood for more Crimson Romance?

Check out *Brave in Heart* by Emma Barry
at CrimsonRomance.com.